Made By Mary

ALSO BY LAURA CATHERINE BROWN

Quickening

Best Wishes!

MADE BY MARY

a novel by

Laura Catherine Brown

Laura Catherine Brown

JUNE 2018

C&R Press
Conscious & Responsible

Cover art: Other Side by Eugenia Loli
Interior design by Laura Brown Design
Exterior design by Laura Brown Design

Copyright ©2018 by Laura Catherine Brown

Library of Congress Cataloging-in-Publication Data

ISBN: 978-1-936196-88-3
Library of Congress Control Number: 2018932452

C&R Press
Conscious & Responsible
www.crpress.org
Winston-Salem, North Carolina

For special discounted bulk purchases, please contact:
C&R Press sales@crpress.org
Contact lharms@crpress.org to book events, readings and author signings.

For Tony, my love
who always believed

A pity beyond all telling is hid in the heart of love.

—William Butler Yeats

EARTH: 1999

Unfortunately, we are unable to consider you as adoptive parents on our register at this time.

Ann couldn't read past the first line before she crumpled the letter in her fist. She hadn't sufficiently protected herself against the flutter of hope that this one would be different. Every afternoon, the piping echo of toddlers' voices from the Little Footsteps Preschool followed Ann home, and filled her with potent, irrational hope. She oversaw the two- and three-year-olds: the Antelopes, as they were called. *Her* Antelopes. Beautiful changelings with bright faces, so good at being alive. At work, she merged with them like crayons melting together in the sun and became, for a while, as vibrant as they were.

Reluctant to file the letter with the others—each agency's correspondence lived in color-coded folders on the shelf by the telephone—Ann went to the kitchen window where she could see the rented backhoe in the cleared field, a hulk that blurred in the wash of her sudden tears. The drip of ice runoff was audible, as if the outside world sympathized and wept along with her. A silly presumption, Ann knew. *Nobody likes a crybaby,* Gran used to say. When McKenna poked his nose into her leg, she was grateful for the diversion. A Beagle-Lab mix, always alert for affection, he had been Joel's dog. Now he belonged to Ann, too. Stroking the silky contours of his skull, she pitied him, poor thing, didn't realize he wasn't enough, and she kissed the crown of his head. His tail thumped against the trailer floor. His gaze was pure love as she speed-dialed Joel at work.

"Slocombe Builders," he answered. She imagined him in the modular unit of his headquarters outside the barn, leaning way back in his squeaky old swivel chair.

"Are you busy?" she asked. "You want to hear what Giggles did today? He was holding his penis at the toilet, waiting to pee and he told me, it's *rewinding.*"

The toddlers said such wonderful things. Today, another one of the children had told her, *I have an eye in my heart so I can see my dreams.* Along with the recollection of their fresh observations, their unrestrained laughter and passionate sobs, came the tactile memory of their soft hands and cheeks, their sticky kisses.

"Did we get another rejection?" asked Joel.

"How did you know?" His understanding induced in Ann a swell of appreciation. Of course he knew. They were in this together, sharing the want.

"Did you call the agency?" he said. "Tell them we were stupid and misguided and it'll make us better parents?"

"*You* were stupid and misguided, not we." She instantly regretted her pettiness. "Sorry. I didn't mean that."

As due diligence, Ann followed up every refusal with a phone call, to plead their case to a human being. The problem was obvious. When Joel was eighteen years old, he had been convicted of a felony: possession of marijuana with intent to sell. Since it was public record, he and Ann had been honest about it on their agency applications. They disqualified themselves. She couldn't blame the agencies.

"You want me to call them? You're right. I was an asshole. A kilo's a lot of dope. I did the crime. I did the time. It was twelve years ago, Annie. You knew about it when you married me. How many ways can I say I'm sorry?"

"It's not your fault," she said. "I'm just disappointed."

"We knew it wouldn't be easy," said Joel. "But we've only been married five months. We're just getting started."

Reassured, Ann walked back to the window. This time when she looked, she noticed shoots had sprung up from the mud around the backhoe. Tiny white flowers bloomed among shrinking patches of snow. In less than a week the ground would be soft enough to break, and they could begin digging the foundation for their planned house—three bedrooms, two baths, a separate apartment for Joel's mother. As soon as this weekend, Ann might plant her bulbs in the soil around the trailer. In an hour, Joel would be home from work. So much to look forward to.

"Someone's bound to answer the ad," Joel was saying. "Are you there?"

"I'm here," she said.

They'd placed the ad when rejections from agencies began to trickle in.

Childless couple with love in their hearts seeks baby for adoption. Can pay legal and medical expenses. Let us provide a stable, nurturing home for your child. Call Ann and Joel collect.

The ad had been running for four weeks in both local papers, plus *The Catskill Shopper*, a free weekly advertising circular. As of April 12, 1999, they had received zero responses.

McKenna barked, and Ann was distracted by the rattling commotion of a lime-green VW bug advancing up the driveway, embellished with a toot-toot on the horn. "Mom's here," she said. "The last thing I need right now."

"Hang in there, Ann Slocombe," said Joel. "I'll be home soon."

Ann Slocombe, she reminded herself as she rinsed her face with cold water so her mother wouldn't know she'd been crying.

Ever since Ann was three years old and became conscious with a sudden jolting awareness that she was *herself* and no other, she had wanted children. Her earliest memory was of being propped on pillows to receive a soft bundle placed on her lap. It would have been one of the commune babies. Warm and weighted, flushed folds of skin, a flower petal mouth blowing air, the slight wheeze of congested breath and the exhilarating recognition that she was holding an infant, all converged for Ann into this realization of herself. *Look how good she is with the baby,* the women murmured from above.

Ann Slocombe. The grounding sound of her married name, its sheer normality, gave her the courage to walk outside and greet her mother.

If ANN HAD BELIEVED in miracles, which she adamantly did not, Joel's appearance in her life might have qualified. They had met over a year ago, in the summer, when Ann, living back home with her mother, answered an ad for a band seeking a rhythm guitarist. She embodied proof that classified ads were answered, which gave her hope that someone somewhere would respond to theirs. Not that she couldn't distinguish between a baby and a rhythm guitarist, a different order of magnitude entirely, but still, she had to recognize that life could offer unexpected openings.

Back then *Little Joey's Toys* played primarily Ramones covers, but also a few staples like *Midnight Hour* and *Louie Louie,* as well as some original songs. Tim played bass and Rick played drums. But Joel, the lead guitarist, with his topaz eyes, curly black hair and chapped lips, was the star.

As naturally as if they'd been doing it for years, she and Joel strummed and sang together, spontaneously harmonizing. They fell into a habit of meeting several times a week outside rehearsals to go for walks. She loved that he built things: tables, cabinets, beds, saunas, porches, decks. To be so resourceful and to do simple tasks well seemed like a great accomplishment. Holding hands for the first time, their fingers interwove with perfect wholeness. But his palm was sweaty and they soon slid apart.

"I have a condition," he said.

"Me, too," she said.

"Mine's palmar hydrosis," he said. "What's yours?"

When she blushed with a heat that made her face break out in hives, he told her she was beautiful.

Together, they hiked every trail in the township. She noticed that he walked with one shoulder slightly higher and thrust more forward than the other, probably from playing the guitar. A few weeks into their relationship, to ease the strange sensation of tenderness in her chest as she watched him stride ahead along the hiking trail, Ann blurted out, "I don't have a uterus. That's my condition." If he intended to dump her, it was best done before she cared too much.

When he turned around in the pollen-scented meadow, suffused in the afternoon light, and said, "Neither do I," she knew it was too late. She loved him already. Her feelings frightened her.

"I'm very small down there," she said. "I was born that way."

"Maybe I'm small, too." He walked towards her, stopping to pick up something from the path.

Afraid to look at him as he came close, aware of the scent of cedar rising off his skin from the sauna he'd been building, Ann stared at the ground. She glimpsed a snake as it slithered through the underbrush. "It's embarrassing," she said. "I have to use a device to stretch myself. I thought you should know because…"

"Because I love you?" he'd said, and handed her a speckled stone, shaped like a heart.

Five months later, they were married by a judge at the Sullivan County courthouse in Monticello, New York, until death do them part, an impulsive action to which their mothers had not been invited. Ann vividly recalled descending the courthouse steps, squinting against the blinding white reflection of the snow-covered lawn below, how she had slipped. Joel grabbed her before she tumbled, lifting her and swinging her off the ground. Airborne, she whooped, *I'm married!* an uncharacteristic outburst.

Ann Slocombe, formerly Annapurna Peace Moonlight, had entered a new phase of life.

MARY MOONLIGHT WAS IN a state of agitation. Driving her vintage green VW bug, with the vanity plates "WCCNWMN" and the "Proud to be Pagan" bumper sticker which she'd slapped over "Clinton/Gore '94" and "I Brake for Hallucinations," she provoked serious hostility from cars sporting the Christian fish. One driver had honked and flipped her the bird. Her transmission was acting up, too. The gearbox slipped through second with an ugly grinding racket, forcing her to shift quickly from first to third. But the real cause of her agitation was loneliness.

Her lover had refused to move in. Her priestess required an appointment to chat. And her daughter might as well have moved to Siberia, since she'd gotten married and isolated herself in this toxic synthetic eyesore of a trailer five miles off a dirt road. The trailer was surrounded by a field of mud, punctuated with stumps where trees had been chopped down. Construction equipment sat in post-apocalyptic readiness to further raze the wilderness. Ann emerged from the trailer, clutching her cardigan tight around her neck.

"Merry meet!" Mary called. Stepping around muddy puddles to the trailer's entrance, she was compelled to goad. "There's plenty of room for both of you at Sunrise. More room than you have here, that's for sure. I'd welcome you both." She reached down to pet McKenna.

Mary had named her house Sunrise to cultivate optimism, then painted the exterior purple and added a giant orange sun with two eyes on the front porch. Her house was an expression of her creative being, as was her car, the jewelry she crafted, and the clothes she wore. Years ago, Annapurna, too—*Ann*—had been an expression of Mary's being.

"Mom, we like it here." Ann's long pale hair, usually held back in a barrette, was tangled as if she'd been pulling at it again, a nervous habit since childhood. Her eyes were red-rimmed.

"Honey, what's wrong?" said Mary. "Did something happen?"

But Ann turned on her heel and walked inside. What clandestine grudge was she nursing now, Mary wondered. She plopped her macramé bag on the kitchen table. The clank as it landed came from her bronze-plated baby shoes, which she'd brought as a gift because she missed her daughter. She missed her mother, too. Her mother had died, her daughter had gotten married, both in the same month.

"I come with an offering," she said, pulling out the baby shoes and placing them on the table, on top of a wrinkled correspondence that she scanned in an instant. *We do not consider applicants with a criminal background, as we are sure you understand.* "Fuck these adoption places!" she exploded. "Do they *know* how good you are with kids? Provident Family Services, my ass. There are other agencies."

"They're all rejecting us." Ann's voice trembled as she pulled up a chair next to Mary.

"Why do you admit to the felony? You have a *right* to lie! These fascist drug laws are out of control!" Relieved that Ann's attitude had nothing to do with her, Mary launched into a tirade about the injustice, the absurdity, and the failure of the so-called war against drugs. But Ann's annihilating look stopped her cold. Such was the power of the contemptuous eye glide, the cruel lip curl, the expression of a child dealing with a mother she'd deemed an asshole. Criticism jumped a generation. Mary's mother, Rose, used to cast the same disdainful glance at her.

"You don't have to give me the dead eye. I'm trying to help. Why do you hate me? Now I'm going to cry." Mary couldn't fight it. Bursting into tears, she dropped her face in her hands. *You do enjoy your whining,* Rose would have said. Never mind that she had died a year ago; her voice still scolded Mary mercilessly. It made Mary feel pitiful. She was an orphan. She had been rejected by her lover. Sniffling, she lifted her face. "America's daughter's back in town. Did you know Cassidy had a new baby girl? *Two* kids now, and America was complaining about the noise and mayhem while she's trying to run her home business. There's so much room in my house! I wanted to take *us* to another level! But she won't move in!"

Raw pain flashed across Ann's face. "What's the baby's name?"

"She doesn't have a name yet. A couple months old and nameless. It's not fair. I can't say I understand your baby lust, but no one deserves a child more than you do." Mary wiped her nose with her sleeve. Her tears had passed, thank the goddess. They were so unpredictable.

"America's a drug dealer," said Ann. "If she lived with you, she'd make you an accomplice."

"She's a purveyor of healing botanicals." Mary carried the bronzed baby shoes around the kitchen counter to the living room, where she arranged them on a small end table next to the sofa. She withdrew a purple amethyst stone that she'd stored inside the right shoe and placed it between them. "This will be your baby altar. Amethysts carry the vibrations of fertility and the shoes symbolize your desire. Visualize what you want and the next communication will be a 'yes.'"

Ann came around the counter and touched the shoes. "Were they yours? So tiny."

"Mother kept them all those years," said Mary. "She loved her *things,* didn't she?"

"Maybe she kept them because she loved *you,*" said Ann.

Crazily, tears welled up again. *Why do you wear such gaudy jewelry!* Rose had said not long before she died. *How could you let yourself get so fat!* "Is it true that you can never outgrow the person you once were because that's the person you're destined to be?" Mary asked. "Once a fat, plain, misfit girl, always a fat plain misfit girl?"

"I don't suppose you kept my baby shoes." Ann sounded like a plaintive child.

"I never imprisoned your little feet in shoes!" said Mary. "We don't need our lives in bronze. Let's have a hug. Please?"

Ann wrapped her thin arms loosely around Mary's waist.

"Hug me like you mean it, sweetie!" The bony protrusions of Ann's spine were palpable under her sweater. How had Mary created such a slender girl? "Beautiful Annapurna," she murmured. "You know how much I love you, don't you?"

JOEL PUSHED AWAY BLUEPRINTS and papers to grab the ringing phone. He'd been sketching out a sauna idea. "Slocombe Builders," he answered, surveying his office clutter, his computer and his collection of mechanical wind-up toys.

"I don't like the girl they gave me," said his mother, Betty. "She treats me like dirt. She won't make the soup I asked for. And she's a slut, always on the phone with the boys."

"You liked her two days ago, Ma," said Joel. Fifteen hours a week to help clean and do whatever needed doing, it didn't have to be difficult. Ever since she'd sprained her ankle a month ago, Betty had been neglecting herself: not eating, not washing. She had type II diabetes and fibromyalgia, didn't own a car, and disliked driving.

And Joel had abandoned her by marrying Ann and moving out.

"I'm closing up here anyway," he said with a sigh. "I'll be over soon."

Betty's call had topped off a day of frustration: undelivered supplies, dithering clients, arguments about billing, and an altercation between two of his guys. He had intended to write up a list of requests for an architect on a second-story renovation job, but it would have to wait until tomorrow. He turned the key on his little plastic monkey toy and watched it totter across his paper-strewn desk and topple into the chair. Then he switched off the lights and locked the door.

Betty lived in Callicoon Center, a few miles from the Slocombe Builders site, a scenic drive along a winding road. Joel rolled his window down, fortified by the cold air. The snow up along the ridge had melted, revealing dark earth. Jack-in-the-pulpit and skunk cabbage bloomed here and there. Having lived in Sullivan County all his life, every landmark was familiar, even the graffiti defacing the barricade blocking access to the unused stone arch bridge. He'd built the buttresses to shore up that bridge for rehabilitation. It would be open by summer, thanks to him.

When he reached the one-story bungalow, he saw his mother standing in the driveway, wearing a housedress over polyester pants. Her fuzzy pink slippers were brighter than any spring flowers. "Ma, what are you doing?" he shouted out his window. "Where are your shoes?"

"That girl is stealing my cigarettes." With frizzy gray hair sprouting around her face and a birdlike quiver to her head, Betty embodied outrage. She was always accusing someone. Pure luck it wasn't him today.

Joel jumped out of the truck. He led Betty along the concrete path to the front door, and she allowed it. The path was cracked and treacherous, laid down years ago by his father. Several times a week, whenever he came by, Joel accused himself of neglect for not replacing the broken stones. Betty didn't have to say a word.

"She's expecting," said Betty. "If you know what I mean. And she ain't married. That dime store ring doesn't fool me."

"There are no dime stores anymore," said Joel, ushering her into the kitchen. The aide sat at the table talking on his mother's phone, her hand cupped over the receiver in a secretive, defensive posture. As soon as she saw them, she hung up. She was much younger than he'd assumed she'd be, with a round face and soft, chubby neck.

"Were you outside, Mrs. S? I told her not to go outside. I'm sorry." She had the hoarse voice of a middle-aged woman who smoked too much, yet she looked like a high school student, big chested in a baggy T-shirt, a kerchief holding back her hair. But with her plump lips and her wide blue eyes, even scowling she was pretty—and arrestingly so, since Joel hadn't expected it.

"Don't get smart," said Betty. "The girl was calling long distance. She's on my phone the whole time she's here."

"Stop calling me *the girl!* My name is *Jessica Lehr!* Got it?"

"See what I have to put up with?" Betty tugged Joel's arm. "What do you care?" A wail circled the room. She had gone through four aides in a month, developing a reputation as "unmanageable" at HomeCare, Inc. She would not permit Joel to live in ignorance of her unhappiness. She would destroy these home health aides one by one.

"Calm down. *Please.*" He led her to her chair with the remote control tucked into the pillow. The living room was tidy. Betty's huge stuffed panda had been given pride of place in the center of the sofa.

Before he'd moved out, Joel hadn't noticed the cloying scent of potpourri from the numerous pomanders and candy dishes. Ann had mentioned it. She'd coughed and choked and laughed. Now he cringed against the dollhouse quality of the place, the framed needlepoints of roses and sunflowers and pithy sayings: *Mi casa es su casa, A smile is a curve that straightens everything, If God seems far away guess who moved out.* Silk-flowered wreaths on the walls, and the overwhelming artificial smell of cinnamon and vanilla. Everything was dusty and yellowed and frayed.

"She's not getting away with anything!" Betty yelled from the armchair.

"I'll talk to her," said Joel. "Stay here."

Jessica was at the refrigerator with a glass of milk. "I'm leaving. I got a ride coming." Her cheeks were flushed, and Joel was afraid she might cry. He didn't want to deal with crying. Among women, it became contagious. The weeping and misery would swirl through the house like a tornado, flinging everything into turmoil.

"Please don't leave," he said. "It's not just you, it's everyone they send."

"She treats people like shit, that's the problem." Jessica drank her milk in a long gulp, regarding him over the tilted glass, licking her lips when she finished. Her frown transformed slowly into a radiant, wide-open smile. "I know where I've seen you before. You're in a band! Didn't you play at The Barge near the community college?"

A touch of fame. A Sullivan County rock star. Joel bit his lip so as not to appear too pleased. "Haven't played there in a while," he said. He hadn't played there since Tim, the bass player, had a kid. They'd tried to revive the band by bringing in a rhythm guitarist, who turned out to be Ann, who'd then stolen his heart. *Little Joey's Toys* had fizzled: rehearsals canceled, gigs postponed, general inertia. Yet they lived on in Jessica's memory! His face was hot as he lowered himself into a chair, noting the ruffles around the chair legs. "I'm building a house with a separate apartment for her so we can keep her close but until then, I don't know what to do."

The phone rang. Jessica leaped for it.

"Who's this?" Betty had picked up the extension by her chair. Her voice spilled out simultaneously from the kitchen phone receiver and the living room, in disharmony with a rumbling male voice.

"You get here," said Jessica. "That's all I'll say." She slammed the phone down. "My ride just bailed. Goddam Sam."

Joel got up to check if the receiver was broken but it was intact and warm. In the living room, the television went on, the volume too loud for comfort. "I could probably take you where you need to go," he said.

She gave him that childlike smile again. "Drop me off at the mall?"

He checked his watch. Ann had been upset lately about the adoption agencies and he didn't want to add to it by arriving late for dinner, especially since she was making chicken and dumplings, his favorite. "Ma!" he called into the living room. "I'm taking Jessica home."

Betty stared at the television, ignoring him. He knew he was expected to kiss her goodbye but he rebelled. Rattling his car keys, he turned to Jessica. "Ready?"

She followed him outside. Hugging her purse, a teenybopper thing with countless studs and rivets, she clambered into the passenger seat. The moon had risen and hung like a toenail clipping near the horizon. Joel pushed a Lucinda Williams CD into the player as he eased out of the driveway. "I appreciate what you do for her," he said. "She doesn't mean to be a bitch."

He speculated that Betty could have gone another way. Before his father had left them, she'd had the capacity for delight. She happily gossiped about the women she worked with at the Sullivan County Gasworks—their strange food habits, their pregnancies and divorces. She used to enjoy watching birds from the porch with her binoculars—identifying them in her book, the kestrels, cardinals, swallows, and jays. She liked cut roses in a vase and taking baths with lavender bubbles. If his father hadn't left, if Betty hadn't been laid off, if she'd had more children as she'd wished to, if Joel hadn't married—each "if" slid into its negative place and created the inevitability of Betty. Only a grandchild might turn it around.

On the stereo, Lucinda sang of heartache and revenge.

"Your mother called it right about me. I'm pregnant." Jessica tucked her hands between her knees, her shoulders hunched inward and nodded, as if to convince herself. "My mom's going to kill me. Unless *uncle* Earl kills me first."

"Is Earl the father?" Joel's palms were suddenly drenched.

"Like hell. The father is an *extremely* rich orthodontist. I thought he loved me but he's married. "

"Sorry to hear it," said Joel. "You have options, don't you? You could give it up for adoption. Or you could…" But to say the word *abortion* seemed presumptuous.

"He hung up on me like ten times." Jessica wiped her eyes vigorously. "I could live or die, he wouldn't give a fuck. And the agency's going to fire my ass when they find out."

"I'll hire you independently," said Joel impulsively. "The hell with the agency."

"I need at least twenty dollars an hour."

"That might be doable." Joel didn't know why he said it. He couldn't afford $300 a week and Medicaid wouldn't pitch in if he didn't use the agency. They had reached the mall. But when he pulled up in front of the Sears entrance, Jessica made no move to get out.

"You're married, right? I like your ring," she said in a rush.

"Thanks, my mother-in-law made it. It's silver and gold, braided." He stretched his hand across his body to show her. He'd been impressed when Mary presented the rings; surprised she made such elegant pieces, given her whole hippie moon-woman, silver-and-stone thing, so different from Ann. What disconcerted him was the prototype Mary had made for herself, as if the three of them were married.

"Are you happy?" When Jessica fingered his ring her touch sent goose bumps along the back of his hand. He got a squirmy, panicked feeling in his gut.

"Sure, I'm happy." His voice seemed to detach from his mouth like a bubble. "This is going to sound weird. But my wife and I can't have kids. We've been trying to adopt a baby since we got married. And here you are, pregnant."

"Here I am," she said.

My wife and I. The words steadied him and he withdrew his hand slowly, as if Jessica wouldn't notice as he put it back on the steering wheel. "We're having issues because I was busted for pot possession when I was eighteen. The police said there was intent to sell. But I was only going to smoke it. I got parole. I did community service. Now I'm stuck with this felony on my record that makes it impossible to adopt." He hadn't realized what a burden this was, this guilt, this thing he had done to make a child unattainable for Ann.

He heard a muffled sort of hiccup. Jessica was laughing. "Were you one of those dudes sweeping garbage off the courthouse lawn? Do you have any pot on you now?"

"No. You shouldn't smoke if you're pregnant anyway." He scribbled his cell phone number on the little pad he always carried in his chest pocket. A hum ran through his body. "If you ever need anything with my mother or your baby, just get in touch."

"Thanks. You're good people." She tucked the number into her purse. "You couldn't lend me a twenty, could you?"

Feeling slightly suckered, Joel took out his wallet and handed her forty, which gave him back the upper hand. "Would that do you?"

When Jessica finally got out of the truck, she walked around to the driver's side, opened her purse, and fished out a flattened pack of cigarettes that she passed through the open window. "Your mother was right about my stealing these. Sorry. I didn't know you'd be so nice."

Joel watched her disappear through the double-glass doors of Sears. She looked more chubby than pregnant but what did he know? As he turned his pickup around and headed home, he remembered the day he got married, how he'd strutted down the courthouse steps, in love, *See, all you people who treated me like shit when my father left, see? You can kiss my ass!* He had been on top of the world because Ann, this slender beautiful woman with a graceful fingerpicking guitar style, loved him. He'd thought that here, at last, is someone I can make happy.

WE LOVE YOU! MARY had written on the card for Ann's sixteenth birthday when she and her then-lover, Cecilia, had presented Ann with her own personal speculum. They were living at the East Village Sisterhood, a Pagan womyn's commune on 6th Street and Avenue B in New York City. In the sisterhood bathroom, in a sloped metal receptacle were *hers, hers,* and *hers.* Ann drew a big A on her speculum, no confusion. She did the same with her toothbrush.

But she had balked at inaugurating the speculum by subjecting herself to a sisterhood pelvic exam. Mary and the womyn, Cecilia, Wren, Asphodel, Raven, and Sage, had scrutinized her for the onset of her period as if they were hungry for blood. *Leave me alone! I don't have it yet!* Although she cut them off, Ann privately yearned for her menarche party: everyone wearing red, diablo sauce on the pasta, red velvet cake for dessert.

The womyn offered to massage her Achilles tendons with black cohosh oil, advised her to sleep with eucalyptus under her pillow until the full moon, to carry a bloodstone in her front pocket every day for a month. Sage dangled crystals over Ann's sacral chakra. *The body has wisdom,* they said. *The body knows when.*

When her body failed to respond, Ann went to a neighborhood clinic where she learned that she possessed a shallow dent, a dead end, no cervix, and no uterus. Cause unknown. Vulva, labia, and clitoris were normal, and as the embarrassing words floated around her, Ann clung to one: *normal.* The doctor performed an abdominal ultrasound. *There's a remnant of a uterus,* pointing to a barely visible gray squiggle on the screen. *And look! You have very healthy looking ovaries.*

While the other pagan girls celebrated their first-blood rituals, and the so-called normal girls at school discussed pads, tampons, pregnancy and sexually transmitted diseases, Ann visited specialists to learn that her body was an utter misrepresentation of herself. She was a freak. Her eggs were released into her body, passing harmlessly through her system, cycle after unrecognized cycle. Diagnosed with MRKH, Mayer-Rokitansky-Kuster-Hauser syndrome, a congenital disorder with an incidence of 1 in 5,000 female births, she refused surgery, renounced the Goddess, moon circles, bloodstones, and anything associated with magic. So it had been for years. She was almost thirty now.

And yet. Over the weeks since Mary had brought over the bronze-plated baby shoes and the amethyst crystal, Ann found herself placing Joel's heart-shaped speckled stone among the items. Joel added a yellow baby bib and a little cabin he'd found at his mother's that he'd made as a child from popsicle sticks.

After the bulldozers broke ground and shoveled out trenches for the crawl space of the new house, the construction stopped for a few weeks while the concrete cured. Ann cleared a small patch of soil for carrots, far away from the debris and mounds of trenched dirt to avoid potential leaching chemicals. The soil in the garden was rocky and difficult but she relished the work, turning dirt over to aerate, topdressing and planting. As the days grew longer and the sun rose higher in the sky each afternoon, Ann planted beets, potatoes, and cabbage.

Since her workday ended earlier than Joel's, she had time in the late afternoon not only to garden and prepare dinner but also, twice a week, to dilate herself. She had owned the dilator kit, with a vinyl case accommodating four cylindrically-shaped plastic objects, tapered and graduated in size, since she was a teenager. An endocrinologist had prescribed twenty minutes a day with a lubricator, demonstrating the angle and pressure with which to insert and apply the object. Through brute strength, Ann could lengthen her vaginal canal enough to have sex without excruciating pain.

God has chosen you because He knows you're strong, Gran told her. *You can use this circumstance to feel sorry for yourself or you can use it to ask Him: If motherhood is not my purpose, what is?*

Mary had crowed, *Lucky you! No birth control necessary. You're free!*

But until she met Joel, Ann had resisted dilation. Sex, she'd decided, was overrated. Now, lying naked in bed, she pressed the object up inside her until her forearms ached, and the pain between her legs became almost intolerable. A year's diligence had graduated her to the third size. *Gaining inches,* the endocrinologist had called it. Better than surgery, everyone agreed. A means to an end, as Ann saw it—necessary to become the sexy, happy, normal woman she wanted to be.

McKenna barked at the low thrum of Joel's pickup truck just before Ann's timer went off. She peeked out the window to see Joel in the twilight, inspecting the trenches at the construction site, and quickly got dressed.

The chicken was cooling in the roasting pan and Ann was setting the table when Joel burst in. "Smells fantastic, Annie! We're one day closer to a house." He headed straight to the shower and emerged within minutes, clean and damp, to kiss her cheek.

Joel ate everything on his plate, unfailingly appreciative. But Ann played with her food, building symmetrical mounds then mushing them up. Cooking was much more fun than eating. She blamed it on her childhood at the Peace Ranch commune where kids chucked handfuls of lentil soup at each other, and the bigger ones stole bread off the smaller ones' plates. Being one of the smaller ones, Ann would create such an unappetizing edifice out of her meal with soggy bits and lumpy piles that no one ever stole it. The trouble was she no longer wanted it either.

You're lucky. It's how you stay skinny, Mary would tell her.

Joel never mentioned her eating habits, which made Ann acutely aware of them as hers alone.

"Remember the pregnant girl I told you about?" Joel put his fork down. His hand was shaking. "She called me today. She wants us to adopt her baby."

"That's out of the blue. Wow. I'm surprised you didn't tell me as soon as you got home."

"I almost didn't tell you at all," he said. "In case she changes her mind."

A flood of hope and desperation caused Anne's heart to thunder through her skull. Her face grew hot. She jumped up to clear the table. "We'll invite her to dinner," she said.

Joel got up and hugged her from behind. Ann stiffened, even as she wished to fall back into the warm cedar scent of him, relaxing into love, into being known and held.

They always cleaned up together. He washed. She dried. He ran his wet fingers along the back of her upper arm, sending shivers along her skin. She snapped the towel at his buttocks.

Later, while McKenna rested in his usual place on the carpet near the heat of the wood-burning stove that Joel had installed, they played their guitars. Playing and singing blurred their edges. When Ann pressed down on the strings of her acoustic guitar, notes flowed from the strings of Joel's. Words floated up in her mind, with a melancholy melody. *Back to Bethel, it's no Bethlehem. A child who belongs to no one.*

"Nice riff." Joel picked out a bass line to run behind it, opening out the tune. But he interrupted his own flow. "We should get the band together, play at The Barge again."

Putting his guitar down, he scooted on his bottom along the sofa until his thigh touched hers. He lifted her long hair off her neck and kissed her. His lashes brushed her cheek. Yet she tensed up. *The sexual act,* the endocrinologist had said, *is more effective than a dilator.* But sometimes, after they made love, Ann would bleed. Soreness would linger for days and with it the terrible sense of being a damaged woman.

"What's wrong?" said Joel.

"I'm sorry. It's stupid."

"Not stupid." Joel unbuttoned her sweater. She unbuttoned his flannel shirt. Then he dropped his face into her lap and she slid further into the sofa, lifting her hips to pull her pants off more easily. When he kissed her inner thigh, she tried to submit to pleasure rather than shame. In her mind, the melody she'd picked on her guitar continued to unfurl.

ANN RAN THE KNIFE under hot water before she cut into the carrot cake, because Gran had always said warm water on the knife made for a cleaner slice. From across the counter the bronze-plated baby shoes caught her eye as if signaling, which was ridiculous since they were inanimate objects. Yet, there on the sofa sat an undeniably pregnant girl. She'd missed dinner but agreed to dessert.

"Can't be*lieve* my mom kicked me out!" Jessica perched forward, her too-tight tank top showing dingy bra straps. "This is a good place for the baby, right, Sam? Sam's my best friend. I love Sam like my brother."

Ann wondered if Jessica was drunk. Her friend, Sam, was slumped beside her, his arms crossed over his chest, fingers tucked in his armpits. Cropped hair stuck out in tufts around his wide, acne-scarred face. His scraggly goatee bobbed when he talked. "Ain't right what your moms did."

"Bad break getting fired, too. We're glad you called us." Joel paced in front of them, nervous and kinetic, distracting Ann. He threw a log into the wood-burning stove and slammed it shut with the iron rod.

"When are you due?" Ann handed Jessica a piece of cake, scrutinizing while appearing not to. Jessica's jeans were unbuttoned to accommodate her girth. Mascara was smeared under her eyes, which were puffy and red from crying.

"November maybe? I don't remember." Jessica gave a harsh laugh. "I heard it never comes out on the due date anyway."

Sam released his fingers from his armpits to receive his cake.

Joel dragged a chair from the kitchen and sat opposite the sofa. "I'll definitely talk to HomeCare, not that I have much clout but I'll do what I can. As for this place, I know it's small but you're welcome to stay here. If it wasn't so dark out, I'd show you the concrete slab for the house we're building."

He gobbled his cake, just as Jessica had gobbled hers. She must have liked it, which was good; it was nutritious for the baby. "Joel can build anything," said Ann. "He cut a hole in this trailer roof with a huge mechanical saw to install this stove. Amazing, right?" Aware of how false and stilted she sounded, and certain that she also was being scrutinized, she searched through the basket of newspapers near the stove. "I guess he told you how long we've been wanting a child. I'll show you the ad we placed in *The Herald* classifieds."

"Not now, Ann," said Joel. "They don't want to read it."

"Sure they do. Why wouldn't they?" She found a page with the ad, folded the paper and placed it on the coffee table. But Jessica was staring at Joel as she played with a tiny pendant at her neck, sliding it back and forth along the chain. Her lovely plump shoulders held the lamplight and seemed to glow from within.

Ann felt awkward standing while everyone else was sitting. "Have you seen a doctor?" she asked.

"The clinic," Jessica answered obediently. Folding her hands in her lap, she appeared utterly sober and eager to please. She addressed Joel. "I got vitamins and such. They were real nice there."

Ann dragged a chair over from the kitchen area. "How have you been feeling?"

"Pretty sick sometimes." Jessica grimaced.

"Not too sick to party." Sam laughed through his nose. His mouth did not smile.

"Party? No way! Not good!" Ann practically screamed.

"It's okay, Annie." Joel reached for her.

Ann shrank away, feeling silenced rather than reassured.

"I wish you were *my* parents," said Jessica with an impulsive toothy smile, allowing Ann to glimpse the preschooler she had once been, innocent and exuberant.

"Can I smoke in here?" Sam withdrew a cigarette from his pack.

"Sure," said Joel.

"Outside," said Ann.

"So, which is it?" said Sam. "Who's in charge?"

"Second hand smoke is bad for the baby," said Ann. "Bad for everyone."

Sam attempted to stand. With a grunt, he fell back into the sofa. Jessica pushed him and he swayed toward the door. "I'm up." He slammed it shut behind him.

"Is he drunk?" said Ann.

"I wasn't thinking," said Joel. "Of course. No smoking."

Jessica shot him her beautiful smile. "You've got a lot to learn, Daddy."

Ann noticed Joel perspiring, the damp at his armpits darkening his T-shirt. "I guess that makes me Mommy." She laughed, wishing she didn't sound so fake, and wishing her shoulders did not feel so painfully rigid.

She wanted to seal in this new, unexpected reality and make it good. But she had no idea how to do that. The situation seemed too fragile. Her role seemed superfluous. Mary might have known what to do. She could have alleviated the tension by drawing energy onto herself.

"I always wanted to play the guitar." Jessica broke the awkward silence, pointing at the guitars hanging on the wall. "Are you playing at The Barge anytime soon?"

"Hopefully," said Joel. "Right, Ann?"

Outside, an engine revved. Ann ran to the door just in time to catch sight of Sam's black Trans Am as it squealed through a turn and bounced down the dark driveway.

"Oh, fuck it. He can't handle anything." Jessica pressed against her, giving off a smell of perspiration and rotting fruit, at first repellent, then almost pleasant. Ann softened into it. Sam's departure was a relief. "Stay the night," she said, impulsively throwing her arm around Jessica's warm shoulders.

"I could show you some things on the guitar." Joel lifted one of his electrics off its storage hook on the wall. "Hey Annie, come play. Ann's really good."

Like an easily diverted child, Jessica slipped out of Ann's embrace. She sat cross-legged on the rug, taking the guitar in her lap. She seemed more wholesome with Sam gone. Ann couldn't control the sudden buoyancy inside. She felt weightless as she cross-picked a quick tune on her acoustic. Joel eyed her over Jessica's bowed head, beaming as if the pregnant girl was a special gift from him to her.

ENORMOUS, WHITE-BEARDED, WITH A tie-dyed T-shirt beneath his lab coat, Dr. Fisher shook Ann's hand, then Jessica's. "Call me The Fish, everyone else does." He had no receptionist, he apologized. "My wife plays the part but today the cards told her not to. I know better than to argue." He had been recommended by Mary, who knew him through America because he had birthed Cassidy's son. After working the bad trips tent with Wavy Gravy at the Woodstock concert, he had simply stayed in Sullivan County and opened an obstetrics practice.

He ushered Jessica into the exam room while Ann sat in the waiting area staring at a wall full of baby pictures. Boy or girl, she didn't care, she would kiss the baby's cheeks and the dimples on his knees, and revel in changing diapers with shit up to her elbows. She couldn't look at baby pictures without a physical salivating rush through her body. Like porn. It was embarrassing.

The Fish opened the exam room door. "Would you like to see the ultrasound?"

Ann squeezed herself into the tiny exam room. She was pleased when Jessica grabbed her hand. "It's mad crazy, right?" said Jessica.

As Ann gazed at the visual on the monitor: a tiny figure all curled up, little fists near its face, she was transported to the endocrinologist's office and the umpteenth ultrasound of her insides. *Your daughter's condition is a medical anomaly. With surgery, she can have a normal sex life.*

What exactly, in your opinion, is a normal sex life? How do you know my daughter isn't gay? I resent your assumptions. Have you never heard of oral?

Shut up, Mom, just shut up.

Ann's longing attacked now like an illness. It was lust. It was desperate. Her head swam. She couldn't breathe.

"You're hurting my hand!" Jessica yanked free. "Next time I want Joel to come."

"You've got a boy in there, all right," said The Fish. "He's twenty-five weeks or so, which puts you in your sixth month."

Ann calculated. "He'll be born mid-September."

"Libra sun sign," said The Fish. "Maybe Virgo, if he wants to come out earlier."

"I wish you could take him out right now," said Jessica.

SAM DROPPED OFF JESSICA'S stuff; her clothes, teddy bear, blow dryer, romance paperbacks, and a makeup case the size of a toolbox all thrown into a plastic garbage bag, making Jessica's move to the trailer official and permanent, at least until the baby came.

"I thought we could let it flow, see what happens," Joel whispered to Ann at night in their bedroom. Sound traveled in the trailer in a way Ann had never noticed before Jessica came. Every cough, every toilet flush and footstep reverberated. "Things don't *flow* without pushing in one direction or another," Ann whispered in reply. She recalled sisterhood members chanting over her, calling down her moon flow. How fruitless. But she wanted to be hopeful.

The bronzed baby shoes and other baby objects had been shoved into a drawer, replaced by a framed photograph of Jessica in an orange prom gown with a corsage on her wrist. In a twinkling, Mardi Gras beads were hung over the lamps and countless metal bangles and gaudy earrings stacked in a little pile on the windowsill. Jessica demanded instant coffee, six-packs of Coke, Lucky Charms, and Count Chocula. *No bran shit,* as she called their cereal. Ann obliged, except for the six-packs of Coke. She bought juice instead.

In the morning, she gently covered Jessica's sprawling naked body with a sheet before allowing Joel to enter the living room area. They tiptoed around her, getting ready for work. If Ann had not insisted, Jessica would never have folded up the sofa bed, just left it open like she left her clothes draped everywhere: underwear, bras, wrinkled T-shirts with the sleeves and collars cut off, all tossed willy-nilly. It offended Ann's sense of order, but she considered it practice for the baby, whose chaos and need she eagerly anticipated.

The concrete on the house site hardened sufficiently to begin work on the floor and the frame. May slid into June. Spring exploded into the heat and dazzle of summer. Seedlings of dill, parsley, and basil cultivated by the Antelopes at Little Footsteps required transplanting. The children spilled dirt everywhere, clumsily pulling the tiny plants from the egg-carton cups and depositing them in plastic pots. When they took turns with the watering can, water spilled everywhere.

Ann didn't mind. She enjoyed wiping noses, bottoms, mouths, and fingers. They stroked her with their sticky hands, kissed her with their soft lips and wet, runny noses. But even in the thick of them, she was thinking about Jessica.

She imagined Jessica flopped across the couch watching television and worried, *What if she changes her mind?* Oscillating between dread and euphoria, she wanted to be there with Jessica, doing what Jessica was doing, whatever it was.

Once a week, at the end of the day, after the parents arrived to swoop up their children in a collective blast of energy, leaving overturned chairs and a floor stained with vivid splashes of color from spilled finger-paints, Shirley, the director, held a status meeting. Swinging her arms as she talked, moving around the room with an enthusiastic rocking on the balls of her feet, she energized Ann just by watching her.

Quieter than Shirley, more critical, long-torsoed with a narrow face and thin, compressed lips, Frances, the other teacher, exuded superiority, talking of pedagogy and child development theory. Ann had trouble following. What was an invariant sequence? Her mind drifted again to Jessica, who had no interest in learning anything Ann wanted to teach her, like cooking. *I'm through with domestic slavery.*

"Theories, theories," said Shirley. "Ann, what do you have to add?"

Ann had received a mere two-year certificate from the local community college, compared to Frances' master's degree at the state university. But in her opinion she was better with children than Frances, who liked structured play and giving them shapes to trace, rather than letting them create on their own.

Shortly after Ann married, at one of these meetings, Frances had teased her about how she'd soon have to enroll a new pupil at Little Footsteps.

Ann had stopped her. "I can't have kids."

Shirley responded with a sharp intake of breath, Frances's hand fluttered toward her heart, and a fountain of pity showered from them both. "Please don't feel sorry for me," Ann had said. "I'm only telling you so we can stop the teasing."

Now, as the meeting wound down, Ann made her announcement. "Joel and I are in the process of an independent adoption. By the end of September, we'll have a baby. I might need some time off." She shocked herself by bursting into tears.

Shirley, who had four children in high school, hugged Ann with flabby arms that smelled like baby powder.

Frances patted her awkwardly. "Be thankful you won't have to give birth. Good God, I wouldn't want to go through that again."

ANN WALKED THE PERIMETER of the construction site. The din of drilling, banging and hammering rattled her bones and she longed to shoot forward into the future when the house would be complete, with white siding, a bay window in the living room and a swing set where the trailer now stood. She wanted to lounge on the wraparound porch with her son, Ethan. She had already named him. Shyly, she waved to the men who paused in their work. Building a house and building a baby, both out of her control. So much of her life occurred beyond her control.

She crossed the dirt to the trailer where Jessica sat on doorstep, polishing her toenails deep red. Mid-June and Jessica had hit the 29-week milestone, bringing her firmly into her third trimester. "I can barely see my feet anymore because of the damn baby," she said. "And I can't go anywhere with my nails still wet."

"Wear my flip-flops. We don't want to be late." Firm but good-humored, like a mom—not Mary, but a mom who cooked breakfast, attended PTA meetings, helped with homework, and never smoked pot or prostrated herself before the Goddess—Ann kept Jessica on schedule. They were going to meet the adoption lawyer.

The sickly stench of Jessica's nail polish filled the car. Ann rolled her window down. Jessica placed her feet up on the dashboard, her toes spilling over the edges of Ann's flip-flops. She seemed in a talkative mood. "Right after we fucked, oh sorry, *made love*, I had this strange fizzy feeling, like a sparkling inside. That's when the baby landed, like magic. Your mom believes in magic."

Mary had paid Jessica a visit while Ann was at work, and regaled Jessica with stories of the threefold Goddess and how her own bronzed baby shoes had channeled Jessica into their lives. Mary had captivated Jessica, as she did almost everyone. Ann took the curves fast. Warm wind whipped through the car window, diffusing the smell. The bucolic blue sky and the wildflowers erupting colorfully along the roadside seemed evidence of a world that conspired with Eros and the Threefold Goddess, causing strange fizzy feelings and babies landing by magic. Ann's big toe cramped as she pressed the gas pedal.

"We were at a bed and breakfast called the Windy Manor. There were so many pillows just piled on this canopy bed, I was like floating on them. And the sheets were soft as clouds. But afterwards, dude dropped me off in Liberty with taxi fare. Said I knew what the deal was."

Ann pulled into the gravel driveway where the renovated barn of Slocombe Builders stood on a small lot. Next to the barn, a prefab building served as Joel's office. He was supposed to be ready. She glanced over, shocked to see Jessica crying.

"You deserve better," she said. "So does the baby." Keeping it neutral, not "your baby" or "my baby." She tried to embrace Jessica. But Jessica thrust out both elbows, violently thwarting her.

Joel approached from the barn in his apron, covered in sawdust. "Be right there!"

"Wow, you're all dusty!" Jessica threw herself out of the car, giggling as if she hadn't just been crying. She ran to Joel and brushed the sawdust off Joel's chest as if the two were on intimate terms.

"THEY SAY THIS IS complicated but it doesn't have to be." Eliza Little, the lawyer who charged $250 per billable hour, settled behind her desk in a kneeling apparatus, her hips propped on a cushioned seat and knees resting on a padded platform. "All of you legally reside in New York, am I right? Good. State law stipulates that adoptive couples can pay not only for medical expenses but also for housing, maternity clothes and counseling for a birth mother, not to exceed three thousand dollars, to avoid even the suggestion that the baby is being purchased."

"I'm not doing any counseling," said Jessica. "That shit will make you crazy."

"Do we know who the father is? Is the father on the same page with this adoption?"

"The father's so cold, he's *freeze-dried*." Jessica had rolled the waistband of her stretch pants down below her belly, exposing her pink flesh. She seemed lit from within.

"I think she means the father's *not* in the picture," said Ann. She saw Joel's eyes sliding along the profile of Jessica's shoulders to her breasts; his lips open in frank admiration, and she clasped her hands tightly, twisting her palms. Her own body had never seemed so bony and sharp in comparison, her way of being so exact and orderly and brittle.

"I know you. You belong to the hippie house. Mary and I used to do the Weight Watchers. I bought this ring from her." Eliza pointed her beringed finger at Ann. A bezel-set emerald in a silver band, the ring looked too thin and delicate for her. "How old are you?" she asked Jessica.

"Eighteen."

"I need to see a birth certificate or documentation."

"Don't have it," said Jessica.

"You should get yourself an attorney, little missy. I can't represent you. It's a conflict of interest. And you two will have to undergo a home study. It's the law. A certified social worker comes to your house and attests to your eligibility. People have nervous breakdowns over this—just warning you."

Eliza Little had drawn up a contract, though it wasn't binding, she said, until she received all necessary documentation. "Mr. Slocombe here tells me you're living with the adoptive couple," she frowned. "Very unconventional."

Joel wrote out a check and they fled the chilly air-conditioned office for the bright warmth of the street. Ann walked alongside Jessica. "I didn't know where my birth certificate was either," she said. "All my life I thought I was born on August 16th. But last year when my grandma died, I found out I was born on August 10th. And I wasn't born at the Woodstock concert but in a hospital in Colorado Springs." *It's just a piece of paper!* Mary had said, not comprehending that it represented the origin of Ann's life.

Jessica flipped up the hood of her sweatshirt. She stalked into the pizza place ahead of them and slid into a booth. When she finally spoke, she glared at them through the slit of her hood. "That lawyer makes this whole thing a big giant hassle. Why can't you guys have kids? Are you shooting blanks or something, Joel?"

"I have a syndrome. I was born without a uterus." Ann stared at the wedding band on Joel's finger. She had left hers on the bathroom sink, often loath to wear a ring identical to Mary's. She didn't mention the other part, the shallow indentation, the cul-de-sac she no longer had the privacy to stretch.

"No uterus? I never heard of that," said Jessica. "Must be a total sucky bummer."

The sympathy surprised Ann. She felt pathetically grateful as she watched Jessica gently place paper napkins on her pizza slice. Oil seeped through, turning them yellow. She glanced up at Jessica's wide innocent face and realized Jessica was addressing Joel.

"Men need to spread their seed," said Jessica. "You don't have an outlet."

"Actually," he said. "It's harder for her than for me. It's hard for me because I love her."

"I wish someone loved *me,*" said Jessica.

"We love you," Joel placed a hand on Jessica's arm. "Don't we, Ann?"

"If she was nicer to me, I might love her," Ann almost said aloud. But she controlled herself, clamped her mouth into a smile and merely nodded.

ANN SAT NEXT TO Jessica on the couch, ostensibly watching TV, but really watching Jessica watch TV. It was the thirtieth anniversary of the Apollo 11 space flight, and Joel had wanted to watch a documentary about NASA. But he sat far away at the kitchen table, poring over estimates and plans. Jessica glared at the footage of Buzz Aldrin walking on the moon. "Come count the kicks with me, Joel!" she said.

"Ann would be a better bet for that," said Joel, barely looking up.

"I'd love to count the kicks with you," said Ann. She could not voice her suspicion without sharpening the potential into hard reality, and she certainly did not want that. She reminded herself that she'd always had patience. She possessed the marriage certificate, as well as the moral high ground. But she found herself analyzing the interactions between Jessica and Joel. He worked late every night, a renovation here, a house addition there, bidding on a building at the Monticello Racetrack. He had never been busier. When he came home, he ate dinner quickly and got right back on the phone with subcontractors and clients. Avoidance.

When Jessica curled up against her, giving tacit permission, Ann felt ashamed of her distrust. However hard she thought she had it, Jessica had it worse. Sure, Jessica could get pregnant while Ann could not, but Jessica was alone, abandoned by her family, while Ann was happily married. So, Jessica had a crush. Weighed against her generosity—giving them her baby! — what did a crush matter?

Ethan kicked and shifted in leisurely organic movements, while the spacecraft countdown unfolded in mechanical sequence. *Ten, nine, ignition sequence starts. Six, five, four, three, two, one, zero. All engines running. Lift-off, we have a lift-off.* Like one person they lay, united by the baby, while history flashed on TV. Ann imagined Ethan reaching from his watery world, and she could almost believe it was possible to dissolve the physical boundary of Jessica's body and merge with her son. It felt delicious, this coalescence, and the softness of Jessica's skin and her tangy smell. If Joel was attracted, how could Ann blame him? She, too, was enchanted by Jessica, carrier of her son.

"HEY STRANGER!" CASSIDY HADN'T changed in the years she'd been gone, still with her wild, curly red hair and multiple tattoos.

Ann had been weeding her garden when the van pulled into the driveway. Now an unpleasant heartburn of envy arose as she hugged Cassidy, careful not to squeeze the sleeping infant slung around Cassidy's front. "Beautiful baby," she said. "What's her name?"

"Sky, maybe?" said Cassidy. "Unless, Star, what do you think? I have to make up my mind! Remember my son, Cody over there? I should have named him Quinn. Isn't he more of a Quinn?" A little boy stared from the open passenger side of the van, America's van, with the license plates spelling CRZYFNGR, from her Grateful Dead-following days. His red hair was wild and unruly like his mother's. The last time Ann saw him, he had been a newborn.

"Come on, little chickenshit." Cassidy yanked him out, righting him when he stumbled in the driveway. McKenna danced and barked around them.

Jessica came out from the trailer, in a string bikini top and black spandex shorts, all her lusciousness exposed. "Who the hell invited children?"

Ann felt physically diminished by her. "Maybe you should put some clothes on."

"Are you going to tell me I'm a whore next?" Jessica yawned and stretched. "Should I harness my tits cause they're hanging out all over the place?"

"I don't talk like that," said Ann. Her vacation coincided with the advent of Jessica's thirty-second week. And the tits, she noticed, had long outgrown the bikini top.

"You got to clear out your negative shit or you'll poison your fetus with emotional toxins," Cassidy said, unslinging the baby and passing her to Ann. Heavy with sleep, floppy in the limbs, and one visible earlobe blushing red like a watercolor, the baby was a miracle. All babies were. Ann touched Sky or Star's downy skull with the tip of her nose.

"Holy shit. What a load of crap." Jessica lay down in a reclining lawn chair, cupping her hand over her forehead like a visor. "Get lost, kid," she said, when Cody sidled over.

"The rhythms you got from your mother, she got from her mother," said Cassidy. "And your baby gets from you. We're all caught up in this great pulsation. So, just think about it. Like ripples in a pond when you throw a stone."

While Ann had survived high school by laying low, studying, and deflecting attention, Cassidy took the opposite tack, pretending to cast spells on other students and chanting loudly in study hall. She painted pentacles in the sky with her fingers, wore a ring with a glass eye for a stone, and was expelled after she left a candle burning in her locker. Ann recalled it now. How fixed their characters were, how little changed. What they'd had in common was their unpopularity, the price of both invisibility and weirdness.

"Give Mommy her space." Cassidy peeled Cody off. He had wrapped himself around her. "Look at those pretty yellow flowers! See at the edge of the driveway? Go pick some buttercups!"

The exchange took Ann back to her own childhood, which she could remember in crystallized moments, when she'd cling to Mary as Mary pushed her away. *Go play!* Like a feral pack of animals, the commune children tore around the fields, hitting with sticks, hurling stones, shoving each other into the creek: whole days spent in unfettered mutual torment. Never would she subject a child to that. She watched the building crew operating their crane to stack custom trusses for the roof frame. They'd finished the inside partitions and covered the outside walls with pink house wrap, like a gift. A truss swung upward, blue sky radiant between the wood slabs.

With a flick of her lighter, Cassidy fired up a joint. The potent smell of marijuana cloaked the other odors of grass and tar. "Can I ask you a favor?" she said squeakily, holding in smoke. "Do you want to take the kids for a couple of hours? I need a break. I'm out of whack."

"I'd love to." Ann refused the joint. She turned to locate Cody, squatting in the grass, his little bottom inches from the ground.

"Can I have some of that doobie?" Jessica piped up from the lawn chair.

"No," said Ann. "Under no uncertain terms."

Cassidy exhaled an aromatic stream of smoke. "Your call. But one hit is no big deal. I smoked when I was pregnant with him. Our mothers smoked. We turned out fine."

"Yeah, and this is so *boring*," said Jessica. "I hate kids!"

"Kids are total entropy but they're our spiritual teachers and don't you forget it," said Cassidy, drawing a counter-clockwise pentacle in the air. "It's a good thing you're giving yours up. At least you have the wisdom for that."

From where she sat, Ann saw Jessica's painted toes tense up.

"Fuck you," said Jessica.

Cassidy laughed, a disconnected, stoned laugh, pushing herself up to stand. "You have to visit Mary. She thinks you disowned her. You know I'm working for her, right? I've been polishing stones and whatever, gluing posts on earrings. But she didn't make her quota so she's emoting all up in my space. Like it's my fault."

If not for Joel and Jessica, Ann might have assisted Mary, which she'd done over previous vacations, sorting stones, cleaning tumblers, soldering silver, whatever Mary needed. But Ann hadn't offered. She'd been avoiding Mary. "Is she mad at me?"

"Who knows? There are extra diapers and some milk I pumped. She'll be hungry in an hour." Cassidy blew a kiss and climbed into the van.

Sky awoke and regarded Ann with a strong, clear awareness. The lawn chair squeaked behind her, then Jessica came over and settled on the ground, cuddling against her like a child needing closeness. "What a weirdo," she said.

"She is a little weird," said Ann. "You're right about that."

For a moment, they were in perfect accord.

MARY LEFT A MESSAGE on the answering machine, *This is your old cast-off mother, checking to see if you're still alive,* but Ann waited until her last day of vacation before she packed Cassidy's kids into borrowed car seats and drove, with Jessica and McKenna in the front, to visit Mary. Startlingly purple, the ramshackle, two-storied farmhouse that Mary called Sunrise stood out among the rolling hills and nondescript cottages like a cry for help. On the porch wall, a huge orange sun flared against the purple background. A spiral between two decorative eyes opened into a line descending to the porch floor. Above the pair of eyes was a third eye.

"Sam calls this the place where hippies go to die." Jessica laughed.

"Why is there a sun?" Cody asked. McKenna trailed behind, panting.

"It's painted," said Ann, hoisting Sky up on her chest.

She hadn't minded when Cassidy dropped off her kids again after the first day, not then or the day after, and she'd finally offered to take them for the rest of her vacation. Much as she disapproved of Cassidy's attitude and didn't want to condone it, Ann welcomed the kids. They diverted her attention from Jessica's body and Jessica's bitchiness, and they seemed to confirm for Jessica that she was making the right decision.

"Monster!" Cody cried at the sight of Mary's trickster, a grinning creature built of wire mesh and papier-mâché. With a long nose and maniacal smile, the statue stood just inside the front door at the foot of the staircase, a taunting welcome. His pointed breasts with nails for nipples jutted aggressively over his large erect penis, upon which hung an umbrella. In his upturned palm lay Mary's pink vibrator with a post-it attached: BUY BATTERIES written large.

"Holy shit," said Jessica. "A dick and balls and tits, that's scary."

"Do you like my trickster statue? I made him myself. Desire unbound by gender, we celebrate him on the Spring Equinox." Mary glided toward them from the kitchen, her green silk robe swanning open to reveal her nudity as she enveloped them in a patchouli-scented hug, breasts mashed against Ann's side. "My desire is fulfilled because you're here!"

"Do you always walk around naked?" said Jessica. "Ann won't let me."

"The naked body is noble in its power and vulnerability," said Mary. "I see Cassidy pawned the rug-rats off on you!"

"Do you mind?" said Ann. "They can hear you."

"They don't understand," Mary and Jessica said simultaneously. "Jinx!" Laughing, Mary hooked her arm through Jessica's. "I'm so sick of working. I'm supposed to meet all these orders for Della, high-end retail—Martha's Vineyard, Cape May, P-Town. I'm not a goddam factory. Let's go swimming."

Ann grabbed Cody's hand and headed outside, down the porch steps and around the house to the path that led to the pond. The field was dotted with goldenrod and Queen Ann's Lace, alive with insects and bees. Sky pushed at Ann's breasts with her palms and pressed her face against Ann's sternum. Cody danced at her side, full of whimsical prattle about flower stalks and worms, his anatomically correct man-doll dangling from his fist. *My children,* she thought, as they skirted Mary's circle of stones for the woods.

The pond lay tranquil, pervaded by quiet greenness. Mosquitoes whined. McKenna paced the shore. Mary slipped out of her robe to slide naked into the water. She rolled onto her back. "It's glorious!"

Jessica peeled off her spandex shorts, let her top fall and waded in, also naked, beautiful. She dove under with barely a ripple.

In her one-piece Speedo, Ann cast a critical eye on herself: a skinny pale woman in a state of refusal. Knots of tension pulsed at the base of her skull. She spread out a blanket before putting Sky down. Cody got caught in his T-shirt. Halfway over his head, arms entangled, he wouldn't let Ann help. "No! I do it!"

"You did it!" she cried when he freed himself. Then she led him to the water and sank into mud all the way to her ankles.

Mary and Jessica somersaulted in the center where the water was deep. "You're the same age I was when I got pregnant with Annapurna!" Mary cried when she surfaced. A mist of droplets held the light around her face. "You're manifesting the great earth goddess."

Ann submerged to her shoulders, holding Cody aloft. She had suffered an ear infection as a child at the commune, causing her eardrum to burst in a pus-filled explosion of pain, and years later she couldn't go underwater without endangering her hearing.

"Is Annapurna your real name? So much nicer than Ann!" Jessica drew Cody away, helping him float.

"Annapurna's the benevolent aspect of Devi, Goddess of Plenty," said Mary. "I gave her that name and she changed it to a boring, plain one."

"Saint Ann is the mother of Mary," said Ann, quoting Gran, who'd supported her name change. When Sky wailed from the blanket, Ann waded back to shore, her hair and face still dry. She scooped up the hot, sweaty baby and brought her into the water, dipping her in and out until the wails turned to shrieks of joy.

They all returned to Sunrise together. While Ann fed the children, Jessica and Mary went upstairs. She heard Jessica admiring the glass and mirror mosaic in the stairwell. "Awesome!"

"Intentional disorder," said Mary. "Disperses the energy so it doesn't fly up the staircase. Have you heard of feng shui?"

When the kids were finished eating, Ann took them into the living room where the air was cooler, shadowed by the oak trees outside, a fan blowing on the windowsill. She wondered how Mary managed to charm people so easily. And why couldn't she do that?

"I'm a hippie chick now." Jessica came downstairs in one of Mary's peasant skirts with the elastic waistband pulled up just under her breasts. "Mary said I could live here instead of the trailer."

Of course she did. "You won't be able to see much of Joel, living here," Ann said coolly.

"I want to give you a gift. You can choose any pair of earrings." Mary dragged her portable display to the center of the room. She unsnapped the latches theatrically, pausing for a moment to allow the full, impressive effect of sparkling stones and polished precious metal against a black velvet-lined board. Ann knew Mary's moves but still experienced a leap of excitement as Mary switched on the small battery-powered light for maximum brilliance.

"Your mom makes such beautiful stuff and you never wear any of it." Jessica touched each pair of earrings, one by one, finally choosing ornate dangling chandeliers, silver with blue crystals—part of the *madebymary*™ series.

"Annapurna has never worn my jewelry. Not even her wedding ring, which I made."

"You're wearing one, too!" said Jessica. "It's beautiful."

"Prototype. Gesture of solidarity." Mary splayed her fingers.

"I don't like things rattling or dangling," said Ann. "Jewelry draws too much attention to itself, and away from the person."

"My jewelry *enhances* the person," said Mary.

"How much would you say this necklace is worth?" Jessica unclasped the gold chain with the heart pendant she always wore. Ann had deduced that it was a trinket from the father of the baby. She watched Mary peer through her jeweler's loupe, turning the necklace in her palm. "Hard to say. It *could* be quite valuable."

The slightly higher pitch of her voice, the forced cheer, and the exaggerated squint with which she inspected the piece revealed the lie. It was worthless. *How kind Mary can be,* Ann thought.

"You should come to our full moon circle," said Mary. "It's at the Sisterhood. We could all drive to the city together. They've been asking about you, Ann."

"We're so busy with the house and the social worker visit. Maybe next month."

"Ann avoids our circles and celebrations," Mary told Jessica. "But you must come to the Autumn Equinox, both of you. Joel, too. It's the season of the mysteries. Only happens every four years. Sage can lay a blessing on your womb."

"Will there be witchcraft?" asked Jessica. Light flashed from her earlobes.

Sky burped warm liquid onto Ann's shoulder. Cody had fallen asleep on the bear skin in front of the fireplace.

"Earth to Annapurna." Mary crawled over to rest her head against Ann's other shoulder. Her hair was wet and clammy, her head heavy: Ann's big child.

I'M IN LOVE WITH you, Joelmeister. I think you're totally hot and that's the god's honest truth. Joel listened to the message again from the relative safety of his office. It gave him that squirming sensation again. Not unpleasant. Jessica had called earlier as he drove from site to site. He was juggling several projects: cabinetry for a kitchen renovation, the raceway building, and an extension with deck for a house outside Cochecton. He hadn't answered his cell phone when he saw the number because Jessica also called during client meetings and inspections. She'd called in the middle of a discussion with a local councilman, too. She called constantly.

She told him about the baby moving, about her sciatica, her shortness of breath, the ache in her pelvis and how glad she was that Ann had gone back to work, freeing her from Cassidy's brats. She said Sam had been fired from his job. She talked about the parties she used to attend at the meth dealer's house, and the snakeskin boots with Cuban heels that the meth dealer wore, how she'd met the orthodontist at one of those parties. But this blatant declaration of love brought a new twist. Joel dreaded her calls. He coveted her calls. He hated her voice. He longed for her voice.

His phone rang again. "Did you get my message?" said Jessica. "You know I love you, right?"

He laughed it off. "We love you, too, Ann and me. A lot."

"That's not what I meant. I see how you look at me. I know what you want. I'm wet for you, like, all the time."

The phone sucked into his sweaty palm. "You're crazy."

"I can make you feel good. I can give you your own baby."

"I got another call coming." Joel's heart rammed through his chest. Sweat collected around his groin. He hung up, dashed into the bathroom and masturbated fast, thinking of Jessica's mouth, her breasts and thighs and pregnant belly. He imagined she knew exactly what he was doing. *You're a cliché,* he berated himself. *You're being manipulated, fool.*

He'd had only one girlfriend before he'd met Ann, one who had slept around and lied. And then she'd moved away, leaving him stupid and heartbroken. He would have to become stern with Jessica. She was only a kid. He was the one with the power.

But he felt helpless. To postpone going home after work, he stopped in to visit his mother. Betty had run through two more health aides over the last couple of months; the first after she suffered from a hypoglycemic episode and fainted. *I'm not a nurse!* the woman cried. The second left after Betty threw a hairbrush at her. Joel had found the latest, Winifred, through Betty's church.

But the women only added to his unease. Winifred bustled about in Betty's pink slippers, dropping ashes from the cigarette that hung between her lips. "I'll tell you one thing that would make your mother happy," she said, cigarette bobbing. "If you would go to mass with her."

I'm wet for you floated through Joel's mind. His whole body went into a heady buzz, pleasant and terrifying. He almost said, *Sure, I'll go to mass,* before he caught himself. "Ma knows I don't go to church. The argument was shelved when Dad ran away."

Betty was sitting at the kitchen table. She jabbed the air with her soup spoon. "How's your Queen Bee? Sittin' pretty, I imagine. Everyone wrapped around her little finger."

"September," said Joel. "You'll have a grandson."

"Head in the clouds," said Betty. "You don't see where this is going, you have only yourselves to blame."

Joel's chest tightened. He was reduced to a kid again, full of foolish notions. She would never understand how the whole world could funnel into the head of a galvanized finishing nail with one slam of a hammer. Life demanded improvisation. Knotholes were strange areas where wood behaved chaotically, unpredictably. He'd always believed that if his father hadn't left, Betty would have chosen joy rather than meanness. Another foolish notion.

As he headed home, Joel remembered lying in bed as a boy, his quilt, decorated with cowboys and lassos, pulled up to his neck and the faces of his parents smiling down on him. Betty and Jake. Hard to believe that moment of tranquility had really happened; he'd gone over it so many times that it was just a memory of a memory, transmuted to a wish. He might have invented it. His father left them for good the weekend of the Woodstock concert, enticed by the music that traveled over the fields. Sitting with his mother in the kitchen, waiting for his dad to come home to dinner, Joel heard the melodies, faint and elusive as a breeze.

Darkness was falling and the lights in the trailer burned fiercely. The subcontractors were long gone. They had stacked the windows and doors against the north wall of the new house. Joel moved everything to the south, wearing himself out, avoiding the trailer.

WHEN HE AND ANN were finally alone in bed, she whispered "I never see you anymore."

Joel had loved her for her shyness and containment. She allowed him to be magnanimous. Not just that. He loved watching her with children, catching the light in her eyes when she smiled, listening to her sing when her voice suddenly broke free and soared, and he had imagined them together, with children, a family singing and bantering and learning together. But now, an electrical current ran through their bodies, down the narrow hall to plug into Jessica on the sofa, and Ann just seemed clueless. "It's not worth it," he said. "We should figure out another way to have a baby. She's like poison."

She went rigid. "We already started birthing classes."

"She calls me at work. It's inappropriate," said Joel. "I don't feel comfortable in my own home." *Joel, will you massage my shoulders? I'm so tense.* Jessica's entreaties carried a potent appeal that he couldn't fathom Ann being indifferent to.

"You're probably the only man who's ever been nice to her so she has a crush on you. You can handle it, can't you?" Ann knelt over him, kissing his neck, his chest, his stomach. "Soon, we'll have a son."

Even though he wanted to kiss Jessica's soft plump lips, not Ann's thin, chiseled ones, Joel felt himself grow hard. Ann moved her kisses to his groin. Her mouth, Jessica's mouth. He stopped her. "I'm sorry, I'm tired."

"No you're not." She straddled him. But she moved awkwardly, still shy. He turned them over so he was on top. Then he feared he'd break her. They made love in tense silence. Joel bucked through the motions, imagining how Jessica would whoop and cry out, spreading her wings, wet and welcoming.

ANN'S THIRTIETH BIRTHDAY CAME a few days before the thirtieth anniversary of the Woodstock Concert. "Goodbye to my twenties," she said, toasting with a glass of wine on the living room rug. Because of rain, they sat inside the trailer—Ann, Joel, Jessica, Mary, and the dog.

"My present first!" Mary handed her something heavy, swaddled in purple tissue.

Ann opened it to find a copper bowl, tapered and curved at one end like a fish, carved inside with a spoon shape, and outlined with oval etchings.

"What the hell is that?" said Jessica.

"It's a yoni," said Mary. "I made it, to give out Shakti energy. Represents female power, childbearing, fertility. They were *way* popular in the '80s. Della says they're making a comeback. It's supposed to go on the baby altar. Hey, where's your altar?"

As a teenager, Ann had chanted to the sisterhood yoni before she found out she had no uterus. After that, the gift seemed almost hostile. A nudge at her leg: Joel rubbing his foot against her calf. She tried to smile. "We put the stuff in a drawer," she said. "That's Jessica's table now."

"Don't undo the magic by hiding the objects away! Bad karma!" Mary became a force of nature, pushing aside the color-coded folders on the shelf above the phone to clear a new space for the bronzed baby shoes, amethyst crystal, heart-shaped stone, popsicle-stick house and, pride of place in front, her yoni.

Ann let her take over. The chocolate cake she had eaten turned and swelled in her stomach.

"Did Ann tell you she was born during Woodstock?" Mary addressed Jessica. "You know, in the movie when John Sebastian announces that some cat's old lady just had a baby, a kid destined to be far out? That was me! Annapurna was that baby!"

"That's a lie and you know it," said Ann. She always had to be the larger person. It was draining. "Why do you do that? It hurts my feelings."

"Looks like she hates your present," Jessica told Mary. "I didn't get her anything because she'd hate that, too."

"You're already giving me the best present anyone could ever give," said Ann.

"Why don't you like it?" said Mary. "I made it for you."

Joel got up and walked out of the trailer.

"Where's he going?" said Mary. "Was it something I said?"

He returned, carrying a guitar case that he placed on the floor in front of Ann. "Happy birthday."

Lined with crushed faux velvet, the case held an electric Fender Mustang with a short-scale neck, easier for small hands to play, instantly the nicest gift Ann had ever received in her life.

"I can't compete with that," said Mary. "He's trying to make me look bad."

"It's not a contest." But it was, and Joel won, hands down. Ann pulled the guitar onto her lap to inhale its new wood-oil-metal smell. She stroked the slick, perfect surface. It was warm, as if alive. When she plucked out the opening notes to Depeche Mode's *Personal Jesus,* the pressure of the strings indenting her fingertips enlivened her, and the notes resonated. "Thank you," she said. "Oh, thank you."

"I got her what I thought she wanted," said Joel. "It wasn't about me."

"I want a guitar, too" said Jessica. "When are you going to give me one?"

Mary, for once, said nothing.

"Turn right here. No!" cried Jessica. "You just passed it!"

Ann made a U-Turn. Jessica's house stood near an auto repair shop outside a town called Rock Hill, about twenty miles away from Bethel. The house appeared uninhabited, its raw wood exposed like naked skin beneath flecks of peeling paint. A torn sofa commanded half the porch. Dead plants drooped in pots suspended from the porch eaves, as if someone had once made an effort.

"Look, I got the shakes." Jessica held out her trembling mani-cured hand. Dressed up in her new maternity pants and pink sweater, her face freshly scrubbed and makeup-free, she came across as conservative and innocent.

"I'll go in with you." Ann turned the engine off.

"Keep your ass in the car. I mean it." Jessica slammed the door.

Ann couldn't shake her dread as she watched Jessica vanish into the house. *What if she changes her mind?* Vibrant orange leaves quivered in the trees, painted against a dull gray sky. Long daggers of yellow grass pointed upward from the roadside. Somehow August had slid right out from under them. She tapped the dash with her fingertips. Minutes crept by. Eight more weeks until the baby. A crow cawed. They had come for the birth certificate.

When she couldn't wait any longer, she got out and crossed the road. The porch steps were rotted and treacherous. She knocked lightly on the door. No one answered.

"Hello?" Ann opened the door. The room was in shadows and smelled of cigarettes and decay. A man was lying on the sofa on the opposite wall. He lay on his side in an unbelted bathrobe and unbuttoned jeans, disheveled and unshaven, his bare chest tufted with graying hair. "What do you know? We got company."

"Excuse me," said Ann. "I'm looking for Jessica."

The man didn't respond. Nor did he seem surprised to see a strange woman enter.

"Jessica?" Ann called. She stepped carefully over a phone on the floor, dodged a TV that flashed with muted images, and ducked a strip of hanging flypaper. A broken swatter lay on the floor near the man's feet, next to a bowl of congealed baked beans. The man watched her as she trod gingerly past him to the next room.

It was a kitchen, with walls the color of mustard. Jessica stood with her back to the doorway, facing an older woman across a table. An unmistakable family resemblance resided in the shape of the woman's full-lipped mouth and chubby neck. The two of them crouched, combat ready with the table between them. The woman's eyes flickered to Ann. "What the hell are you doing with my daughter?"

In an instant, Jessica shot around the table, clamped Ann's arm and dragged her back through the living room.

"Earl!" shouted the woman.

The man was already up, barricading the front door. "Go to your room, slut."

Jessica slapped him. It happened so fast, the room spun in a sickening buzz of dying flies.

Earl opened the door. "Get out before I kill you."

They dashed down the porch steps, holding hands. They flew across the road, into the car. Jessica's mother sprinted after them.

"Step on it!" cried Jessica. "Go!"

Ann couldn't turn the key. Her fingers fumbled. Finally, the engine ignited and she swerved onto the road. But as she gunned the gas, she glimpsed in the rearview mirror a terrible mask of sorrow on Jessica's mother's face.

"I hope you're happy," said Jessica. "Forget the fucking birth certificate. I'm never going back."

Ann didn't know where she was going under the flat, gray sky. She disappeared into a memory of driving when she was only twelve: Mary had dropped acid and sat babbling like a baby, and someone had to get them home. Then as now, Ann couldn't identify a familiar landmark. The road was sucked continuously beneath the wheels. They could be anywhere. Jessica was rocking violently beside her.

Then she saw the Woodstock concert commemoration plaque, brass in stone, and turned off the road, cutting the engine. The fields unfolded beneath the sky. Jessica howled, like the toddlers dropped off by their mothers at the daycare, with helpless, forsaken rage. Amazed at her size and her softness and the weight of her grief, Ann held onto Jessica just as she would have held onto any of the toddlers. Her own tears were silent. "I'm sorry," she repeated. "I'm sorry."

THE SOCIAL WORKER STEPPED primly into the trailer. She took the envelope Ann thrust at her. "I think all the documents are there,"

said Ann, noting that the hem on the woman's skirt was torn and a piece of lining peeked below. It gave her hope that the woman would not judge them too harshly. They'd agreed they would not mention the birth certificate.

They had covered all the doorknobs for child-safety, installed doorstops and bumpers on the end tables, plated the electrical outlets and child-proofed the cabinet under the sink. The fire extinguisher sat prominently on the stove. Emergency numbers were listed by the phone. They'd prepared by the book, no detail left unattended.

Joel poured out decaf coffee. Jessica put out cookies. They sat at the round spool of the kitchen table and talked about the baby. "I'm due in a couple of weeks but he could come out right now if he wanted," said Jessica. Wearing the same pink maternity sweater she'd worn to visit her mother, she looked demure. "Just knock me out cold and wake me up when it's over."

"Goodness." The woman smiled.

"We saw a video in our birthing class," Ann explained. "It looked traumatic but the instructor said it was actually an easy birth." All the women had wept, even Ann, who cried for the loss of what she would never experience. *You'll want to treasure this special event,* the instructor had said in her saccharine voice. The envy Ann kept tamped down—envy of women glowing with the life inside them, of the universal female powers she'd forever be excluded from—was ugly and destructive, and burned like acid inside her.

"Unfortunately, the house won't be finished by the time the baby is born." Joel explained the construction schedule delays. He fetched his blueprints. Ann watched Jessica slide the social worker's coffee mug out of the way as Joel spread the prints over the table.

The social worker looked attentive, nodding when Joel pointed to the baby's room. She declined to tour the construction site.

"What comes to mind," she wearily turned to Ann, "when you hear the word *anger?*"

Ann flashed back to her childhood development theory class. "Management."

"Frustration," Joel nodded. "That's what I think of."

"My mother," said Jessica.

"That's all right," said the social worker. "The question wasn't for you, dear."

She stayed no more than half an hour and never asked for the birth certificate, probably assuming it was in the envelope. Rising to leave, she shook Ann's hand with long, limp fingers.

"Did we pass?" Jessica asked what Ann was afraid to.

"I'm not going to put up any obstacles," said the woman. They walked her outside, waving goodbye to her car until it left the driveway.

"We did it!" Joel yelled. Jessica high-fived him.

Ann exhaled. "It was almost too easy."

BECAUSE THE HOME STUDY visit had unfolded so seamlessly, Ann relented to the Autumn Equinox celebration that Jessica had hounded her to attend. Joel came, too. When they arrived at Sunrise, the driveway was crowded with cars. An altar had been constructed in the field out back, surrounded by Mary's circle of stones. Sage, the high priestess, in a white medieval gown with long, flared sleeves, was arranging baskets of brightly colored yarn. A fire smoldered in the pit. Brilliant red and yellow leaves snapped off trees and danced across the grass. The air reverberated like a plucked string and the sweet sense of soon followed Ann like a song: Jessica was overdue.

Ann placed an acorn on the pile of offerings in front of the altar. Joel set down a pinecone, and Jessica, a long twig shaped like a "J." Sage came over and tied a saffron ribbon around Ann's wrist. "After we bless your surrogate, all initiated womyn will retreat to the forest for the mysteries. I hope you're prepared." The webbed muscle between her thumb and finger displayed a black tattoo of a figure 8, the symbol of infinity.

"Not me," said Ann. "I'm only here because Jessica wanted to come."

But she and Joel had wandered off. Ann saw them talking to Mary.

"Release your resistance," said Sage. "Happy is she among women on Earth who has seen these mysteries. Don't be afraid."

Sage had been a presence since Ann was a child. All the skepticism in the world could be brought to bear and she would label it fear, and bend reality to her will. "I'm not afraid," said Ann.

Scanning the field, she found Joel and Jessica again, no longer with Mary. They were walking toward the house, heads close together. Asphodel and others from the sisterhood were by the fire. America, Cassidy, Mary and her jewelry rep, Della, milled nearby. Even Myron from the Monticello tree farm bore a wreath of chili peppers that he deposited on the altar. "I've taken a new spiritual name!" he declared. "What do you think of Cloud Rider?"

"Cast the Circle." Sage struck a chime three times. "Here is a place that's not a place, between the worlds, in the names of Demeter and Mabon, son of Modron."

Everyone collected around the altar. Joel and Jessica came running from the house, eyes shining and smiles giddy. Ann placed herself between them.

"We give gratitude for our harvest, and we rest after our labor," said Sage. "Day and night face each other as equals. But night waxes as day wanes."

Mary gestured for Jessica to sit in a plastic lawn chair, which had been festooned in vines and flowers. "Autumn's grain is the seed of spring," she said. "We honor Jessica, who brings forth a son. Show us your bounty so we may bless your womb."

Jessica lifted her sweater. Sage passed around body paint and brushes. "Me first!" said Mary, and painted an Om symbol at Jessica's navel.

"Tickles!" Jessica squirmed and giggled.

Envy came at Ann from the backs of the knees and the strange cold air she felt there. All she wanted was to be free of this poisonous feeling. One by one, each person marked Jessica with a visual wish for the health and good fortune of the baby. Ann painted a tiny heart on Jessica's midriff; and dropped her brush into the bucket.

"That which is never born never dies." Sage lobbed a roll of colored yarn into the bonfire. "We have sown, tended, grown and gathered. We thank you goddess and god for your gifts. And thank you for bringing Jessica into our lives. Throw your offerings to the goddess!"

They grabbed their feathers and acorns, twigs and pinecones, stones and leaves and threw them into the fire until all that remained on the altar was a small basket covered with cloth.

"Behold. In silence, the seed of wisdom is formed." Sage lifted the cloth with a flourish and there lay an ear of corn.

Ridiculous, thought Ann. But everyone else focused intently on the corn as if it held the meaning of life. Even Joel regarded it with the seriousness of a disciple. Jessica's mouth hung open.

Sage broke the silence. "Spirits of the north, south, east and west, we thank you and release you. Go if you must, stay if you will." When she genuflected with her palms and forehead on the ground, they all followed her lead.

Cold earth dampened Ann's knees through her jeans. *Now. Stand up. Go home. Plead migraine.* But as soon as she stood, Sage took her hand. "Initiated Women of the Eleusinian Circle. Come, we will experience Mystery."

"I have to go home," said Ann. "I have a headache."

"Please," said Sage. "We need nine for the mystery of the threefold Goddess. She can free you. Let Her in."

"Let Her in," chanted Mary, America, Cassidy, Raven, Asphodel and a few other women. They enclosed Ann in a circle. All of them wore saffron ribbons around their wrists. Ann wanted so badly not to be envious, she couldn't refuse. She wanted to be free. Joel and Jessica had again wandered off, excluded from the mystery.

But Ann was the one who felt excluded from their twosome as she fell in line behind America. They proceeded single file, with Sage in the lead, across the damp meadow grass toward the dark woods. A thermos was passed back. "Three deep swallows and send it to the next woman."

Trekking through the woods drinking tepid sludgy tea, Ann continued to interrogate her inability to refuse. When would she stop being a sucker? Why couldn't she simply do what she wanted to do? Every nerve in her body tightened. Wetness oozed into her sneakers, soaking her toes. She came up with no satisfactory answer, just an insurmountable sense of personal failure. The thermos moved through the line of women and came around again. It was bitter and stank of dirty socks. A form of self-punishment, Ann guzzled huge mouthfuls.

In a moment, the stars, which she hadn't paid attention to, began to melt and flow across the sky. As their procession cut a seam through the earth, energy rolled away like waves, and the sky settled into a vast tapestry of changing, migrating colored forms. Ann realized the hallucinations were a function of the tea. She was in for it now.

They reached a blanket, laid out on the ground with a knife in the center. Who put that there, she wondered, terrified.

"Reside with the goddess in her triple aspect. Maiden, mother, crone." Sage's voice emanated from inside Ann's mind like a psychic ventriloquist.

"The wisdom of the crone fills me." America's frizzy-haired silhouette bristled. "The heat of the sun explodes in my body. Then coolness comes."

"I am the mother," said Cassidy.

"*I* am the mother," said Mary.

The tiny sleeping face of the boy in Jessica's latest ultrasound hovered before Ann like a ghost. "I'm the mother," she said, amazed she could talk.

"That would make me the crone," said Mary. "I'm not ready to be the crone."

"We're all of us, all three," said Sage. "We are born. We die. We are reborn. She is the mystery. We stand in awe."

"That pregnant girl brings darkness," said Cassidy.

"She's wounded," said Asphodel.

"Wounded animals bite," said America.

"Hold your desire lightly, Ann," said Sage.

"No. You need to trust the universe. Have faith." Mary's voice touched Ann like a warm patch in a cold lake. She couldn't feel her limbs. And she dissolved into Mary's flow, becoming three: maiden of Mary; mother of unborn Ethan; and crone, more ancient than Gran, not suffering fools gladly. *Did you know St. Ann was the mother of the Blessed Virgin Mary, whom I named your mother after?* Each kernel in the ear of corn was a microcosm containing a universe. Ann hadn't seen it earlier because she hadn't been receptive.

The knife blade glimmered in the moonlight. "Iakchos!" Sage screamed, rolling up her wide sleeve to slice through the skin of her forearm. The air hummed and throbbed.

"Iakchos," cried America, and cut herself quickly, passing the knife.

Disembodied, Ann watched as she cut her own arm. Blood trailed like an ink-drawn line. Without shouting the name of the atavistic god, she handed the knife to Mary.

"Blood in birth, blood in death, blood in rebirth!" Sage began to stomp the ground and twirl. They all danced then, mimicking Sage in her frenzied gyrations.

Lanced by a cramp, Ann sank to the ground, which shifted beneath her. Wind rattled dry leaves. A shadow slipped through and entered her limbs. Her arms, legs and body solidified again.

"Blessed is she among women who partakes in these ceremonies." The words seemed to melt off Sage's lips like soft wax, no longer in Ann's head. "The great awe of the goddess makes the voice falter. We do not speak of the mystery."

Traipsing back, last in line, Ann experienced a revelation: They were not permitted to speak of the mystery because even though they had experienced it, they didn't know what it was. The shimmering geometric colors of the tapestry faded into night. She almost laughed, so relieved to be herself again.

The mystery is a mystery, she imagined telling Joel, and he would laugh, too. They could write a song. But she remembered how Jessica and Joel had been walking so close together. For a moment, she was isolated in a cold loneliness, stumbling on the dark, uneven ground, remote as the moon. Then she bumped against softness. Mary embraced her. "The DMT is wearing off. We can't know the forces we set in motion."

When they arrived at Sunrise, music drifted out from the windows. Ann held Mary's hand. The party, with its basic human happiness and connection, welcomed them. Upstairs in Mary's workroom where a dim light shone, Ann saw the silhouettes of Jessica and Joel in a pantomime of argument: Joel turning, Jessica grabbing. She knew by the sudden tension in Mary's fingers that Mary saw it, too. It struck her, like a pitch-perfect note on the guitar, that this was the price for what she wanted, this thing between Jessica and Joel, and she could accept it. She squeezed Mary's hand. "It's okay. I'm not jealous. I once was, but not anymore."

"FRIEND OF THE DEVIL" obliged Mary to boogie in her seat. Grateful Dead, Fillmore East, 1970, she had archived the CD from one of her bootleg cassette tapes. She bounced on her stool as she cut a strip of silver on the gouged wooden surface of her jewelry bench. Once the silver was cut, she only had to shape and solder.

She turned on her acetylene torch flame, and quickly painted flux
on the solder chips. With a bushy blue fire going, she warmed the
chips until they were suspended in a honey-like pool of flux. Then
she placed them directly on the ring with her pick, heating the
joint until the solder flowed with a flash of bright silver.

"Friend of the Devil" moved into "Ripple." Dropping the
ring into a pot of acidic solution, Mary danced to her window. *My
property,* she'd never say aloud because it was so bourgeois. But her
thoughts were free and unfettered, and she loved the view of her
field below, undulating like flesh. The circle of stones was coated
in the gold of twilight.

"Hey, girlfriend! You should lock your door! I could be an
intruder." America's tart voice came from the stairwell.

"I'll be right down!" Mary called, turning off her flame. As
she sashayed along the staircase, she caught glimpses of herself in
the shards of her mirror mosaic, an eye here, a lip there, a lock of
long gray hair. She was mysteriously appealing in fragments. Much
nicer, she thought, than her whole.

America was in the living room, crouched at the fireplace,
feeding newspaper into the blaze. Her wild gray hair was held back
with a variety of baby barrettes. Over her yellow stretch pants she
wore a giant black T-shirt with *Will Power* lettered beneath a white
silhouette of Shakespeare. When she stood for a hug, Mary pressed
against her; breasts to breasts. A spark lit up inside. She could evap-
orate in love; she was easy that way. *Oh, patchouli, shrubby mint,
druggy scent of hairy hippie women.* "How about some wine?" she
asked.

"Sure, baby. And I brought over some new wares," said
America. "Just in this morning. Guaranteed to blow your mind."

While Mary opened a bottle of red and poured out two
glasses, America filled her little marble pipe. "I got this stuff from a
one-eyed Tehuantepec bruja on a motorcycle. The karma is good."
She rolled out her tongue to draw in the smoke, her expression
internal, as if tasting fine cognac.

Three hits and Mary's limbs went liquid. She threw a couple of thick logs on the fire, with the foresight to know that soon she'd forget how. Then she lay back on her elbows on the bearskin rug, basking in the warmth and gazing at America's round freckled face. "Are you reconsidering? You want to move in? The offer's open."

America's smile looked surreal, like the Cheshire cat. "Thou art goddess," she said.

One kiss led to a string of them. America pulled Mary's shirt up to scratch her back and Mary's skin came alive. The walls flickered with shivering orange light on electrical impulses. America stroked her buttocks, spooning, sliding her hands around to caress Mary's thighs. Clothing slid off. Familiar with each other's mouths and skin, senses flooding with pleasure and soft explosions of satisfaction, Mary lost herself completely. It had been too many weeks without this.

Afterwards, they lay naked on the bearskin. Mary absently rubbed America's back. Her fingers brushed a series of scabs along America's spine, which she hadn't noticed when making love. "What happened here?"

"Rug burns!" America shook with a muted guffaw. "How about help me unload some of this righteous weed? You'd be well-rewarded."

Sated, stoned, almost dozing, Mary wondered aloud. "How did you get rug…"

"A *man,* sweetie. Can you believe I did the dirty with a man?"

America wound her fingers through Mary's. They were small and soft, not like Mary's large hammer-tipped fingers, which were stained and cut from metalworking. And Mary melted into their softness and the furry bearskin, and the pleasing scent of resin and hashish rising off America's skin until she felt the scabs again. "Why would you do it with a man?"

"Oh Mary. He's a hermaphrodite, like your trickster. It was amazing."

"But I thought you were going to move in with me. Take *us* to another level." Mary's heart fluttered into her throat. She disentangled herself.

America rolled onto her front. "He's my new supplier. We did it, if you can fuckin' believe, on the floor of a warehouse full of sensimillia in the Bronx! Couldn't keep our hands off each other!" She laughed with the sheer cheeky joy of herself. "I'm running amok!"

"What about the bruja?" Mary's mind felt sluggish. She rolled up to sit cross-legged. Oh, she wanted to be an easy-loving open person. But she couldn't reconcile her aspiration with her sense of betrayal. She wanted America all to herself. They had been off-and-on lovers for more than a decade and never once in that time had America been with a man. She wanted America all to herself. "Didn't you say you got the stuff from a one-eyed whatever on a motorcycle?"

"That's my story and I'm sticking to it," said America. "Come on. Don't be a crybaby. I got a lot of love in my heart. Especially for you. You know that."

"I'm sorry but I'm having trouble processing." *Don't be needy, Mary*, her mother, Rose would say. Mary rearranged the logs with the iron poker. It gave her something to do. When she and America spent too many consecutive hours together, they bickered over stupid issues like who was more down-to-earth and honest, boozers or stoners. Or whether the spiritual path was open to a select conscious few or available to all; whether gambling in Sullivan County would be good or bad and when they agreed it was bad, they argued about why. But this loomed larger than any argument. A *man!*

"I still love you, sugar." America wrapped her body around Mary's buttocks. "Come on, I always come home to you, Mary. You're my home."

Tears came with ferocious immediacy. Mary's throat cramped.

America's hands were all over her then. Her hands, her lips on Mary's eyelids, her open arms. Mary surrendered. She felt her tears dissolve into the overwhelming moment. Wasn't she receiving love now? She could cry later. She had plenty of time for that, rattling around in her big house alone. It was better to receive comfort from someone who hurt you than to receive no comfort at all.

You put your right arm in; you take your right arm out. You do the hokey pokey and you shake it all about. Ann was leading the Antelopes in a drumming dance when Shirley came in. "Your husband called. He'll meet you at the hospital. It's time."

The bright blue walls of the preschool with their flowers and rainbows seemed to spin around her. Ann couldn't move. "Happy, joy," said Shirley. "I'll take over here."

Outside it was pouring. Rain slithered up the windshield in silver rivulets. Ann drove all the way home before she remembered, *No, the hospital.* But she stopped anyway. McKenna barked crazily, leaping at her thighs.

Bed sheets trailed from the sofa across the floor, as if Jessica tried to drag them with her. In a calculated panic, Ann collected the envelope with the adoption papers. Shooing away McKenna, she gathered the bedclothes and folded the sofa back up. She washed the dishes. Almost an hour had passed since she'd left Little Footsteps. When the phone rang, it shattered her trance. She grabbed her purse and the papers, and sped to Sullivan County General Hospital.

She could hear Jessica screaming as she ran breathlessly up the corridor to the birthing room. The sounds were primal. A nurse blocked the door. "Family only."

"I'm the mother!" said Ann.

"Annie," Joel called. "They gave her an epidural but it doesn't seem to be working."

The nurse stepped aside. Jessica was perched on the side of a bed, legs dangling, as Joel on the floor, massaged her feet.

"Are you doing your breathing? Have you urinated?" Ann touched her sweaty shoulder.

Jessica slapped her away. "Don't touch me."

The hollow pain of rejection pushed through Ann's bowels.

Don't take anything personally. She remembered advice from the birthing classes. *Just send energy to the laboring woman.*

"You're doing great," said Joel.

The door opened. Backlit, moving side to side as if dancing rather than walking, The Fish strode in. "Almost there," he said.

"I want my mommy!" Jessica cried.

"I'm sending you energy," said Ann.

"Plenty of room here." The Fish was checking Jessica's dilation with a gloved hand. "This guy wants out."

Joel staggered up from the floor. "I think I'm going to faint."

And Jessica let loose another primal scream. It crashed into the walls and seemed to last forever.

"Push," said The Fish. "Get athletic now."

Time accelerated. The baby crowned and emerged, one shoulder sliding out before the other, delivering quickly. The Fish suctioned the mucous off his wrinkled face. He gave a feeble cry.

A short exam later, he was passed to the nurse. "Ten on the Apgar scale."

"He's beautiful." Ann watched the nurse rub him down. He released a high, thin wail.

"Get ready for the placenta," said The Fish. "Here it comes."

With a great bellow, Jessica expelled a baby-sized blob of membranes and blood that The Fish plopped into a metal bowl to inspect. But Ann was intent on the nurse who placed Ethan on a scale: 8 pounds, 2 ounces. "Nice big boy." The nurse wrapped him in a blanket with brisk efficiency, carried him to the bed and placed him on Jessica's chest. Ann shadowed the baby. Indifferent to the bruise on his forehead, he moved his little hands, making sounds as if trying to explain his treacherous, painful journey into the world.

"He sure came out fast, didn't he?" said Jessica.

Ann touched the baby's slick, dark hair. "I have the papers for you to sign," she said.

"Oh Annie. Not now." Joel swayed, dazed and white as the hospital walls.

"I want my mommy," said Jessica. "Where's my mommy?"

"Let's leave this young woman alone with her baby to rest." The nurse took the baby and placed him in the hospital crib. She stretched a blue hat over his forehead and snapped a photograph for the medical records.

"I'll stay. That's my baby." Ann settled into the hard chair by his crib. She couldn't drag her eyes away from his ancient wrinkled face. This was his original soft face. It would soon change, and develop into a mask. But now, Ethan's eyes were open and he emanated radiance.

"Already asleep." Joel's hands weighted Ann's shoulder.

"No, his eyes are open," said Ann.

"I meant Jessica," he said.

Barely aware of his hand sliding off her shoulder, or the soft click of the door as he left the room, nothing held reality for Ann but the baby. "Ethan," she whispered. Happiness rose like waves inside her. At last, the reward: her baby, her son.

Jessica slept. The baby's eyes closed. Time stretched and expanded and ceased to exist. Ann didn't move.

Squeaking door hinges posed no alarm but only pulled her back into clock time. "Where is she?" came a voice, as hoarse as a thousand cigarettes, eerily familiar.

"I saw Margaret in the waiting room. I guess Jessica called her." Joel's hand alighted on Ann's shoulder.

Ann glanced up, and there stood the woman who'd chased after the car, glaring at her with such pure hatred that Ann's blood congealed.

"My little girl." The woman stepped around Ann to jiggle the hump of Jessica's foot under the blanket. Jessica slept through it. The woman moved to the crib. She reached for the baby with proprietary brusqueness, "Christopher. My, what you've been through." The baby bawled. Jessica woke. "Hey, what are you doing?"

"Holding my grandson," said the woman. "What do you think?"

"I did it mom, I did it!" Jessica began to cry.

"Can I hold him, Margaret?" asked Joel.

Ann stopped breathing: one heartbeat, two, three, four. Her vision dimmed.

Margaret held the back of the baby's head in her palm. "Are you the father?"

Momentarily reassured that Margaret didn't know everything, Ann stood and presented the documents. "If you just sign these papers we can be out of each other's hair."

"No one's signing any papers of yours, I can tell you right now."

The reality of the situation filtered down like ashes after a fire. But Ann rooted in her purse for a pen. She could accept anything but this. She would choose her own reality, like Mary did. "You can't just come in here after the work's been done. The baby belongs to us."

"What did you just say to me?" Margaret stepped so close that Ann caught the animal smell of the infant.

"You promised." She appealed to Jessica's worn-out, puffy face.

"My wife and I have an agreement with your daughter," said Joel.

"Get out," said Margaret. "I mean now. Or I'll have you both arrested."

Pressure in the small of her back conveyed Ann toward the door. "We won't solve anything here," said Joel. "We'll call the lawyer."

"Stop pushing," said Ann. "We have a contract. We made a deal. I have a pen. All they have to do is keep their promise."

But she watched helplessly as if from above, suspended near the ceiling in an out-of-body experience, as Joel pushed her toward the babble and whiteness of the hospital corridor. Her fingers lost their grip, the contract slipped and meaningless papers drifted to the floor.

As SWIFTLY AND UNEXPECTEDLY as Jessica had arrived in their lives, she vanished. Their savings account was diminished of $8,000, paid to the lawyer, doctor, and hospital, with nothing to show for it. The trailer was full of her clothes and her food and her personal stuff, reminders to Ann of her own stupidity and loss. She would have endured any price, but she hadn't contemplated failure.

When the alarm went off in the morning, she lay in bed as if encased in gel. Joel brought her coffee, urging her to get up, until she dragged herself out and went to work. But there, the children's voices lanced her temples like surgical needles. When she saw the infants in their row of high chairs in the Chipmunk's room, each face became Ethan's, and she didn't know how to go on.

She sat with the Antelopes in a circle, holding up pictures of faces for the guessing-feelings game. The facial expressions in the pictures weren't subtle. They were easily interpreted by the children. "Happy!" they shouted at the smiling face.

"Sad." Giggles pointed to Ann, with his deep-set brown eyes full of compassion.

She forced a smile. "Now how do I feel?"

"Scary!" shrieked Bossy Boots.

Ann erupted into tears. She covered her face with her hands and sobbed.

Frightened, the children turned on each other. Bedlam ensued. Blue Eyes pushed Sweetheart, who fell headlong into a corner of the play table, cutting her lip and drawing blood. Ann couldn't control them, couldn't stop crying.

Frances marched in and took over, "If you can't do the job, don't come to work."

Shirley called her into the administrative office. Photographs of Shirley's children cluttered the desk in decorative frames; curly-haired high school students with overbites and homely faces like their mother. She planted a box of tissues in front of Ann. "Why don't you take a couple of weeks off?" she said. "You need a rest."

Ann blew her nose. "Am I fired?"

"Let's call it a time-out," said Shirley.

JOEL GATHERED JESSICA'S CLOTHING, makeup, Discman, teddy bear, gauzy scarves and Mardi Gras beads into a plastic garbage bag, prepared for a quick handoff when Sam pulled up in his black Trans Am. He carried the bag as far as the door.

Sam got out of the car. Margaret climbed out from the passenger side, already yelling. "You should be ashamed of yourself, taking advantage of my girl."

"She took advantage of us." They stood on the driveway, watching Sam open the trunk.

Margaret shifted her weight from one foot to the other in her grimy stonewashed jeans, elbows pointing, as if pushing people out of the way. "You'll be sorry you ever messed with her."

"We trusted her, we helped her." Although he managed to sound stern, Joel was terrified. He had to shove his hands into his pockets to hide their shaking.

As the car roared away, he felt simultaneously trapped and boundless. The sensation immobilized him. McKenna barked once, full of dog love, his back leg quivering. "Okay, pal," said Joel. "Okay." And found he could turn and walk back inside. McKenna followed. Uncritical friend. Discovered bleeding and broken at the side of the road as a puppy several years ago, McKenna seemed as much like destiny as Ann did, a union of souls. Joel believed in the union of souls.

Without Jessica's mess, the living room looked sterile, like someone had died. Straightening the sofa cushions, Joel discovered a dingy bra trapped beneath. The subterranean excitement still churned in his blood, a force undeniable. He pressed his nose into the cups, overwhelmed by the scent of fruity perfume and strawberry lip-gloss. *You like my rosebuds, don't you?* She had thrust her breasts at him, but he hadn't touched them. Except for three times when he tentatively pressed his palm on the crown of her head like a benediction, and came into her mouth, he hadn't touched her at all. It was as if reality had opened a chink and he had slipped through to this other place and lost control. Why could he access the past so easily but never the future?

He opened his guitar case, which was empty except for sheet music, and shoved the bra inside like contraband. Pulling his white telecaster down off the wall, he plugged into the amp and started to play. He played ferociously, riff after riff. Lyrics surfaced and he sang himself hoarse. *The succubus sucks, that's what she does.* Unleashing a screaming solo, he lost his pick behind the strings. His fingers bled. *She drains and she pains, she draws out your lifeblood. That's just what the succubus does.*

Halloween arrived, or, as the Eleusinian Circle called it: Samhain, when the scrim between living and dead dissolved, a time for the recognition of death and the remembrance of ancestors. They would honor it with a purifying sweat in Sage's sauna. "Come. You could use a cleansing," Mary told Ann on the phone. *Blah blah blah,* thought Ann, holding the receiver away from her ear. After she hung up, she unplugged the phone. She did not plant her garlic bulbs or transplant her perennials. She lay on the sofa like Jessica used to, except she kept it folded up, with her feet on the armrest. Joel had joined a band again with Tim and Rick from *Little*

Joey's Toys. Now they called themselves *The Contractors,* rehearsing two or three times a week. Joel stayed out late most evenings, just like when Jessica had lived with them. Ann had declined to join the band. Day followed night, one dissolving into the next but there seemed no variance between them anymore. Asleep or awake, dead or alive, what difference did it make? The sound of hammering and sawing, the echo of wood hitting wood, and the sheer industriousness of the construction work outside only emphasized her own lack of vitality.

One afternoon, an outburst from McKenna jarred Ann from a doze on the sofa. The sharp tap at the door indicated someone wearing rings. Mary let herself in. "Why are you lying in the dark?"

Lights flicked on. Ann pulled the blanket over her face but Mary's voice penetrated.

"I dreamed you had a bloated middle and wrung-out limbs. You were almost transparent. You reached for me. A hungry ghost, as the Buddhists say." She whisked back curtains and flung open windows. Cold air streamed in. "There's some clogged feng shui in here."

Despite herself, Ann was drawn from the stupor of her grief. She shuffled to the kitchen where Mary bustled about in her yellow sari like she owned the place. She was carrying her rain stick. Adorned with yarn and beaded elastic bracelets, when Mary turned the stick around, seeds clattered through the hollow inside, sounding like rain on a tin roof. "Let me just say, I *never* trusted that lying jezebel! You know who she reminded me of? The chick in the van who gave us all crabs when I was pregnant with you. Balled every guy there, including the one I was in love with." She peeked out the kitchen window. "Good. Your husband's home."

"How are you, Mary?" Joel came in, hours earlier than usual. His work boots tracked plaster dust on the carpet. "Annie, feeling any better today?"

She shrank back to avoid his kiss.

"Forgive me," he whispered. "I was at the end of my rope."

Mary rapped her knuckles on the table. "The situation has revenge karma all over it. One of you knew her in a past life, did her some injustice. Past life therapy with Sage could help."

Jessica. The sibilance made Ann sick. "That's ridiculous," she said. "Why are we talking about her? It's over."

"If I thought it would work, I'd try," said Joel.

McKenna leaped to the door in a barking frenzy. No knock but Sage's low voice preceded her. "Sorry I'm late!"

"Late for what?" said Ann. "Is this an intervention? Is that why you're all here?"

"We're going to perform a banishing if that's okay with you." In her white priestess gown with long flared sleeves, Sage floated past Ann to the living room. She carried her collection of tools in a drawstring velvet bag.

Before Ann could respond, America burst in , all tie-dye and yellow stretch pants. She carried a plate of cookies covered in cling-wrap. "Hey, hey, hey! Cassidy baked 'em. She wanted to come but I said, nuh-uh, kid-free zone, baby." The squeeze she put on Ann's shoulder felt like a violation. Ann had disliked her from day one, when America guffawed, "I hear your vagina paid for your mother's house!" She'd been referring to the money from Gran, intended for Ann's surgery which, when it didn't happen, became the down payment for Sunrise. Years later, the remark still rankled.

"You don't know how lucky you are that you lose weight when you're depressed." Mary tore the cling-wrap off the cookie plate with a familiar greedy expression that Ann despised. She knew Mary was hungry not for cookies but for America's love, and America was unworthy.

"Those kind of people, Jessica and her mother and that sleazy guy, have no sense of honor," said America. "Ignorant trash. It's their upbringing."

"What do you mean, *those* kind?" said Mary. "What does ignorance have to do with honor?"

"Can we focus our energy?" said Joel. "I really want this malevolent spirit, or whatever it is, out of here."

Ann was four years old again, trapped in some communal rap session with endless doctrinaire bickering swinging back and forth around her. Ann ducked past him to the living room where Sage had placed her chalice, knife and small cauldron on the end table she'd pulled to the center. Sage poured water into the chalice from a frog-shaped pitcher. "Let's cast the circle, shall we?"

"No circle," said Ann. "This isn't okay. I'm not in the mood."

"We're here to provide love and attention so we can repel an unwanted psychic entity," said Sage. "Ten minutes."

The others gathered.

Sage lifted the chalice toward the ceiling. "Blessed be, creature of water. Ann, the salt, please?"

"Ten minutes." Ann picked up the salt dish, reciting by rote the opening convocation to the four elements that preceded every ritual. "Blessed be, creature of earth."

Mary grabbed the knife and stirred the salted water with the blade. "Blessed be, creature of fire."

"Blessed be, creature of air." America lit the sacred smudge stick in the metal cauldron.

"The circle is cast. The quarters are summoned," said Sage. "Do we have an object containing the energy?"

Joel reached between the sofa cushions to extract a D-cup bra with a safety-pinned strap. A violent spasm suctioned through Ann's thorax. How had Jessica's bra burrowed into her sofa? She could smell the girl's strawberry lip gloss, feel the warmth of Jessica's belly undulating with her unborn baby. Ann would have endured any price for that baby boy, but she hadn't contemplated such betrayal, such failure. "How far did you go?" she said. "Did you fuck her?"

"Don't talk like that. You never talk like that." The bra dangled off Joel's fingers for a moment before he tossed it in the cauldron. His face was tense, his cheeks splotched bright red, as he shouted, "The harm you've done my wife and me goes back to you, multiplied by three!"

The smoke darkened. "I don't even *know* you anymore," said Ann.

"Cut the cord, unlock the chains, begone from this house, this land, this space, unwanted guest, begone!" cried Sage. She stepped counterclockwise, pressing Ann into movement. But Ann held her ground.

"Leave this place, evil presence!" America brandished a rattling gourd-like instrument.

Mary shook her rain stick "We banish you, Jezebel!"

"Stop it!" Ann shouted. "Ten minutes is over!"

"I'm sorry." Joel hung his head. "I thought this was a good idea. I guess I was wrong."

"If you'd rather wallow on your sofa, we'll go," said Sage. "Is that what you want, Ann?"

"Wait," said Mary. "I have an announcement. Talking staff, please! We don't have to break the circle. Sit down everyone. This is important." She sat on the carpet with her rain stick upright between her palms. "I'd like to offer Ann and Joel my uterus."

Ann glanced at Joel.

He drew his hair off his face and tucked it behind his ears with an unconscious daintiness that brought a clutch to her throat. "I don't follow," he said. "Did we discuss this?"

"What I'm saying is: I can be your surrogate mother. Your egg, Ann. Your sperm, Joel. In vitro fertilization. My uterus, bang! Your baby!" Mary's cheeks pinked up, her smile widened until her eyes were bright slices in her face, and she looked insane.

"No offense," said Joel. "But if we want a surrogate, we might be better off with someone younger."

"Seems you've had enough problems with young women," snapped Mary. She gazed up at Ann, who was still standing. With her gray hair flowing and her face as full as the moon, Mary seemed a child who'd accidentally aged. "It's not about how old I am, sweetie. I've done some research. Age matters for the eggs, not for the uterus. Let's banish Jessica once and for all. You don't have to deal with a stranger. You call the shots. I'm just a vessel. All I want to do is help."

The vision of a baby with soft folds of skin brought on a hunger that gnawed through Ann's nervous system. It was larger than she was and swallowing her.

"You're so fucking beautiful, Mary," America moaned. "I'm hip to this fertile, green aura all around you. Does anyone else see it?"

Joel thrust out his lower lip. "If you really want a baby, why not use someone else's egg and sperm, not ours?"

"Joel, may I?" Sage grabbed Mary's stick. Seeds and pods clattered like rainfall. "This is the most powerful banishing gesture I've ever witnessed. I've read about this kind of arrangement. A Christian woman in Minnesota gave birth to her daughter's son. I think we can take Mary's proposal as heartfelt and generous."

"If the Christians can do it, the Pagans too," said Mary.

"Goddammit," said Joel. "No way."

Ann had never seen him so annoyed, almost writhing. She imagined the nursery in their unfinished house, pale yellow walls stenciled with butterflies. Little hands reaching from a crib. Energetic little legs kicking. The vision arrived as if the future had sent a reflection backwards in time. If she had a baby, she could let Jessica go. "Is it possible?" she asked.

"Is that a yes?" Mary rose to her knees. "Can I be your vessel?"

"The way we define the world creates the world," said Sage. "We begin with the dream. You're still young, Ann. And Mary's, what, fifty-two, fifty-three?"

"Excuse me! Forty-nine!" said Mary.

"Don't fall for this, Annie," said Joel.

But he couldn't command her loyalty anymore, quite the opposite.

"We can take it one step at a time. Maybe it won't happen." Mary gave Ann a conspiratorial smile. "We don't know if Joel's sperm is viable."

Ann almost laughed.

"My sperm is the least of it," said Joel.

But he kept his eyes downcast, Mary having managed to draw off a portion of his manhood.

AIR: 1999-2000

"OUR SUCCESS RATE STANDS at 45%, the highest in the industry," said Dr. Godwin, the director of the Center for Human Reproduction. "We've had sister surrogates, friends, strangers—but you're our first mother-daughter team, and we're very excited."

They sat across from him, three in a row, Mary in the center. With his prominent ears and boyish smile, Dr. Godwin resembled a leprechaun, a trickster, capable of magic, the kind of man who had turned Mary on before she'd declared herself a lesbian. Which reminded her that America loved her again, and love energized Mary like nothing else could.

"A 45% *success* rate sounds like a 55% *failure* rate." Joel perched on his chair as if any second he'd vault to his feet, shouting, *Put up your dukes!*

"We look at cycle percentages and factor in retrieval rates resulting in live births." Dr. Godwin rattled off numbers and criteria for comparative data, things Mary spaced out on. She splayed her fingers to examine her rings, her force-field of strength, with a ready explanation for each, in case anyone should ask: gold with tiger's eye to guard her spirit, Mother-of-pearl and onyx yin-yang to balance her chi. Jade for healing, lapis lazuli for love and, of course, her mother-ring, identical to Ann and Joel's wedding rings, an expression of solidarity.

She caught Ann's gaze, her daughter's pale blue eyes almost transparent, rimmed by short, blunt lashes as bleached as her straight blond hair. But somehow in the light, enhanced by the mauve upholstery and carpet and walls, Ann was illuminated in a lovely pink aura. *I made you!* Mary wanted to shout. *And I can make another you!*

"How long will the process take?" Joel cracked his knuckles. "Or are you going to throw out smokescreen numbers on that, too?"

Typical man. Mary tried to catch Ann's eye again, to exchange a private communion about men's need to dominate, but Ann was leaning forward, utterly engrossed. "What about the chances of having a baby like me, without a...?"

Mary broke in. "Uterus. Good question."

"I don't think the research bears out a genetic component." When Dr. Godwin smiled, dimples appeared in both cheeks. "As for the timing, let's say everything goes smoothly. Once cycle synchronization begins, we're talking about four weeks for egg stimulation. Then we harvest the eggs and fertilize, that's a day. Less than a week later we transfer the pre-embryos. Two weeks after that we take a blood test. A positive pregnancy means we're done. And you're in the hands of your obstetrician. Which comes to seven weeks. I suggest we work aggressively for the transfer. At your age, we don't worry so much about multiple births, we just want a take-home baby." He aimed his boyish smile at Mary. How appealing he was, even when calling her old!

"What about Mary's weight?" said Joel. "It's not just the age factor. She's carrying some extra weight."

He got her with that one. *Count your blessings,* Rose told her, *overweight women stay youthful-looking longer than slender ones. More flesh, fewer wrinkles, it works in your favor now.* Mary grabbed her blubber through her shirt. "Are you calling me fat? More to love is what I say."

"You shouldn't grab yourself like that," said Ann.

The scolding made it worse. One hundred eighty-three pounds at five feet, four inches, Mary was aware of moisture seeping into the crevices of her flesh. Her hip creases were damp. She nudged Ann. "I think I'm power-surging!"

"Too much information, Mom."

"You're not, as we say, *morbidly* obese," said Dr. Godwin with his quick smile. "You're a healthy woman. And a little extra weight seems to improve the chances of implantation."

"If only my mother were alive to hear this," said Mary. "All these years, I've been healthy, not fat."

Ann jiggled her foot, bumping rhythmically into Mary's chair. "When you said multiple births, did you mean we could have more than one?"

"Twins are not uncommon. I've heard them referred to as 'the jackpot,'" especially if they're one of each gender," said Dr. Godwin. He rubbed his palms together so briskly Mary imagined sparks flying out.

"That's crass," said Joel. "The jackpot."

"Let's think twins. We've got yin on one side..." Mary grabbed Ann's hand, then clasped Joel's sweaty one. "...Yang on the other. And I'm the circle to hold them." They both tried to disengage but Mary had a strong grip. She shut her eyes to call on Demeter as the goddess appeared in the marble likeness on Mary's altar, with her torch and sheaf of wheat. But, instead of Demeter, a vision of Dr. Godwin with the hind end of a goat materialized, consort and son of the universal mother. She opened her eyes. "I'm going to call you Dr. God."

"Oh, come *on*," said Joel.

"It's okay," said Ann. "She's nervous."

"I am not!" said Mary. "You're the scared one."

Dr. Godwin's prominent ears noticeably blushed. "We're happy to work with you. You can settle the finances with our facilitator." He stood and rubbed his palms together, dismissing them.

The facilitator, a nurse in white polyester and foam-soled white shoes, led them to a cubicle where she gave them a pile of paperwork requiring multiple signatures, as well as a schedule of fees and financial policies. Each procedure came with a cost, from the initial consultation ($550) to the semen analysis ($220) to the lab testing

($3,500), egg retrieval ($4,300), embryo transfer ($800), facility fees, evaluation, anesthesia and more. No payment programs. No refunds, no guarantees. Lab testing and initial consultation fees were due upfront.

The numbers made Mary's head spin. "It's hard to believe they can charge this much when girls still get pregnant by accident." She slid her credit card across the desk.

"This is nuts. It doesn't even include the drugs." Joel was punching digits on his cell phone calculator. "We can't afford it."

"You're going to have to make peace with this," said Mary. "Money's a means to an end. I'll take out a second mortgage, I don't care."

"You're doing a great thing," said the facilitator. Her admiration beamed over Mary like a warm light.

"I just don't put a price tag on my daughter's well-being."

"You win. Put half on that." Joel threw his credit card on the desk.

"If only I were independently wealthy," said Ann.

With finances out of the way, the woman handed them folders full of drug protocol information. Mary couldn't focus. The letters blurred and danced on the page.

"Did you forget your reading glasses?" asked Ann.

Joel flipped through his papers. "Producing sperm. That's what they call it. Unbelievable."

"What's unbelievable is that I'm a willing guinea pig in a technological revolution," said Mary. She, who had hated the medical establishment, who imbibed only natural botanical intoxicants, and who aspired to be vegan, was sacrificing her body in altruistic service to her daughter. The idea absolutely thrilled her.

AFTER THE CONSULTATION, SINCE they were already in New York City, a two-and-a-half-hour trip from Sullivan County, Joel, who had insisted on driving, agreed to stop at Della's place, a four-story walk-up on East 7th. Della had summoned Mary to discuss the sales, or lack thereof, of her *spiralmary* jewelry series. Abuzz with the new venture, Mary climbed the four flights quickly, reaching the top before the younger set did.

"Darling!" Della air-kissed Mary's cheek and hustled her to the sofa, arranging chairs in a circle around a low glass table strewn with fashion magazines and jewelry books. Her apartment was divided in half, her office in front and living space in back. Her office walls were covered with photographs of jewelry and bejeweled celebrities. "I must say, I didn't expect the extended family. I thought we'd keep this *entre nous,* Mary. The news isn't good."

"We have our own news!" Mary wiggled closer to Ann on the leather sofa.

"It's none of her business," Ann whispered.

"We have to tell her!" said Mary. "It'll affect my work!"

"How do we know she won't tell everyone else?" The jut of Ann's sharp chin mutated her from adult to teenager, livid that the sisterhood had learned of her condition. Mary, sworn to secrecy, had only wanted to help. Not betray, *help.*

"I guess we need ground rules," said Joel. "No one tells anyone unless we all agree. Though I have to say: we could have ironed this out first."

"You're not listening to me." Della clanked lightly on the glass table with the back of her hand, adorned in silver amethyst and peridot rings, *madebymary*™, which meant Mary wasn't entirely out of favor.

"Not only did you renege on your commitment to supply me with the jewelry for the orders from last spring," Della lectured. "But the work you gave me didn't move at any of the outlets. I was browbeaten into return deals. Apparently, *spiralmary* is not the new black. Nothing sold but the yonis. Very disappointing."

"Look on the bright side," said Mary. "If nothing moved it's just as well I didn't meet the quantity."

"Don't get quippy," said Della. "You couldn't hack the pressure. Over-promised and under-delivered. We'll have to push yonis for the millennium. I need a model by the end of the week. That's why I asked you here. We'll send it out for casting."

"Then it's not handcrafted," said Mary. "We've already been through this." They had become business partners in the 1980s when Mary lived at the sisterhood, making ankhs and yonis, which were all the rage on the Lilith circuit. The only tools Mary owned then were a pair of bevel-style cutters and a rawhide mallet. But over the years, as Mary had honed her metalwork and die-cutting skills, her aesthetics had evolved to high-end contemporary silver and gold jewelry with semiprecious stones and fused glass cabochons. Della got a fifteen percent commission on everything sold, and she always wanted shortcuts.

"I'd think you'd want to sell whatever you could, considering the debt we just took on. Casting or whatever," said Joel from the far end of the sofa.

"Attack from the peanut gallery!" Mary cried.

"There's no room for argument," said Della. "Either we do it my way or you're on your own. I'm talking to my retailers about reintroducing *spiralmary* next season. But I need something from you now or it's bye-bye. I mean it."

"I feel like I'm the only one being realistic." Joel's foot tapped a staccato beat. "Someone has to watch out for the family because this could ruin us financially."

"We'll send the mold to Indonesia for casting," said Della. "All is not lost, my dear."

"Please, Ann? Can I tell?" Mary couldn't restrain herself.

"Cat's out of the bag already," said Joel. "Right, Ann?"

"I'm going to carry Ann's baby!" Mary realized she was patting her stomach as if she were already pregnant.

"My baby, too," said Joel.

"That's fantastic!" Della clapped her hands. "Is it legal?"

"Can we go now?" asked Ann. "Is the meeting over?"

"Let's hope Mary's stuff starts *moving*, as you put it," said Joel. "Because this baby thing costs a fortune."

"A story like this'll *help!* I'll put teaser copy on my web site next to images of Mary's jewelry. Did I tell you I'm doing a website? You *have* to have one these days." Della bounced a little in her chair. "What about the clientele at a place like that? Could you get hold of their list, somehow? A marketing goldmine is what I'm thinking."

"This isn't your story," said Ann. "See, Mom? It might not happen anyway. Maybe you don't have a viable uterus."

"I birthed *you*, didn't I?" said Mary.

Joel stood. "We have a long ride home."

"Two days, Mary. I need a yoni prototype." Della walked them to the door. "And keep me posted on this baby thing."

"Don't worry about my viability," said Mary. "Moonstone will be my gem from here on in."

ALTHOUGH MARY PREFERRED WORKING skyclad, just skin, stone and metal, the cold drafts that gusted through cracks and gaps in the walls of her workroom forced her to don several layers, muffling her creative contact with the universe. She tried to sketch out ideas but only managed to doodle a page of abstract fetal shapes. Normally she loved her workroom and its organized chaos of ongoing projects. She loved her drawers of beads, metals and stones, her faceting machine, drill press, jigs and fixtures in the corner, her polishing station with her buffing wheel vented by the window, her hammers, shears, and scissors hanging from a craft board fixed to the wall. She loved it because she had created the room one piece of equipment at a time. And, normally, all she had to do was sit at her bench, arrange some stones, cut some metal or sketch a few ideas, and off she flew into the realm of imagination. But she wasn't normal anymore. After sending out the yoni mold for casting, she had nothing to do, no commissions, no inspiration. In the wake of her *spiralmary* commercial failure, her tools oppressed. What energized her was the scheduled Lupron injection. No need to get up, she just grabbed a roll of fat and slid the tiny needle in. The drug released a hormone that put her in a menopausal state, which was redundant but so be it. She knew that, five miles away, Ann was also injecting herself and she picked up the phone, eager to connect. "Commencing ovarian synchronization," she said, pretending to be a space-age robot. "Repeat. Synchronization in effect."

"Great. Funny." Ann's high tight voice signified trouble.

"Are you okay?" said Mary, reverting to her usual voice. "You shot yourself up, right?"

"I asked for my job back," said Ann. "Shirley told me to take more time. She said not until after the new year."

"We'll be pregnant by then! Enjoy life, sweetie! Make lemonade from lemons. Open your own preschool. You're young, you don't need Shirley!" But Mary recognized the silence on the other end as disapproval. Genetically unable to back away from perceived disapproval, she filled it with herself. "Is Joel being a nitwit about money? Have you two hashed things out yet? He doesn't like me much or I'd talk to him for you. Why doesn't he like me? What's so threatening about me anyway?"

"I assumed I could return when I was ready," said Ann. "Do you think I should write her a letter, or maybe just drive over and beg?"

"We're in the same boat," said Mary. "I don't have enough work either. Not since I sent the mold to Della. She can be so mean. Why don't you come over?"

"I have to go. I'll talk to you later." The click was abrupt. It meant Mary had failed. She dialed Ann back and got a busy signal. After hitting redial a few times, she gave up. The tide was flowing in her favor so she'd have to trust that whatever grievance Ann was nursing would be short-lived. Now, if only she could figure out some new creative angle with her jewelry.

ANN SAT ON AN ice pack on the couch, watching Joel inject an orange with a long hypodermic needle. "Quick push, no hesitation," he recited like a mantra. The call had come from the Center two days before the winter solstice: Start the drugs. Ovarian stimulation for Ann, estrogen for Mary. Since they entailed intramuscular injections with long syringes, Joel was administering both.

"I'm ready." She rolled onto her front, pulling her sweatpants down just enough to feel a chill, and realized that Joel hadn't seen this part of her in weeks. Extreme tension inhibited her from baring herself. She had always hated getting shots. Suddenly she couldn't breathe. Her sternum wouldn't move. She couldn't swallow. She was panicking.

"Don't clench."

A quick deep stab into her right buttock, and she cringed. "Are we done?"

Dabbing the injection site with antiseptic, he said, "I miss you. I miss us."

Although he resembled the man she had married: the same dark, curly hair, the same thick, untrimmed eyebrows trailing toward his topaz eyes, the same nose that slanted rightward, the same lips, pinker than most men's--his face had changed, become less fluid and expressive, more set in stolid determination.

"Don't look at me that way." He clutched her wrist. "I want you to want *me*. Not just a kid with me. I want to play music together again."

"I'm trying," she said, surprised at his vehemence.

"You think it's easy being the bad guy? I'm going along with this enterprise even though I don't like it. I keep waiting for you to meet me halfway but…" He sat, resting his elbows on his knees, staring at the floor, a lock of hair falling in his face. "Maybe you just don't love me anymore."

The curve of his back seemed to beg for a touch but Ann couldn't. Jessica still overshadowed her. Ann envisioned Joel leaving, right down to the loose flap of his shirt and the hunch in his shoulders, walking out the door. It was easy to see. "I don't know if I believe in love," she said. "Or miracles. Or magic."

"You don't mean that, do you?" He kept his elbows on his knees and his gaze on the dog. He was so remote. "She came onto me and I let it happen. I let her touch me. But I didn't touch her."

"That's pathetic," said Ann. "Now you're blaming her. You're responsible."

He bowed his head. "I'm sorry."

Annoyance sliced through Ann's skull. "I hate you."

"Are we fighting?" he said. "I'd rather fight than drift around each other, to be honest."

"You're an asshole."

McKenna started barking.

"Shit," said Joel. "She's here,"

Mary stamped her feet as she came in, though she tracked in no dirt. Her angora poncho and velour skirt crackled with static as she put her bag down. "Am I late? What's going on? I'm getting a vibe."

As Joel jumped up to prepare the syringe, Ann dwindled down to a child, forced to stifle her emotions. Mary invaded her space, crowding her on the sofa. But instead of the familiar sense of burden and vexation that Mary's presence caused her, Ann was enfolded in a vague, inarticulate memory of being held, and of deft hands wrapping a scarf around her head and neck. The memory comforted her.

"Time for my penetration, huh?" Mary angled herself over the sofa armrest, lifting her skirt and sliding her long flannel underwear down. Joel's face registered nothing as he slid the needle in.

"You're next," Mary rearranged her skirt.

"Already done," said Ann. She caught Joel's eye. *I'm sorry*, he mouthed. *I love you.*

Mary pulled a large bottle from her bag. "Home-brewed beer, gift from Cloud Rider for the Yule celebration, which you didn't come to. So it comes to you." She fetched three glasses from the cabinet.

"I don't know if we should drink with all these drugs we're taking," said Ann.

"A glass of beer. Don't get obsessive," said Mary. "Let's have a toast."

Joel lifted his glass. "To the baby. And to the mothers."

A rush of love filled Ann's heart and she longed for Joel, even though he was right there, sitting across from her. She held her glass aloft. "To us."

"I SAW YOUR GIRL outside the Hotel Claire in Youngsville, smoking a cigarette. Had her baby with her." Betty kept coming back to this. "She made us a laughing stock."

"People have been laughing at us for years. Didn't start with Jessica." Joel forced himself to sip his whiskey, not slug it down. It burned nicely through his throat and chest. Christmas day, and he was sitting uncomfortably in a lumpy-cushioned, straight-backed chair in Betty's kitchen, across from the glassy eyes of Betty's stuffed panda. He'd placed it at the table at her insistence even though it was ridiculous. He thought about the guys in his band, and how they'd be celebrating: Tim with his wife and kid and his extended family of siblings and cousins; and Rick who'd traveled to Boston, to his family. Tim had invited them to his place, but Joel was duty-bound to Betty.

Next to him, Ann wasn't drinking. She played with bits of turkey loaf on her plate, stirring it into her mashed potatoes. *Your mother doesn't cook, she assembles.* Contempt added to her beauty.

"Suppose there's truth in that." Gravy dripped onto Betty's white blouse as she brought a forkful to her mouth. "Your father and that hippie bimbo gave 'em grist for the mill. But I never invited *her* into my home the way you invited...."

Ann's fork clattered on her plate. "We don't even think about Jessica anymore," she said.

"We've been through a lot," said Joel. Under the table, he pressed his foot into Ann's, and was gratified when she reciprocated. He felt reunited, as if she had just recently returned from a long trip.

"You may not think about her but I hear she's thinking about *you*," Betty declared with her mouth full. "Spreading vile rumors from what Winifred tells me."

"My mother's going to carry our baby for us," said Ann. "That rumor's true."

"Excuse me?" Betty blinked several times. "No, I don't advise that."

Joel topped his whiskey and slid down in his chair. He hadn't intended to tell. He shot a look at Ann, who squeezed her shoulders up by her ears in a dramatic shrug. "What Ann's saying is that Mary will be our gestational surrogate, I believe it's called." He touched his mother's arm, taking note of her papery skin. "We're not asking for advice. We're telling you out of respect."

"There's something not right in the head with you," said Betty. She turned to Ann. "Your mother's hard to miss already in that car of hers, flouncing around Main Street like a teenager. Now she wants to become an absolute spectacle?"

"She's going to carry your grandchild," said Joel. "You might think of it that way."

"Like your other scheme," said Betty. "That was no grandchild of mine."

"There's something wrong with you," said Ann. "Can't you ever be kind?"

Joel gazed through the doorway into the living room where Betty's fake tree stood, festooned in silver tinsel, and thought about obedience. Every year, ten days after he erected the thing, he dismantled it and packed it away. No end in sight. Entrapped in the life he'd been born to.

"Don't you talk to me like that," said Betty. "They say your mother keeps goats in that hippie house to sacrifice on the full moon."

"She's a vegetarian," said Ann. "Who said she sacrificed goats?"

"And down the road, her cohort hides dopey in the baby's diaper."

"*Dopey?*" Joel said. "Where do you get this stuff? Not everyone wants to harden their hearts like yours."

"We just want a child like any other married couple," said Ann.

"We?" said Betty. "Or you?"

"Us," said Joel. "And it's been done before. A woman in Minnesota gave birth to her daughter's son. A Christian woman."

"The world's going to end in a week anyway." Betty raised her fork into the air. "There's been sword, famine, and pestilence. The wild animals will arrive on the millennium. I say good riddance. I hope we all die. I might as well be dead."

"Here we go," said Joel. "You don't mean that."

"I'm stating the facts in the Bible," said Betty. "Three years ago now, I was laid off from the Gasworks. Thrown away like an old shoe after decades of service."

"Oh hell. When did you *ever* throw away an old shoe?" Joel swigged down his entire glass of whiskey. He coughed and sputtered, flooded with resentment. Sucked from one abnormal situation into another, from Betty to Ann and her outrageous desires. Well, a man had his limits.

"I just became the designated driver," said Ann.

"You spring this on me today? On the birthday of our Lord?" Betty squeaked. Her right hand shook and she clutched it with her left to steady it.

Joel didn't want to see her tremors. Rage lent him a clarity he appreciated. Pity would only muddy things. "Fuck it." He gulped straight from the bottle.

"We have to prepare for the end of days," said Betty. "We have to forgive and be forgiven."

"The end won't come until 2012, according to the Mayan calendar," said Ann. "That's what my mother says. Not for another twelve years."

He watched her press her palm down on Betty's trembling fingers and was surprised when Betty didn't yank her hand away. Liquor coated the inside of his mouth.

"I haven't heard that," Betty blinked. "Twelve years? Says who?"

"Everyone." Joel slammed the bottle down. He felt good and mad, and he wanted to keep that alive. Ann laughed. What a beautiful mellifluous sound her laugher was.

"You're so skinny compared to me." Mary pressed her thigh into Ann's. The two of them sat side by side on the exam table in their paper gowns with their legs dangling. Splotched versus alabaster. Cottage-cheese-textured versus smooth. Flabby versus toned.

Ann shifted so they were no longer touching. "Let's make a rule. I won't comment on your body and you don't comment on mine."

"But I *love* your body!" So prickly, such a sensitive little animal. When Ann had undressed, she had turned toward the wall for privacy. Mary caught only a glimpse of her skinny little buttocks, bruised from the injections, just enough to jolt her heart.

"I always wanted *more* children," she said. "If I had given you a sister, you wouldn't be stuck with me as your surrogate. Maybe you'd feel freer."

"Does that mean you don't want to do this anymore?" Ann drew herself inward, concaving like only skinny people could.

"I want to do it more than anything. I'm just saying, I would have liked another child, to give you a companion."

"Are we ready in there?" asked The Fish. Rather than driving three hours to New York City every day for blood tests and ultra-sounds at the Center, Dr. God had given them permission to recruit The Fish. "Who wants to go first?" His white coat only partially covered his tie-dyed T-shirt printed with dancing bears.

"You're a kindred spirit. I have a T-shirt just like that." Mary pointed first to his shirt, then to a framed photograph hanging on his wall where a much younger version of The Fish stood in front of a wildly painted vintage VW van. "And that's just like the Mahayana we traveled in, our vehicle of enlightenment. Those were the days, right? We didn't judge people. We took them as they were."

"I'll go first," said Ann.

Mary watched her squeeze the rubber ball to bring up a vein and remembered Ann as a child in the doctor's office, screaming and wailing, terrified of needles. When had she lost her capacity for emotional outbursts? Stoic and withholding, she tilted her face away.

Somehow, it was Mary's fault. "I should have given you a father, too," she said. "A sister and a father." She didn't know who Ann's father was. Mary had been a free-loving woman, and Lars had been the only man whose baby she'd ever truly wanted. But Lars had refused to bring children into a world he judged as defi-cient. By the time he'd entered the picture, Ann was a mature child, already set in her ways. She'd never accepted him as her father.

A powerful memory of Lars arose: the stray hair that slipped from the rubber band of his blond ponytail, the spasm of his Adam's apple as he threw his head back to drink green chlorophyll from a gallon jug, the bony knuckles on his fingers as he wiped his paintbrushes with an oily linseed-soaked rag. "Lars was going to adopt you," she spoke her thoughts aloud. "We were soul mates, two bodies, one heart. No one ever loved me like he did."

"He walked out on you. It's stupid to romanticize." Ann held the cotton on her arm.

As Mary squeezed the ball, she tried to make eye contact with The Fish. She recognized an ally when she saw one. "I can't help it if I love too deeply. Loving never used to be considered stupid. So, I give my heart away, what can I say?"

"Never mind your heart," said Ann. "You gave *me* away."

"Wow, how did we get here?" Mary pressed cotton into her arm as The Fish withdrew the needle. She had wanted to die when Lars abandoned them, sneaking out like a coward while she was working. She came home to Ann's indifferent shrug. *He said he'd be back when the north winds blow,* barely looking up from the guitar she never stopped fiddling with, the guitar that had belonged to Lars. The absence of his Coleman stove and saucepan clued Mary in. "Living with your grandmother does not equal being given away," she said now. "And here we are, so evolved we're making a child together."

"You always forget about the foster care," said Ann.

"Are you two sure you want to do this? It's only going to get more intense," said The Fish. "Perhaps the bickering is a symptom of your collective anxiety? Perfectly natural, but if I can make a suggestion, why not be extra-kind to each other, and to yourselves?"

"I couldn't have said it better myself!" said Mary.

"I just don't want to go down memory lane and start talking about fathers." Ann looked miserable as she got on the exam table for the abdominal ultrasound. She adjusted the sheet over her legs, trying to cover as much of herself as possible.

"I'm sorry," said Mary. "Let's not fight."

"The hormones might account for your mood. I wouldn't be surprised if you're both a little moody." The Fish ran the wand over Ann's midriff. "See those eggs? They're doing great."

Mary stared at the grainy image of Ann's fallopian tubes on the screen, the lighter blobs of gray that were her eggs. It occurred to her that Ann might be reliving her diagnosis, and the same helplessness that had overwhelmed her then might be weighing her down now. She touched her necklace, made of faceted magnetite and rainbow fluorite, a reminder to stay in the moment.

"Ann needs to get back to work," she said. "Look at me. My work pulls me through. See my necklace?" She held it out so they could see how she'd arranged it as a lariat wrap. The stones were cool and smooth, and she pulled them apart for the pleasure of letting them snap together in a line. "Lodestones attract love."

"Well, there's a lot of love in this room," said The Fish, beaming.

ON THE WAY HOME, Ann shivered in the passenger seat of the WCCNWMN. She was caught in a wrenching memory of being sixteen, sitting in the surgeon's office in a cold, white panic. *We take a skin graft from your buttocks and use it to cover a stent, which is inserted into a surgically created space between your bladder and your rectum, and that will be your neo-vagina,* said the surgeon.

Does the stent stay there forever? Ann couldn't stop shaking. The surgery entailed slicing through her labia.

I can't believe this is happening to us, cried Mary. *What did we do to deserve this?*

Everything was always and everywhere about Mary. The heat in Mary's car didn't work but the radio did and, as they chugged along Route 17, commentators on the local station were still marveling that the millennium had come and gone, leaving the known world intact. Despite computers not having been programmed to calculate past 1999, financial institutions had not imploded. The power grid did not malfunction. No breakdown in public safety systems. Four horsemen failed to break seven seals on a scroll. Water-dwelling mammals did not commit mass suicide. Eternal night did not fall. Ann kept her parka zipped and her hood up.

"I regret nothing. He opened my heart and my creative energy. No one ever loved me like Lars did." Mary was swerving from the shoulder to the center of the road as she talked.

"Be careful. Pay attention." Ann sat on her hands so as not to grab the wheel. She stared out the passenger window at the birch trees and maples and oaks along the hills, spreading their leafless branches. Their twigs curled against a crystalline sky like cracks in a blue bowl.

"If you're angry at me, I have to assume it's a case of mistaken hostility." Mary swerved toward the shoulder. "I know we have issues, but don't you see this is an opportunity to get closer and work things out?" She reached over to sweep the hair off Ann's neck.

"Focus, Mom. Look at the road."

"What did I do?" Mary swerved back to center. "It's like you channel your grandmother. I can't do anything right! It's enough to make me stop trying."

"Why can't we just be quiet?" said Ann. *I'll send the sample to the lab. The clinic will call you with your evening dose.* The Fish had pressed his palms together, bowing. *Same again tomorrow.* Tomorrow and tomorrow and tomorrow. What a fool she had been. Every morning, blood tests and ultrasounds; every evening, injections. Each day her eggs matured, Mary's uterus thickened, and the process pulled them irrevocably together until Mary would swallow her up. And she had entered into it willingly.

Mary turned on the hazard lights and pulled over to side of the highway. She twisted toward Ann. "I'm not such a bad mother, am I? You were mostly happy growing up! It was your diagnosis that changed you. Before that you were a bright, sunny girl, dancing around, laughing."

Ann imagined her own child, round-faced like Mary with those wide, innocent eyes. "I don't want to have this conversation," she said. "It's past. It doesn't matter."

"It matters if it interferes with our *now*," said Mary. "You know what? I should never have taken you away from the commune. I was head over heels for Lars and he hated communal living but I should have insisted we stay. You were so happy there, all you kids, running around in your natural state."

If it wasn't Lars Mary idealized, it had to be the Peace Ranch Commune.

"Okay. Reality check," said Ann. "You made me sleep in the children's room where the older kids smothered the younger ones with pillows until they lost their minds."

She remembered several mattresses littered with crumbs and grit, pushed together to layer the floor with bedding. Often at night she awoke with dread in the midst of snoring, coughing, sniffling kids. But that was nothing compared to waking into soft blackness, unable to breathe, unable to scream, suffocating. She held her breath now in recall.

"See? I didn't know that. This is good. We're getting somewhere," said Mary. "It's honest. Don't shut me out."

"You're not hearing me," said Ann. "I wasn't happy. I was terrified."

"The children's room was to discourage ownership and possessiveness. We were all mothers," said Mary. "That was the idea. We let you grow like flowers in the meadow."

"To say 'We were all mothers' actually means there were *no* mothers."

"We failed. That's what you're saying."

Ann stared at her lap, at the crisp creases she'd ironed in her jeans. The hiss and steam of ironing eased her anxiety. Sometimes she pressed sheets and towels, just to smooth something. "I don't know who 'we' is," she said. "There's only you and me here."

"You're saying *I* failed you." With a sob, Mary brought her fist to her mouth.

Ann envisioned the sanctuary of the trailer, neat and compact as the hold of a ship, a fire in the wood-burning stove warming the whole place, McKenna licking her hand. How to get there from here was the challenge. "My experience was just different than yours," she said slowly. "I know you did your best."

"My life was a prison of rules." Mary grabbed her hand. "I thought I was doing better for you than my mother did for me. She was so strict and soul-destroying. It was unnecessary. She didn't like me. She didn't like my company."

Mary's palm was creased with black residue, tough and callused, embedded with flecks of metal, fingernails clipped to the nubs, the hands of a worker. "I must have done something right," she continued. "Look how good you turned out! Right? I was sometimes good."

Ann had always admired Mary's hands. She surrendered to a familiar, oppressive helplessness. "Sure you were," she said. "Of course you were." When they hugged across the gear shift, she disappeared into Mary, her nose pressed against the scratchy wool of Mary's poncho, inhaling patchouli and orange and the medicinal smell of the Band-Aid from the injection and, in the flood of smells and textures, she became a child again, utterly reliant on her unreliable mother.

ANN REMEMBERED HER CHILDHOOD only in fragments, each memory an island surrounded by a void. She didn't recall leaving Peace Ranch but she recollected arriving at the yurt with Mary and Lars. At the end of a dirt road with a mound of grass in the center, bordered by bushes that scraped the sides of the car, the yurt stood in a field, slightly above ground, a giant cylindrical tent with a mounded top.

It was beautiful, with its three-layered walls, rafters, and tension cables. The apex of the roof was covered with a clear dome. The space inside was circular, with dividers to separate the kitchen and the bathroom. No doors but a cozy nook with a single bed for Ann. Boulder, Colorado. *Outside of Boulder. West, if you want to get technical,* said Lars.

Annapurna likes getting technical, don't you? Mary's smile dazzled. Her happiness was contagious. An island.

Ann remembered watching Lars's long fingers press guitar strings, sliding from fret to fret along the neck as he taught her how to play. He called her a quick study. Another island.

He was an artist. To paint from nature, he would roll up his sleeping bag and mat, hoist his backpack on his shoulders with his paints, easel, and canvas, and trek high into the hills. He stayed away, sometimes overnight, sometimes a couple of days.

In his absence, Mary let Ann sleep with her, spooning her in a soft, warm hug. *Play our cards right and he'll adopt you,* she whispered. *And we'll travel all over the country: Oregon, North Carolina, Arizona. That's the beauty of the yurt, we can set up anywhere. We belong together. Me and Lars are soulmates. And soon, I hope to give you a sister or a brother, you'd like that, wouldn't you?* Ann was happiest then, in bed with Mary, listening to their beautiful future, believing Mary's dream.

Lars left one afternoon while Mary was at work. She worked at a self-serve gas station in a little booth, collecting money. When she wasn't doing that, she was sitting at her drafting table with her silver and her beads and her semiprecious stones. *Tell your mother the winds are changing and I have to go.*

Ann was trying to learn chords on the guitar, his guitar. Lars stroked her beneath her chin, forcing her to look into his fierce blue eyes, like an icy lake. *Tell her I'll be back when the north winds blow.*

He left behind his tubes of oil paints, an unfinished landscape drying on an easel, clove cigarettes and two gallon jugs of chlorophyll. His saucepan and his Coleman stove hung off his backpack, clanking as he walked away. But he'd left the yurt, which meant he was sure to return eventually.

When are the north winds supposed to blow? Why didn't you stop him? When Mary came home, she threw a fit, overturned her drafting table so all the beads and stones lodged in the rug. She ran around screaming, then she curled into bed and refused to get up.

For days, as she watched Mary sleep, Ann strummed the guitar and practiced Travis picking until her fingers hurt. It sustained her through those endless, frozen hours. First, they ran out of milk and eggs. Then they ran out of rice cakes. In the morning the school bus stopped, honked, and moved on.

When the truant officers came, they shouted and knocked but Ann wouldn't let them in. By the time the police arrived, there was no food left at all. *When's the last time you went to school?* a policeman asked.

I don't remember.

They found half-smoked joints in the ashtray and seeds embedded in the rug. *Get up, you're under arrest,* they prodded Mary. Magic words, they broke the spell. Mary got out of bed, donned her clothes, and laced her boots.

Ann remembered being driven to a big, shabby house in the center of town. An aproned woman led her down a hall to a bedroom crowded with bunkbeds. On the wall hung a picture of cherub-cheeked children in a meadow with the words: *Suffer the little children to come unto me, and forbid them not, for of such is the kingdom of God.*

The woman was wearing rubber gloves. She was always cleaning something. Ann recalled the contoured texture of rubber against her palm, and remembered how the woman peeled off the gloves to kneel on the floor by the bottom bunk. *This is your bed now. Shall we pray?*

Ann knelt beside her.

Twelve children lived at the house. For breakfast, numerous cereals were lined up on the counter. Before every meal, they bowed their heads and prayed: *Bless us our Lord for these thy gifts, which we are about to receive through thy bounty and through Christ our Lord, amen.*

The man in the house wore thick glasses, magnifying his eyes so they seemed to float away from his face. He was gone all day. Before dinner he added a lengthy sermon to the prayer and the meatloaf would be cold by the time they were allowed to dig in.

On Sunday, no one was permitted to eat until they had been to church. A blue cotton dress was presented, ironed and starchy and too small for Ann; it dug into her armpits. Standing, kneeling, singing, she felt her soul rocked in the bosom of Abraham, as the lyrics of the gospel song went, and she remembered feeling that she would survive. Another island.

Evenings were predictable: Chores, homework, prayers, bed. Chores were designated on a chore wheel. Drying dishes: Annapurna. The sight of her name brought a strange thrill, and she took great care in drying, pressing the towel edge between each fork prong until the woman said, *We don't abide laziness here. You must learn to be more efficient.*

Ann wasn't unhappy except at night when she lay awake, not knowing where Mary was, fearful that Mary was afraid, painfully aware that Mary needed her. Then she sobbed desperately into her pillow until she drifted off to sleep, waking again only after she had already wet the bed.

Even now, as an adult, Ann could conjure the cold fear, the anxiety churning in her stomach, the harshness of the blanket and the crinkle of the plastic sheets, the shame of bedwetting. The other kids jeered. They said she smelled like pee. They called her Cooties, broke her crayons, and pinched her arms.

She missed the yurt then, and Lars. And she began to miss Peace Ranch, too, not sleeping in the children's room, but the brook where everyone swam on hot afternoons, the sweat lodge and full moon rituals when they joined hands and danced in a circle, when Mary was happy, her laugh deep and infectious.

In the morning, Ann felt okay, or, rather, she didn't feel anything, and that became okay. When a letter arrived from Mary she opened it slowly, easing the flap, so as not to tear it. *I love you Annapurna Peace and I miss you.* A drawing of a sad-faced sun. *We'll be together soon, I promise. I'm sorry I failed you. I love you very much. Much love, Mom.* Intricate swirls and doodles of flowers decorated the border. Ann pressed the paper to her face, smelling Mary's patchouli with a longing so deep it suctioned her breath right out of her.

Later, she had no idea what might have happened to those letters. They had slipped into the void between islands. Then came a viscerally memorable moment: *Annapurna, you have a visitor.* And there sat Mary, hands clasped on the kitchen table, horribly out of place in her brightly embroidered denim skirt, her hiking boots and Heidi braids interlaced with purple ribbons.

They were ushered into the visiting room, a first for Ann. She had seen the other kids walking in there with adult strangers, closing the door. Now it was her turn. The parlor was wallpapered with faded pink roses. Two sofas faced each other with two armchairs on either side, a rocking chair in the corner. A stack of Bibles sat on the coffee table.

Wow, a rocking chair! Mary went straight for it, while Ann sat stiffly on the edge of the sofa.

Do you like it here? Mary rocked back and forth with peculiar urgency, an energetic creak-creak.

The inchoate, incommunicable immensity of an answer lay beyond Ann's skill. *It's okay,* she finally said.

Well, I've come to give you a choice. You can stay here for a little bit longer, or you can ride on an airplane to Gran's house. Mary stuck the end of one of her braids between her teeth. She was sucking on it while she rocked and rocked.

I want to stay with you.

I'm sorry. It's foster care or Gran's, just for a short time. I promise.
Mary burst into tears and Ann jumped up, hugging her head, her
soft brown hair, stilling the rocking chair. She clung. She sobbed.
I want to stay with you.

Gran met her at the airport, a stern woman with a sharp gaze
and blue eyes the same shade as Mary's. *Your mother makes a virtue
out of chaos but I hear you're the levelheaded one.*

As soon as Gran said it, Ann was defined.

WHEN CASSIDY CALLED, NEEDING a babysitter, Ann jumped on
it. As she parked in front of America's unkempt cottage that sat
too close to the road, weathered and beaten like a disoriented old
stoner, she reflected that some people's houses expressed their true
selves. She found Cassidy smoking a clove cigarette at the kitchen
table with her feet up on a chair and a large drawing pad in her
lap. Colored wax pencils lay in disarray on the table and the floor.
Several tabloid-sized pictures of fairies in surreal dreamscapes were
taped to the kitchen walls. "Take a load off," said Cassidy, sticking
a pencil behind her ear. "Cody's sleeping. It's a miracle."

"Where's your mom?" said Ann, expecting the caustic voice
to intrude any second.

"Somewhere with Carlos. They're disgusting. You should
hear them having sex, going at it like a couple of chimpanzees.
I have to get out of here. Maybe Mary will let us live with her."

Sky gurgled from a playpen in the corner. "Can I hold her?"
asked Ann. They didn't believe in playpens at Little Footsteps,
too confining, too lonely. Not that she had any connection to the
preschool anymore. *We'll see,* Shirley had recently said again on
the phone, *attendance has been spotty with the Antelopes. Let me get
back to you in a few.* What did "a few" translate into, timewise? she

wondered as she carried Sky around to look at the drawings on the walls. Cartoonish fairies posed in front of colorful backgrounds that undulated mysteriously, implying depth. "I like these," she said.

"Thanks. I have talent but no discipline. There's so much passion in me but I get distracted! Not like you. You know *exactly* what you want. You always did. I envy you."

"Nothing to envy here." Ann wiped crumbs off the chair before she sat, positioning Sky in her lap facing outward.

"And your mom would do anything for you." Cassidy stared at Ann with an intensity that made her uncomfortable.

"Maybe," she said. "But I'm having a hard time. When I'm with her it's like I don't exist anymore. I don't mean to be ungrateful but she's too...." Ann was going to say *needy* but a lump in her throat forced a pause. The crown of Sky's head, the whorl of the pale hair growing out from the center, was so blond and soft she could have been Ann's child, not Cassidy's. Ann was the needy one.

"I can't believe she'll be pregnant in her fifties! Giving birth is the most incredible trip in the universe!" Cassidy pointed to Sky, who kicked her feet and laughed. "My rushes came on with her during a meteor shower. I was having multiple orgasms when I birthed her."

Ann couldn't bear to listen to birth stories. "You said you needed me to watch the kids," she said. "They're giving me the brush-off at the daycare, so my schedule's wide open."

"I'm sorry. I shouldn't have said anything about birthing. I know you're sensitive. Don't look so uptight. Let's do this exercise where I watch you breathe with your eyes closed for five minutes and then you watch me." Cassidy ground her cigarette out. "Come on. I'll time it. Shut your eyes!"

Lacking the energy to argue, Ann closed her eyes. Points of tension pulsed at the base of her skull. The baby was warm and soft against her, ebbing her tension. She became aware of Cassidy breathing and her own breath lengthened. On the crest of a deep, fulfilling inhale, an idea bloomed, miraculous and inevitable as the first crocus in spring. She opened her eyes before the five minutes were up, and noticed how the afternoon light settled softly on the kitchen counters, how Cassidy's smile had brightened and her hair was more red and springy than it had been just moments before. "Will you do it?" she asked. "I can't believe I didn't think of it sooner."

"Do what?" said Cassidy. "Shit, it's late. I have to get ready. Jai will be here soon."

"Be my surrogate," said Ann. "You're healthy and fertile. You love being pregnant. Birthing is a pleasure for you. How about it?"

"That's crazy. Mary would be devastated if she even knew you were asking."

"Mary never *stays* devastated," said Ann. "She'll find something else to obsess about. I know it's huge. We'd pay you what we could. Plus a lifetime of free babysitting for your kids. And eternal gratitude."

"Mommy, look!" Cody pattered in barefoot. He existed at the changeling age between three and four. His limbs had lengthened and his facial features had sharpened to a little boy's. His long hair had been buzz-cut like an army recruit. Bare-bottomed, in a Ramones T-shirt, he held his penis and peed in an arc into the playpen. "I'm a boy!" he cried.

"What the hell are you doing?" Cassidy jumped up, yanking him by the arm. He sprayed pee across the kitchen floor.

"You know how to use a toilet, Cody!" Ann laughed. "You're a big boy."

He wrenched free of Cassidy to hug Ann's legs, poking Sky in her plump little thighs. Reveling in their physicality, Ann rubbed her palm across his buzz cut. "Who did your hair?"

"You have designs on my kids," said Cassidy. "That's your agenda."

Cody pressed his mouth against his sister's leg and blubbered his lips to make her laugh. "You're not serious," said Ann.

"Last summer when you were babysitting every day, he'd wake up crying for you. He didn't want me."

A bright rush of pleasure and Ann knew her blush incriminated. "The world doesn't *owe* you a child," said Cassidy.

Sky pooped in her diaper but Ann couldn't move. She saw herself in an unflattering light, reflected through Cassidy's eyes, a parasite on other people's children. She couldn't seem to get the proper read on reality. "I never said anyone owed me anything."

"Thank you for thinking I'm so good at having babies but I'm getting my tubes tied," said Cassidy. "Now I'm late. Jai will be here any second and I'm trying to cultivate precision." She sprang into action, grabbing her rolled-up yoga mat from against the wall and stuffing it into a canvas bag.

Her new boyfriend entered silently. His head was shaved, his eyebrows thick across the bridge of his nose. He wore a yarn bracelet, a T-shirt decorated with the Om symbol, and brown leather pants. "Namaste, yoginis," he said. "Why aren't you ready? Precision, baby, precision."

"Jai, Ann. Ann, Jai," said Cassidy. "Where are my shoes? Ask Ann why I'm late, she'll tell you."

"It's my fault," said Ann. Cody crouched at her legs. Sky began to fret.

As soon as the door shut and she was alone with the children, Ann stood. Sky needed changing. Cody needed pants. She found clean diapers in the living room and changed Sky on the beanbag chair, gazing into her big blue eyes as she wiped her little bottom. But she couldn't erase the comment: *You have designs on my kids.*

She found pants for Cody in a pile upstairs in Cassidy's bedroom. It was like a room from another era, with a waterbed and a lava lamp, paperbacks stacked on the changing table, an over-flowing ashtray on the dresser with a roach clip resting on its rim. It could have been Mary's room at Peace Ranch. Handwritten Post-it notes were stuck sporadically upon the blue-green walls. "Breathe." "Pause." "Pay attention." "Recognize the sacred."

The dust and mess made Ann's arms itch. She was thankful to find the car seats stacked on top of waist-high piles of magazines in the front vestibule. At last she got the kids outside, strapped them in their seats, and drove to the trailer.

The children were delighted with McKenna. Ann fed them and sang with them, getting Cody to dance when she played her guitar. Later, when they tired, she lay with them in the bed she shared with Joel, positioning Sky in the center and herself close to the edge as a border so the baby wouldn't fall off. She dozed alongside them, feeling closer to them than to anyone else. From outside, the cracking sound of ice dropping off the boughs of the evergreens momentarily jerked her awake, and she knew something was wrong with her, with any woman who loved only children, and came alive only for children.

FOR MARY, THE UNIVERSE flowed. By the end of January her uterus was ready to receive. But first, the surgery to extract Ann's eggs and fertilize them. Mary intended to get an early night because she wanted to be there, but America dropped by with her little marble pipe and Mary couldn't say no.

Flames crackled and quivered in the fireplace. *Surrealistic Pillow* blasted on the stereo. In a stoned tizzy, they danced to "Somebody To Love." As America swayed and bumped against her, Mary shimmied her shoulders and shook her breasts, transported to the wild dances at the Peace Ranch Commune, ecstatic trances and sweats with the bonfire blazing and drummers drumming. She throbbed with the great pulsation of the cosmos. She was drenched when the song ended, and they collapsed into each other's arms, panting and rolling on the floor.

"Where are you going? Kiss me!" cried Mary.

But America disengaged. She had arrived with a large canvas bag that she'd deposited next to the trickster. Now she dragged the bag to the center of the living room and stood over it, arms akimbo. "Do me a solid? Drop this off at the sisterhood?"

In her purple cardigan, her red velvet scarf, and her wild, curly gray hair, America was a gorgeous sight to behold. Mary's spirit widened. Desire flared through her groin. "Anything for you, darlin', what's in it?"

"Two pounds of high-grade, baby."

"Wait a second," said Mary. "I'm an artisan. Not a drug mule." But she was stoned. And guitars twanged out "Plastic Fantastic Lover" and soon, if she was lucky, she'd be pregnant. Nothing was more real than anything else, artisan or mule. Mary didn't know who she was anymore.

"There's a couple hundred bucks in it for you." America dropped to her knees on the rug next to Mary. "I trust you, that's the thing. You and me, we're..." She thumped her chest twice with her fist.

"What about whatshisname?"

"There's always a place in my heart for you. Other people come and go. But you and me, we're forever." America sat on her heels behind Mary and started massaging Mary's scalp, working her fingers through Mary's hair.

"I've heard that before," said Mary. But she was melting under America's touch. Her hair had grown more bountiful from the hormone shots. The hot flashes had faded and she felt young again, malleable and open as her temples succumbed to America's thumbs.

The next day, Mary slept all the way to the clinic, spread out across the back seat of Ann's car. She was still hungover as she stood by the gurney in the pre-op room, where Ann lay face-up, looking pinched, and tiny, waiting to go into surgery. Ovum aspiration, normally done through the vaginal canal would, in Ann's case, require total anesthesia and an abdominal incision for micro laparoscopy.

"I'm scared," said Ann.

"You're brave," said Joel, clenching her hand.

Disoriented from lack of sleep, Mary wanted to add something essential but her mind was a blank, so she watched them as if they were a movie: *Love Story*, but with life instead of death. In the parking garage three blocks away, in the trunk of Ann's car, next to Mary's jewelry case full of samples for Della, sat a canvas bag holding two one-pound bricks of saran-wrapped marijuana covered in foil. In the light of day, Mary recognized that she might have been manipulated.

A nurse appeared, and whisked Ann away for surgery, with a cheerful, "We'll page you when she's in recovery!"

Mary felt guilty because she hadn't been paying attention. "Happy blessings!" she called out, running after the gurney. But Joel pulled her back, depriving her of a last glimpse before Ann was wheeled out of sight.

"What's the matter with you?" he said. "Are you stoned or drunk or something?"

"Don't talk down to me!" As she followed Joel to the waiting room, it seemed he was a thief who had stolen her daughter away. He was the flannel-shirted embodiment of the God Hades. Mythologically, he ruled over the kingdom of death. She sat beside him, trying to deflect her hostility with images of herself pregnant and beautiful, and Joel and Ann kneeling at her feet like acolytes. *We owe it all to Mary.* And she imagined her grandchild cooing at her in private communion: *I know where I really came from.*

Joel cracked his knuckles, beginning with his index fingers and moving outward, with loud pops and snaps that frazzled her. "Do you mind?" she finally asked.

"Sorry. Bad habit. I don't even know I'm doing it." He tapped his plaster-speckled work boots on the mauve carpet. "Technically, you don't have to be here, you know. You could go catch some lunch or something."

"Catch lunch?" said Mary. "My daughter is in surgery. I'm not going to 'catch lunch.'"

As soon as she said it, she comprehended the situation. Sperm-providing time. If she hadn't been hung over she would have laughed. "Oh, I get it," she said. "Just think of it as sacred. At the moment of release, all your chakras open and your body becomes a flute for the music of the life force."

"I'm thinking about work, a job that should have gone to me and didn't." But Joel blushed from his cheeks down through his neck, looking at her sidelong as he loosened and retied his bootlaces.

"Joel Slocombe," said the receptionist.

He stood quickly and tripped. He'd left a lace untied. Not Hades anymore. He was almost endearing. "Good luck," said Mary, watching him trudge down the carpeted corridor like a man approaching his execution.

WHITE CURTAINS PERSISTED IN her vision when Ann shut her eyes.

"Annie, are you awake?" Joel smiled down at her.

Mary reached past him to touch her leg. "Twenty-seven eggs. That's my girl."

She floated in their love, with light shining through the curtains and light in their eyes, and relief flooded through her limbs. Twenty-seven eggs, and on her way to motherhood. "What do we do with them all?" she whispered. "Can we have twenty-seven children?"

In the lab, Joel's sperm was separated from seminal fluid through a process called "washing." Each egg was mixed with the sperm in a lab dish containing a culture medium. The mixture was placed in an incubator set to 97.4 degrees Fahrenheit, the temperature of a woman's body. There, in darkness, examined from time to time under the godlike eye of a microscope, one of the 20,000 or so sperm in each dish would pierce an egg. Then the cells would begin to divide. Within a few days, they'd be ready for transfer into Mary's uterus.

MARY FELT INCOMPLETE STANDING there on East 6th Street, outside the sisterhood's building, watching Ann and Joel's nondescript Ford drive away. They were returning to Bethel. A piece of Mary lingered in their car, a piece sat at the clinic, and a piece still snuggled in bed with America, who'd slept over at Sunrise the night before. Only a fragment of herself existed in the blustery wind to lug the canvas bag and jewelry case into the tenement building.

Asphodel let her in. Immersed in her second-initiation priestess study, she wore her black hair parted severely down the middle, tattooed black liner on her eyelids and, always, deep red lipstick.

"You're looking very dramatic," said Mary. "Like Cruella Deville."

"I'm altering my bone structure through my thoughts," said Asphodel. "Don't mock. I expected you an hour ago."

The sisterhood space, built from two conjoined apartments on the second floor, had not changed much in the twelve years since Mary had lived here. Peacock feathers still bowed from the huge ceramic jar at the entrance. The household rules still hung on the wall of the vestibule, purple marker in swirled, artful script on laminated poster board:

To all those who share this dwelling: No men overnight. Abide in silence before 4 p.m. That means no talking and no noise! Observe nonviolence in language and action. Cooking and/or eating of dead flesh on the premises is strictly forbidden. All residents must share in the preparation of meals. Meals are sacred. No phone calls during dinner. No gossiping. No walking into the living room during yoga in the morning or meditation in the evening. No throwing menstrual products down the toilet. We are all sisters. Om Shanti. Peace.

Mary knew, because a multitude of voices emanated from behind the closed doors of the living room, that a meeting was in session. No one had invited her or even mentioned a meeting. She felt excluded as she followed Asphodel into the kitchen. "I'll be altering my bone structure, too," she said. "Maybe you've heard."

"Let's do business first," said Asphodel.

"Fine." Mary slid the canvas bag across the kitchen floor. "Glad to ditch this."

"Be cool." Asphodel grabbed each brick of marijuana quickly, and shoved them one by one into the freezer. Then she handed Mary a bulky envelope full of cash.

It weighed down Mary's shoulder bag. "Hope I'm not mugged. I hate carrying cash."

"Right, why don't we pay with credit?" said Asphodel. "Grow up, Mary."

"I'm just making conversation. Don't get bitchy," said Mary. "Since when is the sisterhood involved in drugs anyway?"

"Aren't you going to count it?"

"Please, I've already had a long day. Let's not stand on ceremony."

"We don't want to deal drugs, you have to understand." Asphodel opened cabinets, pulling out crackers. She bustled to the fridge for platters of cut-up vegetables, acting busy. "Times are hard. Wren has this new job, but the pay's lousy. I'm the only one earning a decent salary. And these days you have to be marketable. Casting spells and reading tarot cards isn't marketable. Our rent is going up. We're still paying off the Yule event in the public park last year. Raven doesn't work at all. It's all right for you. You've got rich patrons. Your neighborhood's not being gentrified."

"Rich patrons? You've got to be kidding me. I just crossed the line from artisan to drug trafficker. I wouldn't even *be* here if America wasn't paying me a couple hundred smackers." Mary felt less duped by this version of reality.

She heard an argument erupting from the living room, passion-ate voices. *We can't leave them burning all night, it's a fire hazard,* someone yelled.

"Are they talking about Imbolc?" Mary asked. She knew they were. Imbolc was the festival of light and fertility, February second, the feast of torches with lots of candles, fire of the heart and mind. "I'll be full-on pregnant by Imbolc!"

"Aren't you croning?"

"We're doing this expensive high-tech fertility thing. Crazy hormone drugs. My butt's a pincushion. But they got twenty-seven eggs out of Ann this morning! I'm going to carry her baby."

"You don't say." Asphodel stopped and focused her dark eyes on Mary. "That's incredible."

"You know me; I'd do anything for Annapurna. I had to talk her into it. Kids these days are total conformists. They don't think outside the box."

"I remember when she found out about her condition," said Asphodel. "Such a sad girl. So isolated."

"Not sad anymore," said Mary, hearing an accusation. She remembered sisterhood dinners at this kitchen table, night after night with the other womyn, and Ann slouched in a hateful sulk, as if she blamed Mary for everything. But Mary had asked every specialist a million times, *What did I do? Is this something I did? No, no, and no,* they'd said.

"To be honest, when it all went down I thought you were kind of selfish about it. Don't take it the wrong way but you had your jewelry thing and Annapurna cramped your style. You complained about her constantly."

Mary was taken aback. She grabbed a carrot stick off the platter and chomped aggressively, spewing bits of orange. "You've been hostile to me the second I walked in the door and I have no idea why."

"I'm sorry. I'm not hostile to you, personally. I'm against the drugs but I was out-voted. It's great what you're doing for your daughter. Clear up some karma. Seriously. It's like you're evolving. You even look a little different."

The living room doors opened and the din amplified. "Hey Asphodel!" someone shouted. "What about a cross-fashioning ceremony with baskets?"

"They need me in there." Asphodel picked up the platter. "You're welcome to join us. Abundance on Imbolc, that's our theme."

"I wish I could," said Mary. "But I'm supposed to rendezvous with Della."

Asphodel paused in the hall. "I'm amazed. I mean it. I wouldn't have thought you had it in you."

"Thanks," said Mary, simultaneously touched and hurt as she picked up her jewelry case. "A backhanded compliment just like my mother's, but I'll take it."

AT HER DESK, PHONE by her ear, Della waved a bejeweled hand, not ornamented in *madebymary*™ jewelry, but in boxy double-ring contraptions and a bracelet channel-set with emeralds that seemed to burden her wrist. "Yes, darling," she said into the phone. "I'm bowing out of the arrangements. What? Oh, namaste to you, too."

Mary plopped down on the red leather sofa. "I'm sorry to say I don't like that ring or that bracelet."

"Cool your pits, dear. My Soho dealer sold a few pieces, so your *spiralmary* series is back in the catalog. But the yonis haven't flown off the shelves this month, alas. Isn't the year 2000 the designated Year of the Woman? It ought to be! Did you finagle a list from your reproduction center? There's a ready and affluent customer base."

"Let's keep the center out of it. Ann would be upset."

"Oh, come on, Ann is *always* upset. But never mind. I need pictures of your work while you're here. Arrange with the photographer ASAP, if you don't mind. Here's the number." Della scribbled on a Post-it and extended her arm over her desk, forcing Mary to get up off the sofa to fetch it.

Last year, Della would have walked the note over to Mary, but no point in dwelling.

"Don't take this personally, dear," said Della. "But could you skedaddle? I have a conference call. I'm drowning in work." She flapped her fingers in a get-out gesture.

Mary wandered to the back, which Della kept distinctly separate from her workspace. No leather here. Billowing folds of drapery covered the walls. Heavy brocade curtains veiled the windows, hiding the view of the brick wall across the airshaft. Every corner smelled cloyingly of rosewater. The tiny kitchen accommodated two high stools at a small round table. Mary opened the refrigerator—nothing but soy yogurt and a plastic carton of edamame. The freezer, however, revealed an unopened pint of rum raisin ice cream. Mary exerted control and retreated. Sinking into the soft pillows on Della's divan she picked up the phone.

"Yeah," answered America.

"The deal's done, lover girl!" she said. "I'll be back in a few days with your—"

"Is this a crank call? Are you out of your fucking mind? I don't take crank calls."

The click resounded. Tears sprang up. Okay, Mary rationalized, using the word "deal" might have been stupid. Maybe America's phone was bugged. But did she have to be so gratuitously nasty?

She beelined to the freezer, tore the lid off the ice cream, and spooned it right from the carton. Portion control be damned. Nothing to chew twenty-five times, only cold sweetness to suck and tongue and swallow. Raisins lodged stickily in her molars. *No one wants to see a fat girl eat,* her mother had lectured. So, Mary mastered secret eating. How quickly the richness melted, creaming down her throat, how full and timeless the sensations were, until, suddenly, she had consumed the entire pint.

Not bloated, not even particularly full, she tossed it in the garbage. Why, knowing her weakness, did Della stock the freezer with ice cream? The indifference was downright hostile. Overcome with fatigue stemming from shame, sugar and residual hangover, Mary threw herself onto the divan and shut her eyes. She slipped into her past, swinging in the schoolyard playground, pumping her legs, wind slapping her face. She soared so high, the swing chains buckled. Her father appeared at the playground fence, bulky and flat-footed, gripping the chain links, searching for her. He was so much older than the other kids' dads that they made fun of him. *Hello Princess.* He slipped her chocolate chip cookies through the fence, forbidden by Rose. When he smiled, his round face creased with wrinkles like concentric parentheses and his eyes lit up. His unabashed joy at just being with Mary mortified her. *Someone's here to see you,* he said.

"Someone's here to see you!" Della singsonged. Behind her stood a man in a navy pea coat with a camera bag hanging off his shoulder. "This is Peter Shepherd, photographer. Naughty Mary, I told you to call him ASAP." And she receded to her office.

Mary stood quickly, glimpsed herself in a gilt-framed mirror, double-chinned and rumpled, her cheek indented with a wrinkle from the pillow crease, and she became acutely annoyed. "I'm discombobulated," she said. "And I'm a little tired of Della's scolding. She's not wearing a single piece of my jewelry."

With a deep laugh, Peter pushed a tangle of brown hair off his face to peer at Mary's hand. "Your rings are certainly much nicer than the godawful stuff on her person."

A British accent. He was young, not much older than Ann, which put Mary on guard. Young people were so judgmental. And weren't the British also quick to criticize? The last thing Mary needed was criticism. *Are you out of your fucking mind?* America's voice wormed through her brain. She relinquished her hand to Peter, letting him touch her rings and bracelets, then stroke her fingers. He was saying something complimentary about her jewelry but the pleasure from his touch diverted her attention.

She was relieved when he released her. He threw his coat on the sofa but misjudged the distance, and it slid to the floor. Then he stretched his arms up to grip the kitchen doorframe. His T-shirt, decorated with a colorful likeness of Ganesh, slid up, uncovering his smooth, muscular torso. His cotton pants hung low off his hips, revealing a slight tuft of hair above the noosed drawstring.

Mary flashed to Coyote, her first love, with his freak flag of hair and his jaunty saunter, his narrow hipbones and firm, indented buttocks. *I like a woman with meat on her bones.*

Peter's clothing slid back into place when he squatted down to open her bulky jewelry case. "Do you mind?" He withdrew a bust Mary had designed from papier-mâché. Lightweight, androgynous, and pretty, with chokers and pendants looped over its neck, at trunk shows people would ask if it too was for sale.

"Quite lovely," his voice floated up to her. He quickly plucked pieces from plastic bags, unwrapping the anti-tarnish paper, creating a clutter on the floor.

"Don't mix them up, please." She squatted, spreading her skirt out. Her butt ached from injections. Painfully aware of the flesh rolling over her elastic waistband, she tried to organize the jewelry. "Keep the one-of-a-kinds together, not with the lower-end stuff."

He held earrings and bracelets and brooches in turn, examining each piece in his palm as if testing its weight and energy. "They vibrate," he said, brandishing a flexible spiral bracelet inlaid with colored glass. "Picture this one floating in midair with soft color behind it, like a Rothko painting. Blue behind aquamarine and peridot; green behind topaz and garnet. If we hang them on fishing wire and float them in their shadows, their ethereal nature will be displayed." Then, with his index finger, he stroked Mary's collarbone as if she herself were a piece of jewelry.

She stood abruptly. Tiny sparks of light showered in arcs through an enveloping darkness and she staggered into the wall.

"You all right there, love?"

"Just dizzy. Must be the void moon. Or maybe the fertility drugs." She felt protected as he led her to the sofa. His grip on her elbow steadied her.

"Fertility drugs?" His face, his cleft chin and sharp eyes, wavered before her. *Don't be needy, Mary.* She stared into her lap and noticed a rip in the seam of her black muslin skirt. The recycled flavor of rum raisin rose unpleasantly in her throat. "I know what you're thinking," she said. "What's a fat old lady like me doing on fertility drugs?"

"You haven't a clue what I'm thinking," he said. "I'll get you some water."

When he walked away, she tried to establish control, modulating her breath, inhaling and exhaling. But America's harsh voice invaded. *Is this a crank call?* And humiliating tears sprang up again.

Peter returned with two glasses. He sat down next to her, sliding into the declivity created by her body, and wordlessly placed the glasses on the floor. Their thighs touched.

"In a couple of days, there'll be an embryo inside me. I'm going to carry my daughter's baby."

"Della mentioned something. Quite amazing." The scent of sandalwood rose subtly off his T-shirt. Suddenly he snatched her hand and pressed it against his bristly, unshaven cheek. "It's uncanny that you're sitting here so full of life and my mother passed away just yesterday. I don't know why I'm telling you."

"Does Della know?" asked Mary.

Dropping her hand, Peter pressed his fist against his mouth. His stillness, the mottled redness of his face and his glistening eyes, reminded her of Annapurna as a small child at Peace Ranch, just before she exploded in a bawl. Mary threw her arms around him. Even sitting, he was very tall and had to slouch to allow the embrace. She felt the muscles along his back and the warmth of his body beneath his T-shirt. Coyote materialized again, a memory so sharp she could conjure his smell from when he snuck into her sleeping bag at night, the pungent musky odor of another woman. A bed-hopper, he would press his cold toes against her legs and paw her with an urgency enough like love that she always took him in. "I'm glad you told me," she said.

Peter clutched her with a similar compulsion. "Her funeral's in Southampton but I'm skint. If not for flat-sitting I'd be homeless. But I lied to my family. They think I'm famous! What does a funeral matter anyway? My mother won't know whether I'm there or not. I need to sort this out. I can't think straight."

"My mother died around Christmas last year. A month later my daughter moved out of my house and got married, didn't even invite me to her ceremony." Mary felt her own tears coming on yet again. "Here comes my waterpower. I'm like a psychic sponge."

"Her passing wasn't unexpected." Peter sniffed. "She's been ill for years. I'm sure people will say it's a blessing that her son, the ingrate's, not here. You must think I'm a twit."

"You haven't a clue what I'm thinking." She stroked the knotted softness of his hair, which was wispy like the feathers that escaped from Della's pillows, and she recalled her father again, and the cookies. She'd been embarrassed when he came skulking around the playground fence, humiliated by the mockery from other kids. And finally, she had refused to kiss him. She told him not to come. He reacted as if he'd been beaten. Shoulders slumped, he shuffled away, with his hat too big and his feet turned out. He carried himself as though preparing for the next blow. When he was incapacitated by a stroke a year later, Mary blamed herself.

There had been no cosmic effect, no ripple in the universe, no message from the goddess when he died. Rose's letter had been forwarded several times, catching up with Mary in Colorado after he had been dead for three months. She never said goodbye. She sometimes forgot that he was dead. When she shook Peter, his head bumped against her chest. "You *have* to go to the funeral," she said. "I believe in rituals. You have to say goodbye."

"Can't I stay here with you, just like this? You're so good and kind. You're a shining diamond."

No one had ever told her that before. *Are you out of your fucking mind?* Click. With a burst of energy, Mary pulled herself from his grasp, leaving him curled up on the pillows. She grabbed the envelope from her purse and opened it to show him six thousand dollars in one-hundred-dollar bills. "I can get you there. How much do you need?"

"You're mad," he said. "Have you robbed a bank?"

"It's true, I am mad." She laughed. "Get up. Let's get you a ticket home."

As they put on their coats, she was astonished to see a soft outline of gold surrounding his body. All those years, wishing and trying and pretending to see people's auras, and here, unexpectedly, came the real shimmering thing, no mirage. It vaporized more quickly than a rainbow. But she knew she had seen it.

They had to pass through Della's office, which was empty. Peter stepped aside to let Mary descend the stairs first. He took her hand on the sidewalk and their fingers intertwined with a perfect fit. Her hand grew numb in the cold but she didn't care, she was a shining diamond. They leaned forward into the wind for several blocks, ending up at a travel agent on Houston Street, where Peter purchased a round trip ticket from JKF to Heathrow for two thousand dollars of Mary's cash. His flight would leave in a few hours. "Here's some extra money for a taxi," she said, handing him another hundred.

"I love you," he said. "I love you, I love you, I love you." He wrapped her in a hug on the corner of Avenue A and Houston Street in the cold January afternoon while pedestrians swirled around them and a blustery wind blew across their backs. When she tried to pull away, he held her. When she gently pushed him so he'd let go, he tightened his grip. Finally, she surrendered to the shelter of his arms, which were thick and muscular, so different than America's. *To hell with America.* Her forehead fit perfectly in his collarbones.

THE WAITING ROOM AT the Center for Human Reproduction was packed.

"There's a seat. Take it." Ann pointed to an empty chair, almost hidden by the two women spilling over either side of it.

"Don't mind if I do." Mary picked up her portable jewelry display and crammed herself in. Ann followed. She was saying something about why Joel couldn't be there but Mary found it hard to tune in. A Pink Floyd song ran through her head: *Money, it's a crime.* She hoisted the display onto her lap and snapped it open. It held twelve pairs of earrings, twelve bracelets, six necklaces and six pendants, and she knew they were impressive against a black silk backdrop. "Looking is free," she said.

"What are you doing?" said Ann. "This isn't a trunk show."

"Della told me to." Mary adjusted a fabricated necklace of iolite and freshwater pearls with almond-shaped jump rings so it hung in a smooth arc. She was supposed to work the room, pass around her business card, talk herself up and build a new market base. Or was it market share? She couldn't remember. She was on edge.

"What have you got?" The woman on Mary's left reached for a choker of black agate teardrop beads. Her jacket sleeve slid past her wrist, revealing a gold Tiffany watch.

"Wear agates and achieve financial success." Mary slipped into her jewelry-expo self. Pressing the necklace into the woman's palm, she said. "Just feel the energy of the stones. See if they speak to you."

The woman on Mary's right put down her magazine. "Do you have any earrings?"

Mary noted the red blouse, not a good hue; it drained the color from the woman's face. "I see you in rose quartz," she said, unhooking a pair of earrings that combined three collet settings. "*Madebymary*™ jewelry. I think of the work as 'modern talismanic.' It's handcrafted. Each piece is special." Mary passed her a compact mirror.

The first woman opened her purse. "I shouldn't. But I *have* to. Eighty dollars; is that tag right?"

"Actually, it's a hundred. I mislabeled that one."

Mary tucked the five twenties into her bra. As more women gathered around, drawn by the lure of a sale, she wondered briefly where Ann had gone. Her view was blocked.

"I don't think soliciting is allowed in here," An agitated slender woman glared at Mary's jewelry. "It's inappropriate."

"You're probably right. I just wanted to share with everyone." Mary prided herself on bullshitting straights. When she and her tribe had traveled around in the Mahayana, she always dealt with the cops, gas station attendants, toll booth clerks, whatever functionary hassled them, because she understood what they needed to hear. Now she said, "I'm a jeweler and an artisan and I'm constantly in touch with the creative force. But today's the day of my transfer and hopefully soon I'll be carrying my daughter's baby. And that will be the most incredible creation in my life. All this other stuff..." she waved her hand dismissively over her display. "...can't compare."

A murmur of approval ran through the group.

"How much is that pendant? It's unusual." Someone pointed to a piece Mary had created by fusing gold scraps around a rough opal stone. An experiment that she had included at the last minute, it resembled the body of a fetus.

She couldn't let it go. "Sorry, that's a prototype. Not for sale. I don't know how it got in there."

"Are you Mary Moonlight?" someone else said. "I think they're calling you."

She jumped up, slammed her display shut, and scurried down the corridor after Ann. In the locker room, as she undressed and wrapped herself in a hospital gown, open at the back, she was still humming with jewelry-expo vibes. But Ann sat like a lump on the bench, reproaching with her body language. Mary tried to shove her jewelry case into the locker with her clothes, but the case was too wide. "I hate to ask," she said. "But could you carry this? It won't fit."

With a martyred sigh, Ann picked up the case and took Mary's hand as if Mary was a child needing to be led, which she certainly seemed in her foam-slippered state with her flabby rear end exposed. She let Ann lead her to a gurney. Ann held her as she hoisted herself on, and watched her as she lay down. Mary pulled the blanket up to her shoulders. "Stop looking at me like that."

"Why do you do this?" said Ann.

Mary realized she was terrified of falling under Ann's tyranny, getting trapped in Ann's limited and negative little world.

Dr. Godwin came in, rubbing his hands together, all boyish smile and big ears. "How's my mother-daughter team? Are we ready to make a baby?"

"The planets are aligned!" said Mary. "My sacral chakra's spinning."

"Earth to Mary," said Ann. "There's no such thing as a sacral chakra."

Mary heard the terror in Ann's constricted voice and felt instantly guilty. "Honey, life can be a cool sweetheart of a trip if you just open up and see the golden aura."

But Dr. Godwin was walking alongside the gurney talking about the procedure and Mary couldn't focus. She was being pushed along a corridor, under a blur of ceiling tiles, into a large operating room. She saw by Ann's blank face that she wasn't taking it in either.

A nurse helped her off the gurney onto a table.

"Just so you understand," said Dr. Godwin. "Four pre-embryos in one transfer is considered unconventional but at your age the risk of multiples is lower than the risk of no pregnancy at all."

"Whatever!" said Mary. "Where do I sign?"

The embryologist came in, swathed in green, with a mask over his mouth and nose, gloves on his hands. "Are we ready?" His mask moved when he talked.

Dazed, Mary accepted a printout of four cell clusters from Dr. Godwin. "Thanks, Dr. God!" She pressed it to her heart.

"Can I see?" Ann snatched it.

The stirrups were raised and Mary slid her bottom down the exam table. Bright lights hurt her eyes. With the speculum in place, the embryologist inserted a lab pipette up through her cervix to deposit four multi-celled beings into her uterus. The ordeal demanded an incredible leap of faith. If they believed that four invisible little things had just been inserted inside her by a man who called himself an "embryologist," why shouldn't they also believe that a sacral chakra could vibrate?

"I hope they're the right ones," said Ann.

The procedure took five minutes. Then an orderly whisked Mary away to a recovery room where she was transferred to a bed with crisp, clean sheets and pillows. She lay perfectly still so as not to dislodge the pre-embryos. Ann sat in an adjacent chair with Mary's case between her feet, staring at the printout of the cell clusters.

A nurse swished the hospital curtain aside. "Mrs. Moonlight, from now on, you behave as if you're pregnant. You know what that means, right?"

"I'm guessing no alcohol, drugs, herbal remedies, cigarettes… Anything else? I was tripping out on acid when I went into labor with my daughter here."

"Why do you need to tell everyone that?" said Ann. "Do you think it's *cool?*"

"It was during the Woodstock Concert." Mary addressed the nurse, who looked interested. "You know, in the movie when John Sebastian announces that some cat's old lady just had a baby, a kid destined to be far out? That was *me!* Annapurna was that baby!"

"This has to end." Ann chopped the air with her hand. "That story isn't even true."

"Not a good idea to 'trip out,' as you say," said the nurse. "Take your prenatal vitamins. Some people advise eating fatty foods to assist implantation."

"No problem with fat, as you can see." Mary pushed the blanket down to yank on her flesh.

"Stop doing that! Why do you want everyone to know how little you think of yourself?" Ann hissed.

Rebelling, Mary called to the nurse. "Hey, do you want to buy a bracelet? You have beautiful wrists."

"I do?" The nurse turned her hands.

"I see you in blue topaz," said Mary. "Open the case, honey. Show her."

But Ann sat in a strained, still posture.

"The doctor will come by shortly." The nurse slid the curtain shut and Mary heard her at the next bed: *From now on you behave as if...*

"You are far out, you know." Mary patted Ann's leg. But Ann shrank away.

"I wish Joel were here," she said.

"Come on, how about we call a truce?" Mary mimed the lighting of a pipe and passed it. "Peace pipe. Please?"

Ann stared stonily at the imaginary pipe.

"Okay, forget the peace pipe. We're in this together whether we like or not." Mary pointed to the printout in Ann's lap. "What should we call them? Babies? Beings? Little lives?"

"It's just that you always have to make such a scene. I don't get it." Ann relaxed her rigid shoulders.

They were finally connecting! "Blastocyst is their medical name," said Mary. But that sounded more like a disease than a quartet of cosmic particles floating in the primordial universe of her womb. "I know! Babelings. It's poetry! They're our babelings!" This time when Mary reached for her, Ann gave her hand. "Babelings," she said. "Okay. I'll go with it for now."

The jittery light of possibility flashed over them. A little flip occurred in her belly and Mary decided an embryo must have implanted, just then.

ANN DREAMED OF A tiny, shrunken baby who hadn't nursed in so long, her milk had dried up. Terrified the baby was starving to death or, worse, had already died, she hurried along the road from America's house to Sunrise with the infant in her arms. Then she stood in her old bedroom gazing down at the baby who lay on her back under a blanket in a too-large wooden cradle, and she lowered the blanket, murmuring in baby talk. Skinny, wizened and ill, the baby responded anyway, waving her arms and smiling painfully back at Ann. But Ann had been the one who'd let her get sick. She was doubly condemned, not only for neglecting her baby, but for manipulating the baby into showing affection. She awoke in darkness at the dead hour of four in the morning.

Joel stirred. "What's wrong?"

"I dreamed I let our baby starve and then I made her thank me."

"Do you feel like a starving infant?" He was warm and drew her into his arms.

"I'm scared that Mary won't be pregnant," she whispered. "What will we do then?"

"We'll worry about it then," he said, already softening, falling back to sleep.

But she lay wide awake in his sleeping arms, reliving the pregnancy test from the day before, as anticlimactic an event as ever there was one. She and Mary had bypassed the crowded waiting room for a nurse's station in another, smaller room. Ann had watched avidly, jealously as Mary wiggled into the seat. *I know I'm pregnant. I feel it. I don't need proof.* The needle hit the vein, blood bubbled into the barrel, a band-aid was applied and they were dismissed. *You'll get a call tomorrow,* said the nurse. *Take your progesterone.*

We had to drive two hours for this? said Mary. *I couldn't just pee on a stick?*

The home tests are inaccurate this early, Ann had explained, repeating the clinic line. But she had her doubts. Her doubts were abrasive and gave her a headache. She didn't want to be envious or covetous or mired in pessimism. It was as if her presence changed the ions in the air, so that any good situation became tinged with regret, unhappiness, or bad outcomes. Someone had to be in opposition, but why did it always have to be her?

"What?" Joel twitched awake again.

"Go back to sleep," she said.

But McKenna whined and slobbered on Ann's arms. Joel turned the light on. "Forget sleep."

"I'm sorry," said Ann. "I know you have to work tomorrow."

"It's slow. People don't return calls." Joel sat up in bed. "Maybe I should take the day off."

"Great idea." Ann traced the birthmark on his hip with her finger. It held the shape of a long-bladed leaf, hidden from everyone in his daily life except her. Impulsively, she kissed it.

He pressed his palm onto the crown of her head with a moan.

Desire was a fleeting, elusive sensation, disappearing easily for Ann. Sexual urges became an urge to sing, to feel metal strings beneath her fingers, to flick them with her fingertips and hold a pick with her thumb. "Let's play our guitars," she said.

She got up, pulling on sweatpants, socks, sweater, and padded down the hall to the living room to stoke the stove. Outside, the big house was visible only as a hulking shadow through the trailer window. The darkness obscured its surface details of interlocking vinyl siding. It was "dried in," an empty shell, a hollow mother doll overlooking the tiny trailer.

Joel fingerpicked the opening of a Hank Williams song on his old acoustic. The guitar had gone out of tune.

While he tuned it, Ann took up the melody on her guitar. *I saw the light,* she sang. *No more darkness, no more night.* When Joel joined in, they created a fragile harmonious sequence, connected to each other by the hope of a life they'd make between them.

Several hours later, when the clinic called, they were still playing, working their way through sheet music, from "Lovesick Blues," "Wedding Bells," and "Cold Cold Heart." They had moved from Hank Williams to Dwight Yoakam to Reverend Horton Heat. The news that Mary was pregnant became another song. Joel picked out the heart-rending refrain of *Father and Son* by Cat Stevens. Outside, snowflakes danced in front of the window. They sang, *Look at me, I am old but I'm happy.*

PREGNANCY UNLEASHED MARY'S CREATIVITY. Inspired, she hunkered down at her jewelry bench day after day, wrapping rough opals in fold-formed silver wire, each one uniquely curved to resemble a child in a womb. She worked straight through nights, stopping only to eat, sometimes dozing off at her bench with her flame on. Dangerous. A few hours' sleep and she crawled back to her bench. *I'm not playing games. I want my money.* America threatened on Mary's answering machine. But Mary had to ride her creative wave. Her opals came from Indonesia and she couldn't predict when her next batch would arrive, so she stayed with it until she'd used them all.

It was a couple of weeks before Mary finally drove the two miles to America's house with the money in an envelope. As she was pulling into America's driveway, she thought about how this pregnancy was making her feel strong and real. Then she spotted a molted snakeskin at the edge of the driveway. Fragile and perfect, patterned with an infinite number of overlapping scales, the sight of it gave her qualms. She gathered it up carefully before she opened the door to America's cottage, and was immediately surrounded by the pounding bass line of Pink Floyd's "Us and Them."

She tiptoed toward the living room. Through the beaded curtains, she spied America lying on her back on the carpet, eyes closed, arms and legs splayed, appearing peaceful in her red stretch pants and big T-shirt emblazoned with a McDonald's logo spoof: *Marijuana, Over 1 Billion Stoned.*

A strange absence of children's toys, jumpy swing and playpen, struck Mary as another bad omen as she parted the curtains. Music echoed from speaker to speaker. She felt almost stoned as she placed the snakeskin on the rug.

"I left you countless messages," said America without stirring, without even opening her eyes. "I talked to Asphodel. I talked to Della. I talked to Ann. The only person I haven't talked to is the one missing in action with my money."

Mary flopped into the beanbag chair, which spit white pellets from a rip in the seam. "I won't lie to you, some of it's missing," she said, dismayed at the quaver in her voice as she placed the envelope full of money next to America's shoulder. "I was scared to carry all the cash in my bag, so I put some in my bra."

"You put money in your bra. Aren't you the drug-smuggling queen?" America tore the envelope open, letting the bills fall on her chest.

"I went about my day," said Mary. "And a few hours later, the money wasn't there. Maybe it fell out in a taxi? I've been afraid to..."

"Money fell out of your bra, in a taxi. Looks like twenty-five hundred dollars' worth of bra money fell out."

"No, silly! I separated it into a few different stashes and one of them was loose in the outside pocket of my purse." Rose would have known by Mary's high-pitched anxious laugh that she was lying. America didn't deserve the same credit. Still, Mary's story sounded lame even to herself. "The money in my *bra* was safe. But my purse must have opened and..."

"I thought you fucking loved me!" Up in a flash, America kicked over a milk crate, dumping a full ashtray, and upended the beanbag chair, rolling Mary into the ashes. Then she punched the wall above the stereo, and screamed, clutching her fist. "If I was a typical dealer, you'd be *dead!* I got upstreams and downstreams. I'm owed and I owe. And you *fucked* me over, Mary-fucking-Moonlight."

Mary's heart slammed up into her skull. What about the fetus? She shook the ashes off her skirt. She hated groveling but this was a desperate situation. "I do love you. And you love me, too, right? No one fucked anyone over. Love and forgiveness go together. Your hand's going to swell. You'll need to ice it."

"This is so typical," said America. "I can't rely on you."

"I'm not cut out to be a mule." Mary picked up the snakeskin, miraculously unscathed. "I'll pay you back, I promise. Look what I found. See?"

"Get that away from me!" America screamed. "It's a warning! I'm in danger! Don't touch it!"

Mary dropped it. She stood slowly. Her back hurt. "You need to chill out."

"Don't you get it? I need to shed my skin. I need a new identity. Damn straight you'll pay me back." America shoved her, almost knocking her off balance, back into the beanbag chair.

"Don't push me," said Mary. "I'm pregnant."

"Okay, earth mother, here's the deal," said America. "I need product. You have space. You owe me."

"I've never seen you like this." In the kitchen, Mary opened the freezer, and emptied an ice cube tray into a plastic bag. She found a dishtowel wadded up behind the sink faucet, and wrapped it around the ice. "Where's Cassidy? Where are your grandchildren?"

"Gone. Don't change the subject." America stood passively, allowing Mary to wrap the ice-filled towel around her knuckles. "I'm in debt, and these people mean business. Go clean the spilled ashtray."

"Fair enough," said Mary. "Where's your vacuum cleaner?"

"Vacuum cleaner?" America guffawed.

Mary had once loved that laugh for its earthiness but she realized now the love had bottomed out. She went back to the living room where, for the price of peace, she collected ashes and cigarette butts with her bare hands. The warmth of Peter's body and the experience of being sheltered in his arms with her forehead at his collarbones came vividly to her mind. No matter what happened, she'd been a shining diamond for a moment.

"We'll use Ann's old room." America came in and stood over Mary, leaking cold water from her icepack onto Mary's leg. "You'll need grow lamps, a thousand watts each. You can buy them at the mall."

Mary brushed her palms clean on her peasant skirt. "I hope you haven't harmed my fetus with your pushing and yelling. You don't want that kind of karma."

America plopped into the beanbag chair, disgorging more pellets. "Peace pipe." She filled a corncob pipe and lit it, unleashing a familiar pungent scent. "Prepare to enter another solar system."

Mary salivated, but refused the proffered pipe. "I can't. Like I said, I'm pregnant."

"You owe me twenty-five hundred smackers. Don't add insult to insult." America actually bared her teeth. "The game is bigger than the sum of the players, Mary."

Mary understood the necessity of diplomacy. She pretended to inhale but only held the smoke in her mouth until she accidentally inhaled. Then she coughed and became instantly stoned. *Sorry sweet baby,* she communicated silently. *This won't happen again.*

America picked up the snakeskin. "I'll have to meditate on this. I need clarity." Then, she leaned toward the stereo, pipe pressed between her lips, and turned the music way up.

"THANKS FOR COMING." MARY ushered Joel into the living room where a healthy fire crackled in the fireplace. She leaned over to flip her skirt up, baring her buttocks. She didn't wear undies unless it was cold and then she wore long johns. Generally, she liked a little air. Joel's discomfort surprised her, since he should have been accustomed to her ways. He trembled as he dabbed her left buttock with antiseptic. But he was adept and managed to jam the needle in so quickly she barely felt it.

"I asked you to come alone because I have a proposition." She pulled her skirt down.

"You said you wanted to discuss a ritual." He blushed to the roots of his dark, frizzy hair.

"I lied. But it's not *that* kind of proposition. It's business. Have a seat." She explained the situation: America had purchased one hundred Sativa, Delta-9 indoor seeds and wanted to plant a crop. She needed product. Joel and Ann needed money, especially with a baby on the way. Mary supposed even *she* needed money, though she didn't care about money. She left out Peter and the sisterhood delivery. "I can't do this alone," she said. "I bought all these supplies but I don't know the first thing about them. They're sitting up in Ann's room. You're capable. You can install lamps and stuff like that."

She didn't mention that America believed the room was already prepared.

He perched on the edge of the armchair, treading his boots on her bearskin rug. "You want to grow pot in Ann's old bedroom?"

"We already have a distribution network." She parroted America.

"You find me under financial pressure," said Joel. "My land is mortgaged, I've got a mountain of debt on a house I can't get a bridge loan to finish. The city of Monticello doesn't respond to my bids. I had to lay off one of my guys. I don't get it. I maxed out my credit on this IVF process, and the kid isn't even born yet."

"If society is closing you off from so-called legitimate income, you're left with no choice." She had him. She knew she had him.

"Ann would hate it." He shook his head. "The answer will have to be no."

Mary knelt at his feet on the bearskin rug. From this angle, he was impressive-looking, a man of substance. "We're doing it *for* Ann. She doesn't have to know."

"You could keep it quiet?" Joel pressed the sole of his boot into Mary's skirt. "How much money do we stand to make?"

"About twenty-three thousand per lamp." She pushed his foot off. "We have six lamps. We divide with America and whatshisname, whoever she's fucking right now."

Joel looked up at the ceiling. He wouldn't meet her eye. "If I agree to this and anything happens, anyone questions, if Ann ever suspects anything, then we never had this conversation and I walk away."

"Deal," said Mary.

"You deserve better than America." To her shock, he slid off the armchair onto his knees, in frontal contact with her. "I really appreciate what you're doing. I love Ann."

"I know you do, Joel." Mary scooched back to put space between them.

"I just felt it needed to be said." He shifted closer so she was drawn into his energy field and, for a splintered bewildered moment, she feared he might kiss her.

"I'm glad we had this talk." He put his arms awkwardly around her. She was too surprised to hug back.

JOEL TORE OUT THE plasterboard walls of Ann's old bedroom to install wiring for the high-pressure sodium grow lights. They needed extra electrical currency. He understood this sort of work. Problems arose and solutions were found, no open-ended desire, no ongoing issues rising and falling endlessly. One avoided electrocuting oneself, that was all. He installed an activated carbon filter, which he attached to an outtake vent he cut through the wall, grateful for the work. He lay tarpaper down on the floor.

When Mary came upstairs with a mug of jasmine tea, he was touched. "Thanks. Smells flowery."

"I think you mean aromatic," said Mary.

He knew he meant flowery, like his mother's pomanders. His palms warmed against the mug. "Your electricity bill could go sky-high with these lamps."

Mary lifted a corner of her skirt, allowing Joel a glimpse of hairy pubis. He panicked. But she thrust a piece of her skirt up to wipe his chin. "You had some tar or something there. Wow, you're blushing. You and Ann, so alike."

His palms were drenched. He had to put the tea down. He grabbed the mini-vacuum, the first object he saw. It was loud, a boundary of noise. He set about sucking up bits of plaster and debris.

"I could have used that vacuum the other week," Mary shouted. "Cleaning ashes."

A dog barked with a vicious-sounding snarl. Joel turned off the mini-vacuum. He'd regained control. With a knife he cut open the box containing the propagation kits.

"I'm here!" America screamed from downstairs. But the syncopated thump of feet on steps suggested more than one person climbing.

A pit bull trotted into the room, its nails clicking against the wood floor. He butted into Joel, sniffing his pants, the box, the floor. "Hey boy," said Joel. "What's your name?"

"That's Chase." America bustled in. She pulled small, black canisters from her bag. "I brought the seeds. And this is Carlos."

Carlos wore cuffed baggy jeans held in place half way down his hips with a leather belt embellished with an ostentatious studded buckle in the shape of a large "C." "*Sientate,* Chase," he ordered. The dog sat.

"Chase speaks Spanish," America laughed.

"Who cares what language the dog speaks?" Mary cowered against the wall with her knees pulled up and her skirt tented over them. She deflated so easily, Joel pitied her.

Carlos squatted, bumping Joel's arm. He pulled on the slotted tray. "You will want to place these in the dark." His smile showed a flash of diamond embedded in his right canine. Three hoop earrings hung from his left ear. With golden brown skin and dark hair clipped short, he looked almost pretty. But his eyes were as hard and smooth as marbles.

"I know what I'm doing," said Joel.

"If we don't get 95% success, I'll hold you both responsible," said America, plucking seeds from her film canisters and placing them into the rock wool cubes, each of which held a tiny hole for the seed. "I brought some germination hormone, too."

"No need for additives," said Joel. "The trays already have the nutrients. It says on the box…"

"Listen to the expert," said America, pouring the gray substance into the trays.

"95% is not good enough. One hundred." Carlos touched America's neck. She rubbed her face against his palm like a cat.

"Carlos is the son of a Santeria queen," she said, addressing the room. "Mi corazon." And they kissed, long and wet. Chase growled.

"Anyone can act like a horny teenager," said Mary.

"You think this is funny, woman?" said Carlos. "You steal money and hide away like a rat."

"Wait a minute now. That's out of line." Joel didn't get it, the way Mary and her cohorts related to each other, simultaneously intimate and hostile.

"All he's saying is, you can't keep secrets from Carlos," said America.

"Not a good idea to start a business partnership with threats." Joel positioned the seeded trays far enough from the electric heater that they wouldn't burn, but close enough for warmth. He wasn't a perfectionist but he liked to do things well, if possible.

"The psychic gift comes from a lineage." Carlos stood, turning his palms up like a preacher. "My atoms were cooked in the heart of the dark stars. Cannabis is my spirit plant and teaches me vegetable gnosis. America is becoming psychic with my teachings."

"This is a business arrangement," said Joel. "I'd like to keep it that way."

"I am all business, amigo." Carlos flashed a diamond-studded smile.

"Once a day watering, can you handle it, Mary?" said America. "They need to be damp. Not wet. *Moist.*"

"Why do you have to use that tone?" Mary wiped her nose with her skirt. She did it modestly this time, Joel noticed, revealing nothing untoward.

"Don't worry about watering. I'll do it when I come over to give you the injection." Joel stood. He was relieved to find he was taller than Carlos. It meant nothing, but it lent him confidence. Each seedling had been successfully housed in a rockwool cube and there was nothing more to be done. "I think we can call it a wrap for today."

"Aw, he's sweet. Isn't he sweet, Mary?" said America. "Why couldn't Cass go for a sweet man like Joel?"

"If there's one thing I learned from working with construction teams it's the importance of mutual respect," said Joel.

"The man is right," said Carlos.

"May the goddess bless this *professional* crop," said America. "Mary? A word, please, in private."

Joel felt liberated when they all left the room. He stood alone with the trays for a moment, filled with a sense of potential. He remembered the night he got arrested, the siren behind him, flashing red lights, and the crunch of gravel under his tires as he pulled his car over. He knew before it happened that the cop would ask him to open his guitar case. A kilo of marijuana sat in that case and, as he lifted the lid, Joel physically dissolved. What a huge relief to surrender his existence! Just stop fighting and fall into the rapids. He had experienced a similar ecstatic submission with Jessica, and again at the Fertility Center when, to his horror, as he worked his hand, Mary had materialized in his mind, flipping up her peasant skirt, revealing her bare dimpled buttocks pocked with welt marks from injections. Helplessly, in an unstoppable frenzy, Joel shoved himself inside her, taking her from behind, and he toppled over the edge, filling the specimen jar with the image of his mother-in-law.

Now she was pregnant. But he'd done nothing wrong. His need to yield to an undertow could be served by growing marijuana. And he could free himself of debt, too. He turned off the lights and left the seedlings alone to germinate.

ANN WORE A SLINKY red dress for the fertility blessing at Sage's. The dress had been a gift from Mary that Ann had never worn before since the garment was meant, like the birthday yoni, for Mary's colorful fantasy daughter rather than the uptight daughter that Ann had become. But a baby on the way changed everything. Ann could feel the change inside her. She squeezed Joel's hand for the whole twenty-mile ride to Sage's. Mary's car was already in the driveway.

"Merry meet!" Sage greeted them at the door of her A-frame. She was wearing an identical long, slinky red dress. Cats draped themselves over cushions on the floor, groomed each other in front of the fireplace, and crept in and out through the swinging cat door. Sage owned thirteen of them, each one named for a lunar month based on the tree alphabet of the ancient Celts. As cats wound around their legs, drawing sinuous fabric along fur, Ann noticed how the woven sparkles glittered in the candlelight, and she imagined becoming her own version of the fantasy daughter, as poised and confident as Sage.

"Nice dress. It suits you, my beautiful girl." said Mary from the large front room. She was sitting cross-legged on a cushion set up in a circle bordered by flickering candles and she smiled eagerly at Ann, like a devotee. Ann's fantasy mother, attentive, loving, eager to please.

Ann sat on the cushion beside Mary. Her face grew hot as Mary stroked her hair. Grief snuck up on her, prickling across her scalp as she recalled Cassidy. *You have designs on my kids.* Cassidy had left for India without saying goodbye, and Ann suspected her request had played a role. Guilty on all counts, she touched the silver candlestick on the floor in front of her cushion. It held an unlit red candle.

"You've changed," said Mary. "Just receiving my compliment like that."

"We're all changing," said Joel, from Mary's other side. "I think Ann should wear the dress onstage. They won't be able to take their eyes off her."

"Moon mother, we dance your dance. Air, fire, water, earth, elements of astral birth, attend to us." Sage struck a match and held the burning end of her candle toward Joel.

Joel lit his wick with Sage's, extending it to Mary, who stretched her light toward Ann. As her candle flared, illuminating Mary's smiling face, Ann felt helpless with gratitude.

Sage rolled a large lump of wax between her palms. "This is the unformed spirit becoming physical." She passed it to Joel. "Create a human totem," she said. "Just mold it the best you can. Make a hole in the crown of the head."

Ann admired how easily Joel's capable fingers shaped the lump into a female figure: belly, breasts, thighs. He dug his thumb inside, to hollow out the crown of the head.

"Fire of the heart, spark of life, we welcome you." Sage plucked an egg from the center of the circle, where the usual ritual objects of knife, chalice, wand, and cauldron were arranged. She passed the egg to Ann. It felt warm, alive.

"I hold your precious life." Mary extended a little white pitcher. "Just break the egg into it."

As Ann cracked the shell against the pitcher rim, she noticed the glowing eyes of the cats among the candle flames. Mary tilted the spout into the head of Joel's wax figure, pouring egg in. A long slimy glimmer dripped from the back of Joel's hand as he closed the head and reshaped the belly.

"I'll take it now." Lifting the figure toward the ceiling, Mary rose to her knees. "Spirit thrive inside me," she cried. "I am the portal for your soul." Her robe slipped open, revealing her breasts, the shadow of her pubis, her thighs. She was naked.

Was this part of the plan, Ann wondered? She fixed her contemplation at the undulating flame in front of her, but the intrusion of Mary's breasts into her peripheral vision drew her all too easily back into the old current of shame and resentment. She remembered the womyn at the sisterhood, sitting topless around the dinner table. Their breasts—sagging, creped, stretch-marked, hairy-nippled—seemed to mock her anguish about her own body, not only its out-of-control adolescent growth but her uterus, vanished into thin air and the pain of its absence like a phantom limb. How she hated all the exhibitionism.

"Stay in the moment." Sage nudged her. "Tell the spirit of your readiness."

"My whole life is ready." Ann pressed her thumbs into her sternum and imagined her baby's heart, how she'd feel it beating. The memory of the womyn evaporated, and so did her shame.

"Our home is ready," said Joel. "*Will* be, anyway. Hopefully."

"Our hearts are ready," said Mary, as if she, too, imagined the baby's heart beating.

"We're all here for you, blessed spirit." Sage blew out her candle. One by one around the circle they followed her lead and extinguished theirs.

Behind them the cats stepped daintily among the outer circle of tapered flames. Mary began to hum. Ann softened into the sound, surrendering to the sense of a larger power and the miracle of Mary's pregnancy. She wondered why she'd been so upset by the sight of the womyn's breasts. Freedom seemed possible.

Joel asked, "Is something on fire?" And, with an unearthly yowl, a creature dashed across the circle, engulfed in flames.

"Douse it!" Sage leaped up.

"Oh, goddess!" Mary screamed.

Ann acted on impulse. She grabbed a towel, drenched it in the kitchen sink, and heaved it at the flaming cat as it careened toward the reclining chair. The stench of burnt flesh seared the air. Joel had torn his shirt off, wetting it under the tap. Now he wrapped it around the animal and carried it outside. Mary followed him, her screams fading outdoors.

Ann stamped out tiny flames along the floor until her feet hurt. Sage threw more wet towels down. She covered the floor, the chair, the cushions, anything that might smolder. Outside, they found Mary sobbing in Joel's arms. The cat lay in a heap at their feet. Clouds had rolled in, shrouding the stars.

Ann crouched by the cat, horrified to witness the animal's flesh sizzling. It was still alive, its tiny pink tongue hanging limply from its mouth.

"Oh, dear Hawthorne, my familiar." Sage worked the T-shirt underneath to lift the cat. "Run the bath! Please, someone."

"I feel like I'm burning!" Mary bawled in Joel's arms. "America warned me! It was the snakeskin!"

Ann scurried ahead of Sage to fill the tub. She helped Sage lower the cat into the bath, positioning its head above the water line so it could breathe. Then she sat on the rim, watching the water turn gray and red with soot and blood.

Outside, Mary was still screaming.

Joel appeared. "I should take Mary home."

"Go," said Sage. "Do an aural cleansing."

"I'm staying." Ann glanced up, unsettled by the sight of Joel's bare torso, how pale and vulnerable he looked. Of course, he'd donated his shirt to the cat.

"You'll be okay," he said.

After he'd gone, Ann could still feel the press of his lips on the crown of her head.

Sage chanted: *Giver and destroyer of life, we do not fear your embrace. We commend to you, our beloved familiar.* Ann knelt, her bony knees grinding into the bathroom tiles. Sage's chant acquired an always-and-forever quality, pulling her in like a leaf on the wind. Time no longer existed. The other cats prowled near the bathroom doorway, their tails low, growling softly. At one point, Ann got up and rolled a towel to pad her knees. Eventually, Sage lowered her voice and finally it subsided altogether. Hawthorne took his last breath. "So mote it be," said Sage. With a sob, she folded herself onto the floor. Ann stroked her bony back until it occurred to her that Sage preferred to be alone.

Outside, the cold blue light of morning illuminated a world that seemed to quiver with awareness. On instinct, Ann collected twigs and kindling, stacking them in the pit by a black obelisk in the center of Sage's medicine wheel where outdoor rituals were conducted. She worked up a sweat and had to unbutton her coat. One match and the fire ignited. Flames flickered like tongues. Ann tried to breathe through her mouth but the smell of burning hair came back every time she inhaled.

Sage emerged from the A-frame, carrying the lifeless cat. She slid it into the fire. "Hawthorne, my May cat, sacred to the Queen of Love, vanished into Summerland."

Then Sage sat beside her and held her hand, warming it. Ann couldn't have said how long they stayed there on the cold ground, clasping hands, but night gave itself over completely to daylight. She remembered burying a dog on the commune. Everyone stood in a circle to state what the dog had meant to them. She had believed in Summerland back then, a place of eternal sunshine and green meadows. She had wanted to go there herself. Now she believed in nothing but her own responsibility for the cat's death.

The embers were dying when the sound of a car chugged up the dirt road. A toot of the horn, the click of a car door opening. "I managed to sleep a little," Mary's voice rang out. "I was hoping it was all a bad dream."

Sage stood and brushed dirt off her dress. "I need to be alone." She limped up the porch steps and disappeared into the A-frame.

Mary sat close to Ann. The blackened bones of the cat looked indistinguishable from the charred wood, but Ann knew which was which. "He wouldn't have died if I hadn't wanted a baby," she said.

"Don't be silly." Mary slung an arm over Ann's shoulders. "I can't believe I just sounded like my mother. She always said that! 'Don't be silly, Mary, don't be silly.'"

"She never said it to me," said Ann.

"Anyway," said Mary. "We have an appointment this morning with The Fish. The usual urine test and exam. I figured you wouldn't want to miss it."

"I can't go like this." Ann pulled at her dress, which was dirty and stank of smoke.

"It doesn't matter what you're wearing. He'll be examining me. Come on. You need to be with life, not death."

She had a point. Ann let Mary pull her up and lead her to the car.

"Not sure how to say this; don't want to be the person with sad news." Dr. Fisher drummed his fingers on the accordion folder that held their medical history. Ann had decided, after the Jessica debacle, not to call him The Fish anymore but to keep a professional distance, and refer to him as Dr. Fisher. "It would appear from my exam and the urinalysis results that you are *not* pregnant," he said.

Ann felt all the air suck out of her, as if she'd been punched.

"Of course I'm pregnant. The blood test at the center was positive," said Mary.

"It might have been a chemical pregnancy. I'm sorry but you're certainly not pregnant now."

"You did a urine test," said Mary. "Blood tests are more accurate."

"You're far enough along for the urinalysis to be unequivocal," said the doctor. "I'm sorry to say."

"I insist on a blood test," said Mary. "Right, Ann?"

In the bright hard reality of the medical office, Ann could focus only on the dead cat. Her dead dreams. Mary wasn't pregnant, if she'd ever been. She couldn't listen to bickering about blood and urine. The room began to spin, closing in around her, pressing against her, suffocating. Ann jumped up. She fled from the office, through the exam room, through the waiting room, practically colliding with a very pregnant woman. A nimble sidestep and she made it outside where she crouched against the car and tried to breathe. Her diaphragm spasmed, allowing only short, inadequate sips of oxygen. She noticed how the gravel vibrated in the translucent light and somewhere in the back of her mind she marveled at its beauty. *You're alive,* it seemed to say. *Isn't that enough?*

Mary came staggering out. She threw her arms around Ann. She engulfed Ann in sobs. "We have to do a blood test! We have to go back inside."

Ann found it intolerable. "Pull yourself together. We're finished here."

"We'll try again," said Mary. "I'll call the center and we'll schedule ourselves into the next cycle."

"We're not doing this again. Come on. I'll drive you home." She helped Mary into the car. Normally, the WCCNWMN was embarrassing to drive, but the worry seemed trivial now. Ann kept her eyes on the road, unable to think past one task at a time. Follow the white line down the center. Get Mary home. Then what? A black hole. Skirt it. Keep driving.

By the time she reached Sunrise, Mary's crying had dwindled to whimpers. She made no effort to get out of the car. Ann walked around to the passenger side and opened the door. "You're going to help me help you," she said, sliding her arms under Mary's armpits. "One. Two. Three."

They trudged, a two-bodied monster, into the house, past the trickster, to the living room where Ann released Mary onto the sofa. Mary began to blubber again.

"I have to call Joel," said Ann. "Will you be okay here while I do that?"

She sat for a moment at the kitchen table, listening to Mary cry. As if projected elsewhere, she also sat by the fire outside Sage's A-frame. And she also sat in a lilac-sprigged, wallpapered kitchen, in a too-big chair, swinging her feet since they did not reach the floor. *Someone's got her appetite back.* All the wrinkles in Gran's face were misplaced by her smile. Ann shook away the phantoms. She dialed Joel and went right to voicemail. "Mary's not pregnant. Call me. Please, call me."

Without thinking, she called Sage.

"Sage Wisewoman healing ways, how can I serve you?" Her greeting was toneless.

"Are you okay?" said Ann. "I just left you."

"Did you lose the baby?" said Sage.

"We just got back from Dr. Fisher's and he said she…" Ann couldn't continue. She could feel infant skin against her lips, a slippery wet body in her arms.

"Radical action is mandatory," said Sage. "We don't have much time. Come. Immediately. Now."

Ann put the phone down and ran to Mary's car.

SUNLIGHT FLASHED AGAINST THE metal circles hanging from the branches of the evergreens that towered over the A-frame. Sage's Volvo sat in the driveway, with a white "oops" painted into the dent on the passenger-side door. But the house was dark.

A bird lay on the porch amidst a scattering of dark tail feathers. Ann recognized a kestrel from the brown wings and bluish-white head, which was tilted at a strange angle, with the glassy stare of death. Several cats streaked out when she opened the door.

The shades were drawn. When she hit the light switch, nothing happened. As her eyes adjusted, she discerned the reflection of the computer monitor, a gleam in the corner near the massage table and a pile of blankets on the floor. Goosebumps rippled her skin. Her teeth chattered. The cold seemed to emanate from the corner. As she approached, the blanket pile transformed into Sage, curled on the floor with several amethyst crystals arranged in a circle. "Hello?" said Ann.

But Sage didn't stir. A skinny white cat separated itself from the others to stalk Ann, mewling plaintively. Was it attempting to communicate? She tried to recall any scrap of occult knowledge she had tucked away from childhood. Astral projection came to mind. She'd once believed that her astral body could separate from her physical one to fly over clouds in search of her unknown father.

She pressed her fingers against Sage's neck. The cold, moist texture of the skin provoked a nauseating fear but she forced herself to focus. And faintly, she detected a pulse. Reassurance washed over her, a warm bath of it.

Until she recognized the pulse was her own, not Sage's. She listened for breath, but heard only the underlying throb of something electrical. She got up and ran to the bathroom. Without looking at the tub for fear of glimpsing skin or blood or ash, she found a small enamel-framed hand mirror. If Sage were breathing, it would show on the glass.

Squatting down, she angled the mirror toward Sage's mouth. But Sage's body convulsed, her arm slapped the mirror. It shattered against the floor. Sage cried, "Why did you disrupt the journey?"

"I thought you were dead." As she picked up mirror shards, Ann sliced her finger, a thin line of pain she couldn't see. Reflexively, she got up to try the light switch. This time, all the lamps turned on.

"Mirrors hold our other sides. Mine has been broken. I may never find my way back. Where's my athame?" Sage sat on her heels, patting the pockets of her long flowing robe, and withdrew a white-handled knife. She sliced vertically through the air. "I traveled through tunnels and water to reach the sun. Hawthorne led me through a deep forest. I lost my limbs, scattered on the wind. I experienced death and found life."

A tremor ran up Ann's spine, electrifying the crown of her head.

Clutching the knife, Sage stepped out of her circle of amethysts. "Where's Mary? She needs to be here."

Ann left the broken shards in a little pile. Sage's phone sat on her desk next to the computer, objects of the rational, physical world. What a relief to hear a dial tone! The phone rang several times before Mary finally answered.

"Mom. I'm at Sage's. You have to get here right away."

"The Center can't fit us in for two months!"

"Now!" shrieked Sage. "Now!"

"Just come over." But Ann realized she had Mary's car. "If Joel can't take you, ask America. Call back if you need a ride." Ann hung up.

Sage lifted her knife toward the ceiling. "Fill a glass with milk. And chant this: I have been with you since the beginning."

Ann didn't dare disobey. At the counter of the kitchen nook, she poured milk into a glass. "I have been with you since the beginning," she whispered.

"Hold it up," said Sage. "Let Her see. Let Her hear."

Ann held the glass above her head. *I have been with you since the beginning.*

Sage took the glass, dipped her finger in and sucked milk off. "Bring me the bird."

Ann knew she meant the dead kestrel. It lay outside on the porch, the same bird with brown barring and blue-grey secondary feathers. Scooping it up, Ann found it warm. Its blink was so startling she almost dropped it.

She didn't hear America's van pull up until the engine went silent. Mary rolled the window down. "What's going on?"

Ann could feel the pulse of the bird in her fingers. "It was dead," She meant to say. But what flowed from her mouth was, "I have been with you since the beginning,"

"What's the matter with you?" Mary slammed the car door. She trailed close behind Ann. "You're scaring me."

"My little falcon." Sage took the bird from Ann, and cupped it in her palms. "You both need to be skyclad. Hurry. There's not much time."

Mary didn't question, just pulled off her skirt and sweater, no underwear, no bra. But Ann never went naked for any length of time. For her, naked was a transitional state.

Sage seemed to grow imperiously tall. "Now, Ann. Mind what I say."

Ann pulled the fetid slinky dress over her head, unhooked her bra and stepped out of her underwear, crossing her arms over her chest. Her bones rattled with cold.

"Mary, lie on the floor," said Sage.

Mary lay on her back, her flesh quivering. "It's freezing in here."

Sage passed the bird to Ann. Though it seemed sedated, its heat spread through her hands and her arms until she was warm, then hot. She watched Sage pour milk over Mary/s body, while Mary cringed and squirmed.

Sage hurled the empty glass against the wall where it smashed into pieces. Her voice seemed to originate from inside Ann's mind, just like it had on the night of the mysteries. "Place the kestrel on the belly of the mother."

The bird shuddered as Ann set it on Mary's abdomen. It was still, as if dead. "Spirit be free!" cried Sage.

The bird blinked, then hopped and gave a rapid series of sharp cries.

Knifelike pain tore through Ann's groin. She doubled over. *Breathe,* someone said.

"It hurts!" cried Mary.

The kestrel flew crazily, flapping its wings. It swiped Ann's face with its feathered claws.

"I have been with you since the beginning," cried Sage.

"Let me see my baby!" cried Mary. "I want to see my baby!"

The pain intensified, grinding, churning. With dizzying force, Ann exploded into thousands of pieces, mirror shards and broken glass, each a fragmented reflection of herself scattered in the air. She snapped back to Earth to lie alongside Mary on Sage's floor.

Several cats tracked the kestrel as it flew from wall to wall. When Sage opened her palms, the bird settled inside them. The cats dispersed. She walked to the door and flung the bird out. "Be free!" The whoosh of wings, a raucous sound like Hawthorne's cry, and the bird disappeared.

"I'LL BE GODDAMMED," SAID Dr. Fisher. He was holding Mary's urine sample. They had waited two weeks before arriving at his office without an appointment to beg for another pregnancy test. "I can't change reality." He had thrust his face so close to Ann's she saw tiny broken veins in his cheeks. "You're the one with common sense. For your own good, let this go."

In the passing days, the magic at Sage's acquired dream qualities. Ann had been unable to speak about them. She'd open her mouth and her throat would compress. She'd woken naked on Sage's floor next to Mary, opening her eyes to the plaster-speckled brown toes of Joel's work boots. Sage had disappeared.

Mary had waved her credit card in Dr. Fischer's face. "We'll pay you double!"

"You people are crazy." With a shrug of massive shoulders, Dr. Fisher handed Mary a plastic sample cup. "If you're seven weeks, it'll show up in urine. We'll run a blood test if we get a positive."

Mary was so fast in and out of the bathroom, it seemed that Ann had only taken one breath.

Dr. Fisher drooped against the door, color drained from his cheeks. He tugged his beard. He shook his head. "Am I the crazy one? What did you do? You're pregnant. You're undeniably pregnant."

Mary swallowed Ann in a patchouli-orange hug. Ann's joyful yelp was muffled in Mary's soft chest.

FIRE: 2000

SICKNESS OVERCAME MARY WITH sudden viciousness halfway through her seventh week. The acupressure bands with their alleged nausea-relieving properties that Ann had fitted around her wrists did nothing. Several mornings in a row, the swaying of the dream-catcher above Mary's bed made her so queasy she had to hang off the edge of the mattress and vomit into a bucket.

Afterwards, she rubbed a moonstone against her navel until the cool smoothness centered her body and mind. But she was shaky, unable to forget for a second that she was carrying, as the dour pregnancy book Ann had given her said, "precious cargo." It took the better part of an hour just to get out of bed.

Then she only got as far as her altar, which was a table in front of her bedroom window filled with small figures and statues she'd collected over the years. She had propped the computer printout of the babelings against a ceramic statue of the Virgin Mary, whose compassionate face seemed to offer sympathy. Athena, goddess of wisdom, hand-painted resin with gold leaf curlicued in her shield, stood next to the Virgin in an attitude of defiance. Mary moved Athena behind the deity candle for Shri Lakshmi, the Divine Mother; shifted a white resin Demeter to the side, and lit the candle.

Rose would have said morning sickness meant she was having a girl. *I'd be fine with a girl.* Ann had smiled last night when she came over. *I'd be fine with a boy, too. I'm more fine than I've ever been, thanks to you. Maybe there is a mysterious powerful force we don't understand. After what happened at Sage's, I believe in it.* Ann had sat on the edge of the bed, confiding as if they were pals, something Mary had yearned for. But instead of connecting, Mary had to hustle Ann out of the house with lame excuses about needing to be alone when everyone knew she wasn't a solitude person. She'd padlocked the green room door because Ann had taken to dropping in. She kept the key under the Demeter plinth she'd built in the hallway when Ann had left home.

Now she pushed the statue to pluck up the key. She loved unlocking the door, entering the fertile cannabis realm. Transplanted a couple of weeks before, the seedlings had become hardy young plants. They flourished in the warm, perpetually bright room, which was on 24-hour light for maximum growth. The leaves seemed to rustle in welcome, the stems bowed, and Mary's residual nausea vanished.

The line of a poem wound through her mind: *the force that through the green fuse drives the flower.* Amazing how swiftly they grew—over an inch a day. Spidery emerald leaves multiplied. They strained towards the light. Joel had installed the grow-lamps on chains and he'd been forced to raise them already to prevent plant burn. Instead of carbon dioxide, they seemed to exhale peace, enlarged by the white noise of the fans.

As she walked among them, Mary fancied herself the embodiment of Ishtar, Goddess of love and fertility. Their health relied on the power of her presence and the living spirits she carried. They, in turn, nurtured her, as worshippers nurtured deities with their adoration. She touched them one by one like a guru would have touched her devotees.

A BITTER WIND PUSHED Ann's hood back, numbing her scalp, icing the moisture in her eyes. She hunched against it, bowing her head, striding across the snow toward the bright blue entranceway of Little Footsteps. The school building looked silver in the morning light.

Bundled in a down coat and scarf, Shirley waved from the doorway. "What a surprise! Cold enough for you?"

A few early mothers tugged along children swathed in snow-suits and boots. *Good morning!* Shirley smiled her chubby chipmunk smile as more children arrived. Voices rang through the icy air.

Just being here, in the energy, enlivened Ann. "I probably should have called first, but I had to see you," she said. "I miss the children. I'm ready to come back. I want to come back."

"Problem is they changed the rules on me," said Shirley. With her usual rolling walk, she led Ann to the office.

"Have a seat." She perched herself in the chair behind her desk, nodding as if determined to get this thing over with. "Of course, the rumors are ridiculous. I know that. I can't abide gossip. But it's tough to fight."

Ann sat. "What are you talking about?"

"Personally, I don't believe a word," Shirley continued. "But the parents and the board are adamant. I wouldn't have thought so many people…it's collective insanity. We're back in the Middle Ages believing in Satan worship and baby stealing and shape-shifting. I might be able to ignore that or counter it with logic, but the statutory rape? Not so easy, there." She finally looked at Ann, kindly and concerned, her buckteeth pressing into her lower lip. "If you say that girl lied to you, I'll take your word for it. As far as I'm concerned, you helped her. She and her mother want to get on the news, or extort money. I can't figure it out. Everyone wants to air their dirty laundry these days."

Ann heard children laughing in the other room, life and activity and joy beyond the walls of the office—so close. "Are we talking about Jessica?"

"You didn't see the article? She and her mother are claiming you, your husband, your mother, and a lot of other people are in cahoots with Satan. You don't know about this?"

"I've been busy." Ann's jaw ached at a point just below her earlobes. She easily recalled the Autumn Equinox, a theatrical game, painting Jessica's belly, throwing bundles of yarn into a bonfire. But Jessica hadn't partaken in the kykeon tea. She couldn't have known about cutting their arms in the forest, mingling blood. A cat hadn't died there. A dead kestrel hadn't risen like a phoenix. "You won't take me back because she's spreading gossip about Satan? Are you serious?"

"This may sound off the wall," said Shirley. "But have you considered attending church? A few weeks, a few Sundays, word could get out. Give it a little time. I'll appeal to the more progressive members of the board."

The morning had dawned with such promise. Mary's uterus was growing from a fist into a grapefruit. The tadpole would lose its tail. Feet and hands were forming. Sunlight flooded through the window now, irradiating the corner of Shirley's desk. "It was an open adoption," said Ann. "We would never have stolen her baby."

"Your mother-in-law's your biggest defender," said Shirley. "That's why I mention church. But sit tight. We'll give it some time. I'm glad you came by."

When they hugged, Shirley's hair smelled of crayons and Ann wanted nothing more than to snatch hunks of it like the babies did, and scream until she felt release.

MARY WATCHED THE NEW York City bus pull into the depot. She pressed her palm to her tummy, imagining the baby inside, cells dividing, but still a blob. It calmed and excited her simultaneously.

Peter stepped off the bus to embrace her as passionately as he had on the street corner a couple of months ago. "Ah, Mary Moonlight, I've missed you!"

With her face against his chest, Mary felt like a girl.

Della came off the bus behind him. They were spending the weekend at Sunrise.

"You're sitting in back, son." Della popped the front seat up in Mary's car, and Peter clambered behind with his long legs bent. "I didn't know people owned this sort of hippie transport anymore," he said.

"I'll go you one better. You want hippie lore, we'll show you the site of the famous Woodstock concert!"

Della patted her leg. She was bedecked in Mary's jewelry, hard evidence that Mary was back in favor. "Just wait until I show you the mockup of the new catalogue!" she trilled. "What a fantastic job our boy has done with the photography."

My boy! Mine! Mary bit her lip to restrain herself. She took a shortcut off Route 52, and drove along a narrow one-lane road. Bare branches arched toward a gray sky with low, thick clouds. Muted earth tones were interspersed with glimmers of shiny ice.

"Lovely," said Peter. Mary saw through the rearview mirror that he was looking out the window. Sporting a tufted beard, he tossed his head to flick away his hair, which had grown long and shaggy, and caught her eye in the reflection. "Lovely," he repeated, so the compliment included her as well as the scenery.

"I like to think so." She couldn't look at him without smiling. She pulled up in front of the snow-patched fields where the Woodstock festival had taken place. The spot was marked by a commemorative plaque featuring the iconic dove-on-guitar-neck from the original poster and a list of the bands embossed in metal, mounted on a low-lying rock. They stood, gazing at the rock and beyond, at the cluster of barns and silos, and the rundown two-story colonial house of Yasgur's dairy farm. Wind blew across the fields picking up snow in little eddies. Della's bright orange tunic and gauzy orange pants billowed out from under her black coat.

"I gave birth to my daughter here," said Mary. Telling the lie so often had given it truth. Metaphoric, if nothing else. "I was the one they announced onstage, 'Your old lady's having a baby in the bad trips tent'! Now, over thirty years later, I'll give birth to my daughter's child!"

Peter bowed slightly. "I've been wondering about your baby."

As they folded themselves back into the car, Della said, "Do you plan on giving birth in these fields again? Maybe on a full moon night?" She pealed with laughter.

"If I didn't know you better, I'd say you were making fun of me," said Mary.

"You've given me an idea for a book." Peter tapped her on the shoulder from the back seat. "I'd like to photograph you and create a visual chronicle of your surrogate journey called *Mother Mary Come to Me*. What do you think?"

Sunlight diffused through the clouds like an annunciation, momentarily blinding.

"Eyes on the road!" screamed Della.

She swerved to avoid the guardrails. "I thought I heard angels," she said. "But my time's not up until I *see* them. Don't worry. We'll make it to Sunrise." Mary had encountered angels as a young child when she'd been ill with measles. Her fever had spiked to 104° and the winged creatures hovered over her bed, singing with high sweet voices, like castrati. Their faces shone, their lips curved upwards. Colors emanated from their song. Their wings fluttered more like moths than birds, which was a revelation, since Mary had always pictured an eagle-like wingspan on an angel.

"I saw fairies when I was a boy," said Peter. "We walked at dusk through the fields in Sussex and the magic people congregated at the stile between properties. My hair stands on end just thinking of it."

When Rose told Mary that she had almost died, and that the angels had been nothing but a fever hallucination, Mary didn't want to believe it. She had searched for angels in cloud formations, in the glinting tidal water of the Fox River. In church she prayed, *Come back to me. Show yourselves. Please.* She imagined dying would be like floating in the soft, dreamlike love of the angels and their synesthesia song.

As she rounded the bend, Sunrise loomed in all its purple splendor.

"Brilliant," said Peter. "Your house is an expression of you!" He admired the papier-mâché trickster in the hall, pretending to shake its hand. He complimented the mural in the living room and, as Mary led them upstairs to her workroom, he commended the broken-glass-mirror-shard mosaic along the stairwell. His voice affected her like amphetamines, invigorating her with a tingling energy that made her want to dance.

"Lookie here!" Della headed straight for Mary's bench and picked up one of the completed pendants laid out in a row. Foil-flowered lampwork beads in assorted shapes, were wrapped in silver wire and looked uncannily fetus-like. "*Love* it. Love it!"

Even though she'd created hundreds of the pendants by now, the visceral recognition they provoked still surprised her. And they were cheap, simple, easy to make, not like her *spiralmary* series where each piece involved elaborate handwork. "I think I'm inspired by the baby," she said. "If the morning sickness didn't get to me, I would have made even more."

"You. Like that, with your hand right there," said Peter. With a warm, intense gaze, he reflected an amazing woman back at Mary. "We'll do an official portrait this weekend."

Unable to tolerate her own pleasure in his scrutiny, she strode out to the hall. "As long as you make me look beautiful," she called back.

"Flattery gets you everywhere with her." Della followed with a twittering laugh. "I want this series in my catalogue. We'll call it *lifeforce!* We'll add a sidebar, with a picture of you and some copy about this pregnancy thing."

"Why is that room padlocked?" asked Peter. "You've left some lights on in there."

Mary's insides somersaulted. Down the hall, light leaked conspicuously from under the locked door. "My son-in-law is storing equipment in there. He's weird that way, I don't ask questions. You can sleep in the guest room as usual, Della. And Peter,

I'm sorry but you're stuck on the living room couch." She steered them downstairs. "How about a glass of wine? You've had a long bus ride."

They settled in the living room with their wine and snacks, as they always did when Della came for her country sleepovers. But this time, Mary drank herbal tea. And this time Peter was a delightful addition. He crouched at the fireplace, poking the embers with tongs. His shoulder blades spread under his snug T-shirt like wings, toned, defenseless, and irresistible.

"I must show you!" Della withdrew an artist's mock-up of a catalog from a large envelope. She placed it ceremoniously on the bearskin rug. Peter came away from the fire. His arm brushed against Mary's.

The title on the cover, *madebymary*™, sat elegantly in an italic serif typeface above a close-up of a sterling silver spiral choker, flush-set with iolite. It floated, otherworldly, over a background of deep, sensual maroon. Peter turned the pages. Each double-page spread showed several pieces hovering over a background color, casting soft shadows. "It's sublime," she sighed. "You really caught the essence."

"I've been immersed in Mary Moonlight." Peter's expression was radiant, Buddha-like. "Your work is so elemental. If painting was invented in ancient times by someone trying to recreate the shadow of his body in the firelight with lines and shapes, your pieces are manifestations of the spirit recreated. In the ancient days, sculptors believed their work could come to life. I think yours does."

Mary melted under his words like silver under torch flame.

She heard the front door hinges squeak and the scraping sound as it opened but paid it no mind until Joel called out. "You can't leave the door unlocked! How many times do I have to tell you?" He came in, tracking mud on the floor. "Oh, you have company."

"I've known Mary for twenty years. She never locks her door," said Della. "Have some wine."

But Joel stood with his hands thrust in the pockets of his parka. "Good thing it was me who came in, not America," he scolded. "Or worse. Carlos."

"America? Why do you associate with that slovenly woman?" asked Della.

"Joel, you remember Della," said Mary. "And this is Peter, an incredible photographer. This is Joel, father of my child, so to speak." Joel cracked his knuckles. "I'll get the syringe ready."

Mary listened to his footsteps move toward the kitchen. Exaggerating a shrug, she described the nightly hypodermic needle and the bruises on her buttocks, trying to make it sound glamorous.

"Do you mind if I take a picture of you receiving this injection?" said Peter. "It fits precisely with my book idea: A journey in pictures, a unique statement about womanhood and motherhood."

"Love it." Della poured herself more wine. "As long as it helps sell jewelry."

Peter sprang into action, rearranging living room lamps around a portable spotlight he unpacked from his equipment bags. He was securing a digital SLR on a tripod when Joel walked in with the syringe. The needle was almost a foot long. A viscous drop of progesterone oil glistened on the tip.

A sizzle of electricity ran up Mary's spine as she bent over the back of her armchair and flipped her skirt up.

"Lovely!" Peter's spotlight was as hot and bright as the lights in the operating room where the pre-embryos had been transferred.

"Peter's doing a book on us," she said.

The needle pricked her right buttock.

"Why'd you block your face, mate?" said Peter. "The shot was perfect."

Joel threw the syringe into an old cookie tin, separated from the rest of the garbage as biohazard waste. "Private's private," he said. "I don't intend to be in a book."

"Don't be like that," said Mary. "Have a glass of wine."

"Nothing's private anymore. It's a new century!" Holding out her glass, Della burst into an REM song about the end of the world, as we know it.

"I have to check something upstairs." Joel stalked out, stomping up the steps.

"Such an odd person," said Della. "Antisocial. Difficult."

But Mary remembered that Joel had planned to show her how to separate male plants from females. She had agreed to it even though she'd known Della and Peter were coming for the weekend, a fact she hadn't mentioned to Joel. His annoyance was warranted, but he would have to get over it.

Mary had always been this way, avoiding inconvenient conflicts. She loved beginnings. She wearied of relentlessness. Now Peter leaned close so she could see herself in miniature on his camera screen, bending to the side with her bare buttocks exposed. "The feminine principle, embodied," he said softly.

For a moment, she became a goddess.

"Who drank all the wine?" said Della. "We have to open another bottle."

"I'll get it." Mary had to rise slowly, or she'd get dizzy. She strategized. Could she run quickly upstairs, placate Joel, dash to the kitchen for the wine and bring it to the living room without provoking suspicion?

But Joel was already back in the kitchen. He grabbed Mary's arm. "I had to give Ann a song and dance about why she couldn't come tonight, and you have the nerve to invite houseguests?"

"Let's invite her, too!" said Mary. "The room is locked. Chill out."

"Did you know we're being libeled up, down and sideways?" He tightened his grip. "We stand accused of Satan worship by Jessica and her mother. Ann's blacklisted from the daycare. I've lost jobs."

Ann had mentioned something about the ludicrous local rag with the badly-written articles but Mary hadn't listened. She'd been busy throwing up. "Not possible," she said. "We did a banishing. Remember?"

"I say, is this a private meeting?" Peter materialized at the trickster. "Della sent me in to expedite the wine situation."

"I just talked Joel into staying for dinner," said Mary gaily.

"I was just leaving," said Joel.

"MARY," CAME A BRUSQUE whisper. "Can I come in? I'm cold."

She woke like a shot. In her dream, she'd been watching her father through the scrim of a screen door as he mended the wire fence bordering the garden behind the house Mary had grown up in. *Why is he taking so long with that?* her mother asked. *He works in slow motion.*

Floored by an insurmountable fatigue, Mary had conked out early, leaving Della and Peter downstairs, drinking wine. Now she rolled over, silently pulling back the cover to allow Peter in. He nestled his frigid toes between her calves, astonishing yet inevitable. She wrapped her arms around him, and marveled at how utterly different his hard, bony body felt compared to America's. His lips were less malleable. His tongue demanded more. His touch incited white-hot desire. They wasted no time, nakedly entwining. Mary flailed in her mind for rules about sex during pregnancy. Was it allowed? Was it not? Then it didn't matter, she was too far gone to stop.

Peter murmured something about a condom. "Hope it still works. I've been carrying it for eons."

How hard he was, how sleek and firm. With America, their bellies rolled and slapped together but when Peter thrust, his hipbones bumped her. And she was a teenager again; mad about her first love, Coyote. He wanted her! Fat, homely Mary! She cascaded into a wild exultant coming, a fountain of bliss. *Oh, she said. Oh, thank you. Thank you.*

Peter powered on. She recalled the one-pointed focus of men, how they drove until they crashed. He came with a long moan, and fell limp beside her.

Mary stroked his back, as she had stroked America's. "You are you and I am I," she whispered. "I'm not in this world to live up to your expectations and you're not in this world to live up to mine. I do my thing and you do yours and if by chance we find each other, it's beautiful."

"That's the truest thing I ever heard. I feel like I'm home now." Peter slackened in her arms, little by little, his head becoming heavy on her chest. His snores started softly and gathered force, climbing up the decibels until he sounded like he'd swallowed an air compressor. He rattled the walls, swelling the room like a joyous, cheering crowd. Mary pulled her arm out from under him, unable to sleep, amazed that she had just made love to a man who was not Lars: not balled, not fucked, made love.

RECLINING ON THE EXAM table in her paper gown with her legs wide, her feet in the stirrups and an ultrasound wand inside her, Mary was buzzing. A tiny star pulsed in the gray static on the screen, echoed by another star that looked like a reflection.

"Damned if you don't have two," said The Fish.

"Twins," said Ann. "I'm going to cry."

"The jackpot!" cried Mary. "We have to tell Dr. God!"

Peter stood in the corner of the exam room behind them. "All right if I prop the camera here on the counter, Doctor?" he said. "I need a slow shutter speed and I didn't bring my tripod."

"I think you have enough pictures," said Ann.

"Can't have too many pictures," said Mary. "It's a whole book."

"Your pregnancy just became a lot more complicated," said The Fish, moving the wand. "Number three. You see it?"

Mary's excitement verged on terror. Every particle of energy funneled toward the image, as it morphed and undulated. Three lights twinkled.

"Blimey," said Peter.

At the appearance of a fourth star, Ann grabbed Mary's hand. "I'm scared," she whispered, "I don't want them to die."

Four tiny pinpoints throbbed with life in the primordial gray texture. Mary squeezed the violent tremble from Ann's fingers. "We won't let them."

"You're like Boadicea, the warrior queen," said Peter.

"I feel like a warrior," said Mary, turning to smile as the camera flashed. After Della went home a couple of weeks ago, Peter simply stayed at Sunrise, spooning his warm body against Mary's every night. *Don't be needy, Mary*. Reluctant to broach the subject of his indefinite visit, afraid she'd scare him away, Mary opted to let things flow.

"Why did they put so many in? Multiples are serious business." The Fish moved the probe, revealing again: one, two, three, four pulsing lights.

Ann pulled her hand from Mary's. Shiny trails ran down her cheeks.

"Don't cry!" said Mary. "Everything will be fine. I know it!" She remembered when she discovered she was pregnant with Annapurna, the news delivered grimly by the clinic volunteer. But Mary was ecstatic, thrust out of the ordinary drift of her life into the miraculous. Even if abortion had been legal then, Mary wouldn't have considered it.

"Let's hope one or two of them simply expires," said The Fish. "I'm not qualified for this. You'll have to see a specialist. In the meantime, modified bed rest. Nothing even remotely strenuous. No sexual intercourse."

"No sex?" said Mary. "All the pregnancy books say it's okay!"

"Oh, it's better than okay. I'd say it was brilliant." Peter's fingers in her hair sent desire radiating along her scalp.

Ann stood like a shot, the metal stool rolling out behind her. "No, you are not!"

"We're not utterly gormless," said Peter. "We use protection."

"I'm in love!" said Mary, closing her legs and sitting up. Her paper gown was damp with ultrasound goop. "I need to express it."

"I don't think you recognize the gravity of the situation," said The Fish. "Ann, you'll have to help your mother understand."

"Do you hear that, Mom?" said Ann. "I want to help. I have lots of free time but she won't even let me upstairs anymore."

"You sound like a tattletale," said Mary. The locked room was a problem for Peter, too. Secrets were so burdensome. She hated the pressure. "When you're a mother, you'll understand that you don't want your daughter to quote-unquote *help.*"

"You have to let Ann help," said The Fish. "Are you listening?

Mary had stopped listening because she heard a humming in her head, her inner ears tuned to a higher pitch. Four heartbeats. Four babies. Four—the number of transmutation and concretion. The cube, the square, the cross. Reflexively, she touched her necklace of lodestones.

JOEL SAT ACROSS FROM Ann, shoveling down his chicken and broccoli without tasting anything. If he paused, he'd lose his ability to eat. One baby, he would have rejoiced. Two, he would have made peace with. But more than two and his imagination slipped into a wormhole. Stumps, blobs, and fleshy nubbins flashed before him. Under the table, McKenna gobbled scraps. The sounds of his slobbering matched the misshapen images in Joel's mind, a slippery, squishy horror movie soundtrack. Joel felt more kinship with McKenna than with Ann. "They could all die or be damaged," he said.

"I was scared too until I understood that it's a miracle! Four! All these years I didn't believe in magic. I thought everyone was full of shit. But how else to explain?" Ann talked in fast, feverish bursts. Puffy-cheeked and red-eyed, she'd cut her chicken into bite-sized pieces, arranging them impulsively around a stack of broccoli centered on her plate. Now she halved each bite-sized piece, knife clinking.

Her delusional state rattled Joel more than the fact of quadruplets. He relied on her being grounded in the same reality he was. "We can't go off into la-la land," he said. "Please don't get goddessy. Stay with me."

"No. I'm sick of losing hope. I refuse. Come hell or high water, I am going to be a mother. And you know what else? I *will* get my job back. She can't destroy me." Ann pushed her plate away. A stranger, she seemed to give off light.

"I just don't know if I can be the father of four possibly damaged children," he said.

"You already *are* the father."

It was as if a steel door shut. But Mary wasn't his mother. This did not have to be Joel's problem. What would his father have done? He would have walked away, just walked away. "If you had to choose between me and them, which would it be?"

"But I don't have to choose," said Ann. "Do I?"

When he shrugged, he realized his shoulders ached. "As if I could walk away from children I fathered by masturbating in a windowless room," he said, and wiped his hands on his pants. Irony felt corrosive. His palms hurt as if he'd slapped something.

"You're just afraid." She touched his wrist.

"Not necessarily," he said. Equal warring factions struggled within. Wrench away and be free, not afraid. Or succumb to this insanity and let her inhabit him more deeply.

"Let's go look at the house." She stood and moved toward the door. McKenna leaped out from under the table. "Come on," she said. Then she was out, the door closed quietly behind her.

Joel sat alone before his empty plate, abandoned by his wife and the one creature with whom he'd felt kinship. He snapped then, pushing his chair out. "Wait for me!" The waning moon hung low and plump. An owl hooted. Ann's spectral figure floated ahead, surrounded by darkness.

THE AIR WAS COLD against Ann's bare arms. She'd run outside without her coat. Yet just the day before, in the slushy fields behind the trailer, in a patch of rimy mud beneath crusted ice, she had noticed snowdrop flowers blooming. Tiny buds were sprouting on branches, simultaneously tentative and tenacious. Her boots squelched along the ground.

The space inside the house smelled of newness gone stale. Joel and his assistant had installed a one-piece tub and shower unit, attached to rough plumbing and main water lines. They'd filled the tub to allow it to settle, and the water lay as still as a mirror. The staircase led to the raw plywood frame of an incomplete second floor.

Joel came up behind her and she let her weight fall, feeling the warmth of his chest as it expanded and contracted against her back, breathing in unison with him.

They kissed in their dark, unfinished house. When Joel slid his hand up her sweatshirt, Ann refused to succumb to a familiar knot of panic. A chemical pregnancy had become four pulsing lights and she was damned if she would cringe in fear of physical contact. Impulsively she lifted her sweater off, then his. He raised his arms to help her. Shivering, they lowered themselves onto the cold concrete floor, with its damp, settled odor. His breath in her ear, his palm on her thigh, his soft, springy hair, his lips on her neck, and she was transported to a sensual realm of touch and smell and taste, lips, fingers, tongues. The concrete fell away, the walls vanished. She lifted and dropped with Joel, wrapped around Joel's mouth. Then she wanted him inside her. He took it slow, her tissue stretched and she expanded to let him in. She could feel the opening like flower petals unfurling, and she came with a shudder that felt magical, as if the earth itself moved with her.

Afterwards, smoothing Joel's hair off his forehead, she'd never felt such tenderness. They lay together in the darkness surrounded by their own breath. But in her imagination, Ann strode from room to room holding a child in each arm, followed by Joel, who also carried two children. She could hear them crying, healthy, lusty, lung-developing cries. And she believed in them. She believed.

McKenna barked with sudden fury at who knew what.

ANN LOOKED UP AT the sky where a flock of geese flew in formation, honking to herald the return of spring. *Happy Easter!* People passed by them in the parking lot as Ann helped Betty from the car. She had forgotten it was a special Sunday. Friendly smiles were cast their way. Betty heaved forward, righting herself by thumping into the ground with her three-pronged cane.

Billowy white ribbons were affixed to the sides of the pews. The notes of the organ struck and the congregation stood as one to sing a hymn that Ann didn't know, except for one word: *Alleluia!* As a child, she'd attended church with Gran in Oshkosh every week for almost a year, and sometimes on weekdays. And during her sojourn in foster-care, she had gone to Pentecostal service twice. But those forays into organized religion happened a long time ago. *Alleluia! Rejoice, heavenly powers! Sing choirs of angels! Exult, all creation around God's throne!* Everyone stood.

Betty alone stayed seated, her prerogative as a woman with a three-pronged cane. Ann turned to watch the priest glide up the aisle in a long, white gown with the altar boys swinging their censers behind him, and she glimpsed among the rows the friendly face of Shirley with her four children, two on each side. Shirley's chin dimpled with approval. *Alleluia!*

Ann followed the mass with the paperback provided in the pew. Standing, sitting, kneeling. Call and response. It was easy to relax into scripted formality. The altar and the chancel were decorated with baskets of beautiful lilies and hyacinths, filling Ann with hope. Betty elbowed her with a stiff, conspiratorial jab like Gran's, making Ann feel like a child again, in a good way. A tilt of Betty's chin signaled toward a woman in a wrinkled, calf-length coat stepping furtively up the side, fifteen minutes late. With a shock, Ann recognized Jessica's mother. The back of her neck prickled.

"With Christ's death and resurrection, the gates of heaven are now open to man." The priest's mouth was fringed by a thick, white mustache. He looked kind and sincere. "God, full of mercy, moved by the infinite compassion with which He loved, gave us Christ and He raised us with Him. Easter is the celebration of our Redemption."

Betty nodded ferociously. But Ann questioned whether Betty believed in this arrangement with God, or whether she simply enjoyed being among people once a week.

"...Thou hast prepared the body and soul of Mary, glorious Virgin and Mother, to become the worthy habitation of Thy Son; Grant that by her gracious intercession, we may be delivered from present evils and from everlasting death..."

Mary would laugh about the term "worthy habitation," Ann thought, even if she'd be annoyed by Ann attending church.

"Let us offer each other the sign of peace," said the priest, and everyone in the pews turned toward each other.

"Peace be with you." Betty patted her hand. "Good you're here."

Impulsively Ann embraced her, pressing the delicate shoulder blades under the polyester sweater, and she was filled with affection for this woman who had raised Joel, and who was unafraid to claim her space no matter who disliked her.

The mass swiftly ended after the communion rite, for which Ann stayed on the sidelines. She hadn't lived long enough with

Gran to make her first communion. She watched the congregants form a line down the center aisle to receive the host, and noticed how they politely allowed Betty to cut in.

Outside after mass, a cold drizzle was falling. Dark clouds had gathered. The priest stood under the shelter of an enormous black umbrella held by an altar boy. "Good to see you, Betty," he said.

"My daughter-in-law, Ann," said Betty. Ann thought she detected a tendril of pride.

"Good to see you," he said, pleasantly impersonal. She didn't feel obliged to shake his hand, just give a friendly nod. She supported Betty, who clung to the rain-slicked railing along the steps. Halfway down their slow descent, Betty stopped short. "Fancy meeting you here."

A ruddy-faced woman climbed toward them. Her bright, floral-patterned scarf covered a headful of curlers. Ann recognized Winifred, Betty's aide. "I missed the ten o'clock, as you see," said Winifred. "I forgot to set my alarm."

"I don't need an alarm on the Lord's Day," said Betty.

"You're a funny one, merry sunshine." Winifred let out a peal of laughter.

Betty moved on, her imperious manner belied by the tentative dipping of her toe to the stair below. If they had not been delayed by Winifred, they would not have bumped into Jessica's mother lighting a cigarette at the edge of the parking lot.

"Good morning, Margaret." Betty's superiority was manifest in her unblinking stare. Her fingers twitched on the crest of her cane. "I quote Matthew when I say: Do not give dogs what is holy and do not throw your pearls before swine, lest they trample them underfoot. Of course, Jesus doesn't discriminate, even if I do."

"You're a pious old bag who should mind her own business," said Margaret. But she slunk off toward the snow-covered church-yard. Smoke trailed from her cigarette. Betty wore a gloating smile as they moved toward the car, her opinion not only of Margaret's lowliness but also of the general baseness of human beings confirmed.

"I appreciate how you stood up to her," said Ann.

"She drinks," said Betty. "Of course, she forgot to set her alarm."

It took Ann a second to understand she was talking of Winifred, and another second to recognize that Betty couldn't accept appreciation. The silence as they drove home was not tense but companionable, and Ann wished she could preserve it.

She pulled into Betty's driveway and got out to open the passenger door.

"I'd ask you in for coffee if I thought you'd bother accepting," said Betty.

"Thank you. I accept." said Ann. As she helped Betty out of the car, the icy drizzle on her face refreshed her, washing her clean.

"I HAVE TO TELL you something." Peter threw his cigarette into the fireplace. "I'm in trouble."

Mary was basking on the bearskin, flushed and open after making love. Like a she-bear with her young in her womb, she had roared with desire on hands and knees, arching her spine and spreading her toes while he took her from behind. Her every cell oscillated with the aftermath of pleasure. "What kind of trouble?"

"Wait, let me capture you, just like that. You look so lovely. Do you mind?" Peter went for his camera. "Just stretch out on your side like you did a second ago."

Mind? She was willing to pose for every photograph he would ever want to take. How novel to be lovely when all her life she'd been, as Rose maintained, fat and plain, not even a pretty face to compensate. With America, she hadn't been lovely either, that wasn't their thing. But Peter had effortlessly transformed unappealing, disappointing Mary into beautiful, transcendent Mary. "So, what's this trouble, darling?" she asked.

He would have been a hot item thirty years ago at the Peace Ranch Commune. Back then Mary had been perpetually unchosen during the nightly pick-and-choose sexual undercurrents at the communal dinner table. It was the story of her life. But now, Peter's love appointed her the most favored woman in the universe.

Peter spoke from behind his camera, bracketing his shots. "Visa's-expired-sort-of-thing. I squeaked back into the country after my mum's funeral. The authorities can't find me, not that they're searching. But I can't open a bank account or work anyplace that requires identification. It's a bit of a quandary. I'm afraid I've imposed on you long enough, not to mention the dosh I still owe you. I may have to leave soon."

If he left, he'd take the beautiful goddess with him, leaving Mary with the plain, plodding self nobody wanted. Her nerves fired. Electrical synapses coursed through her energy field. She felt herself proliferating. "Let's get married!"

"You're mad." He put the camera down.

"Just say yes!" said Mary.

He prostrated himself, with his forehead on the floor in a child's pose. "I worship you, Mary, the almighty mother. I am your slave."

"My goodness. Not necessary." But she burned for his adoration. A geyser of energy thrust upward along her spine, from her groin through the crown of her head, a white-hot electrical charge that triggered vibrations through her body. The floor dissolved beneath her. "I think my kundalini just awakened!"

"Should I call an ambulance?" said Peter.

Mary laughed. She shook. The bearskin quivered. Peter seemed to wobble in front of her. Laughter filled the room as if it came from outside herself. She couldn't stop. She rolled backwards, and couldn't catch her breath. The uncanny energy infused her with such vitality she could fly, sing, run, dance, and birth four babies effortlessly.

Peter circled his arms around her, kissing her cheeks and her neck. Her mother hadn't liked kisses or hugs or holding hands, none of it. Mary would clamber onto her father's lap, but he would push her off because she was too big. And from the basis of that experience, she had assumed no one would want her. How ridiculous to carry this weight of unlovability year after year, just because her parents had been so limited. She cast it off. Tears of laughter ran down her cheeks. "If my mother could see me now!" she cried. "She always wanted me to get married! I told her I was a dyke!"

"World! Listen up," shouted Peter. "Mary Moonlight and I are getting hitched!"

"Okay," said Mary. "Since no secrets should be kept between betrothed, I'll show you the 'Bluebeard room,' which is actually a grow room." Mary led Peter upstairs or, rather, he pushed her up the stairs from behind, since technically she shouldn't have been climbing stairs at all, or even bending down to pull the key out from under her plaster Demeter plinth. She unbolted the padlock.

Joel had been curt last week when they performed their usual evasive dance for Peter's sake, tit-for-tat and tea-for-two and Joel would head up to the room by himself to check on his "equipment."

The plants bowed and rustled, dazzlingly green. Thigh-high, thick with vegetation and wide at the base, shaped like Christmas trees, they were flowering now and needed only twelve hours of light rather than twenty-four.

"Blimey." Peter strolled among them. "What a bloody perfume. Miraculous. Joel's quite the green thumb." He aimed his small digital camera.

"No photos." Mary passed her hand over his lens. "Only me."

"You're my muse," he said.

"I'm amused to be your muse. But I'm not sharing the role with Mary-Jane." Flinging herself against the wall, Mary vamped.

THE SOUR TASTE OF beer set Ann's teeth on edge and bubbled queasily in her mouth. She was drinking it to calm herself but it only heightened her alarm. These days she seldom went to bars and she rarely played her guitar for an audience, but here they were at The Barge: Ann, Joel, Rick, and Tim, after only one rehearsal.

The evening featured several bands, each one scheduled to play for half an hour, with theirs, *The Free Radicals,* slotted at midnight. Joel had decided on the name.

But the program ran late, each band amped up louder than the preceding one, and as midnight came and went, the noise level hit a deafening pitch. Black Strap Molasses finished to applause at half-past twelve and, finally, Ann and the others took the stage, plugging into amps, positioning microphones, tuning guitars. She loved her new guitar when she played it at home, picking around with the first position C-D-G chords, getting the open string sound that pulled her into the music. But now the neck of the Fender Mustang felt heavy, unbalanced by the guitar body, bumping against her front. The strap dug into her shoulder.

She was wearing her slinky red dress, the dirt stains invisible to anyone but her, and it felt like bad luck. But it was the nicest garment she owned. She looked at Joel in his black western-style shirt, his hair hanging in his eyes as he calmly tuned his guitar. When he glanced up, his smile was a refuge that told her she was lovely and there was nothing to fear.

They opened with "Ring of Fire." The entire world shrank to the stage. The people at the tables, the shouts and clink of glasses, the intermittent tock of balls on the pool table—all that happened far away. Gone were the fey days of *Little Joey's Toys,* with its burden of irony and Ramones covers. *The Free Radicals* played rhythm and blues, Gene Vincent and Johnny Cash, as well as some rock classics from their previous incarnation: "Sunshine of Your Love" and "Louie Louie." Ann somehow remembered her harmony parts. Her anxiety dissolved and she homed in on the task of pressing strings and keeping her pick between her thumb and index finger.

Tim, on bass, chewed gum in time to the rhythm, rocking forward and back as he played. Rick's drumsticks vanished in a blur. And Joel's smile lingered with Ann even as she looked down at her guitar. The next song in the set was an original. It belonged to Joel. *The succubus sucks, that's what she does.* He sang with a delay on the chords and unleashed a Nirvana-like screaming guitar behind the refrain. *She drains and she pains, she draws out your life-blood. That's what she does.* During his solo, his fingers darted over the strings. His demeanor was somber, delicate, a cross between goth and folk. When he'd first played the song for Ann in the trailer, the screaming guitar triggered a headache. He had admitted the lyrics were a little bit about Jessica and a little bit about Mary. Ann hadn't particularly liked it. But now, attuned to him, she lost herself in the song just as she'd done when they met, falling in love not only with him as a person, but with his take on life, and with herself inside it.

A smattering of applause and they moved on to "Fast as You" by Dwight Yoakum, a rocking country song. A couple of women got up to dance. How satisfying! Ann felt hot, glancing at the others as they transitioned into her song, "Back to Bethel, It's No Bethlehem." The rock-steady beat drew out a few more dancers. With everyone smiling and good feelings flying, the guys gave Ann space to take a solo and she stepped right into it with a snapping, flat-picking wander through the frets. She sensed rather than saw the guys nodding, appreciation flickering.

The realization of happiness arrived like a melody playing in her body, thrilling and new, and she jammed with it, buoyed by the bright lights, cigarette smoke and the incredible energy pushing her into the future.

They closed with Gene Vincent's "Be-Bop-A-Lula." Applause crashed around them as the emcee grabbed the microphone to announce the next band. With a porousness that made her feel almost ecstatic, she melted into Joel as he threw his arms around her. "This is my wife!" he shouted to the bartender. She pressed her cheek against his drenched T-shirt, reveling in the lightness that lifted them both. Her ears were ringing. A thousand songs buzzed through her head. Her fingertips ached, callused with indentations. When she showed them to Joel in the dim light of the bar, he kissed each finger.

"We can't stop now. We're fucking great!" cried Tim, lifting his beer bottle.

Tim's wife, Lisa, sat alone at a table, drinking orange juice. She pulled her earplugs out when Ann sat down. "The babysitter's costing fifty dollars," she shouted. "And Tim will wake up cranky tomorrow from not getting enough sleep. He'll have a hangover, too." She pressed her shoulder to Ann's and confided that she was pregnant again.

"I'm pregnant, too!" shouted Ann. She'd have an entire brood soon.

Lisa pointed to Ann's beer, eyebrows raised, just as the next group launched into a Metallica song, beyond deafening. She covered her ears. Tim sat down and Ann saw an argument about to ensue—Lisa wanting to go home, Tim claiming the party just started, all of it in a silent choreography of fierce glares and hunched shoulders. Ann got up to follow Joel, who'd slipped outside with Rick. She floated on the revelation. She had told someone. *I'm pregnant, too.*

Joel and Rick were sharing a joint in the parking lot. "Smooth on the throat, crazy on the mind. That's the kind of stuff we're harvesting. Oops." Joel covered his mouth, as smoke flowed out between his fingers.

"I see you smoking pot," said Ann. "Why pretend to hide it?"

"Hey, great playing," said Rick.

"You, too." Laughter bubbled like beer, no longer sour.

At 4 a.m., still elated, music ringing in her brain, Ann couldn't sleep. She had driven home, the designated driver. Not stricken with insomnia but simply awake—there was a difference—she sat at the kitchen table, eating an apple. McKenna lay at her feet, content with her company. Joel had passed out fully clothed in bed. She turned off the kitchen light, checking the sky for signs of the impending sunrise. The unfinished house was a shadow against the darkness, the glint of glass windows barely apparent. Every morning, a new world bloomed, but especially now, this morning. Springtime was nigh, their house would soon be livable and overrun with children. She sat in the dark, waiting for dawn. Then she noticed the message light blinking on the answering machine.

Mary sounded drunk on the recording. "Where are you. I'm bleeding. I don't know what to do." Click.

THE CRAMPS BEGAN AT night, low in Mary's gut, while she and Peter lay in bed listening to Sage's interview on the local radio station. Peter was the best lover Mary had ever known. She was supremely content.

The word "witch," said Sage, *describes an individual of power. It stems from the Old English word, Wik, meaning to bend or to shape. A witch shapes reality.*

How? said the interviewer. *Can you give an example?*

We don't believe in power over others but in self-empowerment. If we wanted to manifest, for example, a car, we need to see the car as the composite of a pattern of energy, not the end result of our personal desire.

"Can you massage my lower back? I have weird cramps." Mary rolled onto her side.

Peter was good at massage, pressing his thumbs deeply into the tense spots at the crest of her sacrum. She moaned in gratitude.

For pagans, the deities aren't distant, but within us, and all around us. Every tree, every stone, every blade of grass manifests the glory of the Great Mother. We're interconnected. A moth flutters its wings in one hemisphere and causes changes in the other. You want to label and compartmentalize and convince yourself of the solidity of things when all we are is energy, particles of energy.

"She comes off very well," said Peter.

"She'll do our wedding rites." When Mary rolled over, she spied red spots on the sheet. "Is that blood? Maybe I should call the doctor."

"Don't tell him we've been naughty," said Peter.

His flippancy relieved her. Less worried than diligent, she left a message with the doctor's service.

The phone rang while Sage was explaining the history of persecution going back to the Burning Times, when the power of the Inquisition was unleashed against the Old Religion. "Probably nothing," said The Fish. "What does your neonatologist say?"

Probably nothing. The words alone seemed to ease the cramps. "I haven't met him yet. Couldn't get an appointment right away."

"Stay in bed for now. Monitor it. Come see me first thing in the morning. I'm here at seven."

Although the question of matriarchal emphasis in WICCA might be cause for argument, we certainly need to restore balance. Patriarchy and dominion over the planet has brought us war, famine, slavery, and the threat of complete annihilation.

Mary arranged her pillows to support herself, sitting cross-legged. Her belly had developed a distinctly pregnant shape and, having gained forty pounds, Mary was enormous. Fifteen weeks tomorrow. Peter lay on his side, his eyes half-shut as Mary spread out her tarot cards in a runic cross on the blankets. *We no longer represent a handful of cranks engaging in a bizarre hobby, but widespread prejudice still endures. A California couple was firebombed from their home after appearing on a talk show. We're your neighbors, your co-workers, your classmates.*

"Hear, hear!" said Mary, just as she flipped the death card over in the "near future" spot. Thirteenth in the greater arcana, the card displayed a skeleton in a black suit of armor riding a white horse over a battlefield strewn with corpses. Fear swarmed through her body like a thicket of black flies migrating up through the crown of her head toward the netting of the dream catcher hanging above.

Calls from crazies were coming in. *There's only one God and that's God the father, maker of heaven and earth. You deserve to be burnt at the stake.*

"What's wrong?" said Peter. "You look like you've seen a ghost. You're not scared of the fascist caller, are you?"

"Death." Mary pointed at the card.

"You can read that card as life renewed," he said.

"Wow, you know the tarot deck. How perfect are you?" He didn't entirely vanquish Mary's fear, but eroded it.

Another caller came on. *As a Christian, I say live and let live. We may not like the sin but we can offer love to the sinners.*

"That sounds like Joel's mother," she said.

"Let's go to the green room," said Peter. "The green room cures all anxiety."

"You go. I want to hear the callers." Mary scooped up the cards and returned them to their box.

I just want to say that I think it's great. How can I join your, what do you call it, your coven? I love that you're right here in Sullivan County.

We're out of time for now. If you want to get in touch with Sage Wisewoman, just go to her website, at www.wisewomanhealingways, no space. You heard it here first folks, from a genuine witch.

Mary felt dizzy as she turned off the radio. Since when did Sage have a website? How did she get internet access along that dirt road? "I want a website," she said aloud, kneeling at her altar. She couldn't resist moving the printout of the babelings from behind the Demeter statue into the arms of her Barbie doll. She positioned Barbie to embrace the statue of Aphrodite, who smiled seductively from a ceramic clamshell. Then fatigue slayed her like an opiate and Mary had to stumble back to bed.

MARY DREAMED SHE WAS a child holding her mother's white-gloved hand as they entered the dayroom at an old folks home. Age and decrepitude seemed to seep from the walls, the shabby sofas and card tables where the elderly played Go Fish with arthritic deliberation. An old man in sagging pants moved painstakingly across the room with the help of a walker. He'd missed a belt loop and Mary spied telltale white puffiness peeking out above his waistband. *A man in a diaper!* Overcome with giggles, she nudged her mother. Rose frowned. *I'd rather be dead than come to that.* Sprouting blue-feathered wings she turned into a falcon and flew frantically through the room, wild and frightening, calling, *Killy killy, killy,* her beak aimed at Mary's face.

Mary awoke to shooting pain. Midnight. Peter snored beside her, whistling like a bird. She turned on the light and dialed Ann, rambling into Ann's answering machine, "Cramps. Bleeding. I don't know what to do ..." Then she turned off the light, folded herself in the fetal position and prayed: Let the falcon be a symbol of renewal. Let me wake to wholeness and freedom from cramps. Dozing, she was nineteen again, pregnant with a baby she would name Annapurna because Coyote, the man she loved, had shown her a picture of a mountain range before he left for Nepal on his spiritual trek. Mary didn't need to go to Nepal because the cosmic journey unfolded in her body.

She rolled over, saw a silhouette in her bedroom doorway, and screamed.

"It's me. I came as soon as I got your message." Ann approached the bed. She stank of cigarettes and beer but her presence gave Mary a profound sense of safety.

Peter stirred. "What's happening?"

"Go back to sleep," said Mary. "I'll get up." She swung her legs over the side of the bed but a deep twinge in her groin halted her movement. Sweat poured from her forehead into her eyebrows and along her hairline. Her body seemed to generate heat. Yet a cold wind rattled the windowpanes.

"You're sweating." Ann came around to Mary's side. "Do you have a fever?"

"I need to pee." Mary appreciated Ann's reinforcement, the arm slung over her shoulders as they headed down the hall to the bathroom. A loud click sounded from the green room just before intense white light flooded the hall and the bathroom. Mary had to squint against it.

"That's weird," said Ann. "What's going on?"

Mary realized that Peter had left the green room door wide open. She clutched herself. She was still bleeding. But the calamity of Ann, a slim shadow surrounded by luminescence tiptoeing toward the green room, canceled out Mary's physical crisis. She screamed, an expedient reflex. "Ow! My cramps! Blood."

Ann walked back to the bathroom with a halting, rigid gait. Like a windup toy, she snapped her head from Mary to the green room, from the green room to Mary. "I'll call the doctor. Then the police. That's what I'll do."

"The Fish says to come in at seven," Mary held onto the towel rack for support. "I already talked to him."

"What's going on?" Peter ambled out, rubbing sleep from his eyes.

"Go back to bed, honey," said Mary.

"*You* put her up to it! You think she's stupid!" Ann quivered, a nerve end with a face.

"What's she talking about?" said Peter.

"He has nothing to do with it!" said Mary. "It was Joel! Joel's my partner."

"You're lying." Ann covered her face with her hands.

"Are you talking about the plants?" said Peter. "She doesn't know?"

Mary recalled with a terrible clarity the day she put Ann on a plane bound for Oshkosh to go live with Rose. They had let her walk up to the departure gate at the airport because Ann was only ten. She watched her little girl step through the telescopic corridor, burdened by the weight of a brown vinyl suitcase she refused to check because she feared she'd never see it again.

"Things have gone pear-shaped," said Peter.

"Why didn't you shut the door?" asked Mary. "How could you be so careless?"

She reached for Ann. But Ann recoiled.

"Honestly, I thought I was the reason it was locked." Peter's hand looked strange as he grasped hers, the top knuckle of his index finger yellow from nicotine, the hand of a demon.

"Not now." Mary shook him off. She remembered that Ann had forgiven her, ultimately. After a year with Rose, Ann was overjoyed when Mary arrived to pluck her away.

"BABY ONE AND BABY TWO," said The Fish.

Ann sat on a metal stool, anxiously at odds with her body as she listened to the watery rhythm of two syncopated heartbeats.

"I wish Peter were here," said Mary. "But see? I respect your wishes. Who cares what I want? I'm just the vessel."

"You have no leverage," said Ann. She'd relived the shock of her discovery several times an hour, filled over and over with impotent rage. Listening for heartbeats washed the rage away. But she felt as if every muscle and tendon were inflamed. She'd walked among the plants briefly, touching their drooping, tattered leaves. She'd assumed the wilting had been caused by heat from the lamps until she touched the drenched soil in the pots. Over-watered, at risk for root rot. Pathetic. Mary and Peter were not only conniving but also incompetent.

A third heartbeat sounded much softer than the other two. Ann held her breath for the fourth. The tension of the passing silence tightened. She carried the quadruplets in her psychic uterus, taking better care than Mary ever could. She collected pregnancy data obsessively and knew that the fetuses could now move spontaneously. External genitalia were developed enough to reveal their sex. Their urine made up Mary's amniotic fluid. "Where's Baby Four?" Her throat hurt.

"Stop screaming," said Mary.

"You can't always hear the heartbeat at this stage," said The Fish. "Doesn't mean it's not there. We'll do a vaginal."

He attached a long wand to the ultrasound device. Within seconds, two embryos appeared on the monitor. They had evolved from mere pulsing lights to visible humans with oversized heads and tiny bodies curled up, resembling Mary's *lifeforce* cabochons, but much bigger, about the size of apples. "Looking good," he said.

The third one revealed itself closer to Mary's pubic bone. The doctor moved the wand. He passed the two again, then the one.

"Where is it?" said Ann. She couldn't swallow. Her tongue felt clumsy.

"It seems to have disappeared," he said.

"Then there were three," said Mary softly.

The urge to slap her was so fierce, Ann had to shove her hands in her pockets. "You killed it," she said. "You made it disappear."

"No one killed anyone. It's probably a natural reduction," said Dr. Fisher. "Might give the others a better chance. Make an appointment with the neonatologist. I'm sorry to take a hard line but I refuse to see you anymore."

"Mary told me he didn't have any appointments open."

"He didn't!" said Mary with a high-pitched voice that revealed her lie.

"I'll call him myself and insist that he see you," said Dr. Fisher.

"I can't do celibacy," Mary said. "I'm sorry. I want to be this receptacle of life and everything but there are limits to my obedience. I'm getting married on Beltane, the day the young god becomes a man, falls in love with the goddess, and they consummate."

"You don't believe in marriage!" Ann's voice cracked. "State-sanctioned permission to screw, useless piece of paper, remember what you told me? What does Peter want? Does he need a green card?"

"Don't bully me." Mary was ashen, sliding off the exam table. "There may be immigration concerns but it's my problem. Not yours. I don't need the criticism."

She shuffled to the curtained cubby where her clothes hung.

"I'm going to give you a prescription for anti-anxiety medication. You don't look so good, yourself." The doctor placed a firm hand on Ann's shoulder.

The wheeze of his breath was audible. Ann longed to confide in him. The Fish, not Dr. Fisher. But what would she say? *Mary's growing pot in my old bedroom.* It didn't matter, weighed against the loss of Baby Four. *I shouldn't have allowed myself to be happy.* The urge to confess flared and died. She was being punished for wearing her death dress, for allowing Joel's smile and the applause of drunken people to send her floating on a sweet haze of euphoria. She'd lost her vigilance against misfortune.

She had grown accustomed to four babies, two on each lap, four babies napping in a playpen, fighting over toys, tattling on each other, becoming friends. But if one could disappear, they all could. "We'll set ground rules." She addressed the closed curtain. "Peter has to get his own place. I'll move back to Sunrise until you give birth. After the babies are born, you can marry. In the meantime, I will put my bedroom back the way it was." She enunciated this last, just as Mary came out, pulling her skirt.

"You can't tell me what to do. I'm your mother."

"Then stop acting like a baby!"

"Do you understand how serious this is, Mary?" said The Fish. "Would it be easier to accept the loss of these fetuses if you knew that at least you had lived exactly as you wanted?"

"Don't talk to me like that! It's not my fault!" Mary coughed, then gasped. "Goddess, I can't breathe!"

"Don't force the inhale," said The Fish. "Just relax and let it come."

Lord, I am not worthy to receive you. Recited every week before communion, the prayer arrived in Ann's mind like a rope thrown over a chasm. *But only say the word and I shall be healed.* Even the memory of Betty sitting righteously in the pew brought solace. And she recalled another time when she'd experienced the rush of pure elation like the one she'd just had onstage, the irrepressible jubilance when she realized Lars had gone for good and she had Mary all to herself. But her happiness had been premature, dwindled to nothing when she recognized that without Lars, Mary didn't want to be alive anymore, whether Ann was there or not. Ann had never been enough for Mary.

"ONE LESS TO WORRY about," said Joel. He seemed to cave in on himself. "Why didn't you wake me? I would've come with you."

"Come with me where?" Ann unbuttoned her coat, surveying him on the sofa; his tangled hair sticking out over his ears, his torn, coffee-stained T-shirt, the guitar in his lap. She had delivered the news abruptly. *Baby Four disappeared. Mary lost one.* "Are you okay? You haven't slept. Come here." He patted the cushion, gazing at her with guileless topaz eyes.

"You think you're so smart," said Ann. "I know about the marijuana. You and Mary in cahoots."

His eyes glazed over, he strummed a desperate, half-formed tune on his guitar. Guilt seeped from his pores. "I could've come with you to the doctor."

She swerved past the counter and slipped outside, shutting the door quietly. Ann never slammed, no matter what. McKenna ran ahead, panting. Sparrows darted along a breeze close to the ground, and an undertone of warmth held the promise of spring. Ann again marched over the slippery mud to the unfinished house. The trees with their young green shoots remained majestically indifferent. She had never been enough for Mary and she wasn't enough for Joel.

Ever since the night she and Joel had made love in the empty space of their future living room, Ann visited the house regularly. She liked the smell of damp cement and the idea of children filling the place. She approached the kitchen window, where one day she would gaze out while washing dishes. And there on the windowsill sat Mary's bronzed baby shoes, along with the bib, the yoni, the popsicle-stick house, the amethyst crystal and the heart-shaped stone. Joel must have arranged them, cultivating his own private faith. She picked up a shoe and pressed it against her cheek, flooded with impressions of Jessica, her freckled smile, strawberry lip gloss, heavy walk, and the hope she had embodied.

McKenna dashed behind her in a fury of barking.

"We did it for you." Joel's voice rang out. "Hell, I jumped on the idea when Mary brought it up. I knew you'd be mad and I did it anyway. Don't you see? It's all for you!"

"She said it was your idea, so I guess someone's lying."

"She would have done it with or without me," said Joel. "She already had the seeds and equipment."

"I expect lying and manipulation from Mary, okay? But not from you." Ann placed the bronzed shoe on top of the yoni and covered them both with the bib. "You and Mary. You and Jessica."

"I put those things there because I want the babies to happen concurrently with the house. Sage suggested it. I don't want to get stuck living in a trailer next to some decaying half-built dump. I'm sorry I didn't tell you about the pot plants." Joel sat on the bottom step of the staircase, talking louder. "I'm sorry about Jessica. I'm sorry I'm doing everything wrong. I wish we could just get married again and start over from the beginning. I wanted Baby Four as much as you did. Please, I wanted it. Come here, *please?*"

The plaintive urgency of his "please" compelled her to the stairs. He shifted to make room. She fit perfectly on the step beside him.

"Maybe we can ask Sage how to bring back Baby Four," he said.

Ann gathered her knees up and folded her arms around them. "Mary could kill them all. Then she'll cry about 'her' loss. It's all about her."

"We can't just sit back and act helpless because, guess what? It *is* all about her." Joel gripped her hand, bruisingly tight, crunching her knuckles. "Don't *let* Mary take over. You think you're so breakable, but you're as tough as she is. Tougher." He released her.

Ann shook her fingers. She had been under Mary's thumb all her life, had shaped herself in reaction to Mary. She pulled on the railing to get up. "I know Mary a lot better than you do."

Joel pulled her back down. "Annie, I'm on your side. I love you. Don't you understand that?"

"Maybe love is something you learn developmentally, like language or motor skills," she said. "There's a period in early childhood when it's supposed to happen and if you miss it then you're stunted forever. Maybe I missed my love window. When I saw those plants, that's how I felt. I'm one of those people. I *need* children."

"Then it's all about *you*," said Joel, bumping her shoulder. "It's never too late to learn about love."

"I just don't understand why you'd want to grow pot when your involvement with pot is what made this so complicated."

"Yeah, well, I don't have any work coming in and we're up to our necks in debt." He bumped shoulders again. "I'm glad you know! It's a relief. For Mary, it's a game. Peter's an idiot. America vanished off the face of the earth and she's the one with knowledge and connections. There's a giant padlock on her front door, have you driven by there recently? The plants are drooping and turning yellow and I don't know what to do. Maybe the carbon dioxide tanks were a bad idea."

"America, too?" said Ann. "Everyone's in on it."

McKenna rested his chin on Joel's knees and stared lovingly at both of them.

"Over a hundred and thirty thousand dollars. We need the money." Joel tentatively touched her hair. "But they're not thriving. I don't know why."

"You guys are over-watering," she relented. She was so tired of holding herself apart. "Stop watering so much, they'll be better within a week."

On May 1, the air held a chill but Mary, dressed in a floaty white frock with lace eyeholes, hardly felt the cold. *I'm loved,* she told herself. *I'm ecstatic.*

"I purify your feet to walk the goddess path," Sage chanted, bending to anoint Mary's bare feet with rose oil. Sage wore a thick alpaca sweater over her ceremonial saffron robes. "Blade into cup. Let these two join in everlasting union."

"May desire wed delight!" Mary cried, according to their script. Her feet tingled where Sage had anointed them. "All nature is renewed with our love."

Her recitation was punctuated by the same few chords on the auto harp, played with a zithery flourish by Della, who had driven up from the city for the occasion.

Also in bare feet, wearing black jeans and black turtleneck under a yellow silk cape he'd created from Mary's old sari, Peter looked heroic. His cape billowed in the wind that swept across the Sunrise field.

"Blimey," he said. "What's my line? I'm..."

Mary whispered, "Say: 'I Merge with the moon goddess, who never dies but only changes from bright to dark and back again."

"I merge with the moon goddess..." He gripped her hand. "What? Bloody hell. I'm so nervous."

"Be the God inside me. Like the waters of nature, the tides propel me forward and draw me back!" Mary shouted. Wind blew her hair around her face. "Say anything. Be spontaneous."

He cleared his throat. "You are you and I am I...how did that go?"

"No, that doesn't really apply because we already—"

"Wait. I am not in this world to live up to your expectations and you are not in this world to live up to mine. I do my thing and you do yours and if by chance we find each other, it's beautiful." He clasped her hands, crossing wrists. Lifting his face to the sky, he shouted, "I love Mary!"

They totaled thirteen people. Cloud Rider brought a supply of home-brewed mead. Asphodel, Raven, Wren and a couple of the others had driven up from the sisterhood in a minivan, along with America, who'd arrived in disguise, with her hair dyed as black as a hole in the universe. Mary's heart constricted to look at her; she seemed so small standing next to Carlos in his leather jacket and baggy jeans. And he was less threatening without his dog. A festive mood prevailed despite the wheelchair that Ann had placed conspicuously outside the circle. *In case you get tired.* Twenty-four weeks to go, and Ann hovered behind Mary like a probation officer.

The wedding rings were simple: no bezel, no stone. Mary had chased a pattern of the infinity symbol along the outer bands. Peter's ring adorned his long muscular fingers beautifully. But Mary's only went down as far as her middle knuckle because of swelling.

"As your hands shall be bound," said Sage. "So shall your lives be bound together."

Ann stepped forward, cardigan buttoned up to her neck. Not only had she ironed a crease in her jeans but she had also bleached her white sneakers whiter, and looked about as straitlaced as a human being could. With a sure touch she tied a red ribbon in figure eights around their wrists, not too tight, not too loose, knotting it firmly, ever capable. But she wouldn't meet Mary's eye.

Acceptance is a process, Mary told herself. She was grateful Ann had agreed to participate at all. In exchange, Mary had promised to stop climbing stairs. For the rest of her confinement the living room sofa would serve as Mary's bed. Lumpy in the middle cushion, frayed at the armrests and not exactly roomy for sleeping, it was her concession to her daughter, the doctors, and the three remaining babies.

Sage said, "May the blessings of Demeter and the Corn King be upon you as you jump over the broom like you will jump over obstacles in your lives."

The sisterhood members laid down an exquisitely crafted double broom made of hawthorn, the handles twined together at the root where a thick set of bristles fanned out. Mary and Peter, bound at the wrists, stepped rather than jumped over it because of Mary's condition.

For their purposes, this handfasting only covered a year and a day, in keeping with the Wiccan tradition to allow them room to reconsider before a soulmate ritual, in which they would vow to be together for the eternity of future lives; legally, if Mary and Peter wanted to sever their ties, they would have to divorce.

Everyone clasped hands and circled them, chanting. "We are the circle of life and rebirth, with no beginning and never ending."

Faster and faster they danced. They made Mary dizzy. When she tried to settle herself by looking at the ground, the sight of her swollen ankles gave her heart palpitations. She shut her eyes. The world spun and she remembered how she'd go twirling around the yard as a child until she fell flat on her back on the grass. The sky circled above and a deep, resonant voice rumbled, *Hello.* She had staggered inside to tell her mother. *The sky just said hello to me!* Rose dismissed her. *Don't be silly. Shut the door before the flies come in.* As if flies were avoidable.

When Mary opened her eyes, the footrest of the wheelchair protruded into her range of vision. "Sit," said Ann.

"I'm fine," said Mary.

But the others had stopped dancing. "Rest when you need to," said Sage, and everyone concurred. *Take care of yourself. Accept support. Trust your body.*

Mary conceded. With Peter's help, she maneuvered her hands from the ribbon that bound their wrists together. Unknotting would have brought bad luck. As soon as she flopped into the wheelchair, she recognized the extent of her exhaustion. "Thank you, Annapurna," she said. To dispel anxiety, she punched her heart twice and raised her hand in a peace sign. "Let's feast!"

A cheer went up. Ann, Joel, and Sage unwrapped the food they'd set out on a covered card table: cheese and bread and hummus and grape leaves, with mead and beer and seltzer and an urn of hot jasmine tea. The wedding cake, a fruitcake with marzipan icing, like the druids would have eaten, sat on a doilied platter to be cut later with Sage's ceremonial sword. As Mary watched them all, a wave of gratitude made her sleepy.

America pulled away from Carlos. She came over and kissed the crown of Mary's head, her breasts landing in Mary's face. "Not doing the Great Rite? I know you love that sexual feeling!" And she chortled like the friendly, bawdy woman Mary had once loved.

"What's the Great Rite?" Peter massaged Mary's shoulders. "Shall I be shoved into a wicker effigy and burnt alive in the field?"

"You should be," said Mary, "for screwing up your lines." She would have loved to enact the Great Rite, the sacred sexual union, disappointingly off limits, another concession. She hadn't anticipated the grief that followed the loss of the quadruplet, though it manifested less as mourning the lost fetus than as mourning her lost sex life. Not that her carnality had absolutely caused the absent fetus, but now she was sticking by the rules.

She caught sight of Ann in a folding chair, tuning her guitar. Next to Ann, Joel strummed and sang "All You Need Is Love." A yearning for Ann to drop everything and shout, *Mommy, I love you!* like she used to as a little girl brought tears to Mary's eyes.

Della danced over, blocking her view, and Mary steeled herself for the inevitable, overpowering perfumed hug, but Della embraced Peter, not her. "I'm the source of it all because I introduced you two! You'll get your green card and live happily ever after."

"Our love transcends nation states, Della." Mary hated this entrapment in the wheelchair with everyone looming above, ignoring her while she craned her neck to converse. "Bureaucratic documents are nothing but paper and dust. We eat the meal, not the menu."

She was mollified when Asphodel kissed her cheeks, European-style. "I'm not a sun-god person, but this was beautiful. May your triplets be born in health and joy."

"Quadruplets," Mary answered, repeating the line Ann insisted on. "Losing one doesn't make them triplets."

She heard no sirens, saw no flashing lights, nor sensed any negative vibes, except for the pang about Baby Four, so she was stunned to see two sheriff deputies. They came striding around the laurel bushes from the front of the house. In their green uniforms, with their sunglasses reflecting the wedding scene, they looked like a hallucination, not a physical reality. A collective gasp went up. The guitars stopped. Singing ceased. In an instant, Della and Peter retreated toward the circle of stones, along with everyone else. Only Ann put her guitar down to stand near Mary.

"Ma'am, are you acquainted with the owner of the house two miles east of here?" the officer spoke to Ann, as if Mary was invisible. He pointed in the direction of America's house. "Down the road a piece? The door's padlocked."

"Excuse me! Hello! I've just gotten married!" Deflect and distract: that was Mary's tactic. She hoped her dazzling smile didn't appear too false. "And I'm pregnant with three! I call them my 'three-tuses!'"

"How well do you know Amy Kray?" One of the deputies addressed her. "Were you aware of suspicious activity at that residence?"

"Who is Amy Kray?" asked Ann.

"Are you talking about America? All these years, I never knew her real name!" Mary laughed heartily. Her throat hurt from the effort. "Goes to show, no one *really* knows anyone! We barely know ourselves!" In the dark lenses of their sunglasses, she saw an image of her mother. *Contain yourself,* said Rose. And she conceived the extent of what she could lose—freedom, happiness, love, Sunrise. To avoid an inadvertent glance upstairs at the foil-covered windows of the green room, she stared at her toes, which were bluish with cold though she couldn't feel it.

Sage approached, orange robes flowing beneath her sweater, and Mary almost wept with relief. "This is a private party," said Sage. "Is there a problem?"

"Aren't you the county witch?" One of the deputies spat out a brown jet of chewing tobacco. "My wife wants to be a witch ever since she heard you on the radio."

"We have evidence that Amy Kray is involved in drug trafficking," said the other. "You don't want to become an accessory."

"This is a peaceful gathering on private property." Wren from the sisterhood strode forward, scolding. A lawyer, she specialized in housing.

"If you think of *anything* you might know about your neighbor, we'd appreciate your cooperation." The tobacco-chewing deputy tossed a business card in Mary's lap.

As quickly and mysteriously as they had arrived, the deputies turned and marched away, around the laurel bushes toward the front drive.

"I refuse to be intimidated." Mary turned, craning her neck to find Ann.

But everyone was watching the police car roll down the road until it disappeared. Everyone except for Ann, crouched and dry heaving in the grass.

"Careless!" Carlos hissed. "Now we must move our little garden."

"We can't move anything," said Joel, snapping his guitar case shut. "They'll be watching us like hawks."

"I'm wiggin'. Come on, baby." America grabbed Carlos. "We gotta split."

"There's no need to panic," said Sage.

But she didn't know about the green room. Mary's adrenalin was churning. "Where's Peter? Let's cut the cake! Wait! Della, play some more harp!"

Della was already putting away her instrument. Sage dismantled the altar, touching each item to her heart. Ann was putting away her guitar.

"We're leaving, Mary, lovely party." Asphodel waved but kept her distance.

Cloud Rider said, "Don't forget to drink the mead wine. It won't keep."

The others didn't even say goodbye. The sisterhood van gave a cheerful beep as it pulled out onto the road.

"The hell with this. I'm not an invalid." Thrusting the wheelchair out behind her with a vigorous shove, Mary discovered she could walk rather quickly after all, without dizziness. She headed straight for the driveway where Joel sat behind the wheel of his idling truck.

Ann came over, carrying her guitar case. "We're going," she said.

"Stay for cake!" said Mary. "The pigs are gone."

"I'm a convicted felon." Joel leaned across the car seat to shout at Mary. "The plants are ready to harvest. But you had to get married, right? You had to call attention."

"Getting married has nothing to do with this," said Mary. She could feel tears welling. What an awful way to end her wedding.

"Did you ever once consider the consequences of this harvest?" Ann's nostrils pinched and her mouth tightened, just like Rose.

Mary heard a keening in her head. As a child, she would hear it when her mother left the room, taking Mary's center with her. *Where's me? Where's me?* She would cry after Rose. Now she was crying after Ann. "Please stay. Please be happy for me. I'm in love."

Peter appeared from behind the house, swinging the red ribbon from the crook of his finger. "There you are! I've set the tripod on the porch. Sage agreed to rebind us for a photograph."

"I'm just manifesting my waterpower," Mary sobbed. "These aren't tears."

"Please don't cry," said Ann. "Go on, Joel. I'll be home later."

Joel gunned the engine.

Touched because Ann loved her enough to stay, and Peter loved her enough to marry her, Mary reached for both. Her legs buckled as she waddled to the porch, where the camera faced the railing like a weapon. The wedding cake sat on a wicker table, a sad, untouched edifice.

Sage quickly bound Mary and Peter together at the wrists and stepped behind the camera to press the shutter. Ann slipped into the house and Mary felt a piece of herself follow. "Where are you going?" she called after.

"Smile," said Peter.

When the picture was done, Mary sank into a wicker chair. "You'll stay for some cake, won't you, Sage?"

"I'm fasting until the moon transits Aries. Take care of yourself, Mary. Tell Ann to come visit." Sage carried her box of sacred objects to her car. It took four tries to turn the engine over. Each strangled attempt heightened Mary's sense of failure until, finally, Sage drove off in a cloud of smoke.

"Why do you and your friends have such crappy cars?" Ann came out with a pair of sweat socks. She sat on the porch to pull them over Mary's feet. Her little Annapurna, so caring and forgiving. "Thank you sweetheart," said Mary.

Sage had taken the ceremonial athame with her so Peter cut the cake with an ordinary kitchen knife. Curled up in her wicker chair, sheltered from the road by the juniper bushes that grew thickly over one side of the porch, Mary ate, chewing each bite twenty-five times until a glob of mush stuck to the roof of her mouth. The air grew colder as the sun lowered behind the hills. Suddenly, a strange, thrilling series of flips and taps signaled from her interior. "Oh, Shakti!" she cried. "The babies moved!"

"What did they feel like?" Ann slid onto her knees. "I want to feel them!"

"Hold it, right there!" Peter dragged the camera on its tripod. Light exploded as his flash went off. "That one will be captioned: *Life Stirring*. Both of you looked holy, for lack of a better word, with a medieval grace like the annunciation in a Giotto painting."

"You cheapen the experience when you do that." Ann sat back on her heels. "It's not a performance."

"If you hate the picture, I'll delete it," said Peter.

"They felt miraculous," said Mary. She imagined three heartbeats pulsing around the absence, three nodes of energy. From a cube to a triangle; harmony, wisdom, and understanding; the first true Pythagorean number; the tripod of life; the goddess in her triple aspect. As if in response to her thoughts, the moon materialized in the sky above the tree line, a lovely drooping crescent, a shadow completing its circle. "Look!" she said. "The moon Goddess is blessing us!"

And a rumble of what sounded like thunder turned out to be the Slocombe Builders truck rolling back up the road, returning to Sunrise, to the fold of his family. Ann's whole body seemed to exhale, Mary perceived it as profoundly as she'd felt the babies. "I knew he couldn't stay away," she said, though she hadn't. But saying it made it true.

We've had an influx of infants, Shirley had said on the phone. *We need you for the toddlers. Please, come back.* And there she stood now, waving from the front door, which had been newly painted with flowers and butterflies. Ann hurried to embrace her, delighting in Shirley's scent of crayons and Clorox. Frances nodded curtly. Children tore around the grass, screaming: *Mommy, she hit me! Did not! Did too!*

A mother marched toward them, pulling a little girl in pink boots. "I don't want to report you to the state, but it's a public health issue when you serve yogurt to the children."

"Ah, this is one of yours." Shirley touched Ann's hand with a tenderness that made her feel nurtured.

"What's your name?" She crouched down.

"I'm two!" The girl lunged, flinging her hands.

"Tell the teacher your name," said the mother, above them.

Ann preferred the energy of tempestuous toddlers to that of their parents. More children arrived, yanked along by mothers. Fathers were rare but Joel would be an exception, Ann thought. She felt senseless with happiness to be back.

"Are you hiding?" she called to another little girl who'd pulled her skirt over her head, revealing her tights all the way to the waistband. As she rearranged the girl's skirt she was distracted by a quick movement at the curb where a woman in a blue sweat-shirt wrestled with a stroller. She noted something familiar in the woman's bulldozing motion and, in dreamlike paralysis, she recognized Jessica.

She was still pretty with her hair dyed blond, her chubby cheeks, light freckles and large dewy eyes, but fat, now, too; she hadn't lost her pregnancy weight. Jessica shoved the stroller forward. "I thought they fired you."

Ann forced herself to look at the gnome-faced baby in the stroller, his face awash in snot. Moist coughs exploded from his mouth. He tilted his head, knit his brow and, in that instant, absorbed her into his mind: *I could have been yours.* "Ethan," she said.

"Christopher." Jessica kicked the grass with threadbare, laceless sneakers. "You were trying to steal my Christopher."

"You were trying to steal my husband," said Ann.

When Jessica narrowed her eyes, she resembled her mother. "You put your black magic on me. Made sure I'll never be happy."

Ann recalled the wanton girl lounging in the trailer with all her bravado and entitlement. "Magic can't do that," she said, and understood as if she'd known all along that magic was simply the recognition of the unimaginably vast and complex mystery of life.

"Hi there!" Shirley tramped across the grass. Full of professional efficiency, she stooped over the stroller to dangle a plastic bell in front of the baby. "Goodness, I hope he doesn't have a fever."

"The doctor said he wasn't contagious," said Jessica.

He would be almost nine months now, one of the Chipmunks. Not Ann's domain.

"Your Antelopes won't wait," said Shirley, keeping her eyes on Christopher.

Ann forced herself to move across the grass, which still sparkled with dew. The Antelopes dashed about with zig-zags and high-pitched voices. Inside, the infants' caretaker washed the changing tables. Frances was already ensconced on the sofa with the four-year-old Lions.

"Come on, all you Antelopes, choose a center." Ann clapped her hands. The rule was that once they chose, they played in their selected center—the dollhouse, the ornamental fireplace nook, dress-up area, coloring corner, or blocks space—until breakfast. But rules were merely blueprints. A crying boy needed a hug. One of the twins peed in her big-girl pants. Kim, the two-year-old with food allergies, declared that Ann was beautiful and leaped up several times from her blocks to affirm it. Ann remembered how smart the children were, how demanding and keen to exploit adult weaknesses, the instinctive push and pull that made them grow.

Breakfast was the usual messy affair. Ann was caught in the fray: food in fists thrown at faces, milk spilled, spoons dropped, cereal overturned, and clamorous voices piping a din to the ceiling. After breakfast came cleanup, potty, and playtime. Lunch followed playtime, then cleanup, potty, and naptime. Only once did Ann hear a cry from the infants' room that pierced through the tumult of two- and three-year-olds, provoking a jarring crunch of longing in her bones because she knew it was Christopher: *I could have been your son! I should have been your son!*

At the end of the day, perched in a tiny chair, Ann struggled to record activities in the state-mandated log. She had fallen out of practice. By the time she finished, the infants were gone. Good. She could do this. She straightened the room, picking up over-turned chairs, pushing the tables together. Tomorrow, she told herself, she would bring her guitar for a sing-along.

Shirley came in and dropped a folder on the desk. "We've got a pile of lesson plans here if you want them. Seems like you're in the swing of things?"

"It's good to be back." Ann picked up the folder. If Shirley wasn't going to mention Christopher or Jessica, neither would she.

But as she drove home, Christopher's cry echoed through her mind. *I should have been yours!* Her hands began to shake. She couldn't hold the steering wheel. Mistakenly hitting the gas instead of the brake, she lurched and panicked, then pulled over to the side of the road. She turned the engine off and cried for several minutes. When she covered her face, tears ran between her fingers. The windows fogged. She rolled hers down and saw that she had stopped in front of a little cemetery, which she passed every day without really seeing. It was animated now with daffodils and crocuses and a velvety layer of grass. A kestrel swooped above the windshield, wheeled around, and flew past again. When it glided by a third time, Ann wiped her nose with her sweater sleeve and instead of going to Sunrise as she had planned, she drove to Sage's.

THE PLACE STANK OF cat pee, causing Ann's nostrils to vibrate.

"Who's there?" Sage called weakly from the loft bed. She was covered in blankets. "Oh! I'm glad to see you. Could you do me a favor? Go through my messages and cancel appointments? The numbers are in my Rolodex. Tell them I'm running a healing circle in Sedona. No, Costa Rica. No. Tulum. New Paltz. Wherever. Don't say I'm sick."

Dust drifted like plankton in the light streaming through the slanted roof windows. Cats circled the massage table, mewling. Papers were scattered on the floor, and the reclining chair was torn as if someone had knifed it. As soon as Ann sat at Sage's desk, a fluffy gray cat with a pink nose leaped into her lap, kneading her thighs with sharp claws. There weren't many appointments to cancel. Sage did her best business in the weeks between June and September when the Catskill resorts filled and summer homes were rented. It was too early in the season.

Afterwards, Ann fed the cats. They surged toward the food from every nook and hiding place. It seemed the dead one had vanished from their awareness. They lived in the present. With a prick in her heart, she thought of Baby Four. How quickly dailiness closed in over loss. Ann swept the floor, grateful to be of use, and she remembered Mary's frail step over the double broom, how

Peter had lifted their bound hands, practically yanking Mary's arm from the socket, revealing the torn seam at Mary's armpit. Ann was cursed to notice Mary's discomfort even when Mary did not. She boiled water for miso soup, then carried the soup up to the loft bed on a tray, a precarious one-handed balancing act that made her feel capable.

Sage had fallen asleep. Reluctant to wake her, Ann set the tray on the bed and watched her slumber. Wrinkles netted her face. The familiar oval shape, with her upper lip that never quite closed over her top row of teeth, morphed into Mary's round, homely face, and Ann was carried to her childhood, sitting on Mary's bed, watching her sleep, safeguarding her. She would curl herself up beside Mary and pull Mary's arms around her. Submerged in the warm bouquet of Mary's exhalations, back when she had still yearned for Mary.

Sage moaned. She pulled herself up to sit, an alarming profusion of gray hairs adhered to her pillowcase. "Was I asleep?"

"Eat." Ann slid the tray toward her. "You need a doctor."

"I don't believe in doctors." Sage's lips were blue, her skin almost translucent, as if moonlight shone beneath it. "When I was sixteen, I was sitting on the rocky shore of Lake Superior, where I grew up, and it started to storm. But I sat there, letting rain pelt down on me. All I remember is an explosion of light. I woke up in my bed, completely deaf. I lost my hearing for a month. But everything shimmered with a light that dissolved into silver liquid."

A string of seaweed slicked against Sage's lip as she waved away the soup. "Thank you. I'm done."

"Then what happened?"

"I'd been struck by lightning and, suddenly, magnetic fields were visible to me. It sounds cliché but I was terrified. I didn't want this power. But I learned how to use it. I devoted my life to its service."

Ann's legs ached suddenly, as if her tendons and ligaments were inflamed.

"When we lost Hawthorne that night, I lost access to the quantum world," said Sage. "The light has been extinguished for me. But you have the gift. You must use it."

"It'll come back to you," said Ann. "I can't have this power. I'm not like you."

"It's not about what *you* want. Stay awake." Sage gripped her arm. "If you bring forth what is within you, what you bring forth will save you."

With a shock, Ann saw Sage's hand mutate into the down-covered claw of a bird. *I'm witnessing this,* she thought.

"You need to bury the totem with the egg yolk," said Sage. "The ground is soft enough. Mary keeps it on her altar. Call on the powers of the lost one. The gods and goddesses are rooting for you. Also: What you do not bring forth will destroy you."

In a blink, the articulated structure of the bird toes became, again, Sage's fingers. Ann's wrist was hot where Sage had grabbed her. She started to say, "I just want to be normal." But what issued from her mouth was, "In our beginning is our end."

"Take care of Mary. Her prana is weak. And Peter is heedless."

"What about *your* prana?" said Ann.

But Sage shut her eyes. She looked ancient.

Ann carried the tray back down the loft ladder. The words of a prayer from Sunday mass looped through her mind as she washed the soup bowl. *Lamb of God, you take away the sins of the world, have mercy on us.* And another line followed that, not from church but from so many Wiccan rituals: *We are a circle within a circle with no beginning and never ending.* The cats reclined on the floor, under the armchair, on the kitchen counter and the table, regarding her languidly, as if they knew that words could merely point to the infinite source, but never embody it.

Outside, the wind had picked up. In the shadows under the evergreens that bordered the driveway, Ann glimpsed a baby squatting in the dirt. "Hey!" she called. Her heart hammered blood to her fingertips. But when she rushed over, the branches lifted in the cool draft, revealing nothing beneath but their pale undersides. They did not question or resist the wind but acquiesced, because it blew, as it should.

ANN FOUND MARY IN her usual spot on the sofa with her legs tucked under her, thumbing through *The Tibetan Book of Living and Dying.* "This has been on my list since it came out in the '90s." Mary lifted her face for a kiss. "Now's my chance."

"Have you taken your meds? How have your sugars been?" Ann pushed aside the pregnancy books and tarot cards, reading glasses, box of runes, I Ching and crossword puzzles to find the prescription medications. Such a mess. But she managed to root out the Glucophage, the iron tablets and high-powered pregnancy vitamins. "Where's the Aldomet? Where's your blood-sugar device?"

"I'm a boon for the medical establishment." Mary waved her hand. "Peter keeps it under control."

But there was no sign of Peter. "You can't rely on him," said Ann. "Where is he anyway?"

"He finagled a job in the city," said Mary. "Didn't you notice my car's not in the driveway? He's photographing hedge fund executives for an annual report. He'll be telling them: Look left, look right, lift your chin. Not that we don't have our own hedge fund to harvest up in the green room. Ha, hedge fund! Get it?"

"Forgive me for not finding that funny." Ann discovered the thin black device for measuring blood sugar between the sofa cushions. The vial with the blood pressure pills had rolled under the couch. "You didn't miss a dose, did you?"

"Why are you in such a bad mood?"

"I'm sorry." Ann went to the window where Mary's altar had been arranged on a card table for the duration of her confinement. Outside, she saw the grass and reeds and wildflowers in the meadow swaying in a breeze she couldn't feel. The trees were so lush with foliage they seemed burdened by their own abundance. "I ran into Jessica," she said. "Her son's enrolled at Little Footsteps."

"Her karma will catch up to her," said Mary from the sofa. "We don't know how, we don't know when but, trust me, it'll happen. Do you know anything about the bardos? I've been reading about them. Bardo means transition but it's associated with dying. We can't grasp the truth of impermanence. It's the human condition."

Ann moved the Virgin Mary statue to the right of the brass Kali. Then she positioned Barbie against the seated Demeter. As a child, she'd enjoyed organizing Mary's icons, and she felt childlike now, secretive, vulnerable. The printout of the blastocysts remained tucked in the Virgin's elbow. Which one had disappeared?

"Hey, I've been meaning to ask you," said Mary, from behind her. "Peter's using my social security number for this job but he really needs a green card. Can you write a letter on our behalf?"

"Sure, Mom." The box that held the totem was hidden behind the Shri Lakshmi candle. Hugging it tightly, feeling as awkward as a teenager when she'd slink away to use her dilator, aware that everyone at the sisterhood knew what she was up to, Ann strode to the front door.

"Where are you taking that?" Mary called after her.

"There's something I have to do." Late afternoon was evolving into evening. Amber light spread out over the meadow, calling up colors then redefining them. It was chilly enough to require a sweater. Ann picked up a shovel at the back of the house and headed down the path through the field, to Mary's stone circle. Wind flattened the grass. Leaves resembling small birds twirled here and there. Everything seemed disparate and futile. As she pushed the shovel into the ground with her foot, she heard Sage: *When intention can't be summoned, gesture will suffice.*

A whiff of sulfur rose from the carved wooden box when she opened it. The clay had cracked. She held the crude figure in her hands for a moment, feeling the rough texture before she placed it in the hole. *You have the gift.* Scraping up dirt with the shovel, she wished for an infusion of wisdom, or light like liquid silver. The lichen and dirt on the rocks quivered in the wind. She shivered. The moon hung at apogee, waning. Crickets were calling. The frogs began their chorus in the nearby pond. Birds called to each other from the trees.

Seized with a ferocious longing for her children, and for a larger force in the universe to align itself with her puny desire, Ann threw the shovel down and tore up dirt with her bare hands. "Baby Four, I wanted you!" she shouted. "I want all of you! I want! I want! I want!" Soil swelled and compacted under her nails. Dirt got in her hair.

"It's done," she said, as she filled the hole, and buried the clay figure. She wanted Sage's blessing. Streaked with mud and dirt, she trudged back toward Sunrise.

In the plasticky rustling of the laurel bush leaves, she heard a child laughing. "Who's there?" With a lunge, she swept the branches apart, but encountered only silence and shadows and the moist sweet odor of flowers. But she accepted the laughter as a sign of Sage's benediction, and an indication of her own gift.

MARY STOOD BY HER altar, watching through the window as Ann hurled dirt around like a wild woman, and she recalled Annapurna, her child, busily tidying corners, creating orderly little houses from cardboard boxes, like a soldier, her kit and cot aligned. While the other commune children ran boldly and nakedly through fields and woods, Annapurna swept wood chips or scrubbed kitchen counters. She never went naked. And even though her uptight behavior reflected badly on Mary and seemed to prove the rap-session allegations of Mary's hang-ups, Ann had created a safety zone for Mary, keeping her in check. It worried Mary to watch her now, acting crazy. *The curse of Jessica,* Mary thought.

THE NEONATAL SPECIALIST'S WAITING room featured no photographs from the original Woodstock Concert, no psychedelic posters or pictures of babies, just beige walls and tan chairs, neutrality as decoration. The receptionist sat behind glass, thoroughly impersonal. "You're late."

"Honey, we operate on pagan time." Mary interrupted Ann's apology. She had to counter the sense of herself as an invalid. She was strong. She was woman. The flesh on her hips swung side to side as she lifted one heavy swollen foot, then the other.

Ultrasounds in this office were performed in a separate exam room by a technician, rather than the doctor. Mary donned her paper gown and took her position on the table. The video monitor angled down from above.

"Cold!" She recoiled as the technician applied gel to her belly.

"It'll warm," said the dispassionate young woman, moving the device. "Your chart says you're twenty-two weeks. I would have guessed a lot further. Did he put you on total bed rest yet?"

"Modified," said Mary. "I'm going crazy."

The technician slid the transducer over her flesh. "There's your girl. See the labia?"

"Don't tell us!" said Ann. "We don't want to know!"

But Mary thought she discerned a scrotum on one of the larger fetuses. "Is that a boy?"

"I asked you not to," said Ann. "I'm the mother. I should get a say."

"What's the third one? What's the third one?" Mary was clapping her hands.

But the third, smaller, fetus curled away. "That one's shy," said the technician

The door opened. Light from the hall poured in as Dr. Stark entered. A tall thin man with wispy gray hair and a sour face, he wrapped a blood pressure cuff around Mary's arm without looking her in the eye, even as he asked, "How are we doing?"

She recognized his type, a man stuck in his own preconceived notions.

"Your technician told us the genders when I asked her not to," said Ann.

"A girl, a boy, and a shy one!" cried Mary. "It's silly not to know."

"I thought they already knew," said the woman.

"Everyone's different," said Dr. Stark as he pumped the armlet. "Some people want to know, some don't."

"Don't you understand?" Ann's voice went hoarse. "They could all disappear!"

"I doubt that," said Dr. Stark. "Disappear? No."

"Mary's not taking care of herself," said Ann.

"I'm being good," said Mary, stung. Following orders, taking her meds, what more could she do?

Dr. Stark offered neither assurance nor threat as he poked and prodded. "Time for the amnio."

While he palpated her uterus, swabbing her with antiseptic, Mary shut her eyes. The needle was painful, sucking out amniotic fluid and taking her life force with it. She suddenly understood Ann's anxiety, though she didn't experience it herself. She felt for Ann, a profound pity.

The needle was withdrawn and Dr. Stark took her pulse again. "No bending, lifting, or carrying," he said. The threat of complete bed rest hung in the subtext. "I'm instituting the 50/10 rule. Each hour, you can engage in ten minutes of *light* activity and spend the next fifty minutes resting."

Ann was asking something about fetal development and they talked as if Mary weren't there. She felt the strange looping aquatic movement inside, and the babies soothed her while Dr. Stark spoke of her deficiencies: her elevated blood pressure, anemia, protein in her urine, edema, blah blah blah, accompanied by the scratch of Ann's pen, busily taking notes.

She remembered holding baby Annapurna, gazing at her little face. When she opened her mouth, the baby's lips parted. She tilted her head, and the baby's head tilted. She raised her eyebrows and the baby mirrored that, too. Annapurna had been her refuge. If she lost herself, the baby drew her back in.

"Stop spacing out!" Ann pulled her back now. "You will have to keep better track of the medications."

Mary felt dizzy as she shuffled into the curtained cubicle where she'd left her clothes. She groped for the little netted bag of stones she carried for protection in the pocket of skirt. "Jade, garnet and opal," she blurted through the curtain. "Those are the babies' names. They're as real as you and me. Opal's the shy one."

"We can't name them yet," said Ann. "What if we have to do a selective? I can't believe I'm calling it a *selective!* What if we have to kill one?"

There was a wooden bench inside the cubicle and Mary sat to catch her breath before undertaking the formidable task of getting dressed. She was so tired, falling backwards into a time tunnel. She was thirsty, terribly thirsty. She rubbed her sandpaper tongue against the dry roof of her mouth. She was absorbed into her younger self, lying on the floor of a jostling van, the fetus kicking against her ribcage, a mildewed pillow beneath her head, and the smell of other bodies all around her. A rough carpet beneath her caused unbearable itching on her legs. Sweat trickled in streams down the backs of her knees and the insides of her elbows. Hot wind blew in through the open windows.

A man in green sneakers, the toe-tops cut out so that five long, crooked, hairy toes poked through each shoe, kicked a canteen across the van to her. Mary hoisted herself up to drink. The water was warm, tasting of metal, smelling like the inside of an old tent.

"Mary," said the guy. Orion. Her heart overflowed with love. She'd had sex with him. His big lips were too lazy to close over his teeth. Tufts of blond hair sprouted along his jaw. "Mary," he said. "*Mary!*"

She opened her eyes, and there stood Ann, filled with light. Rays streamed from her heart and her forehead. She didn't appear pitiful. She shimmered and rippled.

"What happened to you?" said Mary. "Your aura is so—"

The doctor peered at her from behind Ann. "She's fatigued."

A glass of water appeared, with iridescent droplets quivering along the edge. Mary knew she would eventually die, and all her friends would also die, as her mother and father had died, and new lives would wash over them like waves over footprints in the sand. But she didn't often feel it so close. She didn't want to get old. She didn't want to die. She sucked up liquid, shivering as it flooded her mouth and, thankfully, revived her. "I'll be fine," she said. "Just give me a minute."

MEMORIAL DAY WEEKEND MARKED the start of high season in Sullivan County. Joel didn't know whether that was good or bad, whether they'd be more closely surveilled by the police or less. But the plants couldn't wait. He left work early, picked up Ann, and parked the truck a quarter of a mile down the road from Sunrise. They hiked through the fields to the house. Precautionary measures. Joel was nervous. He carried a bag, heavy with pruning shears, clippers, and grafting knives. Ann held several drop cloths.

When they got to Sunrise, Peter was ensconced in an armchair in the living room, typing crazily on Mary's laptop. Mary nestled in the sofa, as if today was any other day.

"Where's America?" said Joel. "I thought we'd get right to work."

"What do you think of this opening sentence?" said Peter. "The visual journey of a surrogate mother, the real mother of the mother-to-be, has never before—No. Has never been so intimately portrayed *before*."

"I love the repetition of the word mother!" cried Mary. "What do you think, Ann? It's the book proposal."

"Did you take your blood-pressure meds?" said Ann.

"The trichomes are withering," said Joel. "But I'm the only one who gives a shit."

"America's on her way," said Mary. "She said, and I quote, 'Must be the season of the witch.' I cracked the code. Don't you get it? The witch. She's coming from Sage's."

Joel hated waiting around but America was the expert. They couldn't do it without her. He grabbed a pair of hedge shears from the bag. Snapping them open and shut created a satisfying *shh-click* sound that alleviated his annoyance.

"...takes an unflinching look at a fifty-year-old woman carrying quadruplets," Peter read from his book proposal.

"'Unflinching' implies ugly," said Mary. "How about 'sympathetic' and 'mature' instead of fifty? What do you think, Ann?"

"I think I hear the babies." Ann snuggled with Mary. Joel had been profoundly relieved when the doctor stopped the injections. But now he felt excluded. Ann and Mary didn't need him anymore.

A light tapping came from the back window like the brush of twigs. Joel saw her shadow first, then the window slid up. America hoisted a yellow stretch-panted leg over the sill and climbed through.

"Sneaky!" Mary clapped.

"I drove Sage's car." America yanked at her pants, which had cinched around her butt. "Bad scene. I'm scared of the pigs."

"Where's Carlos?" said Joel. "We need all the help we can get."

"Can you believe that scumbag was hiding a wife and son behind my back? Had the nerve to tell me a man *needs* a wife! I said to him—"

Joel had heard enough. He would not place himself at the mercy of idiots. Gathering up drop cloths and shears, he marched upstairs to the green room. Oscillating fans created a running rustle through the emerald leaves. With less water, the plants had flourished. Their aroma was intoxicating. He shut his eyes to allow a peaceful photosynthesis to permeate his body.

But instead of peace, what permeated his body was the memory of a dream from the night before. He'd been searching for his father, wandering through muddy fields. The Woodstock concert was over and people filed out in every direction. He fought the human tide, kicking through trash and pushing through people. *Joel! Over here!* Mary beckoned from an empty stage. Then he was on top of her, floating as she swelled beneath him like a waterbed. They were naked. She moved her belly out of the way so he could push his penis up inside her. *Oh, good,* she said. *You're such a good boy.*

"Earth to Slocombe," America intruded. "We gotta turn the fans off, don't want leaves blowing around. Wow, you're sweating!"

He wiped his forehead with the back of his hand. Sweat poured down his spine. Peter came in behind America. "We've appeased her Majesty for now. She's not coming up."

Ann carried the rest of the tools. "She *knows* THC can seep through her skin and endanger the fetuses. And she's crazy if she thinks I'll let her climb stairs."

"I say make her work," said America. "THC seeping through skin, come on! The fussbudget generation."

"I don't know how she ever thought she loved you." Ann threw down the bag with a loud clank, and stalked out.

"Where are you going?" said Joel. "You saved this crop."

"Someone's transit moon is opposing her natal sun," said America. She grabbed a plant and hacked it off at the base. With clippers, she removed the lower leaves, piling them on a drop cloth, then the secondary leaves, creating a second pile. Lastly, she gathered trim leaves surrounding the buds. "Keep the quality levels separate. These are the sweet ones. This here's the shake, for the hashish. Preliminary manicure for now. Cloned cuttings in the corner. We'll deal with them later."

Joel tried to match America's speed, snapping stems, separating leaves. But his palms grew sticky with resin. His shear blades gummed together.

Peter worked slowly, milking each plant. "My mum always gardened," he said. "I wish I'd paid more mind."

"I bet she never had a garden like this!" America guffawed. "We gotta expand this operation, go for a three-harvest year. Those clones are fucking gorgeous. Joel, you could bust through the wall into the guest room and double the space, double our output."

"I'm not working with you again," said Joel.

"You'll reconsider when you see the cash-ius clay," said America. "How about we put the next grow in your house? It's just a shell, right? Never be livable. We'll fit it with lights and no one will know."

"Of course, it'll be livable," said Joel. "The insulation's installed. The drywall's coming next week. As soon as the vapor barrier's up, the sheetrock's ready." He knew he shouldn't let her get to him, but she'd hit his weak spot. He couldn't sleep from worry that he would never finish the house. Maybe the dream about Mary was really a dream about the house. The thought reassured him.

Ann returned. She took a pair of shears from the bucket. "Mary's drinking her protein drink," she said. Then she stepped across the row to kiss Joel on the mouth. Love was an ache in his chest, his gut, his groin.

"Okay, lovebirds," said America. "We can start taking some cuttings downstairs."

"How long before we smoke?" said Peter.

"Not for smoking, dude. It's for selling." Joel gathered one of the canvas spreads by the corners to fold it. Ann took the other end.

Night had fallen by the time they transferred all the leaves to the basement, where they hung the cuttings by the crooks of their stems. The plants would have to dry before curing. Joel had wiped his palms so many times on his thighs that his pants were sticky too. He washed his hands at the kitchen sink, taking his time, scrubbing his palms, noting three broken fingernails, which irritated him. His fingerpicking would be clumsy now. The strings wouldn't snap the way he liked.

"I'm fucking exhausted," said America. She threw a fistful of buds on a plate and put it in the microwave. "Let's sample our wares. Job well done."

"We shouldn't smoke it," said Joel. "We have to keep our heads clear, maximize profit." But the sweet scent of marijuana filled the kitchen and he salivated.

"We take our perks where we can," said America.

"Oh, that smells good," said Mary. She waddled in and settled herself at the kitchen table.

Peter peeked through the glass door as the plate rotated inside the microwave. "Clever. This is quite exciting."

The oven beeped. America packed a wooden pipe. "Who wants?"

Peter sucked in a hit and coughed harshly.

"Don't be greedy, boy toy! You inhaled too much." America nudged Joel with the pipe. "Take some. Don't be a twerp."

"Where did Ann go?" said Joel.

"In here!" Music seeped from the living room. Ann had put on Gillian Welch.

"Oh, what the hell." Joel inhaled a slow burn down his throat. His mind softened.

"I feel like a prop," said Mary. "It's like you're all actors in a play and I'm onstage doing nothing."

"That's how I feel," said Joel.

"You're doing more than the rest of us put together, making babies!" Peter giggled, a high-pitched alien sound.

"What a strange laugh," said Mary. "I never heard you laugh like that before."

Ann appeared in the doorway. "You can't be in here, Mary. Second hand smoke. Come on guys, help me get her to the living room."

Joel and Peter positioned themselves on either side of Mary. It took two men to hoist her up. She was heavy and huge and solid, not the waterbed of Joel's dream.

"Sorry. I need a pulley." Mary swayed between them.

America followed with the pipe. "Anyone want?"

"Don't bring that in here," said Ann. She was wrapping a blood-pressure cuff around Mary's arm. Their symbiosis forbade intrusion.

Joel stayed with Peter and America, at the entrance to the living room. The pipe went around too quickly. He took too many drags.

"How's that mother of yours, Joel?" asked Mary from the sofa. In the lamplight her smile was a coy curling of plump lips, identical to her smile in Joel's dream. It was like she stepped inside his mind and mangled it. "Why do you look so terrified?" she said. "His eyes look yellow, don't they Ann?"

The inside of his mouth was like a lint-filled sock. "Mom's the same as she ever was," he mumbled.

"My mum is dead," said Peter, sniffling.

"Aw, come here, you," said Mary.

"Your blood pressure is high," said Ann. "Too much exertion."

"Her blood pressure's not the only thing high!" America burst into peals of laughter. When she refilled the bowl and the pipe began its round again, Joel took it. He had nowhere to go but deeper in. His mind blobbed and dripped.

Peter and America blathered about atoms and molecules and time going backwards. Mary and Ann were singing along with "Orphan Girl". They looked like one entity. Joel couldn't recall which one he was supposed to be close to. He yearned to be with

Rick and Tim, jamming, just to have his guitar, to feel the body of the instrument hanging off his shoulder. Then he remembered: he couldn't pick out melodies because his fingernails were broken. He stared at his hands, twisting his wedding ring. He would be trapped in this stoned mind for hours. "I know the difference between dreams and reality," he said aloud.

"Sure you fucking do!" America and Peter laughed like hyenas.

Then Ann extricated herself from Mary and came toward him. She was familiar, beautiful. She held out her hand. "Come on. We have to trek through the field to the truck, remember?"

"I love you," he said.

WHILE THE COFFEE BREWED and Joel slept, Ann stared out the window at the bare dirt surrounding the big house, which was shrouded in the early-morning mist. Work was underway again. The ductwork components sat on the porch, huge metal flanges and valves. With subcontractors hired and parts delivered, full installation of the duct system would be complete by the weekend. Days slid by, overlapping one another, but Ann was suspended in a state of unremitting tension.

No chromosomal damage had been evident through the amniocentesis. But Ann's euphoria had been quelled by news of Baby Three, or "Opal," who had revealed herself as a girl at their last visit to the neonatologist. Opal was smaller than the other two and didn't move as often or as vigorously, which was "worrisome" according to Dr. Stark, and more like nerve-wracking for Ann. The trees behind the house undulated in a breeze, their luxuriant leaves fluttering. Sun slanted through the mist. Then she saw a baby in a yellow sunsuit crawling through the silt near the porch steps. She lurched forward, her breath in her throat.

"Should I pour the coffee?" said Joel.

She jumped. "Do you see the baby?" She pointed out the window at nothing. The baby had vanished. She brought her hand to her chest. "I'm hallucinating babies."

"It's probably normal, given the circumstances." He handed her the mug. "Good day for working. The guys should be here in an hour."

"But the babies seem so real." She stared into his eyes, seeking stability. Instead, she saw herself expand, igniting like a solar flare, consuming him in flames.

"Sometimes, you seem to have a light in you." He touched her cheek. "I used to think you were easy to read but you're a mystery. That sounds like a line, except it's true."

"You're right," she said. "It sounds like a line." When she embraced him, she felt normal again, and the babies, too, seemed normal under the circumstances. No conflagrations here.

They turned in their hug as if a dance moved through them, until he faced the window and she looked past the counter at McKenna lying on the living room rug. "How far along are we?" he whispered. "I always forget."

"Their skeletons are hardening," she said. "They can frown and make faces. It's like Mary is a skin between them and me and I want to go right through her. Then I feel guilty."

"I'm scared of Mary." Joel's voice tickled her ear. "Sometimes I dream about her. It's not pretty. I'm scared that you and Mary will cut me out. I'm sorry I hurt you. I'm so sorry."

She touched his neck, his shoulder blades, the curve of his lower back. The hurt seemed distant. The babies loomed close. "I'm not hurt anymore," she whispered.

ANN CARRIED HER GUITAR into Sunrise. She'd led a sing-a-long at Little Footsteps, a raucous, joyful hootenanny.

"Annapurna, is that you?" Mary lay on the sofa, in a fetal position, varicose veins running like a topographical map of rivers along her swollen calves. The windows were wide open. Warm breezes whirled through. In the corner, a fan rattled.

"You're alone." Ann perched on the edge of the sofa. "Why aren't you wearing your support socks?"

"I hate them," said Mary. "His Lordship's upstairs, working on our book. I'm glad you're here. Why don't you play something?"

Ann angled her guitar toward Mary. The babies were developed enough to recognize sound. Suggesting the bass line with her thumb, she picked chord fragments with her fingers and began to serenade her children with lyrics that materialized as she sang: *Three beating hearts. She feeds you breath. We wait for your coming, the coming of light.*

Peter bopped into the living room, wearing only gym shorts. He carried a thick envelope under his arm. His hand-rolled cigarette bobbed between his lips. His chest hair quivered the fan's breeze. "Sounds brill," he said. "When's your next gig?"

Joel must have told him the Free Radicals had been offered a spot at The Barge. But Ann associated the place with losing Baby Four. She'd been reluctant to commit, and the guys refused to do the gig without her. She was holding them back. "Not sure," she said.

"Has Mary told you *our* news? I got an agent for the book!" Peter bristled with self-satisfaction, seating himself cross-legged on the floor, placing his envelope in front of him. "The magic word was triplets. Jade, Garnet, and Opal. The woman went bonkers. She's shopping my work to several publishers already. Della predicts huge success."

For a moment, panic roared in Ann's skull, and she was transported to her childhood. Strange how her competence and hard-earned mastery and all the ensuing years could vanish instantly, as if they had never existed. *You're going to live with Gran for a while,* Mary had said. *Mommy needs a break. It's either Gran or the foster home. Those are your choices.*

Ann told herself she was no longer a child. She had the gift. Hadn't Sage declared it? "You can't do a book," she said. "I won't let you."

"Look at the photos before you judge." Peter slid several 8x10 prints out from the envelope and arranged them on the floor. Ann noticed deep yellow nicotine stains inside the top knuckles of his index fingers, which signaled a sort of depravity, and revolted her.

Mary leaned forward. "Some of these are new to me."

Reluctantly, Ann put her guitar down. The photographs were black and white. One of Mary with her skirt flipped up to receive the progesterone injection was an evocative study of curves and shadows. Another of Mary at her jewelry bench in a silk robe, her expression self-consciously mysterious, captured her at her most beautiful, childlike, and conspiratorial. Ann had to admit, the prints showed Mary at her best, highlighting her softness, her guileless joy, her plump flesh and fertility. Then she came across a picture of herself on the porch, kneeling at Mary's feet, her hands like claws on Mary's belly, as if she wanted to puncture the flesh and rip out the babies. And a picture of Joel crazed around the eyes, gripping a syringe like a weapon. "Mary looks like a goddess," she said. "But you make Joel and me look mean and weird."

"I capture a moment," said Peter. "I strip away the nonessential to allow the true spirit through. I do not make anyone look like anything."

Ann despised the sneaky way Peter had wormed into Mary's heart. "Don't you see what's happening, Mom?" she said. "He's using you!"

"As if *you* aren't using her!" said Peter.

"We're all using each other," said Mary. "It's called love."

"That's not love," said Ann.

"You defend yourself against the lens. Just surrender." Peter aimed a small digital camera at Ann.

She imagined a shield dropping down from the air to protect her. Amazingly Peter cupped the camera in his hands with a perplexed look, as if he'd forgotten why it was there. "This book will bring money, attention," he said. "You can use it as a platform to help other women like yourself."

"I don't need a platform," said Ann. "Do a book on your own life."

"This *is* his life," said Mary. "We're all living through this."

"Sorry to have bummed you out with good news." Peter sat back, extending his legs, and taking up more space than he had a right to. "Can't you see this is my gift to your mother? Don't you care what *she* wants?"

"Ann never liked my partners, no matter who, no matter when," said Mary, with the weary, authoritative voice Ann recalled from childhood. "It's not about you, Peter. She's bound to be oppositional."

"Just because you're carrying my babies doesn't mean you can exploit them!" Ann picked up the print of herself and tore it in half. Vibrant energy ran through her limbs.

"What are you doing?" Peter crawled across the rug, gathering photographs.

But Ann ripped up another one as Peter tried to snatch it.

"Admit it," said Mary. "You have a grudge against *anyone* who loves me. Remember how you'd go through Orion's pockets early in the morning? And later, with Lars, the same thing. You snuck into my bedroom and stole cash from the pockets of my lovers."

Even now, remembering, Ann experienced the racing pulse and trembling emancipation she'd experienced as she quietly extracted coins and bills from the pockets of jeans crumpled on the floor. That Ann—the survivor, the taker—had disappeared somewhere in the years of growing up.

One morning at the commune, Lars caught her in the act. She darted to the kitchen but he dragged her out from under the table. Everyone awoke. Mary screamed from the bedroom doorway. And in the chaos, Ann slipped from his grasp to dash barefoot down the dirt path, quicker than Lars, whose feet were soft. She waited, hidden behind a boulder until Mary came and got her. She hadn't thought about it in years. "I was a child," she said. "I don't want to fight. I know you were just looking out for me, getting money for us." Mary slumped back into the sofa. The glow in her cheeks revealed itself as acne. "I just want you and Peter to be friends."

"I don't need friends," said Ann.

"Luckily, I already sent a batch to my agent so I don't have to make new prints." Peter carefully slid the remaining 8x10s back into his envelope. "You're like a suit of armor, Ann, darling. It's not healthy."

When the phone rang, they all started. Mary answered. The threatening male voice on the other end projected outward, audible to Ann and Peter. The pot drying in the basement came immediately to her mind, with an image of police bursting in, some sting operation that would render their puny personal disagreements to nothing.

"I don't know who you are," said Mary. "But the police are tapping this phone. There's no one here by that name."

"That's good," Peter whispered. "Now hang it up and unplug it."

"What's going on?" said Ann. "Is this about the green room?"

"Don't worry, we're changing the number to an unlisted one," said Mary. "Plus, I'm getting internet service. You and Joel should do it, too, for Slocombe Builders. Sage has a website, so does Della."

"What are you involved in?" asked Ann.

"Honey, it's nothing to do with the green room," said Mary. "Peter has some corporate work. Remember I told you about the hedge fund? Everything's under control."

What Ann heard was: *Take care of me because I can't take care of myself. I'll throw my life away on worthless people who will use me as they see fit.* Ann had never been able to fix Mary's life but she was unable to stop trying.

THE WIND CHIMES TINKLED *now, now, now,* but true contentment eluded Mary. Firmly into her sixth month, the babies punching and kicking like tantrums inside her, she had nothing to do but loll about in her maternity support sling. She sat with her feet up on the porch rail, feeling undeserving of the beauty of the grass, which was golden in the sunlight.

It was not just her physical discomfort, or the midsummer festival canceled because of Sage's illness. Nor was it the threatening calls for Peter, as they'd finally ceased when Mary had her phone number changed. *I owe the blokes some dosh,* Peter had finally admitted. *My worry is that they tracked me here at all.* The true source of Mary's anxiety was immediate. As she shifted her position in the wicker chair, she saw a police car appear over the crest of the hill as it did several times a week. Pasting on a fake smile, she waved as they glided past, but her stomach roiled in panic. "Peter!" she called.

"Ready?" The screen door slammed behind him. It never failed to alarm her.

"The police drove by again. Help me up." With one hand on the banister, the other arm slung around Peter, and her heart palpitating madly, Mary lumbered down the porch steps. Short drives were permitted, though they felt transgressive. Mary could barely squeeze herself into the passenger seat of her car anymore. They passed America's deserted, padlocked cottage. Then the road spread itself before them. The wildflowers and fields alongside were warm, green, and luscious, and gave Mary the sensation of being in a movie. She rolled down the windows, elated by the wind.

When they arrived at the bank, Peter parked in the handicapped slot. He helped her out of the car and held her securely with his arm around her upper back and his hand tucked under her armpit. Mary had to deposit a check from Della for $3,800, Mary's share of the *lifeforce* profits, with a percentage and vendor fees deducted by Della. She had sent the pendants out for casting—set them on low-grade silver chains purchased cheap from Indonesia, and shipped them to Texas, South Carolina, Missouri, and southern Illinois, where they sold immediately. Even as Mary protested—*They're not handcrafted if they're made from molds*—she couldn't argue with the money. Her trademark, *madebymary*™, was still engraved on the back of the cabochons, but the work no longer belonged to her. Only the money did. Peter had received $1,500 for his corporate photography, and they deposited both checks into the joint account they had opened for immigration purposes. In the quiet solidity of the bank, the police car seemed very far away, and Mary's panic an overreaction.

As for Peter's debts, Mary had hatched a solution. Peter carried the documents they had brought along to notarize: the deed to Sunrise with his name added and an application for a second mortgage that Peter had filled out. As Mary waddled to the customer service desk, she sensed the ripple of attention from other customers, the rubbernecking and whispers. She couldn't tell if she looked gorgeous and munificent, or like death warmed over; she'd lost all perspective. The hasty offer of a chair in a cubicle clued her in that it was probably the latter, but she wasn't going to freak out about it.

A fresh-faced young man examined their documents. He explained that she had already taken out a second mortgage on Sunrise, though he didn't call it Sunrise but "your domicile." It was for the in-vitro fertilization process, she recalled now. Because Joel had done the paperwork, she had forgotten. She had also forgotten that she couldn't add Peter to the deed without Ann's signature.

"Mary, darling, what a muddle," said Peter.

"I'm not a capitalist, I'm an artisan," she said, defensively.

"We can offer you a home equity loan," said the bank officer. He slid brochures across the desk and talked of balances, adjustable interest rates and the latest securitized products. She couldn't pay attention. Once numbers were bandied about, a fog rolled through her brain.

Ultimately, the process was simple and immediate. Mary took the loan, which meant a credit line of $25,000 would be available to their joint account within a few weeks. Peter hugged her, nuzzling her neck with his nose. "Anything's possible with you, Mary Moonlight," he whispered.

"Ah, love," she murmured, exhausted. This was more activity than she'd had in weeks. She felt like she was sleepwalking as they made their way back to the car, and she dozed off on the way home, lulled by the car's vibration.

SHE AWOKE ON THE sofa with tingling in her fingers. "Wakey wakey." Peter pushed aside the clutter on the end table to make room for a sandwich and a can of Ensure.

"Thank you. I'm starving." The sweet thickness of the protein drink made her gag. But Mary loved the sandwich; the salty chicken and stickiness of the bread, the crunchy lettuce and ooze of low-fat mayonnaise, all created a delicious constellation in her mouth.

"You're holy," said Peter. "The way you eat a sandwich like nothing else exists in the universe."

Her laptop was on the floor but Mary didn't have to lift a finger. All she had to do was glance at the computer and Peter was so attuned to her desires that he picked it up and placed it in her lap. "You were sound asleep when Ann came 'round," he said. "She didn't want to disturb you. But she didn't believe me when I said you were sleeping. She had to tiptoe in and see for herself."

Her brittle little girl. "I just want her to be happy," said Mary.

"If she's unhappy, it's not because of you," said Peter. "You're too good. Look at your sacrifice."

"It *is* a sacrifice," she said. "But I do it for love." A long cable attached the computer to a phone line and a modem, installed when they'd changed the phone number. Keeping up with technology, when she clicked on "connect," the modem emitted a friendly beep-beep followed by fuzzy white noise. She loved that sound.

Magically, she had received an email from the listserv for surrogates, an online community she'd signed up for. *We welcome all stories, please tell us yours,* said the listserv moderator. Peter took her empty plate out to the kitchen. Mary heard water running. He was washing dishes. Ann claimed he didn't love her, what did she know? *I knew as soon as my daughter was diagnosed, this was something I could give,* she typed, before the unpleasant image of Ann's disapproving frown gave Mary pause. But Mary couldn't base her actions on others' approval. Though Ann wasn't exactly a nonspecific "other." The line of thinking stressed her out.

Peter was on the phone now; she could hear his voice on the kitchen extension. Probably with his agent, whom he called daily for updates. Even Mary, who loved him, would have considered him a nuisance if she were the agent. She closed out of her email to visit her page on Della's website, watching the photographs slowly load. An image of a ring appeared, an experiment from early in her pregnancy when she tried to expand her *lifeforce* series to include rings and bracelets. Silver with a bezel-set rough garnet, it hadn't accomplished the fetus-visual she was aiming for, yet it was elegant on its own terms. *I did that.* She remembered soldering the bezel after making a ledge for the stone to sit on. Her fingers twitched. She could smell the flame.

For a second, fiery energy crackled inside her. Peter and Joel had moved her jeweler's bench downstairs and parked it across the room in front of the bookshelf. Oh, she missed her work. She would do it again!

But the bench was a mess of pliers, hammers, and shears. The bench pin lay on top rather than clamped on the block and her flex-shaft sat on the floor by her chair. On casters, its upholstery torn, the chair was not enticing. She'd have to set up the workspace first, which was far too much activity, against the rules. Her energy dampened as quickly as it had ignited.

Peter came in, carrying spotlights on spindly metal frames. "I just spoke to my agent. She suggested a naked photo. Starkers. A surrogate Demi Moore of the millennium. You don't mind showing the whole monty, do you?" When he turned the spotlights on, they glared at her, emitting an unwelcome heat.

"Come look at my jewelry on Della's website," she said.

"Another bloody rejection from another ignorant publisher. Now she wants me to collaborate with a writer," said Peter, inspecting his camera. "The marketplace is cruel. Rip my soul and hand it to someone else to call their own. Like the Yeats poem about the coat, how does it go? 'The fools caught it, wore it in the world's eyes as though they'd wrought it.'"

Garnet pedaled his feet against her uterus wall. She knew they were his because she'd seen them on the ultrasound. "He's kicking!" Mary cried. "Come feel!"

With a sigh, Peter put his camera down to perch beside her on the sofa. But Garnet stopped. "Yes, I remember shooting those in a box with a light above and the camera lens inserted in a hole to isolate the piece in the light." Peter was peering at the website. "That's how I got those reflections."

"I'll do it again, won't I? This hiatus from my work is only temporary, right?"

"You're a forger of metal and stone. No need to doubt yourself. You're the creative source."

His words were a balm. He touched her face lightly. She let her hand drift to his crotch, wanting to please him. But he brushed it away. "I want you naked, making love to my camera."

"How could I refuse? I was *born* naked." Mary closed out of the website, put the laptop aside and pulled her T-shirt over her head. She had to draw her elastic-waisted skirt up over her paunch before yanking it down and stepping out of it. When she unhooked her maternity sling, she was amazed by her abdominal area—so huge, a mountain with runnels and ridges and crevices. She ran her fingers over the stretch marks. "I *earned* these."

Peter adjusted the height of the lights. "Why don't you go over to the altar, by your statues? Prop your tummy with your left hand and cover your breasts with your right. Like Demi."

"I don't know what you're talking about." Mary pushed herself up. With the lights behind her, she was confronted by her reflection in the window, looking lumpy and old.

Peter laughed. "Don't you know the Leibovitz photograph?"

A painful twinge in her sacrum compelled her to lean. The card table buckled, overturning Demeter. Barbie tumbled to the floor. "Don't laugh at me," she said, suddenly tearful.

He pushed the table back into place. "Right here, a nook for you to stand in. I wasn't laughing at you, Mary, love."

Mary put one hand on her breasts and the other at the base of her belly. "Like this?"

"Michael Thompson's pic of Cindy Crawford pales in comparison. Nice try, chap but no go," said Peter. "Gaze upward, as if you're seeing a vision."

The camera was practically silent. She noticed paint peeling in huge flakes from a spot above the window. How had she not seen this before? She was always looking down. Was that a sign she had become too submissive?

"No, no, no!" said Peter. "Give me beatific, not battleax."

He never used to instruct her. She'd simply always done it right. "That's it," she said. "The battleax is calling it quits."

"Please don't get temperamental." Peter wheeled her bench chair over, blocking her path to the sofa. "I'm sorry, poor choice of words. You're the goddess incarnate."

"Let's just get it over with." Mary sat. She couldn't take a deep breath because the babies blocked her diaphragm.

He handed her the statue of the Virgin. "Can you mimic her expression?"

With the statue in her arms, Mary recalled Annapurna as a child in the grassy meadow behind the main house at the Peace Ranch compound, painstakingly wrapping her doll in a blanket. *I'm her mommy.* She'd kissed the crown of her doll's head. *So nurturing,* said one of the other women. And Mary took credit: *Takes after me.* Her pride caused heat to rise to her cheeks.

"Beautiful. Perfect," said Peter. He kept shooting as he talked. "Our children will treasure these photos of their mum in years to come."

"*Our* children? What a thought."

"Not so farfetched. You're a marvelous mother and I should like to try my hand at fathering. You and me, a family." He finally put the camera down. The light fractured in his dark brown eyes like subtle flames.

Mary would be better at raising a child now, than she had been with Annapurna: no getting crabby if the child whined. No rage or despair when the baby shat its just-changed diaper. No getting stoned to endure the tedium. Oh, to do things *right!* To not be alone! "You're making me cry," she said. "I'm so touched."

"I bet Ann and Joel will beg us to take one." Peter ran his fingers through his hair, a seemingly careless gesture that handsomely tousled his tresses. He hadn't showered and gave off a pleasant manly pungency when he embraced her. Her face was level with his stomach, pressed against him, and she heard his voice above. "They're actually yours. Aren't they?"

"Right now they are," she said, disengaging. "But I intend to let them go." And she got up off the chair without his assistance, weightless, as if lifted by angels who transported her to the sofa and placed her down with grace and dignity.

ANN SAT CROSS-LEGGED ON the floor in Sage's A-frame. She didn't know why Sage had asked her to come. She couldn't have refused. "I've been seeing children who aren't real," she said.

"Don't be frightened. They won't harm you," said Sage. She lay in her reclining chair, wrapped in a blanket and shivering in the summer heat. "The power to see and understand the unknown is something to be grateful for."

The cats lay in various stages of sleep on the floor, under the armchair, on the kitchen counter, and one of them in Sage's lap. Cat hair floated in the shafts of light. "But I don't understand the unknown," said Ann.

"It's awkward when you begin to listen to your deeper self. It doesn't make sense to your logical mind," said Sage. "I've seen a child in my dreams. This bodes well for you."

She brought the reclining chair into an upright position and seemed to glide slowly off, floating to her glass-doored cabinet, from which she gathered three thick green cords that she draped over her arms like snakes. "These are consecrated to the goddess, Hathor. They can symbolically weave the three elements—your will, the universe, the guardians—into correspondence with your wish." She dropped them into Ann's lap.

They were heavy. Ann touched them. "Is this why you asked me here?"

"I've been diagnosed with stage two cervical cancer," said Sage, standing above her in a long white tunic, looking like a ghost. "The cancer has spread to my uterus. I'm going to the city for tests and treatment options and I'm going to ask you to feed the cats while I'm gone."

"Does Mary know?" Ann was stunned. The sounds of the solemn, incessant grooming of the cats amplified. "Of course, I'll take care of them," she said.

"Come to the sauna," said Sage. "It's been heating for hours."

Ann followed her outside. The air was still and heavy. No birdsong broke the silence. The branches of the fir trees were decorated with shiny metal circles that reflected ellipses of light. Wildflowers proliferated below, dwarf cornel and chokecherry, shinleaf and periwinkle. Sage walked slowly along the path, without moving her arms.

Joel had built the sauna to face south toward Sage's garden, which was overgrown with mint, basil, and lavender, spreading perfume. Around the garden, a path of loose stones seemed to vibrate. Ann took off her clothes and hung them on the rack outside the sauna. Her usual self-consciousness at being naked was gone. In the face of cancer, what was the point?

The odor of cedar was intense in the close, hot space. She began to sweat profusely as soon as she entered. She observed the stove, the rocks, and the wooden handle on the door, which wouldn't burn the flesh like metal. All the details invoked Joel, a true craftsman.

"Spirits of the south, of heat and purifying fire, we call you here to cleanse and purify the sauna that cleanses and purifies us." Sage pointed to a bucket. "Just sprinkle some water."

The bucket sat on top of the stove with a wooden ladle, which Joel had also made. Ann splashed the sauna bench and steam rose with a sizzle. Her eyes teared. Sage called the spirits of the west to lead them like water to life's flow. She called on the north to ground them to the earth. She invoked the east to breathe sweet air upon them. "Spirits and guardians, empower this sweat lodge to clear the space for Ann and Joel to raise their children."

Ann ached with the need to speak. "And heal Sage, and give her back her power." Her voice sounded full and resonant, like someone else's, someone powerful.

"Very good." Sage took her hand and the world seemed to bend. "You've been chosen and I'm sorry to say that it comes with responsibility."

Ann sensed a subterranean shift from mundane to divine, from dead to alive. Her thighs adhered to the wooden slats. Her flesh was melting. "What am I supposed to do?"

"You'll know when the time comes. Trust your instinct. Braid the cords when you get home. Bring the universe into alignment."

WATER: 2000

RAIN CAME AT THE end of June. It fell for several consecutive days, drenching the stacks of lumber stored at Slocombe Builders, a loss that Joel tried to ignore. His greater worry was the marijuana plants drying in Mary's basement, where water had been seeping up through the ground cracks to form huge puddles on the floor. Mary called him at work to say that Peter had salvaged the "lettuce leaves," which, if their phones were being monitored, wasn't very subtle. "It's cool," said Mary. "He brought them upstairs. But I don't know where 'our country' is? Get it? I tried calling the sisterhood. They haven't seen her."

"We'll have to figure it out, but right now I have a call coming in on the other line," Joel lied. "I gotta go."

The rain caused flooding in the crawlspace of the new house, creating an indefinite delay to moving in. Frustrations abounded. Joel had reached his credit limit, so he signed up for a new card and shifted his debt, raising his interest rate. Meanwhile, he'd been neglecting Betty and kept expecting her to call with a demand or an accusation. Not hearing from her made him nervous.

After work, he drove to the bungalow with a dozen red roses, a peace offering. Winifred's car sat in the driveway, which surprised him. He assumed she came earlier in the day. As soon as he opened the door, he heard voices from Seinfeld blaring on television. The house stank of cigarettes. He put the roses in a vase with water and carried it into the living room where Betty and Winifred sat, wreathed in smoke, ashtrays overflowing.

"I was fast in high school," Betty was saying. "I ran track for those two years, even with the shin splints, I had the two-mile race. But I quit when I fell in love. To be honest, I never liked all the sweating."

They were playing cards, drinking Frangelico liqueur from tiny fluted glasses, not even looking at the loud TV, but shouting over it. They didn't acknowledge him. Joel stood there with his vase full of roses, feeling like an unseen child.

"You remember, I was the highest jumper on the cheerleading squad," said Winifred. "Being small, I was always the top of the pyramid. V for victory."

"I never made the squad," said Betty. "I should have. I had a lot of personality, everyone said so."

"Because you couldn't do a split," said Winifred. "Splits were mandatory."

"Hey, Ma," Joel put the roses on top of the television, and turned the set off.

"Put it back on!" said Betty. "You can't just come in and mess with my things."

"Look at that," said Winifred. "He brought you flowers."

"They're red. I like the pink ones."

"They didn't have pink ones," said Joel. "I thought you quit smoking."

"I did. And I'll quit again!" Betty laughed.

Winifred tittered.

"I pay you to look after her," said Joel. "Not enable her."

"I've been meaning to talk to you about that," said Winifred. "Betty and I are friends. Taking money for a friend, it's not right. I give it back to her anyway. And she has something to tell you, don't you, dear?"

"Yes, I do," said Betty. "I don't appreciate being used. How do you think it feels when Ann comes to church with me for a few weeks, and then decides to never show her face again? She thinks she's so smart with all those babies coming out of her mother."

"She doesn't believe in it. She gave it an honest effort, but she couldn't lie. I'll take you to mass like I used to." Joel couldn't say that Ann had seen visions of children, that she had braided three green cords together in a ritual. How incredible it felt to watch her; she conveyed a strength that heartened him. *She'll know what to do,* he found himself thinking when he feared for the future.

"I don't want someone to drop me off. I want you to sit with me in the pew."

"It's what she wants," said Winifred. "Not so much."

He couldn't be shoved back into his childhood, the designated little man of the house, obedient to a fault. "I'll go to church for the occasional Sunday but it won't be a regular thing."

Winifred downed her glass. "I'll see you tomorrow, dear. We'll finish the game then. You be good to your mother," she said sternly to Joel. "Make sure she takes her antibiotics with food."

With Winifred gone, Betty seemed to shrink. She pulled a needlepoint from her sewing basket. "I suppose your mother-in-law has to stay in bed now, a fifty-year-old woman having a litter, it's unseemly. Knowing her, she's probably proud of herself."

"But you *don't* know her, do you?" said Joel. He sat on the sofa, inhaling shallowly against the cloying scent of Betty's lotion and acrid cigarette smoke. His friends didn't judge him. Tim had heartened Joel the other day, saying you want a kid, you do what you got to do. I didn't know what love was until my kids came along. It's not about me anymore, it's larger than that.

"Do you know what people are saying about her?" Betty focused on the needlepoint, pushing her tongue between her teeth in concentration, an unconscious habit so familiar to Joel he could have been doing it himself. "They say she's shacking up with a gigolo, and there's drugs involved. You don't want to get mixed up in this, my son."

For the first time since the rain started, the delay on the house brought relief. With her living next door, he'd never be free of gossip. "Is he still a gigolo if they're married?" he said. "The house is delayed again. Maybe six weeks before you can move in."

"I don't want to live in your house." Betty jabbed her needle. "I'm staying here, thank you very much."

"We already talked about it," he said. Damned either way. She'd find fault. He could imagine the accusation if he hadn't included her in the house plans. "The property taxes on this place are too high. You need revenue, not a money pit. And I'm building the apartment so we can visit each other across the porch. You'll have privacy. Believe me. Winifred can come anytime she wants. And your grandchildren will be right there."

"This is my home. There's room here for visiting grand-children," said Betty. She flattened the needlepoint on her lap, presenting the design for Joel's benefit. She had only just started it: an illustration of a beribboned lamb and, in stylized script, *Baby Sleeping*. "We'll have to change that to plural. I'll mark it when I reach it," she said.

Just when Joel got fed up, she'd go and do something unexpectedly sweet. "It's pretty scary, three of them," he said.

"You'll rise to the occasion," said Betty. "You always do. But you don't need me to tell you that."

"You're wrong, Ma, I do need it." Joel pulled the needle-point across to his own lap. He realized his tongue was poking out between his teeth, just like hers did. Maybe the children would have the habit too. It made him happy to imagine that.

ANN TOUCHED MARY'S HOT, taut belly. She loved to imagine the babies curled up inside, the lumps as someone's elbow or knee. Outside, rain lashed the ground. Water slid down the windows, leaking through the walls and pooling on the sills. A tarp covered in drying marijuana leaves lay partially unrolled near Mary's jewelry bench, safe from the wet. But the damp air threatened mildew. Peter and Joel had gone to the basement to gather the rest. The dried bud was ready for curing.

"I'm suffering from *pre*-partum depression," said Mary. "I'm a damp slug. I have some kind of fungus on my boobs. My nipples itch like a motherflapper. So does my tummy. Dr. Stark, Mr. Cold-heart, told me not to scratch. That's all he could do for me."

"But the babies are healthy, thanks to you," said Ann. Two days ago, Dr. Stark had shone a bright light on Mary's uterus and Ann watched on the ultrasound monitor as Jade shielded her eyes. Her baby was seeing! Reacting! Alleluia!

"I called the number in the Bronx where America was staying when she and Carlos were together," Mary said now. "And a woman went off on me, swearing about America, the fat whore. It was awful."

"After this crop, you never have talk to America again," said Ann.

"Why does Sage have cancer?" Mary pouted. "What is there to believe in if my spiritual teacher can get cancer?"

"She asked us to visualize her whole and well, Mom."

"You're being relentless! I'm telling you how I feel. Don't squash my emotions." Mary pushed Ann's hand away.

"I'm trying to help," said Ann.

"I'm sure they could use your help in the basement," said Mary. "Please, just go."

Ann was reluctant to leave. But Mary shut her eyes as if willing her away, a trick she'd used when Ann was a child. "Why are you still here?" she said.

"Okay, I'm leaving," said Ann.

Before she'd descended halfway down the uneven basement stairs, she was hit with the potent stench of hemp. A large puddle at the foot of the stairs reflected one bare light bulb and a forest of upside-down branches hanging off fishing wire. Behind the drone of the dehumidifier came a steady drip-drip-drip from somewhere. Peter and Joel were shadows, moving among the branches. "Be a love and take the other end, would you?" Peter flung an old bedsheet across to Ann. Because the floor was damp, they held it like a hammock while Joel unhooked plants off the wire and let them drop. They didn't have to talk. When the sheet sagged with buds, they rolled it up and carried it to the living room, repeating the process a few times until they had moved all the dried plants and leaves upstairs.

Mary, meanwhile, had put a CD on the stereo. Nestled on the sofa with her laptop, she bobbed her head and sang along with Bob Marley to "Easy Skanking." "I'm feeling better," she said. "I got an email from my surrogate group, and I'm skanking it slow."

Mary's moods were contagious. Ann's spirits lifted as she fetched a cardboard box full of canning jars from the kitchen. But if Mary sank into moroseness again, Ann would sink again, too. She knew this.

Joel plugged the dehumidifier in, and they all sat on the living room floor with the marijuana spread out on sheets to begin filling the jars. "Don't cram the buds in," said Mary. "They need to breathe. I've seen America do it. Just fill them about two-thirds."

Clipping buds off brittle stems and dropping them into jars, Ann was reminded of the good days at the commune, when she and the other children shucked corn in the afternoon. She got into a rhythm. Peter's scissors flashed. Joel sang along with "Soul Shake Down Party." They filled the space with harmony that Ann recognized as unusual and worth preserving.

When "No Woman No Cry" came on, everyone sang. The heft and stubble of the buds satisfied Ann's sense of touch, promising *everything's gonna be all right*. She belted out the words. The reggae beat thrummed, absorbing the knocking sound until it escalated into an unmistakable banging on the door. They all stopped.

"Do you think it's police?" said Peter.

"Red-handed," murmured Joel.

"They can't come in without a warrant," said Mary.

"Stop it. All of you." Ann jumped up to answer the door. Her heart slammed so forcefully against her ribs, her whole body reverberated. She thought she heard a child crying. *They won't harm you,* Sage had said. She opened the door a crack.

"I knew you were here. I saw your car down the road. Why'd you park so far away?" Cassidy stood on the porch. Rain dripped off the end of her nose. She had shaved her head. Water clung to patches of bristly growth along her skull. She clutched Sky, who was crying. Not an imaginary child.

Ann was still vibrating with residual terror. "I thought you were in India."

"Why is my house padlocked? Where's my mother?" Cassidy pulled the bawling Sky inside. Her green eyes were luminous.

"Who's that?" Mary called from the sofa.

"Mary?" Cassidy was already peeling her clothes off, discarding them in a waterlogged pile at the trickster's feet. She undressed Sky next; ignoring the towel Ann thrust at her, and headed, naked, into the living room, pulling the sobbing toddler along.

"Hey, don't drip on the buds." Joel pulled the sheet away. "Sit down and help us out. There's a lot of marijuana here."

"Clothing optional, I guess," said Peter.

"Mom, do you have anything for her to wear?" Ann followed.

"I want to be naked, too." Mary pulled off her T-shirt and raised her arms, enormous and stretch-marked, an affront to Ann's modesty. She banged her pimpled chest like Tarzan. "Oh yeah! Tits are powerful! Hey Peter, get a picture!"

"Calm down," said Ann. "You're supposed to take it easy."

"I'm afraid I am a photographer," said Peter. "Which means I must capture you both."

"No photos of the bud," said Joel.

"And why is there a photographer?" Cassidy wrapped the towel around herself. Sky grabbed her legs, still weeping.

"That's my husband," Mary crowed.

"I thought you were a lesbian," said Cassidy.

"Love transcends gender," said Mary.

"I thought you loved my mother," Cassidy said as Peter disappeared through the doorway to fetch his camera.

"You just left without saying goodbye," said Ann. "Where's Cody?"

"You are so fucking big and beautiful!" Cassidy leaned against Mary.

Ann caught Joel's eye in a brief alliance. "It's like we don't exist," he shrugged.

"Sky must be hungry," said Ann, escaping to the kitchen.

"We're both fucking starving," Cassidy called after her.

Ann had made a large batch of gazpacho that she'd left for Mary in the refrigerator. Pouring out a bowl for Cassidy, she pondered why Mary's nakedness so offended her. She wanted to be over it. She grabbed a box of animal crackers from the cabinet, and carried the food into the living room.

"Where's Cody?" she asked again.

"Mary was telling me about Jade, Garnet and Opal. I mean, holy shit!" Cassidy refused a spoon, and slurped directly from the soup bowl. "If anyone can handle three of 'em, it's you," she said with a disarming smile. "Cody's with his dad. He didn't want to go to India."

"Look at the sores I got from eating all those nightshades." Mary opened her mouth wide, as if for a dentist. Ann willed her annoyance away. Begone.

"Maybe you can contribute since America pulled a no-show," Joel raised his voice. "The question is: How long do we keep the buds in the jars? What's optimal?"

"If they're Sativa Delta-9s, probably three weeks before they're good to sell." Cassidy let the towel drop at her feet, her colorful mandala tattoo sagging around her navel, her legs flopping open. "Mom would know. Where is she anyway? Why's the house padlocked?"

"I don't remember what kind of seeds they are," said Mary.

Ann sat on the floor and bent herself around Sky, a plump dimple of a girl who snatched the cracker she offered. How she loved those soft cheeks! But Sky pushed her away and hurtled toward Cassidy with the undeveloped, speedy run of a toddler.

Peter reappeared, a camera bag slung over his shoulder and a lit cigarette hanging between his lips.

"Got an extra cigarette?" said Cassidy.

"I don't have extras," said Peter. "But I can roll one for you."

Let Mary be naked. Let Cassidy sit with her legs open. Let them smoke their cigarettes. Ann envisioned three cords, which she had knotted, nine knots in each, murmuring words of a spontaneous spell. *Knot of one, spell's begun, knot of two, may it come true, knot of three, my will shall be.*

She picked up Sky and twirled her around. Sky laughed with her whole body.

"There are hundreds of buds here," said Joel. "I could use some help."

"Once you got 'em in the jars, you should open the lids every day for a few hours or you'll get mold," said Cassidy. "You don't want mold."

Peter moved crablike around Cassidy, snapping photographs. "Lovely. Now bend forward a little."

"Ahem," said Mary. "Don't forget about taking pictures of your muse."

"Is Mom still with Carlos?" said Cassidy. "I hate that guy."

Ann carried Sky out to the vestibule. She put her down to scoop up the wet clothes, and took her soft little hand to descend the basement stairs. One step, pause, next step, pause: everything took a thousand times longer with young children. But if Sky wanted to throw her own T-shirt into the dryer, pick it out and throw it back, fine. Sky pressed the button to turn the dryer on, then opened the door to stop it. Press button, open door, repeat. Sky's delight grew with each repetition until she was gasping with laughter.

By the time Ann trekked upstairs, Mary had put her shirt back on. Cassidy was wearing Mary's *Got Soy?* T-shirt with the picture of a cow, which fit her like a dress; and she was sitting on the floor with Peter and Joel, busily filling canning jars while Bob Marley sang "Lick Samba Lick Samba."

"Come here, you!" Mary spread her arms out for Sky. "You, too, my baby, Annapurna."

"I should help." Ann deposited Sky with Mary. She squeezed in next to Joel on the floor and began filling jars with marijuana buds.

"I learned reflexology in India," said Cassidy. "The bottoms of your feet correspond to your vital organs. I'll massage yours later, Mary. It'll be excellent for your babies."

"Our babies," said Ann.

"We can cut that padlock at the house for you," said Joel. "Whenever you want to go home."

"Stay here. That place looks desolate," said Peter. "We've plenty of room."

"Open invitation," said Mary. "As long as you want, Cass."

Joel picked up several full jars. "I guess we'll store these in the kitchen for the duration."

Ann followed him. In the kitchen, they opened cabinets, removing plates, blender, glasses, and Mary's failed alfalfa sprout farm in a tray full of rotting water. They moved in tandem. Joel talked quietly. "I'm trying to be cool but the vibe is annoying."

Ann stood on the stepladder as he handed her jars. "Just let it go," she said.

"You know, once, in high school, I kissed Cassidy," said Joel. "We were drunk at a party in the field near the graveyard in Jeffersonville, remember the keg parties?"

"I never went to them, but sure," said Ann. "Do I want to hear this?"

"It's funny but I forgot about it until we were sitting there and "Stir It Up" came on, and Peter was taking Cassidy's picture and you were down in the basement, and it took me back. She used to carry a flask of tequila in her purse and she invited me to drink with her that night. I don't think she remembers. It was a sloppy kiss, accidental. And you know what happened?"

"No?" said Ann. "Should I?"

Joel gazed out the kitchen window as if hypnotized by something. "She said, 'Ew!' And pushed me away."

Ann laughed. She stepped down and looked out the window with him. Behind the rain, beyond the hills, the sky had brightened. "What did you do then?"

"I forgot about it until now," he said. "I'm not a masochist."

"I love you," she said.

THE SUN FINALLY EMERGED after weeks of rain. The green fields were luscious and shiny. The birds sang with vociferous cheer as if they were celebrating. Ann and Joel, too, were celebrating as they carried their bed across the expanse of squelchy mud from the trailer to the new house. The reek of paint and polyurethane intoxicated. Ann strained under the burden of the mattress and giggled when she almost lost her grip as they struggled to get it upstairs.

Fully assembled, the double bed, which had occupied the entire space of their room in the trailer, shrank to a miniature of itself in the vastness of the master bedroom. "We're like Lilliputians playing in the giants' house." Ann's voice echoed.

"When the kids come, the place won't feel big enough," said Joel. "That's what my clients say."

The adjoining bathroom with its shiny blue tiles and oversized tub intimidated Ann. It was too fancy. She had to run downstairs and outside, across the dirt to the vinyl-walled trailer toilet with its plasticky smell and tiny sweating window. She was more comfortable there.

Joel sat on the steps of the spacious new porch, strumming his guitar. He sang with an exaggerated country twang. *My girl's no high-falutin' ass-kisser. Only takes a dump in a tiny trailer pisser.* "How long did it take you to compose that?" Ann fetched her guitar. Steel strings shuddered beneath her fingertips. Music flowed between them, a bubbling creative pool generated just by noodling around. Time disappeared, one riff leading to another. But inevitably, the sky darkened, fireflies flickered along the horizon, and they reached a stopping point.

Ann summoned the nerve to go upstairs and draw a bath. The luxury of sinking her body into a deep tub filled with almost-scalding water suffused her with a sense of plenitude. "I could get used to this," she said. Her voice rang out against the tiled walls. Soon, she would have her babies in the tub. It was big enough for Joel, too. Family bath. The prospect was so delicious, so enticing and palpable, it frightened her. She remembered bathing at Gran's house, being scolded for failing to clean the ring around the tub. *Too scared to be happy,* lyrics floated through her mind.

"Annie!" Joel called from below. "I have a surprise for you!"

She wrapped herself in a towel and walked downstairs to the bare space of the living room, sliding her feet along the shining floorboards, and found Joel on hands and knees, studying plans he'd spread out on the floor. Slabs of unfinished wood were piled near him.

On the windowsill stood the bronze shoes and other objects, encircled now by three knotted cords. Ann stopped, pressed her palms together and bowed to the altar. *May our children be born healthy and thriving, I call on Ishtar, Brighid, and Lilith, mother of all living.* She held her bow until she imagined a release that signified she'd been heard.

"I'm building a cradle big enough for three." Joel pointed to the drawing. "It's important to create the basket first. See? The suspension system works with dowel pins. It's designed to swing on this stand. Three infants can lie in a row."

McKenna reclined beside the stacked boards with a satisfied groan, laying his chin on his white tufted paw. All around them, the house breathed and settled. So what if mildew was growing in the basement and their debt was unsustainable? Sitting on the floor, watching Joel mark his drawing with notes, muttering about lathing and cutting, Ann saw three babies fast asleep. Hovering above them was the spirit of the fourth. She saw herself and Joel occupied by the lovely chaos of children and she believed for an evening that the future might be trusted.

TRAPPED IN A HARD, wooden chair in her kitchen, naked and covered in thick, clammy plaster from breasts to pubis, Mary questioned her sanity. The itch was tortuous under the hardening plaster and she could do nothing. A pregnancy belly cast had seemed like such a good idea in the abstract. Ann had warned her against it. But Mary had assumed Ann's negation stemmed from pregnancy envy.

Not only was Mary suffering from a chronic, low-grade fever giving her extreme fluctuations from hot to cold, but worse, according to Dr. Stark, her gestational diabetes might persist for life. A scary prospect that would be even scarier if she wasn't distracted by the premature contractions she had to monitor constantly.

She could hear Cassidy and Peter chatting about the day and about Sky, who was, apparently, playing with a puzzle on the living room floor. "I can't take it anymore!" she screamed. Her groin spasmed, snapping like a rubber band. Now, it seemed only the plaster held her in place.

Cassidy strolled in wearing too-short cut-offs and a halter top flaunting tanned, peeling skin. She carried Peter's camera, a fancy

German make that she peered down into rather than through a lens, shoving the apparatus in Mary's face. "You have ten minutes left," she said. "Try smiling. You look fantastic."

"Where's Peter?"

"He'll be right down. He's fetching yoga mats so we can pop into a class after the darkroom."

"Didn't you go to the darkroom yesterday?" Daily, Peter and Cassidy drove the WCCNWMN to the community-college darkroom where they stayed for hours while Mary sat by herself, stewing in envy and checking her blood sugar. A thump in the living room preceded a shriek from Sky.

"Go," said Mary. "She might be hurt."

Cassidy moved without urgency. Never mind that Sky could have been pinned beneath a fallen bookcase. Mary was alone again, caught in an upsetting, judgmental state of mind. If she couldn't dissolve this negativity, it would kill her.

Things got quiet. Sky's screams dwindled to sobs. "Peter!" Mary called, wary not to exert too much abdominal pressure.

But Cassidy returned to the kitchen with the child in her arms. "He's doing email or something," she said. "Peter!"

He came on Cassidy's call, and took Sky, as if they were a couple, accustomed to sharing childcare. "I think my writer's gone a bit purple," he said.

Cassidy tapped Mary's plaster. The stubble on her scalp had grown into soft fuzzy ringlets. "Five more minutes wouldn't hurt," she said.

"She's been free-associating with her magnetic poetry," said Peter, shifting the baby to read his printout. "What do you think of this? *Baby bumps hard hurt on bad goddess smells.* Maybe if she takes out 'hurt' and 'bad' she's onto something?"

"I didn't know you'd settled on a writer." Mary lifted her arms as Cassidy pried beneath the cast with her fingertips. The tickling diverted her attention from the itch.

"My worthy rep decided," said Peter. "Stop it right now, rug rat."

Sky had been sticking her finger in his ear.

"I think you should take out 'smells' too," said Cassidy. She loosened the cast and in a quick movement, lifted it off, a huge round tub.

Air cooled Mary's damp abdomen but further ignited the dreadful itch. It had a name: Fifth disease. Scraping her nails across her skin only intensified it. Her belly was covered with welts. "I don't see the point," she said. "I like poems but that's not a poem."

"It's jazz improv with words," said Peter.

"I think there's a place for it," said Cassidy.

Were they fucking? Mary couldn't ask. The question contradicted her open spirit. His answer would prove nothing. She couldn't handle an affirmative and she'd disbelieve a denial. She was trapped.

"This is between me and Peter," she said. "It's our book."

"Why are you so shirty?" said Peter, finally looking at Mary with warm, curious eyes.

"Maybe it's time for Cassidy to move back home," said Mary.

"But we're all good chums, Mary," said Peter. "And Cassidy helps lots with chores and all."

"Don't make me leave. I love it here!" said Cassidy, lifting Sky from Peter.

"Do you realize I'm fifty years old and carrying three fetuses? I'm a prisoner in my own house while you walk around freely, getting stoned as if life was one big party! Do you have any idea what I'm going through?"

"Stop scratching or you'll draw blood," said Peter.

"Please don't get upset." Cassidy put Sky on the floor. "We want to help."

"What do you mean 'we'? What's going on between you?"

"Mary darling, have you gone daft?" Peter walked behind Mary's chair to massage her shoulders. He kneaded her muscles, placating her. "You're just tired."

She dropped her chin to her chest and sighed, "I'm sorry. I'm on edge."

"We'll paint the cast together tomorrow, okay?" Cassidy took Mary's hand, massaging her palm, her fingers, the mound of Venus at the base of her thumb. "I'm a good artist. Ask Ann. She's seen my drawings."

Mary relented. The massage soothed the itching. When she wiggled her shoulders, Peter pressed his thumbs more deeply into the knots at the base of her neck. "You guys love me, right?" she said.

"As if you have to ask," said Peter.

"WELCOME." ANN STEPPED BACK to let Mary in. She felt shy as she surveyed the new house through Mary's eyes, the pristine walls, the glossy wooden floorboards, and the great height of the cathedral roof that diminished them all.

Huge and breathless, Mary shuffled through the vestibule, without looking at anything. "It's okay for a McMansion," she said. "I sure do like the central air."

With a low whistle, Peter came in behind Mary. "Nice digs. Very posh."

Peter had shaved his head. His shiny skull was bumpy, dented above his left temple. His handsome features, the sharp nose, deep-set eyes, and cleft chin no longer seemed precisely chiseled but soft in the context of his hairless visage. He resembled the man in the moon.

"It's smaller than Sunrise, hardly a McMansion," said Joel. He was kneeling with the hand broom, sweeping sawdust from the half-built cradle into a dustpan. "Whoa, dude, did Cassidy shave your head? The look isn't for everyone."

"Bubblehead." Mary dropped with a grunt onto the sofa. "At least the bleeding cuts have healed."

"Piss off," said Peter. He circled the cradle. "What's that? A cage?"

It was a first, Ann noted. She'd never heard Mary speak derisively to Peter. "Are you guys in a fight?" she asked.

"Mary's shagged," said Peter. "She's a bit cranky and a bit paranoid."

"It looks like a cradle to me." Mary spread her legs and fanned her skirt. "You're so good with your hands, Joel."

Ann noticed Joel's blush as he answered, "You're right. It's a cradle for three." He swung the basket in the half-frame.

He's proud, she thought.

"Of course, I'm right," said Mary. "Can I have my purse, please, husband?"

"The papers are in the side pocket." Peter placed the macramé bag in Mary's lap.

Mary rummaged through it, withdrew a saltshaker and sprinkled salt all over the sofa cushion and herself, though she probably meant to fling it about the room. "May the goddess bless this dwelling."

The forlornness of the gesture worried Ann. She brushed off salt before she sat. "Is everything okay, Mom?"

"Couldn't be better," said Mary. "Don't I have the pregnant glow?"

Ann observed Mary's lipstick-clotted lips, her inexpertly applied rouge, and the bits of black mascara that speckled the pouches under her eyes. Pity pierced her heart. "Why are you wearing makeup?"

"*I* think I look good and that's what counts," said Mary. "I've had *amazing* energy all day."

"How much weight can it bear?" Peter jostled the cradle. "Seems a bit flimsy."

"He's just jealous he can't build anything so nice," said Mary.

"Give it a rest, mum," said Peter.

"Don't call me mum," said Mary. "I'm not your mother."

"The spindles keep it lightweight. I know what I'm doing." Joel briskly rubbed the curves of the cradle headboard with sanding paper.

Ann felt supremely fortunate, compared to Mary. Ann loved a good man. Their devotion would strengthen as they became parents. The two of them would intertwine like two trees growing toward the light. But Mary would always be searching for something that didn't exist, demanding what couldn't be given.

"You always had the need to build things, is that right?" said Peter.

"It's something I'm good at," said Joel. "I guess you could say it's a need. Come on, I'll show you upstairs."

McKenna trotted after them. As soon as they left the room, Mary whispered, "Can I ask you something? In your opinion, are Peter and Cassidy...you know?" And she gestured, poking her left index finger through the circle of her thumb and right finger.

Ann had witnessed Mary's lovers come and go. She had seen the way Mary collapsed into others until they had to leave. "Don't waste your heart on him," she said.

"You know me. I'm a free spirit, not the jealous type," said Mary. "But they do yoga together *naked*. I love the nude body in all its pure wisdom but I—"

"It's your house," Ann interrupted. "Tell them to put clothes on."

"It's not just that." With thumb and forefinger Mary mimed toking a joint. "I mean, *all* day. They get so stoned, they don't make sense. He calls me 'mum' like I'm his mother. You heard him. She does, too." She wiped her eyes, with a catch in her voice. "It's insulting. Help me get her out!"

"You invited her," said Ann. "You can uninvite her."

"You know what she told me?" said Mary. "That *you* asked *her* to be the surrogate. After we were already doing our injections together, you went and asked *her*! She didn't know what to say to you because of how much she sympathized with me!"

The guilt was visceral, a convulsion in Ann's solar plexus. A heartless ingrate, she stared at her flawless polyurethaned floor, no longer superior or fortunate. "I'm sorry."

"So, it's true? Oh goddess. I feel so betrayed."

"It was impulsive," said Ann. "I'm sorry. I'll help you get her out, okay? Whatever you need."

McKenna came in, sniffing at Ann's hands. She unfolded her clenched fingers to pet him and he dropped a string of drool on her foot.

Peter and Joel came downstairs shortly afterward. "Lovely bathroom up there," said Peter. "And the nursery is quite beautiful as well. You're a couple of DIY whizzes."

"Is everything okay?" said Joel.

"They were just having a natter," said Peter. "Did you mention the papers yet, Mary love? They're in your purse."

"We were discussing the babies," said Mary. "Not nattering. Discussing. What is the nursery like? I wish I could see it."

"I'm putting up wallpaper. A butterfly pattern," said Ann. She wanted a perfect fairytale room where the children would be safe to dream and grow. "It's taking me a long time. I don't want to tempt fate."

"If Sage said you have the gift, then why worry about fate? The universe is on your side," said Mary.

"Sage could be wrong," said Ann.

"You have to trust," said Mary.

"It's good to be skeptical," said Ann.

"The babies will sleep in our room at first, not the nursery," said Joel. "Unless they're in the neonatal ICU."

Mary gasped. "They will not spend time in the ICU."

"Sorry," said Joel. "But Dr. Stark mentioned it the last—"

"If they're born now, they'll survive a lot better than if they were born last week," said Ann. "We could look at that aspect. You made it to your third trimester."

"Stop being morbid. Let's change the subject." Mary groped through her bag and pulled out a stapled sheaf of papers. "I need your signature on these documents, if you don't mind."

"Joint ownership is key. They seek that on the interview." Peter crouched down on the floor near Mary. He looked uncomfortable. But there were no chairs for him to sit on. All their furniture, which had crowded the trailer, had been consumed by the immense space of the new house.

Ann examined the documents, which appeared to be the deed to Sunrise. A clanging erupted in her skull.

"It's nothing," said Mary. "I put Peter's name on the Sunrise deed. We just need your signature."

"What do you mean, 'It's nothing'?" said Ann. "My money paid for Sunrise. It belongs to you and me."

"Gran's money," said Mary. "Come on, you have a brand-new McMansion. Don't be selfish."

"The money was for my surgery. Just because I didn't have the surgery doesn't mean you can hand the house to him." Ann's foot jiggled of its own accord. How could she finally stop being drawn into these archaic grievances? If she had this clairvoyant gift that Sage had spoken of, how come this betrayal shocked her? Was it a betrayal? Or was she being selfish? Mary always twisted Ann's reality.

"I wish Cassidy *had* said yes," said Mary. "Then I wouldn't be sitting here like some deformed monster carrying a fucking litter."

"I think the timing's bad," said Joel. "This is one of those huge emotional deals that needs thought and preparation, and we have too many huge emotional deals happening. There's no reason to rush it."

"We have our interview coming up," said Peter.

"It's the principle." Ann's lips were quivering, which made her voice tremble, which made her sound weaker than she wanted to sound. "Mom, you're doing this great thing for me, and I'm thankful. Beyond thankful. But you can't just assume it absolves you of not loving me."

Out of nowhere, she was overcome with harsh, dry sobs. She clamped her palm over her mouth, but the noise came from deep in her chest. She couldn't stop.

"Maybe you guys should leave," said Joel.

But no one moved. Ann couldn't stop crying. She sounded like an animal. She was ashamed.

"I've *always* loved you," Mary gasped. "Always. Always."

Ann heard the words but they couldn't penetrate her unloved armor. She was aware of Mary's warmth, the patchouli orange smell of her. She heard Peter and Joel leave, their whispers vanishing with the click of the front door. But Mary stayed. Ann could hear the wheeze of Mary's breath and the snuffle of Mary's tears.

TO KEEP HER PROMISE, Ann offered to help Cassidy clean out America's cottage and make it livable. The house had been shut for months, and stank of stale smoke and mildew. Ann and Cassidy didn't have to talk. They just set to work. Magazines were piled inside the front door—*High Times, Utne Reader, Cannabis Culture, Relix,* and various pornography rags. Ann tied them into bundles for disposing. She kept an eye on Sky, who sat at the foot of the stairs, tearing out pages. Cassidy stalked through the beaded curtains from the living room to the hallway to the kitchen, dragging out trash. Together they dumped ashtrays, old Castaneda and Terrence McKenna paperbacks, junky knickknacks featuring penises and toilets, and ash-strewn clothing no one would ever wear again. They worked quickly. Ann enjoyed the ruthlessness. In no time, they were ready to tackle upstairs.

Sky climbed one step at a time, clinging to the banister. Cassidy followed, then Ann. As soon as they came to America's room, which was empty but for an unmade double bed and a broken dresser, Sky darted beneath the bed.

"No you don't." Cassidy dragged her out by the ankle, though Sky shrieked and kicked.

"What's in her hand?" Ann pried something from the toddler's fist. It took a moment before she recognized a used condom. She hurled it away. "Gross!"

The bedsprings creaked as Cassidy sat. She bowed her head, her slender neck curved like the stem of a flower. Sky was still screaming. Ann felt sorry for them both.

She sat on the bed next to Cassidy. "At least she used protection," she said.

Cassidy burst out laughing. She wiped her eyes, and her laughter turned to sobs. "Yeah, protection. She's nothing but nasty. Doesn't love anyone, not even herself. She never loved *me*, that's for sure."

"She probably loves you as much as she can, even if it doesn't feel like enough," said Ann. "We're in the same boat. Our mothers are flawed."

"Your mother loves *you*. Look what she's doing for you."

With a whimper, Sky hugged Cassidy's legs.

"Your *daughter* loves you," said Ann. Sky's love seemed pure and undiluted compared to anything Ann felt for Mary. She reflected how much simpler it was to be angry at Mary than to love Mary. It was easier to think that Mary had injured her than to think Mary had done her best, and to acknowledge that carrying Ann's child was an act of love that transcended any wrong Mary might have committed. That line of thinking led to obligation somehow.

"It's not love, it's a survival tactic." Cassidy pulled Sky onto her lap, and kissed the top of her head.

Ann was engulfed by a familiar longing. As a reflex, she changed the subject. "Do you remember kissing Joel at a keg party in high school?" she asked.

"Oh please. You're going to act jealous of me, too?" Cassidy rested her chin on Sky's head. "When I was in India, I was the bottom of the barrel. All the people at the sangha could practically levitate with their feet behind their heads, their yoga was so amazing. But I never got a one-on-one meeting with the guru. One day, he just told me to go home because I wasn't getting it. It was devastating. I thought Jai was my soulmate. But as soon as we got to Mysore he was all about bramacharya and serving the guru, and I respected that. Really. Until I found out he was fucking someone else."

Ann surmised that bramacharya related to celibacy. "Mary thinks Peter's her soulmate," she said. "Let her have him. Leave him alone."

"What kind of person do you think I am?" said Cassidy. "You have no idea how he gloms onto me. You're the one who went behind her back. Shit, that could have been me, trapped on the sofa like a beached frigging whale."

"I could ask you the same question about what kind of person you think *I* am," said Ann. "For the record, I *never* had designs on your kids. Maybe we can stop assuming the worst in each other."

Cassidy began to sob again. "I'm so lost! I think I went to India because I've been searching for my father. I found nothing. It's like he's a phantom. My mom's no help. She doesn't give a shit. Don't you ever wish you knew your father?"

"If Mary had better taste in men, I might want to know my father," said Ann. "You're not lost. You're here. You're home."

"When did you get so wise? Peter's not bad. He makes her feel young." Cassidy stood, causing Sky to slide to the floor. She strode from the room. "I need to get stoned."

Ann took Sky's hand and followed Cassidy, who'd gone into the bathroom to crouch at the sink cabinet, rifling through a box of menstrual pads. Feverishly Cassidy tore them apart, littering the floor with ragged bits of fluff until she extracted a hidden baggie of marijuana. "Bingo!"

"The cops are watching this house." Ann tried to snatch the baggie but Cassidy dodged and ran downstairs. Ann grabbed Sky, who began to shriek and pummel. She carried Sky downstairs in a firm hug—a preschool technique to calm hysterical children. The reek of marijuana came from the kitchen. Cassidy laughed exultantly. "Bring my little girl in here."

"Not while you're smoking pot." Ann tightened her grip on the child, feeling the taut energy of Sky's little body. She knew she sounded prissy. *Uptight,* Mary called her. *Born square.* But Ann was sick of feeling bad about herself. "You have no idea how much I envy you," she said. "And no idea how lucky you are, to have your kids. So, take responsibility. Act like a mother."

"Shit, that's harsh." Cassidy sucked in another hit. "I guess I should appreciate straight talk from a friend."

Ann lowered Sky to the floor. "I'm here because Mary guilted me out. If we were friends, you would have kept my request to yourself. If we were friends, you would have told me what happened to Cody."

"That's enough. Don't talk to me about Cody. He *bit* Jai. I couldn't take him to India. Sky's young enough to stay in a room with all the other kids. She doesn't cause trouble. But Cody, well, you can imagine." Cassidy threw the pipe down. "I'm not feeling anything. This is bullshit pot."

Sky had found a dishtowel on the floor near the sink. She draped it over her head. "Where Sky?" she said.

Ann swept the towel off. "There she is!"

"I've been fighting some custody shit with Cody's dad," said Cassidy. "First he says I'm an unfit mother. Now he says he doesn't want Cody. You know what my mother says? Chickens come home to roost. That's how much she loves me. What am I supposed to do? I have no money. No car. Nothing."

"Where exactly is he?" Ann sat and pulled Sky onto her lap, letting Sky lean back with her head toward the floor. A memory arrived like a shaft of light, when Ann was held in Mary's lap, falling back just like this, with the wide expanse of Mary's skirt and the movement of Mary's thighs beneath. Being in physical contact with her earthy, unpredictable mother had made Ann so radiantly happy, she couldn't contain her joy and had to shriek and kick to release it.

Dust motes spun into jewels, diffused in the sunlight hitting the smudged glass of the kitchen windows. *You have the gift,* Sage had said. *You must use it.* Maybe the gift was something obvious, like recalling moments of lost happiness, or seeing the beauty in everything, or knowing exactly what to do. "If Cody's father doesn't want him, we need to go get him," she said.

"That's impossible. He's living up near the Finger Lakes. I don't even know the exact address."

"A few hours' drive? That's nothing. Where's her car seat? Let's go."

"What's gotten into you?" said Cassidy. "We have to let him know we're coming."

"We'll call him on the way," said Ann. She remembered spotting a car seat in the living room, torn and dusty, but it would do.

THE ROAD UNWOUND BEFORE them. Warm air blew through the windows. Cassidy fell asleep, slumped against the passenger door, just like Mary would have done. Sky nodded off, too. Ann slipped into a meditative state: awake, breathing, driving.

About halfway to Aurora, she pulled into a service station and shook Cassidy awake. She filled the tank while Cassidy strolled to the convenience store to call Cody's father, stretching her arms overhead, lifting her cut-off T-shirt to reveal the tattoo of the threefold goddess across her back, mother in the center, flanked by maiden and crone. Cassidy attracted glances and did a little dance, obviously reveling. Style over substance, thought Ann.

Drivers pulled in, gassed up and left. People entered and exited the store, their shadows long. Ann saw a little girl skip alongside her mother toward a nearby car, not an imaginary child, yet she seemed unreal, far away. Cars whooshed past on the highway, heightening Ann's sense of unreality and disconnection, forcing her to question her meddling. Cassidy was so careless, Cody might be better off where he was.

Perhaps Ann wouldn't be as good at love and nurturing as she'd always assumed. She might intrude on her children, control and limit them. What if, once they were birthed, she failed at raising them? Easy to call Cassidy a lousy mother when she herself was untested.

"Cwacka." Sky offered Ann a chewed-up piece of soggy cracker, pulling Ann into the present.

"Thank you. So generous." She gave Sky a new cracker. As she listened to Sky's simultaneous humming and chewing, Ann imagined three small children presenting their globby crackers: how fun that would be. She would never be alone, and always be needed.

"Bad scene." Cassidy opened the passenger door. "That man is a moron and a shithead. He said Cody's not his son and now he's going to sue me to get his child support back."

"Mommy!" cried Sky.

"What are we waiting for?" said Cassidy. "Let's get my boy back."

Ann took the second exit after Cayuga Lake and drove past a health food store, a check-cashing place and a thrift shop, past well-kept houses with brilliant flower gardens and rainbow flags. They proceeded through the town proper and up a hill with a hairpin curve, then down a narrow one-lane road. "Go slow," said Cassidy.

Just after a thicket, a small white house came into view. Ann pulled over. A little boy sat alone on the porch steps, his hair in an old-fashioned crew cut.

Cassidy ran from the car. "Sweetheart? Mom's here!"

Ann walked around to the passenger side to lift Sky out. She carried Sky to the porch, where Cody sat, chewing on his upper arm. They should have thought to bring him a toy.

"Honey, it's Mommy."

But Cody wouldn't look at Cassidy.

A man with hair as short as Cody's swung the door open and stepped out onto the porch. He thrust an envelope at Ann. "Here's the proof. Now get off my property."

The door slammed as the man disappeared into the house. Ann thought she was lucky never to have known her father, if her father had been a man like that. In the envelope, a single sheet of paper displayed the results of a lab test. Blood type, chromosomes, plus and minus numbers. The comprehensible section was contained in a paragraph stating that no blood relationship existed between Cody and the man. Was that the measure of connection, after all the days and nights this man had spent with him? If Ann had not been holding Sky, she would have screamed.

They walked back to the car. Ann placed Sky in the car seat in back. Cassidy slid in beside Sky, and Cody sat rigid as a doll next to her.

"We missed you," said Ann. His eyes flickered.

Alone in the front seat, Ann drove like a chauffeur. She peered frequently at Cody in the rearview mirror. His face was squeezed shut against the world. The babbling joyful boy was gone. Cassidy put her arm around him and he pushed her away.

"Fine," she said. "You let me know when."

Ann remembered being reclaimed as a child. She recalled the crucifix on the wall in Gran's living room in Oshkosh, and the palm fronds tucked around it. *The people laid palms down for Jesus when he entered Jerusalem,* Gran had said, *Next year, we replace them with new ones.* She courted continuity.

Ann had lived with Gran for a year, and she'd had the chance to replace the old palms with new ones. She adopted Gran's schedule. She wore a uniform to school, and she enjoyed the orderliness.

One day, Mary showed up, a painfully familiar stranger. Mary sat in the living room, getting scolded by Gran. Ann hid. She was afraid. Then she heard Mary cry, *But I'm her mother!* And that cry ripped her open. Ann had hurled herself at Mary then, knocking over the tea and cookies Gran had set up on a tray, provoking a reprimand from Gran. But Mary had never cared about spilled tea or stained upholstery. She squeezed the breath out of Ann, *Oh, you're so big,* and Ann wrapped her legs around Mary's torso and they twirled away together, into magic only Mary could offer.

She watched Cody eye his own mother suspiciously. He was younger than Ann had been when she'd gone to live with Gran, and she imagined the inchoate riot of his emotions, how overpowering they must be for him. She wasn't surprised several miles later when Cody erupted in a paroxysm of choking sobs, thrashing and kicking the seat. "Holy shit," said Cassidy. "What's up with you?"

"He's feeling you," said Ann. The light was golden along the horizon, looking less like a sunset than the luminous promise of morning.

MARY WATCHED PETER UNSCREW lids. She had no strength in her hands and couldn't have twisted them open herself—swollen tissue pressing against nerves, according to Dr. Stark. She plucked a moonstone from the small dish of stones on her end table, and held it against her cheek as she watched Peter overturn jars of weed onto the scale on the living room floor. The scale was old-fashioned, with two plates stabilized by a shank, resting on a beam.

The aroma of cinnamon and nutmeg wafted from loaves of zucchini bread cooling on the kitchen counter. Peter had baked the bread at Mary's request, in honor of Lughnasadh, the Feast of Bread, or August Eve, adding walnuts because Mary needed extra protein, though the Moosewood cookbook didn't call for them.

Normally, everyone in the Eleusinian Circle would have gathered for a ritual marking the time of waiting between the waning of the year and the reaping of the harvest. But with Sage sick, America disappeared, and Mary confined, there was only a small gathering at the sisterhood, too far away for Mary to attend.

"That's another pound." Peter dumped a batch of buds from the scale pan into a plastic trash bag and carried it to the sofa. It should have been a joy to have Peter all to herself again, but Mary was irritated by his sloppiness. He dropped bits of leaf everywhere, working too quickly. She felt paranoid, remembering how she'd been busted in the yurt with a few seeds all those years ago, her daughter taken away.

"Are you sure we shouldn't wait for Joel?" she asked.

"I'm aware that Joel's supposed to be the expert but we don't need to consult him on everything," said Peter. "Shall I bring you a slice of bread? It's probably cooled sufficiently."

"I'd love that. I'm going insane. I'm a prisoner." Mary gathered the garbage bag he'd filled with pot. She tucked the excess plastic around itself and taped the edges. Her fingers were fat but she managed to make the package neat enough. She cut a section from a roll of fiberfill foam, slid in a few incense sticks and swaddled the bag, creating a bundle that she secured with packing tape. Sliding the bundle into a pink cotton pillowcase, she was cheered. Pink perked her up. She asked, "Is it marijuana, or is it a lovely throw pillow? You tell me."

Peter took the bolster off her lap, replacing it with a slab of bread smeared with honey. Then he lay on the floor with his head on the faux pillow. "Not the comfiest, but it looks genius."

His hair was growing in. He resembled anew the handsome young man who'd declared her a shining diamond, rather than the skin-head betrayer who'd shadowed Cassidy. Mary had him back. Cassidy spent all her time with her children, as if she'd renewed her mother vows. Mary bit into the bread, a textural heaven: moist and sticky with honey, punctuated with the crunch of walnuts.

The front door rattled. "It's us." Joel called.

Ann came and kissed Mary's cheek. The babies stirred inside, as if they knew Ann was close, and Mary shut her eyes to surrender her body to these beings who kicked and shifted willfully, jolting her bones and tendons.

"Are they dancing in there?" said Ann.

Mary barely felt Ann's palms through the riotous action of the infants. They wrestled for space. Even timid Opal managed to kick Mary's bladder. "They'll all be dancing soon," she said. "Out here in the world."

"Is that pillow what I think it is?" said Joel. "Nice work."

Mary felt the sofa shift and knew Ann had moved away. Blood was pooling in her ankles, she could feel the swelling, and she adjusted her position to bring her feet up. A burning sensation arose behind her breastbone, and she wished she hadn't devoured her bread so quickly.

"It's all in hand," said Peter. "Under control. That's eight pounds so far."

"America's not going to be happy with that yield," said Joel. "Only sixty thousand."

When Mary opened her eyes, she saw Ann sitting on the floor on her heels, reaching for the pillow, her eyes downcast. She looked so sweet and lovely that Mary almost regretted the impending birth. The babies kept Ann close. After they were born, she would drift away. "Doesn't my daughter look beautiful?" she said. "That's a picture for the book. If only you could see yourself right now, honey."

"Great idea. Make sure you get the marijuana in your book, too." Ann's beauty vanished in a fleeting expression of scorn.

"Why do you give me that look?" said Mary. "It's so hurtful."

"It's my face," said Ann. "I'm not giving you a look."

"I was feeling full of love and wonder," said Mary. "But when I expressed it, you mocked me. I felt annihilated."

"This is stressful." said Ann. "I have a long drive ahead. I could go to jail."

"We're small fry," said Mary. "I should come with you! I dare the establishment to arrest a pregnant grandmother!"

"There's no such thing as the establishment," said Ann. "And being pregnant doesn't magically protect you from arrest."

Peter dumped another jar on the scale. "Cass told me we could bank closer to five thousand a pound. She worked for a grower in Oregon. And the plants in the green room are ready to flower so we'll have another yield soon. Shouldn't we change the lighting or something?"

"Yeah, they're ready for twelve-twelve lighting," said Joel. "I'll set the timer."

Ann placed another pillow on the growing stack. "We can't do another grow. It's too risky."

"I'll take over the farm," said Peter. "Mary and I can do it."

"That's the last of 'em," said Joel.

"Let's pack the car," said Ann. "Get this over with."

Everyone talked around Mary as if she was a piece of furniture. "What can I do?" she said. "Someone give me a task."

But Ann had already walked outside.

Mary picked through her dish of stones. Amethyst wasn't right. Moonstone was too emotional. Black onyx was perfect, the stone for protection. "Help me to the porch, please," she said.

Transitions caused the most discomfort. Mary felt like a rucksack full of rocks. Leaning heavily against Joel, since Peter didn't get up to help, she appreciated his solidity. "I'm about to sound like an old lady," she said. "But your mother's lucky to have you as a son."

"Thanks. I'm kind of your son, too, huh?" He helped her into the wicker chair near the porch railing where she could inhale the sweet scent of the juniper bushes. The air was hot and still. The cloudy sky was tinged with yellow, auguring a storm. Mary watched Ann, who stood by the open trunk of her drab, nonde-script Ford, her arms wrapped around herself, turning back and forth like a weathervane.

"You should take one of my portable displays," said Mary. "In case you get stopped you can say you're on the way to the city to sell your jewelry. Della will back you. She won't even need coaching but I'll call her as soon as you leave."

Peter and Joel emerged, each carrying pillows. They were arguing. "No, you can't," said Joel. "This is serious business."

"I must go. I really must," said Peter. "Ann needs a backup."

"Not negotiable," said Joel. "I'll be her backup."

"I'm going alone," said Ann. "We already discussed this. You have a felony. Peter could be deported."

"Cassidy could go," said Peter. "If she wasn't saddled with her psycho son."

"How dare you!" said Ann. "Cody's wounded."

"Peter, please go get my jewelry case?" said Mary.

Peter slammed the door behind him.

"Why is he acting like a spoiled brat?" asked Joel.

"Because he is a spoiled brat," said Ann.

"He just wants to be involved," said Mary. "Come here."

She pressed the onyx into Ann's palm. "Keep it in your pocket. Be careful. Drive just above the speed limit and stay calm."

Ann embraced Mary with a tearful clutch, as if she were leaving forever.

Peter came outside. He tossed the jewelry case in the back seat, then he threw himself into the chair beside Mary. Joel got into his truck. Ann got into the car. It seemed solemn and momentous, watching them drive away.

"You're very trusting of your daughter," said Peter.

Mary said nothing, holding her breath so she could listen to the sound of their engines recede.

ANN TURNED ON THE radio as soon as she hit the Quickway. The enclosed space filled with insistent voices. George Bush had chosen as his running mate the man he had hired to choose his running mate. She drove grimly, barely listening as pundits discussed Cheney's history of heart disease. Wildfires raged in California, Arizona, Colorado, Idaho. England's Queen Mother would turn 100 in a couple of days.

Her mind drifted to the cradle and the baseboard she and Joel had sanded the night before. Afterwards, she had lain awake in bed, rigid with worry and praying to a blue-robed vision of the goddess, a deity who looked like the Virgin Mary statue in the church she'd attended with Gran. *Please don't punish me for looking forward.*

Time passed. Towns passed. Investigators concluded the crash of the Concorde near Paris might have been caused by a fire. Planes had been grounded indefinitely. Ann didn't hear a police siren until the hard, granite reality of New York City loomed into view. Flashing red lights slid across the seat and dashboard as she hit traffic on the inbound lane of the Thruway. Her mouth became a dry cave. Her hands shook, her fingers went limp. She was terrified of losing her grip on the wheel.

Deep breaths, long exhale. Nothing to fear, she imagined Sage saying this. But her mind went woozy. Sage wasn't here. The police were on her tail. She pulled over, clicking on her hazards. She watched through her rearview mirror as an officer approached, and her mind became a rush of nothingness. Her scalp went numb, her face dead. The sharp rap of knuckles against her window detonated through the car.

"Ma'am, is there a reason you were going twenty miles an hour in a fifty-mile zone?"

She tried to answer but a tiny wail trickled from her mouth.

"License and registration, please."

Her arms were like rubber and wouldn't obey. She couldn't move. "Goddess, protect and save me," she whispered.

"Do you have health issues?" he said. "Phobia? Anxiety?"

As she reached for the glove compartment, she felt the onyx in her back pocket. The pressure snapped her back to functionality. "I was driving and suddenly I couldn't breathe," she said.

The policeman took the documents to his car, its lights still flashing behind her. Ann cupped the onyx in her palm. Through the rearview mirror, she saw a baby in a blue onesie lying on its belly on the hood of the police car. It was a sign. She wasn't crazy. *They won't harm you.*

When he returned, handing her the documents, he ducked his head inside to glance at the backseat. "What's in the case?"

"Jewelry. I'm taking it to the city to sell. Want to see?" Ann reached back to unclip the fasteners but she opened it the wrong way, displacing necklaces and earrings. "Silver's one of the seven noble metals. Corresponds to the brain," she jabbered, just like Mary. "That's amethyst. Attunes the healing forces. These are modern talismanic pieces, they're called *lifeforce,* and…" She pulled out a small plastic bag containing silver rings. Her fingers were shaking as she removed a spiral snake ring. She didn't know what she was doing. She thrust it out the window and heard the baby laugh. "Please, a gift."

"Are you trying to bribe a police officer, ma'am?"

"Sorry," she stuttered. "I'm not in my right mind, I—"

"It was a joke," said the policeman. "My mother has the same phobia. She takes a pill before she drives. Here, put it back. I'm giving you a warning. You might want to talk to a doctor."

"Thank you, sir, thank you," Ann gushed, just like Mary would have. She checked the rearview mirror though she knew she wouldn't see the baby. She no longer needed its protection. Gripping the gearshift, she cruised back into traffic. "Under control," she said aloud. "It's under control."

Heavy congestion on the east side cleared up after she passed the United Nations. The streets were full of cyclists, pedestrians and cabs weaving through the lanes, requiring so much concentration she had no time to dwell on phantom infants and close calls. She turned onto Avenue B and parked in front of a hydrant. After turning on her hazards, she jumped out, leaping up the steps three at a time.

Raven opened the door. Dressed in a long black skirt and black T-shirt with a red half-sweater tied around her chest, she followed Ann down to the car. Her dark hair hung like a curtain in her face "You can't park here," she said in her gravelly voice. "You'll have to find a space."

"I thought we could do this quickly." Ann opened the trunk.

"What the heck? Pink pillows?"

"Mary's idea," said Ann.

"That's so Mary!" said Raven. "I haven't talked to her since the handfasting but we've been casting protective spells ever since. Keep the police away! Stay away! These are heavy!" Hugging two pillows, she headed up the steps.

Asphodel appeared on the landing. "Once we unload, you need to come in. We have to talk." Her authority forbade argument. A few more women emerged from the building and came down to the car. It took only two trips to empty the trunk.

Ann didn't have to go any further than the front door. Asphodel slid into the passenger side. "You'll find a spot faster with me here," she said, and began to chant *nam-myoho-renge-kyo,* as Ann circled the block. Lo and behold, within minutes, a pickup truck pulled out from the curb on East 7th Street, and Ann zipped effortlessly in. "The Goddess is with us," sighed Asphodel. "Can you feel her?"

"Sure," said Ann, and she did. She felt buoyant as she followed Asphodel inside, and the burnt-vanilla scent of sweet grass transported her back to when she'd lived here as a teenager, powerless to control her own body. Not a place she'd ever wanted to return to.

"Come, dear." Asphodel beckoned her down the narrow hall to the large airy bedroom Ann had shared with Mary years ago. They'd slept on mattresses on the floor and painted the walls midnight blue with stars on the ceilings, creating an eternal, oppressive night. Her relief at leaving the sisterhood and the city had been akin to happiness. It was weird to return here, larger in spirit, older, wiser. The room was smaller than she remembered and now the walls were painted a monastic white. A king-size bed with an ornate wood frame dominated the space, pink pillows heaped on the bedspread.

Asphodel lifted a black cloth that covered a metal scale on her dresser like a consecrated object. "Twelve pounds, right?"

"I don't know," said Ann. "I'm just the driver."

Raven came in, brandishing a small pocketknife. "How did you get mixed up in this anyway? You were always so straight-laced." She sliced through the tape on the foam fiber and placed the garbage bag of pot on the scale.

"You have a different energy now," said Asphodel, bringing her face close to Ann's. "We could use someone like you here at the sisterhood. Clairvoyant. Responsible."

The oddness of her thick eyebrows, which were joined together at the bridge of her nose, would have caused the former teenage Ann extreme discomfort. Now, she noted the light burning in Asphodel's eyes, and she met it with her own flame. She could feel the heat between them.

"I'm not going to weigh each one," said Raven. "Just a few random pounds. This one's short by a half an ounce. Sloppy."

Asphodel reached under the bed, pulled out a small backpack, and unzipped it, revealing small bundles of cash. "You should know that America took three thousand dollars of this money. She said it was hers. I don't know where she is because she's no longer welcome here at the sisterhood. You should also know that we owe you an installment of fifteen thousand, which we intend to pay within the month." With that, she passed the pack to Ann. It was frayed at the seams.

Unlike drug deals in movies, where crisp bundles of 100-dollar bills were exchanged, these were twenties, haphazardly rubber-banded. Ann felt no need to count it. She couldn't recall how much she was supposed to receive. Fifteen thousand still owed— she retained that number. It sounded like a lot. The entire project seemed badly planned, executed by a bunch of amateurs.

"Raven, could you hand me…" Asphodel gestured toward a shelf on which consecrated objects were stored: the familiar ones, chalice, knife, pentacle, but also a collection of stones and crystals.

Raven handed her a chunky blue stone embedded in rock. "Sodalite," she said. "For Ann."

Ann squeezed the stone so the protrusions bit into her fingers. It was too big to fit in a pocket. "I already have an onyx," she said. "What does this do?"

"Transformation and physical healing," said Asphodel. "We hear you're awakening your power." She kissed Ann's forehead with cool lips. "Don't try to block it. The universe is with you."

"I should go," said Ann. She heard chanting from the hall. The double doors to the living room had been shut when she'd arrived. Now they were open. She saw Sage, lying on her back on the floor surrounded by women who stood over her, each one dangling a crystal over Sage's body. Frankincense smoldered from an iron cauldron, spreading thick aromatic fog through Ann's mind.

The chanting stopped. The women looked frightened. Ann realized that she had just said, "I have been with you since the beginning." She dropped the backpack. Sage's eyes were closed. She looked at peace. The women made room for her. Now they chanted: *Since the beginning.* All of them, along with Ann, began to walk counter-clockwise around Sage's body.

When Ann was younger, she had lain on the same living room floor for healing sessions that promised her a uterus. And she had believed desperately, because she'd desired it so much. When nothing happened, she'd dismissed it all. Now she understood she'd taken everything too literally. They'd been attempting kindness. There had been no failure except her own failure to accept herself. Now, she surrendered to the floor, to the women around her and to the energy of stones, and led a chant of healing: *Thou art she between the worlds, in all worlds blessed be.*

She was imbued with a sense of connection, along with a glimmer of understanding that her mind could generate endless phantoms and fantasies all on its own while reality unfolded independently. True magic resided in the miracle of consciousness, of being born, living, dying.

MARY LAY IN DARKNESS in Dr. Stark's office, breathing shallowly against the pain in her sacrum. Ann touched her lightly on the calf, which irritated Mary like a fly landing. The ultrasound display flickered with the image of three babies, their eyebrows, fingernails, and toenails discernible.

"Just getting measurements," said the technician. "Hold tight."

Jade, the biggest, covered in visible fuzz, was up nine ounces from the previous week. Garnet up seven. The smallest, Opal, was in a vertex position and weighed three pounds, up four ounces from last time.

"We want to get them each to five pounds, if possible," said Dr. Stark. The lights came on, exposing Mary's enormous thighs and arms. She didn't want to see so much of her own skin, all those lurid veins and bruises. Groaning, she rolled over so the doctor could inject her buttocks with steroids to assist in the babies' lung development.

"Avoid being on your feet entirely," said Dr. Stark. "No more car rides, except for doctor visits. Move as little as possible. You can get up to use the toilet."

"Permission to crap," said Mary. "That's what I've come to."

"Whatever you need, just call me or Joel." Ann slung the maternity harness over Mary's shoulders.

Mary couldn't twist to snap the fasteners. She to sit while Ann did it. "This is rehearsal for when I'm old and infirm," she said. "Oh wait, I *am* old and infirm." And she let out a long, resonant belch, which she was entitled to do in her condition. She expected Ann to recoil. But Ann didn't respond, which made the experience less satisfying.

At the payment desk, Mary watched Ann pull out her wallet. "Hope cash is okay," Ann said to the woman, her chuckle as fake as a lounge act.

"Uncool," Mary whispered. Ann dropped the cash, scattering twenties. Since Mary couldn't bend down to help, she rested against the counter, shrugging at the bland face of the receptionist as if this foolishness had nothing to do with her. Then Ann had to count again from the beginning, excruciating to witness, especially when the receptionist had to tally it up once more, four hundred dollars' worth of grubby twenties. The babies, meanwhile, seemed to have fallen asleep inside her.

As they walked out, Mary whispered, "You need to learn to maintain."

"I'm doing my best," said Ann.

"Deposit the money and pay with a check." Mary looped the seatbelt under her arm but didn't latch it because she needed to breathe. She was desperate for her sofa but the drive was an hour.

"Joel said we should deposit little by little, a hundred here, a hundred there. Make only small purchases," said Ann. "I thought the doctor was a safe place to use cash. You being a pregnant grandmother, above suspicion and everything."

"Joel's Mr. Money Launderer now." Mary yawned. With Ann and Joel in charge of the money, she didn't have to think about it, which suited her because she was no longer capable of thinking. She noticed the leaves were turning color. Dazzling yellows and vivid reds made them appear more vibrant and alive in their demise than they had been in their prime. Before she could point out the contradiction, she drifted into sleep.

She awoke with a lurch, and toppled out of the car. Peter tried to catch her. Ann was screaming. "What are you doing? Be careful!"

"I didn't realize she was sleeping." Peter had opened her car door.

"No big deal," said Mary. She had landed on her side, unhurt. But she couldn't bear their effortful grunting as they hoisted her up. "Can you cool it with the sound effects? I don't need to hear the hernias."

"Sorry, love. Come along." Peter yanked her toward the porch.

"Stop pulling her," said Ann."

"Two people I love, fighting over me," said Mary. She dropped gratefully into the sofa, appreciating the musty smell and softness.

"Did you bring our share of the money with you?" said Peter. "Mary needs it."

Ann bustled about, trying to nestle pillows around Mary. "You need to keep your hips elevated, remember what Dr. Stark said?"

"It's not fair," said Peter. "You can't keep it for yourselves."

"Don't be silly," said Mary. "Ann and Joel will safeguard the money. They're like a holding company."

"Ha!" said Ann. "Who sounds like Gran now? You just said, 'Don't be silly'!"

"She doesn't like that pillow under her head. She likes this one." Peter tried to pull Ann's out and insert another.

"Both of you stop it, right now," said Mary. "I'm taking a nap." All she had to do was shut her eyes and she was gone, falling into a field of poppies, letting disagreements and complications carry on without her. If the babies could sleep in their little world, she could damn well sleep out here in hers.

ANN SAT ON THE living room floor, stacking twenty-dollar bills into equal piles of ten while Joel attached rockers to the underside of the cradle.

"Ma's talking about baptizing," said Joel. "I told her we'd rather have a wiccaning."

"I bet she loved that," said Ann. Her fingers were grubby from the money. "I feel sorry for her, for everyone lately, even Peter."

"Maybe you're just feeling fortunate, and that brings sympathy for others," said Joel. The buzz of his power drill prevented further conversation. Ann lost count as she watched him secure the rockers. Then the phone rang. *The babies!* she thought, and ran to the kitchen to answer.

A robotic voice intoned from the receiver, "Destroy the green room. The man with the dog has gone down."

"Who's this?" said Ann. "What man, what dog?"

"Don't be fucking stupid." The electronically-altered voice hung up.

McKenna thumped his tail on the floor as if to say, *I'm the dog.*

Ann felt queasy as she crossed the hall to the living room.

"It rocks!" Joel laughed over the swaying cradle.

"That was weird," said Ann. "A voice ordered me to destroy the green room. They said the man with the dog has gone down."

Joel stilled the cradle. "We better get to Sunrise."

They took his truck. Ann tucked her shaking hands beneath her thighs.

The door to Sunrise was unlocked, as usual. In the living room, Mary lay on the sofa, propped on her side, with a pillow under her hip. Her laptop was open on the floor. She glanced up, unalarmed. "Hey there, I just emailed my support group. Everyone loves my testimonial. Want to hear it? 'As soon as my daughter was diagnosed, years ago, I said to her, we can make a baby together. It hasn't been easy but our faith in the natural energy of the universe, in the flow of the moon and the power of the sun, has led us through.' Do you love it?"

Her obliviousness reassured Ann. "The man with the dog has gone down," she said. "Does that mean anything? We just got a call."

"Did you even listen? Moon flow and sun power. How about 'lent us strength' instead of 'led us through'?" Mary was panting.

"Goddammit," said Joel. "This is important. Someone said, 'Destroy the green room!'"

"Don't yell at her," said Ann. She knew Mary's diaphragm was hindered by the fetuses. "Are you all right? Just breathe."

"Help me sit up," said Mary. "The man with the dog is probably code for Carlos. Gone down...got arrested?"

"Where's Peter?" said Ann. "He's supposed to be taking care of you."

"He's at Cassidy's." Mary made air quotes with her fingers. "'Practicing yoga.' Why can't they practice *here?*"

"Stay focused," said Joel. "If Carlos got arrested, we could be next."

"Don't harsh my mellow," said Mary. "Why does he have a crush on *her?* I'm the creatrix."

"Where's the blood-pressure cuff?" said Ann. "Your pulse is high."

"We'll have to burn the plants in the back field, and tear out the lights upstairs," said Joel. "We'll carry them through here and throw them out that window."

Ann couldn't find the cuff anywhere. She threw off books and stones, tore through the sofa cushions.

"We don't have time," said Joel. "Go upstairs and start bringing down plants. I'll get Peter, and be right back."

"Found it." Mary wrapped the inflatable bag around her arm. "Stop panicking. I've got this covered. Go. Deal with the plants."

The rare side of Mary emerged, so rare that Ann had forgotten it existed: Mary, calm, capable of checking her own blood pressure. Ann dashed upstairs, glimpsing herself in the mirror shards along the stairwell: a panicked eye, a pale lip. She didn't recognize herself. She looked like Mary.

In the green room, the plants were flourishing, each over five feet tall; full and beautiful. She gathered one up. It was heavy. She had to stop at the stairs and rest. She was careful not to bump it as she descended. It hadn't asked to be cultivated. To kill it seemed senseless and violent, and she pitied the plant as she placed it in the living room.

"Blood pressure's no higher than usual," said Mary. "But if you don't figure out how to manage your own stress, three kids will kill you."

"Remember this anxiety," said Ann. "The next time you want to do something illegal. No money is worth this."

"I don't give a shit about money. It's a source of strain between me and Peter. He thinks we're being cheated."

"Cheaters are always afraid of being cheated." Ann pulled the plant across the room toward the window. Access was blocked by the makeshift altar.

"Right back at me!" said Mary. "Pot *should* be legal. We answer to a higher power, like Antigone. Didn't she bury her father contrary to government edict?

Ann began clearing statues, the easy ones first: Barbie, Demeter, the Virgin Mary.

"Give her to me!" said Mary. "She'll keep us from harm."

Mary's lap was dominated by her belly, with no room to hold a statue. Ann placed it beside her. "There's your Virgin."

"Nothing chaste about her," said Mary. "She's virgin as it was defined in antiquity. 'Woman unto herself,' meaning she knew her own needs and had lots of lovers."

Ann tried to move the bronze Kali statue. All those arms, that protruding tongue, the necklace of skulls and girdle of dead men's hands, the statue wouldn't budge.

Mary laughed. "Her hymen wouldn't have been intact anyway what with all that donkey-riding!"

"Mom!" Ann could feel laughter bubble up.

Footsteps sounded on the porch. Joel charged in, followed by Peter and Cassidy. Peter's tank top was drenched in sweat. Cassidy wore red spandex pants and a jog bra. Perhaps they really had been practicing yoga.

"Let me help you." Joel grabbed the base of the Kali statue while Ann took the head, and they moved it to the jewelry bench.

"Mom always said Carlos would sing like a bird if they caged him," said Cassidy. She and Joel dragged the table away from the window.

"Where are the kids?" asked Ann.

"They're old enough to stay on their own," said Cassidy offhandedly.

Every muscle in Ann's body tightened.

"Kidding!" Cassidy hooted. "Mom's playing grandma. She took 'em to Mickie D's so they could eat toxins and get crappy plastic toys."

"America's back?" said Mary. "Why isn't she here?"

"She's probably the one who called," said Joel.

"But the voice didn't sound human," said Ann.

"She got back day before yesterday," said Cassidy. "Bail was a bitch. Now she wants to go to law school. She brought home all these books."

"Law school?" said Mary. "She's older than me."

"Age is irrelevant. You're living proof," said Cassidy. "Soon we'll live forever. They're working on it already. I mean, the world is all waves and particles and strings."

"Come on, people! We have work to do." Joel grabbed Ann's hand and pulled her toward the stairs. His palm was clammy.

"You're not the boss," said Peter. But he followed them, leaving Cassidy with Mary in the living room.

The plants stood in orderly abundance under the lamps, with an empty spot where Ann had removed one. Joel carried two, trailing leaves and dirt. Peter seized another. "A damn shame," he said. "Such a waste."

Ann held hers like a heavy child in her arms, supporting herself on the banister as she negotiated stairs. As soon as she'd placed it by the window, she turned and headed back up. Cassidy followed. "Why is Mary so paranoid? I was never paranoid when I was pregnant."

"Why does Peter have to go to your place to practice yoga?" said Ann. "It upsets her."

Joel and Peter had dragged the plants closer to the door, grouping them in a cluster. "Mary interrupts," said Cassidy. "Whenever we practice. Talking and talking, and she needs a response."

"She can't just be in her own space," said Peter, who seemed to know exactly what Ann and Cassidy were talking about.

"Less talk, more work," said Joel.

Ann hoisted a plant to her shoulder. She knew how Mary demanded a constant witness. She'd lived it. But her loyalty lay with Mary, not with Cassidy or Peter. Behind her, Peter tipped his plant forward so the leaves brushed the top of Ann's head. She could hear clods of dirt landing on the steps. "Mary needs a new car," said Peter. "She needs her cut of the money."

In the living room, Mary was on all fours on the bearskin rug. "I have to dislodge Jade's foot from my ribs," she said, rounding her spine.

They detoured around her. Peter set his plant below the window next to Ann's. "I'm a member of this family, too," he whispered. "That money belongs to all of us."

"Why does everyone whisper around me?" said Mary.

Joel brought in another plant. "Hey, Peter, let's deal with the stuff upstairs. Ann, you and Cassidy start throwing these guys out the window."

The window was loose and slid open easily. Ann pitched a plant out onto the grass.

"Mom wants to defend people in court," Cassidy was saying. "Marijuana cases, that's her cause. It's healthier than alcohol."

Ann flashed on Cassidy's breasts, then her hips and her paunch. "Are you pregnant?" she asked.

"You're the first to notice!" Cassidy grinned. "I'm glad you're not mad."

"How far along?" said Mary. "Will we give birth together, me and you?"

With broken fingernails and dirt-caked palms, Ann threw another plant out the window. "I thought you were getting your tubes tied," she said. She felt no grief, no rage, no sense of exclusion.

Peter and Joel trekked in, dropped two plants by the window, spilled soil on the rug and turned back around. "I hope you guys aren't just shooting the breeze," Joel called back as they disappeared.

"I'm four months." Cassidy folded one leg up into a tree pose. "I'm trying to locate Jai, let him know he's going to be a father."

"You don't have morning sickness?" said Mary. "Lucky you."

Ann shoved another plant out the window. Her shoulders ached. She braced herself for the onslaught of envy. Peter and Joel came and went. Plants accumulated. Outside, they lay in a sad, shrubby pile. Behind her, Mary and Cassidy chatted about their pregnancies.

But nothing happened. No bitterness arose. Squinting at the circle of stones, trying to pick out where she had buried the totem, Ann felt sad for Baby Four but eager for One, Two and Three. In burying the totem, she had buried her rancor. She understood that she'd idealized the pregnant state, just like the patriarchy tended to do. The miracle of motherhood was not just about birthing, as wondrous as every birth was. No, the true marvel lay in the absurdity of rearing children, the mundane tasks performed, endless and tedious and done with adoration. And she would have that.

"You look so beautiful there, by the window," said Mary. "What do you think of me and Peter raising one of the babies as our own, just to help you and Joel?"

Ann turned. "I don't understand the question."

Joel and Peter came in, depositing two more plants. "Only a few left," said Joel.

"I just brought up the parenting thing," said Mary.

Instead of running back upstairs, Peter curled next to Mary on the sofa. "Technically and physically," he said. "These are Mary's babies. And she's obviously a devoted mother."

Cassidy stood there with her mouth open. "I don't see you as the fatherly type," she said.

"Am I missing something?" said Joel.

"I think Mary just said she wants to keep one of the babies for herself," said Ann. "Did I hear that right?"

"I wouldn't put it that way." Mary flashed her fake and dazzling smile, the one she used on cops and bureaucrats. "Peter and I are making an offer that comes from the heart, to *help*. It takes a village. That's what they say. And Peter will make a great dad."

"You're carrying them. You're birthing them. You even named them. Of course, you think they're yours," said Ann. Her voice seemed to come from a great distance.

"What the hell? We have a lot of work to do here." Joel kept blinking, as if to wish the distraction away.

Ann heard the words in her skull before she spoke them. They came from somewhere dark and powerful. "I will die before I let you have custody of my children."

"Wow," said Cassidy.

"It's just an idea," said Mary. "I don't mean it to be threatening."

Peter stood. He approached Ann, but kept a few plants between them. "Give us our share of the funds and this conversation goes away."

"You think you can bribe me?" Ann picked up a plant. She wasn't going to throw it, but Peter jumped back.

"I have to intervene." Joel wrestled the plant away from Ann. He wrapped her in a tight embrace. She struggled against him. He tightened his grip, barking out orders. "Peter, take the plants to the fire pit. Cassidy, go with him. Annie, no one is taking our babies. Right, Mary? No one."

"Let go." Ann twisted and elbowed. She couldn't get free. But she could see past him, to Mary.

Mary tore the wrapping off a protein bar. "Is Cassidy pregnant with *his* baby? Go. Use me up. You think I won't be a good mother? You're wrong. It's his baby, isn't it? What planet are you living on?"

"You're crazy!" yelled Ann. Joel was stronger than she was. He dragged her outside.

"I'm a fucking great mother!" Mary screamed.

Out on the porch, Joel kept hold. "She's desperate to keep Peter. And to keep us. It's fear, don't you see that?"

With the sun sinking, a chill set in, summoning a more urgent reality. Ann went limp. She understood Mary's terror. She felt it too.

"There's a can of gas in the truck. Let me talk to her. I'll meet you out back," said Joel. He walked up the porch steps and went inside.

Fetching the gas allowed Ann a moment to appreciate Joel's insight and kindness. Of all the griefs she could list in her life, Joel was the gift that outweighed them. She strode around the laurel bushes, gas can in hand, wishing to hear children's laughter. Instead, she heard her mother weeping.

Joel and Peter pushed a wheelbarrow full of plants across the field. Cassidy shoveled a trench around the fire. Ann circled the pile of marijuana bushes, splashing gas. The can became lighter and lighter, until it was empty.

Peter lit a cigarette before he threw the match. Nothing happened. He struck another match, then another. Finally, flames shot up. The odor of marijuana grew intense. Joel slid his damp palm against Ann's, intertwining their fingers. Ann became dizzy in the flickering orange light. She could still hear Mary sobbing. "Goddess of fire," she shouted. "Liberate and purify us!"

THE TOUCH OF PETER's fingers as he buttoned her smock-top caused Mary to shiver with delight. She wanted the act of dressing to last forever. It couldn't, of course. Soon she was fully clothed. The stretchy front of her hideous pregnancy skirt expanded beyond capacity, tearing the seams. Her thick support socks, without which her feet would swell to mammoth size and throb painfully, were rolled up past her knees. Double-wide Birkenstocks were the only workable shoe option.

"I must look a sight," she said, wanting him to protest.

"Shall we go, love?" he replied. They had an appointment with the Immigration and Naturalization Service. Peter had polished his shoes and slicked back his downy hair. He carried his documents in a leatherette folder. In an old suit with frayed cuffs that made him look both decadent and dashing, he escorted Mary to the WCCNWMN. A rented wheelchair filled the backseat.

They were breaking Dr. Stark's rule with this twenty-five mile journey to the county seat. For Mary, it was an act of love. Dropping her chin, she inhaled the essence of violet she had dabbed between her breasts, and a delicious, fleeting sense of transgression lifted her spirits.

When they arrived, Peter parked in the handicapped spot. He unfolded the wheelchair clumsily, catching his finger in a lever. "Bloody hell! Arsehole!"

He's frightened, Mary realized. His fear should have given her a greater sense of power. Instead, as she squeezed herself into the wheelchair, she was alarmed, and helpless.

A guard directed them to the elevator. They were only going to the second floor. Mary's former self would have taken the stairs.

The elevator doors opened onto a large, crowded room, every chair occupied. The metallic smell of nervous humanity clung to the walls. Mary was no fussbudget, but this room was filthy. She couldn't help comparing it to the hushed mauve waiting room at the fertility clinic, a place where she'd been a rock star.

Peter abandoned her in the middle of the room while he approached the front desk, and Mary became aware of a collective curiosity about this colossus in her wheelchair. The armrests were too high, not easily adjustable; they caused her shoulders to hunch up by her ears. She put her hands in her lap, trying to maintain a soft, compassionate expression as she examined her rings, one on each finger, as well as several bracelets from her *spiralmary* series. She had also donned two *lifeforce* cabochons and the lodestone necklace she never removed. Her jewelry fortified her. Let them stare.

Peter returned from the desk with a number on a bit of paper. "Now we wait."

"It'll be okay." She wanted to soothe him and to feel loved.

But the wheelchair seemed to erase her influence. It made him pull away, and this turned her resentful, like a child. "I have to pee!" she cried. "Or maybe give birth! I can't tell which!"

He propelled her from the room, wheeling her down a corridor, and stopped with a jolt at the public bathroom. Mary pushed on the armrests to lift herself off the chair. When Peter tried to steady her, she elbowed him away. Thrusting her shoulders back, she felt energized. The hell with doctor's orders. Movement was good, stimulating her chi.

But alone in the stall, sitting on the toilet, she experienced a frightening head rush. Vertiginous darkness swirled. She braced herself against the wall, aware suddenly of the sulphurous smell of the water and the underlying stench of industrial cleaner. Then she heard her mother's crisp voice, as if Rose were sitting in the next stall: *Some women use their pregnancy as an excuse to malinger. But we do not.* The floor tiles stopped spinning. Mary staggered back out to her wheelchair.

"All sorted?" Peter rolled her to the crowded room. He stood next to the wheelchair while she sat. And sat. She grew hungry. Peter fetched pretzels from the vending machine. The pretzels made her thirsty. She had to check her blood sugar. He brought her a bottle of water. She had to pee again. But she was exhausted. The fluorescent lights gave her a headache. She dozed off, skimming back through the years to her childhood, swinging in the school-yard, soaring so high the swing chains buckled. Then she was lying in her parents' bed, sick with influenza, running her fingers over the nubbles on the quilt. Angels assembled at the foot of the bed and burst into song. Their chorus gave off heat. When she woke all her eyelashes had fallen out. But she wasn't really awake. She was still in her dream.

Peter shook her. "Stay alert, love, please. Our life together depends on it."

She adjusted her weight to ease the ache in her sacrum. Her thighs were numb. Peter's eyelashes were long and dark, beguilingly curled. *Wasted on a boy,* Rose would have said. But were pretty traits ever wasted? "You're so handsome," said Mary. "Is that why you're ashamed of me?"

"Ashamed? Whatever gave you that idea? I was thinking of the grow room. Don't you wish we could have saved one or two plants? At the very least, we might have kept the equipment intact. We might want to try again in future."

"Let's not rehash that, please," said Mary.

Two adjacent seats came free. Peter helped Mary move from the tight, sagging wheelchair into the hard, plastic seat. She grabbed his hand, and he rewarded her with an apologetic smile. One by one, she removed her rings and slipped them onto his fingers. None of them slid further than his first knuckle. "You have very knobby digits," she said.

"I'm a nob," he laughed, wriggling his fingers. Then he bowed his big head so she could insert her earrings through the holes in his earlobes. "Do they suit me?" he asked.

His bowed head conferred an uncharacteristic humility, and Mary apprehended with sudden clarity that Cassidy had rejected him. "Are you in love with her?" she said. "Did she spurn you?"

"I'm lousy at relationships." His lips brushed her cheek. "I thought I could change. I'm sorry."

She blinked back tears as he opened her palm. He stroked the lateral crossing of her heart line. "Our love is the only thing real," he whispered.

"Mary Moonlight. Peter Shepherd," called the officer at the desk. "Are those your real names? Moonlight and Shepherd?"

"No sheep were harmed." Peter chuckled nervously into the man's impassive face. Mary heaved herself back into the flimsy wheelchair. A sharp cramp in her side stopped her breath for a second.

They were ushered into a cubicle by a curly-haired woman in a stern gray suit and gray pumps. *The establishment,* thought Mary. Here it was, embodied. *See?* she imagined showing Ann this scene. *And you said there was no such thing as the establishment.*

"Do you want to sit in the chair, or are you fine where you are?" asked the woman.

"I'm good for now." Mary clenched the armrests. The thought of Ann had triggered anxiety. If she knew Mary was here, she would have an absolute fit. *Relax your jaw,* Mary told herself. *Relax your shoulders.*

The woman leafed through documents. "Looks like the deed to your house was transferred quite recently."

"It's been in the works for a while but..." Peter was trying to pull off his rings.

"We wanted to do it as soon as we married," Mary interrupted. "You might notice my daughter's on the deed, too."

"Your daughter's named Anna...*purna?*"

"Yes, but no. But yes. She changed her name when she was sixteen to Ann. Rejected the name I gave her." Mary stopped. The name change still upset her.

"And you're pregnant. Obviously. Are you two starting a family?"

"Bit more complicated than that." Peter rattled the rings in his folded hands, as if shaking dice. "Though I *am* a family man, my wife is a surrogate for her daughter. She was just beginning the process when we met."

Mary splayed her fingers for him to put the rings back on, but he didn't take the signal.

"Let me get this straight. You're pregnant with your daughter's child? And you're…" The woman flipped through papers. "…fifty years old."

"Not *fifty*-fifty!" cried Mary. "Age is a construct."

"You should know the age discrepancy between you two raises a red flag," said the woman. "It's usually the other way around, gender-wise. You've been married how long?"

"The marriage license is with the paperwork," said Mary. "We had a lovely ceremony in the field behind our house. I don't know why people get so obsessed about age. Peter and I are devoted to each other. And I have a friend who's fifty and she's going to law school."

"I must say I love how Mary's neck wrinkles when she turns her head." Peter laughed. "It's true. I'm besotted with your neck."

"I don't exactly feel flattered." A foot wriggled itself between Mary's fifth and sixth rib. *Maintain,* she told herself. *Act natural.*

"Your income statement indicates that you—" The woman pointed to Peter. "Aren't contributing financially."

"In my profession—I'm in the arts—it's often said that you can't make a living but you can make a killing."

The woman's raised eyebrows indicated skepticism. "So, you pay the bills, ma'am."

"Pretty much," said Mary. "Me and my wrinkled neck." The items on the woman's desk wavered in front of her, a jar with a couple of pens and a pair of scissors melting like the objects in a Dali painting.

"How big is your house?" the woman's voice vibrated.

And Mary was back in the playground again, sitting on a bench near the seesaw with her friends. *Our house isn't big enough to swing a cat in,* she told them, repeating what her mother would say. With a start, she experienced the rigid terror of a screaming cat spun around by its tail.

"...four bedrooms, a large kitchen with rather ancient appliances," Peter was droning. "Though I'm not, as you say, the bill payer, the bulk of household chores does fall to me."

"What exactly *is* 'Sunrise'?" said the woman. "Are you running a bed and breakfast?"

The establishment was always belittling what it did not understand. "Sunrise is just a large welcoming abode, not a bed and breakfast," said Mary. "I almost named it House of the Rising Sun, after the song. Except it's not a brothel." She tried a friendly laugh, but yawned instead. She couldn't seem to draw enough oxygen. If she stayed in this tiny cubicle much longer, she was going to die.

"What's your wife's favorite food?" The woman pointed her sharp chin at Peter.

"Don't be disgusted, but since she hit her third trimester, she likes cold refried beans, straight from the can."

"It's true," said Mary. "Beans are complex carbohydrates. Doctor-recommended. I'm confined downstairs until these three are born but Peter waits on me hand and foot. Is it hot in here?"

"Mary and I are collaborating on a book about this pregnancy," said Peter. "I believe I included a letter from my agent for your perusal. In fact, I recently sold a photograph of Mary to a magazine called *The Lively Dialogue,* highly respected. They publish poetry, fiction, essays and artwork."

"When?" said Mary. "You never told me that!"

"The Demi Moore portrait." Peter unhooked Mary's earrings from his ears. "My photograph will be featured on the cover in November. The flesh issue, flesh as landscape, flesh as metaphor. I'm quite excited."

"By November the babies should be a month old." But Mary couldn't envision her life after pregnancy. She barely remembered her life before.

"The bad news is, I get fifty dollars and a year's subscription," said Peter. "Lousy money, good exposure. So, my wife will continue as the bill payer for now, alas."

"You could have aimed higher," said Mary. "Why send it to some unknown publication no one reads rather than, say, *Vanity Fair?*"

"It seems you're surprised, Ms. Moonlight," said the woman. "And not exactly pleased."

"He didn't tell me he was submitting it. As the subject, I should have a say." Mary's discontent magnified as she voiced it. "What's the circulation of this magazine?"

"I thought you'd be happy," said Peter.

"I see in my records your mother recently died?" said the woman.

They both nodded. Mary said, "Mine died just before the winter solstice, two years ago. His passed away more recently."

As if her mother were standing behind her, Mary heard a familiar harrumph of contempt. She was jackknifed by another cramp. Her skirt stuck to her legs like cheesecloth to slabs of meat. Had she brought her anti-contraction medication? Maybe a stray pill lay at the bottom of her bag?

"Are you all right?" cried Peter.

"Oh my god! Are you in labor?" The woman stood. "Should I call an ambulance?"

"Just a little Braxton Hicks." Mary shut her eyes to inhale. She imagined pure oxygen traveling through her blood, to her uterus and the babies. As she exhaled, she imagined spewing out poisonous toxins. *In. Out.* The pain passed like a brief, violent thunderstorm.

"Mary was very kind to me when my mother passed away, but I loved Mary before I even met her. I loved her work." Peter opened his palms as Mary opened her eyes, and the earrings and rings lay there in a vibrant jumble, oscillating in a golden light. Artful spontaneity, a beautiful accident. "Are you seeing what I'm seeing?" he said.

"Your aura," said Mary. "If only we could reproduce it in a photograph."

The thwack of a stamp on paper startled them both. "You passed," said the woman. "You can't make this stuff up. You're approved for the green card."

"Thank you! By God!" said Peter. "I'll send you the first copy of our book, hot off the press!"

Mary hadn't realized the tension she'd been holding until relief arrived and the stress drained out, leaving only a twinge deep in her pubic bone. She braced herself against it. But the twinge broadened with grinding violence, heaving her up in an arc, somersaulting through her. She moaned as it crested and crashed like a wave in the surf, throwing up swirling sand and foam before it weakened, eventually becoming a small lip of water tugged back with the undertow, allowing her to breathe again. But her chair was soaked and her skirt, too, humiliatingly wet as if she'd peed her pants.

MARY AWOKE TO HER mother's face. Rose looked angry. But she was young again, Mary's mother from childhood. The lines of disappointment around her eyes and mouth were merely superficial. Then the sharp features rearranged themselves into her daughter's anxious visage.

"You're in the hospital," said Ann. She wiped Mary's forehead with a damp cloth. "You needed an emergency cerclage. You know what that is? A thread holds your cervix shut."

The cloth felt refreshing on her forehead, and awakened Mary to the tension at her groin. She touched her neck and found her lodestones gone. No rings on her fingers, no bracelets. She remembered the woman at the immigration office stamping the application. She tried to push the covers off but an IV yanked her left arm. "Where's Peter?"

"You went against doctor's orders," said Ann.

"I couldn't let Peter down." Mary tried to curl into a fetal position, twisting her hospital gown and exposing herself. Cool air brushed across her buttocks. Ann dragged the chair close, and the abrasive sound of its legs against the floor jarred Mary's bones.

"Peter went home hours ago. He doesn't love you. He doesn't love anyone but himself."

A nurse wheeled in an ultrasound machine. She seemed far, far away. "Time to visit our babies," she said.

The ghostly images brought a lump to Mary's throat. The smallest fetus barely moved. "Opal's sleeping," she said.

"Perhaps." The nurse said. "I'll be right back."

"What do you mean perhaps?" said Ann. "What's the matter? What's happening?"

But the nurse had placed the wand in its holder and left the room, her mouth set in refusal, leaving Mary greasy with gel. Who could parse a "perhaps?"

Mary saw that Ann was crying, her fist in her mouth, transformed back into little Annapurna. "Don't assume the worst," she said. "Please, sweetie, don't."

But she was drifting, a piece of flotsam, powerless to stop the flow from carrying her away. Five years old again, sick with fever, her mother's voice scolding: *Mary can you hear me? She's burning up*, then fading, as if she'd moved to another room. And most wondrously, here in this hospital, crashing through the ceiling in a clattering thunder of wings, several angels alighted.

How disorderly they were, angling for space! Large and boisterous, they hovered with huge thrumming wings like hummingbirds, but amplified to helicopter decibels. Their faces shone. One blew a trumpet. They burst into a crazy, unfamiliar hymn. Each note issued forth a plume of vivid color. With warm, collective breath, they bathed her in their synesthesia. Their song grew louder, the harmonies so beautiful they pierced Mary's heart.

"Go away!" she heard Ann scream. "Tell the ghosts to go away!"

A persistent ache pulled deep inside her. Mary opened her eyes. The sun against the windows cast a blinding slant that made the glass appear metallic. Her belly was covered with round stickers that pinched her skin. She was belted across twice. A monitor sat on a trolley at the side of her bed, split into three screens. The liquid rhythm of syncopated heartbeats filled the room.

Dr. Stark stood there, his pale eyes blinking in his pale face, moving his pale lips. But Mary couldn't hear him. Ann clasped her hands like she was praying. Joel held her around the shoulders. And Peter bowed his head, with his camera slung around his neck. *Mary, can you hear me?* said her mother.

"Angels came," said Mary. "I saw angels."

"Are you listening?" Ann's voice rang like a crystal chime. "Fluid leaked. The small one is dead."

"The other two don't appear distressed," said Dr. Stark. "We're not going to induce."

"Opal?" Mary couldn't understand how the baby had died while safe inside her. "The angels came for me," she said. "They should have taken me."

"We need to get her to a better hospital," said Ann. "This place isn't equipped for these high-risk—"

"Too disruptive," said Dr. Stark. "She can't be moved."

"She can't stay here. They'll all die!"

"She's receiving the best possible care."

Mary had forgotten the constant dread she'd endured as a child and then as a young woman, that any moment the edifice of her life could crumble, leaving her utterly helpless. She'd learned to push away that fear. It came back to her now, a malignant reminder, not only that her life could crumble and she could die, but that she could cause other lives to crumble, and have to live and bear the cost.

ANN FISHED THE DEAD child from Mary's womb and kissed her. The infant's color changed from ash-blue to healthy pink. *She's alive again, look,* she lowered the baby so Mary could see. But Mary turned monstrous, with hundreds of eyes and tongues, her hair a mass of wriggling snakes, her mouth a bloody wound. With a shriek, she spat a white crystal that speared Ann's chest.

Ann awoke in a chair beside Mary's hospital bed. Instantly remembering how the dead baby had come to life, she touched her sternum where she felt a sting. Mary was snoring, attached to a pump that delivered anti-contraction medication through a needle in her leg, connected to an IV to keep her hydrated. With her acne-covered cheeks and gray hair strewn across the pillow, she was unrecognizable as the all-powerful mother Ann had lived her life in opposition to. *I should never have let you do this,* Ann whispered.

One vanished, one dead, two living, and Mary incapacitated—everything coexisted in a swirl of sadness and anticipation. Ann felt she had gotten to know Opal, who would have been a quiet girl with an inner strength not obvious to those who didn't pay attention, the kind of girl people overlooked, a bit like Ann herself. The dream had been so vivid. Perhaps Opal wasn't dead, but trapped between life and death, searching for a portal?

It will have to be carried to term. Dr. Stark had called Opal an "it." According to the doctor, Opal was blocking Mary's cervix and couldn't be disturbed without endangering the others. His thin authoritative lips had tightened when he talked. *Each day in utero is two days less in intensive care.*

Joel returned from an excursion to the snack machine, and handed her a packet of crackers. She couldn't remember when she'd last eaten. The crackers were salty and stale. Opal appeared in her mind as a fetus in a jar, and she realized the baby was dead and there would be no portal, no resurrection. The food turned to dust in her mouth.

Peter slunk in, stinking of cigarettes. "I know, I pressured her to go to the I.N.S.," he said. "I'm a weak person. I'm hypocritical. I'm shallow. But I never anticipated this."

"Don't," said Ann. She folded forward over her legs. Her sneakers were scuffed. Her fingernails, she noticed, were dirty. She would have to wash her hands. Soon, she thought, she would stand up and go to the sink.

"Mary is my shining diamond," Peter continued after a pause. "I wouldn't ever want to hurt her, you have to know that."

"Ann and I would like you not to talk," said Joel.

"But I respect Mary so tremendously," said Peter.

"Respect, my ass," Mary piped from the bed.

"Mom." Ann held onto Mary's foot beneath the blanket.

Mary didn't move. Her eyes were still shut. "Garnet and Jade," she said. "I'm thinking of you. Ann, my baby, I'm thinking of you. And Opal, my sweet."

"Mary, love. I'm here." Peter stepped forward. "Your husband."

Ann stood. She felt herself expand. She widened, lengthened, branched out. *I'm alive. Mary is alive. Two quadruplets are alive.* She pointed to the door. Jagged light flashed from her finger. "Get out."

Peter backed out of the room, and Ann dropped her arm, not victorious, just drained and grief-stricken.

"How did you do that?" Joel was pressed against the wall, aghast.

"I don't know." Ann gently brushed the hair off Mary's damp forehead. She could do her vigilant best to ensure the last two babies emerged intact, and her mother survived unscathed. Pain in her chest brought a vivid reminder of the crystal. Angel quartz, she thought, remembering its whiteness, and wondered how she knew.

"You're the queen now," Mary whispered. "I gave you my power."

THIRTY-TWO WEEKS AND TWO days. Thirty-two weeks and five days. In the otherwise timeless tedium, Mary was aware of the accumulating days only because the doctors and nurses kept a running tally. One day in utero, two days less in NICU, they repeated like a mantra as they came and went. Because of gestational hypertension, Mary's blood pressure was measured several times a day. Pricked for blood sugar before and after eating, hooked up intravenously to magnesium sulfate to prevent preterm labor, subjected to daily ultrasounds and fetal monitoring, Mary had become a specimen in a scientific experiment.

She lay, as instructed, on her left side, hour after hour, gazing at a piece of rough coral on the bedside table. Pink as a heart with its end cut and polished, a burst of red veins radiating from its center, the coral came from Sage. *I took it from her cabinet,* Ann had confessed. *She would have wanted you to have it.*

Ann had transformed the bedside table into an altar, presenting not only the coral but also the bronzed baby shoes, Mary's ceramic Virgin statue, and the copper yoni Mary had given Ann on her thirtieth birthday. With shame, Mary remembered the flourish of her presentation, how badly she'd wanted to make a good impression not just on Ann and Joel, but also on Jessica. She cringed to think how hurtful the gift of a yoni must have been to Ann, who didn't have one.

"I'm sorry," she whispered.

The Virgin gazed at her compassionately. *Life, life, life,* the Virgin seemed to say.

Propped against the wall was the painted plaster cast of Mary's belly, decorated by Cassidy with a fairy landscape. Mary was twice as large as that dome now. On the walls around her bed hung several paintings and drawings created by Ann's daycare charges. Supposedly portraits of Mary, they were bright splotches of color and, in principle, Mary was grateful. She had the brightest corner in the hospital. Yet the hopeful naiveté of the pictures seemed inappropriate. The Scotch tape couldn't hold the heavy paper so they fell and curled into scrolls on the floor, which made them depressing rather than hopeful.

Ann spent most nights in the hospital. They didn't talk about the death of Opal. Mary was afraid to open the floodgates of grief. Ann left early in the mornings, after re-hanging the paintings. The fuss and snapping sound of sticky tape annoyed Mary. "You really don't have to," she said.

"I know they cheer you up." Ann kissed Mary's cheek before leaving Mary alone to brood. Mary could have said "Too risky!" and refused to go to the immigration office but it had never crossed her mind.

A couple of hours later, the coast clear of Ann, Peter showed up looking like a rock star in his black Levi's and T-shirt silk-screened with a picture of the queen. "We got an offer on the book!" he said. "Thirty-seven five! The book is alive! Fame and fortune! You're going to be the mother of the year!"

All the excitement about an inanimate enterprise seemed not merely misplaced but deluded. "Let's not tell Ann," said Mary.

"I've been seriously worried that I'm not a real artist," said Peter. "But the world has validated me!"

"Such a silly waste of time, fretting about whether you're a real anything." Though Mary knew she had wasted the better part of her life on precisely that. Her past life.

"Artists obsess about things your average human being deems silly." Peter dragged a chair to the foot of the bed and stepped up onto the seat, aiming his Rolleiflex camera at her.

Mary was aware of herself as seen from above, intubated and immovable, a yellow stain on the front of her hospital gown. Her half-eaten breakfast of powdered eggs and canned pineapple coagulated on her food tray. "Your concerns are not deep and unusual or even artistic." She addressed the camera lens. "Just self-absorbed."

"I'm absorbed with you. I'm trying to cheer you up." Peter stepped off the chair. "Help take your mind off it a bit."

"If you actually believe my mind can be taken off a dead baby pressing against my cervix, you are completely out of touch." Her anger felt healthy. "You come here, sneaking around Ann's schedule and you have not once mentioned Opal."

"I'm grieving, too," he said. "We're all sad. I take my cues from you."

But she didn't have the strength to teach Peter about the nature of sorrow or responsibility. Instead, she asked him, "How about the picture? Did you forget it again?" She had requested several times to see the photograph he'd sold to the magazine.

"No, no, I brought it. I'm quite proud of it. I think you should be, too."

She watched him as he put his camera down to open his black messenger bag. He moved stiffly under her scrutiny. He slid the photograph facedown across the blanket, yanking it away when she reached for it. "I submitted a huge bloody batch," he said. "That's the one they chose."

"Enough false modesty!" said Mary. And he finally relinquished it.

She turned it over. The top of her face was cropped off. She was a grotesque mountain of flesh in black and white, multiple chin folds visually echoing a coy smile. She was a freak of nature.

Was this how Peter saw her? The statue in her arms with its sweet expression and smooth edges was more sharply focused and beautifully lit than the lumpen ugly background of Mary herself.

"I think it portrays every angle of the complex creature you are." His laugh quavered in his throat as if he were choking on a feather.

"Creature is right," she said.

"Should I have lied and brought you the soft-focused goddess pic they rejected?" Peter sat on the edge of the bed. He plucked the coral from the nightstand, turning it over in his palms. "I'm too honest for that. It's not about me or my image of you, but about you, radiating your beautiful, resilient spirit."

She had engineered her own heartache, Mary recognized. Unable to create an appealing vision of herself, she had abdicated to an opportunist with only a superficial capacity to love. Basking in his adoration, she hadn't considered what might happen when adoration faded. Now he was saying something smarmy about her courage and generosity. Despite her resistance, his voice lulled her. She didn't want to be alone!

And she glimpsed an elusive truth: that love flowed outward from the heart, not the other way around. "Put the coral down, please," she said. "Get off my bed."

"Is something wrong? Should I call a nurse?" His handsome face was held in a pose of concern, complete with pouting lips and furrowed eyebrows, the epitome of a spoiled, selfish child running on charm. But she had encouraged him. Never asking him to pay for anything, tolerating his games and trying to please him, threatened by the idea that he could thrive in the world without her; she too, had been a spoiled selfish child. Her own fault.

"Go practice yoga or something." Rolling over, she stared at the colorful toddler depictions of herself on the wall, the newsprint already sagging off its tape. "I relieve you of, whatever, your marital duties."

Yet, she was disappointed when Peter slid off the bed. He dropped the coral on the table, grabbed his bag and camera case, and sidled away. "Just leaving, just been asked to leave."

"Excuse me. Mary Moonlight?" Her range of vision was invaded by a hairy wrist protruding from the cuff of a gray sleeve. Thick fingers grasped what appeared to be a badge. "Do you mind answering a few questions?"

A precipitous dryness in her mouth left her mute.

"I'm Detective Blandsky and this is Detective White." Another man in a suit came forward, both with thinning comb-overs and beady eyes. "We're in the state narcotics unit. We won't take up much of your time."

Mary unclenched her body and took a sip of water, briefly wondering if she should ring for the nurse. Perhaps Peter was fetching her now. "I come with these attachments," she said. "If you're going to arrest me, you'll have to take the bed and IV, too."

"You're not under arrest," said Blandsky. "We'd like to question you as a witness. We know about your business relationship with Amy Kray."

"My only relationship right now is with these babies. One of them is dead. Think how that feels."

"As you're probably aware, we have Ms. Kray in custody," said the detective. "She seems to believe you two are very close. She implied that a whole slew of people right here in Sullivan County are involved in the trafficking of illegal substances. Are you acquainted with a Carlos Cubano?"

"I'm not close to Amy Kray," said Mary. "My husband and I have been kind to her daughter who's alone with those two kids."

"Your husband?"

"The man who was just here," said Mary. "I know, I never should have married him."

"Ma'am. Do you mind if we take a look around your house over on East Hill Road?"

"Do you have a warrant? Can't you see I'm not well? I need to sleep." She shut her eyes. The scratch of pencil on a notepad indicated they were still there. *Suspect refuses to cooperate and appears depressed,* she thought, remaining motionless.

The squeak of their rubber-soled shoes brought relief, but she didn't move, even after the sound faded. Only after she heard the flip of one of the paintings falling off the wall, did she open her eyes. She had lived her whole life seeking reflections of herself, and here they were, blobs of color dropping to the floor.

Peter sidled back into the room. "That was a close one. What did they want?"

"I thought you left," she said. "You must have known America got arrested but I have to hear it from the law."

"We wanted to protect you. Mind you, your daughter knows full well. To be honest, what's most appalling is your son-in-law. He refuses to give up cash to pay America's bail. Cassidy's beside herself. You're lucky you're here. Everyone's at sixes and sevens back home."

Mary knew that somewhere inside she must be terrified, but physically she felt only swollen and sore. "You never really loved me, did you?" she said. "We were both just looking out for ourselves."

She heard him exhale with a faint whistle. He was afraid to touch her, she knew. "You're tired," he finally said.

"Yes, I am. It's true." When she closed her eyes again, he left so quietly she didn't hear a sound.

AFTER FILLING A BUCKET with water and detergent, Ann got down on her knees to wash the kitchen floor. The floor was newly tiled and spotless, but she splashed it with soapy water anyway. She had held it together in the hospital, held it together for the children at Little Footsteps, would hold it together until her two living babies were alive and safe in the world, and then she'd have to hold it together for the rest of her life to mother them. The physical act of cleaning released her from all that holding for a time. Galvanized by the bitter odor of ammonia, she washed and rinsed and washed and rinsed.

Until Joel's scuffed work boots stepped in front of her. She hadn't heard his car or the door, or McKenna barking. Her shoulders ached as she crawled around his feet, vigorously scrubbing. "You're home early," she said.

"I figured out how to divvy up the cash." He backed away from her scrub brush. "Subtract the missing installment from Mary and America's share. We keep our twenty-five grand and let the rest go. I'm sick of arguing with Peter. Why are you washing the floor?"

She pushed at the soapy puddle with fierce satisfaction. "I don't know."

"I don't care about money anymore." Joel dropped to his knees in the spill. "I regret losing the green room because it was a place where I could be useful. Funny, but taking care of those plants made me believe I could be a father. They gave me hope. Now your room at Sunrise is a stripped-out wreckage and all I can think about is the dead baby girl. It's my fault. I thought there were too many. I built the cradle to stop thinking about it, but I still thought there were too many. She probably felt unwanted."

"Thoughts can't kill." Ann threw the brush into the bucket. "Her name was Opal, not Baby Three. And I'm glad I don't have to worry about the green room anymore."

"I don't know what to believe," said Joel. "Ma said she and Winnifred started a prayer circle. She paid the priest for a special announcement at mass. Now everyone in the county knows we lost one. But can't you bring her back to life? Like you and Mary did with Sage, remember?"

Ann recalled the penetration of the crystal in her dream. A diamond-shaped bruise marred her skin there. "Do you want to pray? I'll pray with you."

"I saw lightning come out of your finger," said Joel. "I saw you grow into some huge, powerful I-don't-know-what. But it was scary."

Ann fetched the onyx Mary had given her. She took the braided cords and the chunk of sodalite from the windowsill. She and Joel sat across from each other with the rocks between them. Joel slung the braided cords over both their shoulders and they joined hands. Ann couldn't absorb the whole of his face, just individual characteristics: a topaz eye, his girlish lips, the flare of nostrils, the lines on his forehead. He wavered before her like a projection, separate and unknowable. His face mutated into Mary's. And Ann recognized that the crystal she'd dreamed about had been transmuted from Mary, a jagged piece of motherhood shot right through her heart.

Joel became himself again, soaking Ann into his stare. They were irrevocably bound. No one else had seen the grainy black and white visual of their lifeless baby, with Mary lying in a trance in the hospital bed.

"Guardians of the four directions, we beg you to protect our babies and our mothers." Ann's invocation rang out. The late afternoon sunlight reflected on the wet floor, giving the impression they were kneeling on a lake of light. "Align your force with our deepest wishes. Two are gone. Let two live. We're begging you."

"Let them live," Joel repeated. "We'll do anything."

"Lend us your force and strengthen us…" Ann stopped, unable to find the right words for the enormous well of their longing. The cords lay heavily on her shoulders. "We're like children trying to control chaos through magic. But we can't control anything."

Joel squeezed her hands. "Stay with me."

She glanced up and saw a baby perched in the kitchen sink, slapping his palms against the rim. His intelligent gaze widened to take her in, and she experienced an unaccountable acceptance, as if all the space she occupied on Earth, all the weight she placed on the ground, was worthy.

"Do you see the baby?" Joel slid along the wet floor toward the sink. "Do you see?"

Ann blinked. The baby evaporated.

Joel clambered to the sink, touching the basin, the taps, and the counter. "I saw it. I saw a baby."

They stood laughing together at the sink, joined by the cords around their shoulders, by their mutual desire and their shared vision. It seemed most wondrous to Ann, who'd nursed a healthy skepticism all her life. She knew now that even in the middle of a tragedy they couldn't escape, they could still be suffused with hope and happiness.

SPIRIT: 2000

"I RELY ON MY internal wisdom," Mary said aloud, trying to believe it. But she was living in a passive hell in a hospital bed where wisdom was nonexistent. The ongoing drama of the presidential election blared throughout the ward, first the conventions, now the debate. Even though Mary kept her own television off, news and commentary filtered in from nearby rooms, and from the tinny-sounding radio at the nurse's station. Fuzzy math and finger-pointing. Mary told herself she was lucky the neighboring bed was empty, but luck was a relative notion.

The babies moved with such turbulence she imagined them freaked out about sharing the space with their lifeless sister. She was staring at the metal slats of her bedframe, which resembled a cage, when she heard a familiar hoarse voice from the doorway. "This hospital's more toxic than jail! Something's wrong with our society when this is the kind of place we put sick people."

There stood America, silver spiral *madebymary*™ earrings glinting from her earlobes. She approached the bed, talking as if they were back in the Sunrise living room. "The whole goddam country's shot to hell," she said. "Cass thinks Nader's our man and I'll tell you one thing: if he'd been in charge, I wouldn't have landed in jail. Legalize it, I say. You're smart, your TV's off."

Her musk-oil scent suggested home, normality, and contentment. "You smell nice," said Mary.

"Can't say the same for this place but it's better than the county jail. Shit, piss and cigarettes, that's the stink of jail." America let out a raucous chuckle. "You won't be doing *this* again, willya?"

Mary tested a giggle, and a cramp knifed her ribs. "It hurts when I laugh," she said.

"No fucking picnic, is it? Fifty fucking years old! How the hell did *that* happen?" America wheezed with laughter. "I sure do appreciate your generosity. You did me a solid. I'll never forget it." Mary didn't know what generosity America referred to, but she basked in the gratitude anyway. "That's me. Selfless. Look at me." America kissed Mary brusquely on the cheek, adding an affectionate but painful knuckle twist to her skull before sitting in the chair next to the bed. "What a couple of sad sacks we are. Next time you see your husband, tell him to go home, would you? He's over at the house all the goddam time. No one wants him. At least I never *married* Carlos."

"I'm not ready to laugh about Peter yet," said Mary.

"Did I tell you I met *la esposa de Carlos?*" said America. "She's pretty hot. Shame she's a bitch. She turned us in. Seriously, I'll need you to get on the witness stand. Attest to my character."

"Your character! 'She's corrupt to the core, your honor.'" Mary laughed, pushing right through the cramp.

"What's so funny?" A nurse entered, brandishing a blood pressure cuff.

They went quiet as the nurse tested Mary's blood pressure, which was was elevated, as usual.

"Laughing's good," the nurse said as she left. "Keep laughing."

"Not for nothing, but you're true blue. Putting up Sunrise for the bond. Good people, I always said that about you." America chewed the inside of her cheek, an unconscious tic that made her look both infantile and elderly.

What about Sunrise? Mary noticed that America's normally springy gray curls were limp and greasy. She also noticed a tremor in America's hands, though America kept shaking out her fingers, trying to make it look deliberate. Mary wanted to grab those soft hands and squeeze them until the quiver vanished. But she'd lost the strength to squeeze anything.

"You look like hell, sister," said America.

"I was thinking the same about you. But I still love you," said Mary. "Even though you're obnoxious."

"You could have stopped at 'I still love you.'" America laughed. She stamped her moccasined foot.

Mary couldn't help laughing, too. Hysteria rippled through her. She saw the ripples in colorful waves. It felt so good to laugh, it made her feel almost normal.

She was shocked to see Asphodel from the sisterhood gliding into the room with a djembe drum under her arm. Her fingers were taped up as if she intended to do some serious drumming. Joel came in behind her, holding his guitar by the neck. Ann followed, supporting a frail, skinny Sage, who wore a turban settled low on her forehead.

"Sage!" Mary choked up. "Amy Kray, did you arrange this?"

"Not me, girlfriend." America was beaming. "Someone else."

Peter straggled in, carrying his camera on a strap around his shoulder. "Sorry I'm late. Had a confab with my writer."

"Was it you?" said Mary.

Joel maneuvered his guitar across his chest and picked out a simple tune as the others crowded around Mary's bed.

Asphodel began beating her drum. Ann chanted in a mellifluous voice, joined by Sage in a delicate, reedy one:

Great Goddess, Mother of Life
Goddess of Mercy and Healing,
Send strength to Mary and the infants.
Restore her body to sacred balance.
Great Goddess, Mother of life.

Forgetting the IV, the medicine pump, all the devices, and her own monstrosity, Mary inhaled deeply the aroma of frankincense released by the candle. She harmonized with the vibrating energy of everyone, her discomfort lifting away. "I adore rituals!" she cried.

"Mary, queen of fragrant Earth, giver of gifts, give us your grace. Ann, fairest maiden, we offer our song." Asphodel hit out rhythms like the patter of rain. "Let mother and daughter embrace as Demeter and Persephone, and find strength in love."

America held the IV line out of the way so Ann could step forward and press her warm lips on Mary's forehead. With her hand on Mary's belly Ann sang. "Mercy. Heal. Balance. Life."

"Hare Krishnas or something." The comment came from the doorway, crowded with nurses and orderlies. Mary's pulse accelerated. Ann had arranged the ritual—her pessimistic, distrustful daughter had come around. Mary remembered the van they'd named the Mahayana, stopping for gas, how she tumbled out of the back doors, hugely pregnant with Ann, and danced around the gas pumps. She'd hadn't known she was already in labor. *Are you people part of some cult?* a guy had asked. *The cult of humanity!*

"What's going on?" A security guard barged through. "Extinguish that right now. It's a fire hazard."

Ann blew the candle out.

"This is a healing ritual." Sage's head wobbled. "We're not bothering anyone."

Her frailty seemed to rile the guard. "Do you see the sign that says quiet? Everyone out! Visiting hours are over."

In the room and in the corridor, everyone fell silent. Not a beep nor a voice, only the clicking of Peter's camera. Mary hadn't felt this animated in weeks. She watched her daughter rise like a priestess.

"We call on our power and the power of the goddess to let them live," said Ann. "We lost two. Two are alive. Let them live."

"Go, girl," said Asphodel. "Let them live."

The others chanted, *Let them live.*

"I'll give you ten minutes to wrap it up." Waving away the crowd clustered at the door, the guard stationed himself there.

Ann leaned close to Mary. Her face was soft and open. "It's weird how people respond, isn't it?" she whispered.

"I'm proud of you," said Mary. Jade and Garnet kicked and turned, and Mary experienced the oceanic sense of being loved, that feeling she always longed for.

"May the goddess heal thee and keep thee strong." Asphodel placed her palm near Ann's, a cooler touch. America put her hand on Mary, too. Joel added his, then Sage. Peter held his camera aloft like a beacon, pushing the IV pole out of the way to slip behind Mary's bed and take a photograph, capturing them all as they touched her.

"This is so perfect," sighed Mary, just before pain sliced across her body and everything disintegrated.

A CORPOREAL MASS OF muscle and blood writhed in a hospital bed.

But a divine energy lifted Mary from that wretched heap and carried her through light and air, to deposit her into a much younger body, whose soreness was finite and bearable. She was in the van they called the Mahayana, lying on her side, bumping against the carpeted floor. Jimi Hendrix blasted "The Wind Cries Mary." She was among her tribe of hippie nomads, careening down a highway. After hours of jostling, the van finally stopped at a gas station.

Mary clambered out, dazzled by the sun. Giddy and dizzy and tripping on acid, she watched Sage dance around the gas pumps, waving long sinewy arms. Sage had changed her name from Nina, expanding her consciousness, reshaping the bones of her face and altering her destiny. Mary desired that transcendence for herself.

Cramps cycled through her body on the periphery of her awareness, until a ferocious spasm crushed her in its giant teeth. *My old lady's having a baby,* said Orion, her old man. They both knew the baby wasn't his. She'd been pregnant when she met him.

Someone pushed her. Mary opened her eyes and fluorescent lights blurred above, moving quickly past. "Orion?" she cried. "Sage?"

She was being conveyed along a corridor, streaming past greenish ceiling lights, a confusion of wheelchairs against the wall, a man in a hospital gown dragging his IV. She saw the austere visage of Dr. Stark, and remembered she was Mary Moonlight, fifty years old, containing multiples.

Sage appeared in the corridor, neither young nor dancing. Her face was gaunt. A turban sat crookedly on her skull. "You're giving birth," she said. "The only problem with your pain is that you view it as a problem."

"Remember the gas station?" Mary tried to reach Sage but her arm wouldn't move. "You were named Nina then. Remember, Orion? How I adored him?"

Mary's vibes had melded with Orion's. He claimed to dig the fat chicks. Other cats asked her, *Where's Orion?* And Mary always knew where he'd gone. That's how she came to have an old man. It meant she wasn't alone. Until that fateful afternoon, she threw open the van doors to find Orion entwined with the blond girl who'd given everyone crabs. *She's a Pisces,* he'd said. *We flow like water.* Or was that another man for whom she'd flung away her heart? In a twilight state between sleeping and waking, Mary witnessed her wide-open youthful self, wearing a colorful peasant skirt with tiny mirrors woven into the fabric. *You fool,* she wanted to say. *They threw you crumbs, you called it love.*

She had no inkling that this stop for gas in the middle of Bumfuck, Nowhere would be the place that marked her destiny, while Orion's fate lay elsewhere. In the bright white world of the gas station, as sun sparkled across the pavement, Mary was felled by pain, deeper and more ferocious than anything she had ever experienced.

Don't push, someone dictated. But Mary bore down helplessly, tumbling along a current, until the torture ebbed. Her legs quaked. Only Sage stayed with her. The others took off in the Mahayana for the great happening scene, which turned out to be historical: the Woodstock concert. They abandoned Mary in a community hospital in a tiny town in Colorado.

They lost their humanity, said Sage. She had folded her T-shirt up under her breasts. The hem of her wraparound skirt drooped around her calves. Her Mexican huarache sandals squeaked as she stepped around the bed.

"I always loved you, Sage. So much more than..." Mary trailed off, unable to remember who she loved Sage more than. Peter, for one. America. Annapurna? No, she couldn't admit that. Sage turned aside with the eyes of a sly feline.

White-coated people darted incomprehensibly about the room, only their eyes visible above white masks. Mary's lips had gone numb. An icy stethoscope pressed against her breastbone. Dr. Stark loomed over her. "We'll have to perform a Cesarean," he said.

Then the room filled with light so intense it burned her retinas, and the scent of lavender, her mother's perfume, permeated Mary's senses. She discerned, in the corner, a woman in a severe navy suit who examined the procedure with tightly pursed lips, and shook her head in disappointment.

"Mother!" cried Mary. An upsurge of pain slammed her against rocks, then dragged her through shards of glass. *Where is my baby?* she pleaded. *Let me see my baby.*

Hands held out a bluish creature. *A girl,* they said. *You have a girl.* And a wail trickled out of her. But no, the keening came from the baby. Someone laid it on her chest, magically alive, sniffling like an animal, sweet and slimy, a brand-new human being.

Mary didn't know that giving birth to Annapurna would be the pinnacle, the most intense, cosmic experience by which all others would fall short. Metalworking, love, music, drugs, sex. Nothing compared. Then they whisked her baby away. *Where are you taking her?* she shouted. *Bring me my daughter!*

Something prodded her. She tried to roll away but the shoving persisted, pushing and jostling, and she was back in the Mahayana. *Stop!* she cried. *I need to get out.* The others agreed. They'd been driving too long, cooped up in the van. They needed air. The music was too loud.

Joel stood over her. He moved his chapped lips but no sound entered her sense doors. *Don't be silly, Mary,* her mother said. But they used to call them sense doors. Like the doors of perception. *You'll never understand me, Mother.*

"Do you know where you are?" Joel's voice burst in. "Do you know who I am?"

Lacerating pain cut through her middle.

"Is she awake?" Peter appeared beside Joel, tall and very handsome. "Ah, Mary. You did it, you *did* it."

Then she saw the quiver of Ann's shadow along the blanket, and slowly turned her head, letting her eyes rest on Ann, who was slumped in the visitor's chair, her face hidden behind her hair. That protective posture was so familiar, Mary felt she was watching a part of herself. Ann was crying. Her face was mottled and puffy. Life took a harder toll on her than on the other children at the commune. Of course, they were no longer at the commune, but now, as then, Ann's presence anchored Mary in time and place. In Ann, she sought the true assessment of the situation.

"A boy and a girl. They're stable," said Ann.

"Garnet and Jade," whispered Mary. Her throat burned. Her mouth hurt.

"Not Jade. I want to name her Maria, after you, Mom. Four pounds, three ounces. Breathing on her own. The boy is Ethan, not Garnet, I'm sorry; he's on a vent. Three pounds, twelve. They say the odds are decent." Ann delivered the news softly, already fluent in neonatal ICU lingo. "I have Opal here. They said I could hold her as long as I want."

Mary hadn't noticed the bundle in Ann's lap. Ann pulled the blanket down to reveal a tiny dead baby, doll-like in her stillness. "Maybe you want to hold her. Peter could get a picture."

A glance at Peter, and he nodded. He was holding the tip of his nose with his curled hand. His eyes were wet.

"He already took a lot of beautiful pictures," said Ann.

A cold, clammy darkness threatened to engulf Mary. "You hate pictures," she said.

"It's all we have," said Ann. "Plus, handprints and footprints, ultrasound print-outs, and memories."

The clammy chill was supplanted by a fire that burned from Mary's belly to her chest, searing up into her skull, until she was sweating torrents. The hot flash erupted in full conflagration, as if her biological clock had to compensate for the lost months. "Maybe I'll hold her after all," she said.

When Ann laid the baby on her chest, Mary was astonished at how light Opal was, how rigid and tiny. She could fit into one cupped hand. Veins stood out in blue threads along the baby's skull. Ann dabbed Mary's eyes with a tissue, wiping away tears Mary hadn't known she'd shed.

"Mary, you're so brave!" cried Peter. He was sobbing.

Strange to see him cry. She remembered how his tears had moved her the day they'd met. Now, as she stroked the baby's cold, soft, delicate skull, his weeping seemed like so much histrionics. "Please take the baby," she said. "I want to see the living ones."

Joel came around to hold her in a kind of embrace, supporting her as she sat up and brought her feet to the floor. He was solid and helpful, a stable force. Peter tried to shoulder in. But his need to assist carried a destructive element. Had it always been so? Or had Mary just now recognized it? As she pulled her IV to the side, she tried to hold onto the question. It seemed important. But it slipped away. Peter bumped her with his camera hard enough to cause a bruise.

"Be careful," Joel scolded.

"You caused it," said Peter. "I'm trying to help my wife."

Mary settled into the wheelchair, opening her arms so Ann could put Opal back in her lap. Except for the birth, which didn't count because she'd been sedated, Mary had not left her hospital room for several weeks. The light in the corridor hurt her eyes. The noise was overwhelming. Peter pushed the chair. Nurses, patients, visitors all turned to stare as she rolled by. Joel wheeled her IV alongside, and Ann strode on ahead. They stopped in front of a large window. Visible behind the glass were the tiniest infants Mary had ever seen.

The girl, who Ann had announced she'd name Maria, who should have been Jade, was dwarfed by her incubator, attached to a network of wires. She was covered in dark hair, monkey-like.

"She's an animal," said Mary.

"They say it'll fall out. They let me touch her. You can, too. There's a method to it, to help her grow quicker." Ann smudged the glass with her fingertip, pointing. "There's Ethan on the vent. See, with the oxygen mask? He has a staph infection." His tiny body was hooked up to an enormous machine.

A harsh cry, like the call of an injured bird, came from Joel, so primal and uncensored it shocked Mary.

"I won't let them take him off the vent." Joel pressed his face and palms against the glass. "Tell her. Don't lie to her. The odds are not *decent,* they're shit."

Mary couldn't enter his energy stream—it had changed too abruptly from its former steadiness. She touched Opal's perfect miniature eyelids, her beautifully crested lips. She held the noodle of an arm between her fingers.

"If you don't tell her, I will." Joel knelt on one knee and, gripping the armrest of the wheelchair, stared fiercely up at Mary. "Our son is in a vegetative state. Brain dead. They want him off the vent."

"No." Mary was desperate to return to the van, to the birth of Annapurna, and young, vital Sage with long wavy hair, to go back to when Orion had been her old man and, most of all, to her young, hopeful self, when life beckoned like a sparkling jewel.

SAGE'S CAT HAWTHORNE LEAPED into the cradle and spoke. *There is a bardo where unborn babies go.* Another dream. Ann awoke in the chair next to Mary's bed and knew, blinking in the glow of the never-dark room, beside the mound of sleeping Mary, that they would have to let Ethan go.

Later, she was somewhat prepared when Dr. Stark stopped on his rounds at Mary's bedside. "If you take him off the vent, he'll expire naturally," said Dr. Stark. "If you keep him on the vent, he could live indefinitely but he won't improve. He is essentially in a coma."

"Maybe you're wrong. How do you know for sure?" Joel pressed against Ann. She smelled his fear and sadness, his stale breath and unwashed hair.

As Dr. Stark explained about motor response, Ann glanced at Mary, whose face was bruised, yellowish. A burst blood vessel reddened her left cornea. Peter had gone home for the night. None of them said aloud that they didn't want him present, but the urgency was there, to do it before he returned.

Ethan lived for an hour after they detached him from the ventilator. Ann held him in a nursing chair in the intensive care unit with Mary and Joel beside her. The hiatus between Ethan's fragile labored breaths lengthened, each inhale weaker than the last until the moment stretched, interminable and silent.

"Amazing that he lasted as long as he did," said a nurse, not unkindly. "He's a hardy soul."

He stayed warm for another half hour. Joel draped his arm over Ann's shoulder while Mary, in her wheelchair, kept her hand on the baby's skull. In this way, they were one person divided into three bodies, absorbing the loss.

DAYS PASSED IN A blur between home and the hospital, until the morning finally came that Mary and the surviving baby would be released. Ann and Joel had arranged that Mary would stay with them for a couple of weeks. They'd rented a hospital bed and prepared their living room to accommodate her. Ann anticipated repaying Mary, nursing her, bonding with her daughter and her mother simultaneously.

Five pounds six ounces, no longer covered in dark hair, Maria slept in her carry-case, her lips puckered as if to nurse. Irrationally, Ann could hardly wait to show Maria the new house. Yet she couldn't gaze at her daughter for more than a few seconds without weeping. She roller-coasted from wonder to fear to grief.

Mary sat with her swollen feet dangling off the hospital bed. Dr. Stark had claimed that Mary's edema would resolve itself but he couldn't say when. One of her slippers had fallen off. Ann bent to put it back on. "Are you ready?" she said. "There's the wheelchair."

"I'll walk like a dignified human being to the car." Sliding slowly off the bed, Mary swayed into the wall.

When the nurse entered with release papers, Ann signed quickly, keeping one arm linked through Mary's, in case Mary fell. "I'm sorry, ma'am," said the nurse. "But I can't authorize your release unless you agree to the wheelchair."

"You can't make me," said Mary. "I've been through enough."

"Take the ride, Mom, please? For my sake? Let's just get you home. We stocked up on all your favorite foods. Your favorite live Dead CDs. What's a few minutes in a wheelchair?"

"Your sake," Mary muttered. "All for your sake."

"Do you have a car seat for the infant?" said the nurse.

"She's in it," said Ann. "It fits into the base, which is in the car."

The nurse examined the carry-case, comparing it to a diagram with a checklist. Her fastidiousness annoyed Ann. "We're not going to risk our baby's life on the ride home!"

"Our baby," said Mary. "Do you mean yours and mine, or yours and Joel's?"

"Yours, mine and Joel's," said Ann. She hadn't realized she'd used 'our.'

"You answered correctly, my dear." Mary shuffled into the wheelchair. "I'd like to hold our baby now."

Ann placed the carry-case with the baby in Mary's lap. She noticed Mary wince. "Does it hurt? You don't have to hold her."

"Just get me the hell out of here," said Mary.

Pushing the wheelchair along the corridor brought a lump to Ann's throat. Mary's hair had gone completely gray. Her part was crooked. When the nurses and orderlies lined up to wave goodbye, the lump expanded. She hadn't expected leaving would magnify her sense of loss. She had been looking forward to life with Maria and Joel and Mary, far away from the hospital. But the spirits of Opal and Ethan still lived here. Their tiny bodies had been cremated through a service connected to the hospital and their ashes were contained in two biodegradable urns shaped like shells that Joel had taken away a few days before. The urns didn't hold their essence though, only dust.

"You don't do me any favors naming her Maria," said Mary, as the doors opened before them. "She's a Jade, I can't believe you don't see that. And Ethan will always be Garnet to me."

"I hope we can argue about it for years to come!" Ann gripped the wheelchair as it rolled down the ramp. Gusts of wind whipped trash and dust and leaves, swirling them around the parking lot.

Peter's camera stood on a tripod at the base of the entrance ramp. "Smile please. Say cheese!" he cried.

"Oh, sweet air. I can taste the clouds." Mary lifted her face toward the overcast sky. Heartened by Mary's blissful expression, Ann cupped Mary's chin with her palms and kissed her forehead.

"That's lovely," said Peter. "Gorgeous."

He'd taken such beautiful pictures of Opal and later of Ethan that Ann couldn't hate him anymore. Begrudgingly, she recognized a depth in his photographs, through which he seemed to transcend his immaturity and selfishness. He stripped away the nonessential to allow the true spirit through, as he'd once told Ann he aimed to do. Much of the nonessential, Ann saw quite clearly now, was Peter himself. But this was true of everyone, in some respect, she thought.

Joel pulled up to the entrance. He stayed inside the car with the engine idling, though Peter gestured for him to join the photograph. "Take the baby, please," said Mary. "I'm getting up now. This wheelchair is bullshit."

"Are you sure?" Ann lifted the carry-case from Mary's lap.

Peter hopped to Mary's side, throwing his arm around her. "Five second timer. Smile!"

But Mary pushed him away and trudged toward the car. Her dismissal seemed to diminish Peter. Ann felt sorry for him, as he concentrated excessively on disengaging his camera from the tripod, a lost soul. She slid the baby carrier into the back seat.

"Can you open the boot, mate?" she heard Peter ask.

Maria began to cry as Ann adjusted the harness of the car seat. "Sorry sweetie," she said.

"Her crying hurts my breasts," said Mary. "They gave me an injection to stop the milk but I'm still leaking."

"It'll pass, Mom," said Ann. But she focused on Maria. She stroked Maria's forehead and the baby stopped crying, which filled her with pleasure that she could comfort her daughter. She unfolded the blanket, to shelter Maria from the chill of Mary's open window.

"We're trying to figure out how to end the book." Peter slid into the backseat on Maria's other side. "We never envisioned a sad ending. Not that this little one isn't cause for joy but..."

"It's not yours to envision and it never was," said Joel as he pulled out onto the highway.

"I know you're going through hell, mate," said Peter. "But I'm on your side."

"I don't appreciate calls from reporters," said Joel. "And I don't like hearing from freaks far and wide who want to join this goddess crap. Next time, give them your own number."

"What calls?" said Ann.

"Mr. P.R. back there wants the world to know all about him so he gives out my phone number." said Joel. "I had to unplug the phone. You're paying for the number change, dude."

"Fallout from the article, I'm afraid." Peter passed Ann a folded-up copy of the local newspaper. *Grandmother is Mother until Birth,* read a small one-column headline. Just beneath was Peter's photograph of the ritual around Mary's hospital bed: Sage in her turban, Asphodel with her djembe drum, Ann appearing otherworldly.

"Has Betty seen this?" she asked.

"That's where I found out about it," said Joel.

"I said I was sorry," said Peter. "I didn't know Associated Press would pick it up. I never imagined the response."

"Could everyone please shut up?" said Mary.

Silence reigned for the rest of the journey. Ann devoted her attention to the miraculous universe of Maria, her soft exquisite face, those lips, those ears and eyelashes. She couldn't drag her gaze away, though tears ran down her cheeks. Their arrival at Sunrise unsettled her, it seemed just a blink from the hospital.

"Your stop, dude." Joel turned the engine off. Peter was out in a flash, opening the trunk to fetch his camera.

With a groan, Mary opened her car door. She swung her legs out.

"Where are you going?" said Ann. "You're coming to our house. That's the plan."

"I changed my mind." Mary hung her head, slumped sideways in the front seat. "I want to be in my own home."

"But you're still recovering," said Ann. "We all decided you'd stay with us."

"Come on, Mary, love," said Peter. "I'll make you a nice cup of tea."

"Okay, we'll spend the night *here* if that's what you want."
Ann's voice turned shrill. Maria uttered a thin cry.

"If Mary changed her mind, let her go," said Joel. He turned
with his arm over the back seat. "Let's not make a scene. We'll
come by tomorrow."

"If Mary needs us, we stay here," said Ann. "Please don't do
this, Mom."

Peter had carried his tripod and camera case from the trunk to
the porch. "Mary should do what she wants," he said. "I'll escort
you inside, love."

"Leave me alone, all of you." Mary pulled herself up. When
Peter attempted to help, she slapped him away and stepped across
the gravel, slowly shuffling towards the house. The shawl slipped
off Mary's back. Joel started the engine and, as they accelerated
onto the road, Ann watched her mother from the rear window.
The hunched, heavy figure grabbed the porch railing. Ann craned
her neck until the last tiny sliver of purple disappeared.

MARY'S BREASTS ACHED. SHE held them in her palms to ease the
pressure.

"Let me help you to the sofa," said Peter. "I put new sheets on."

"Hell no. I'm sleeping in my own bed." Mary grabbed the
trickster for support but his arm broke off in a cloud of plaster. She
stumbled onward. She had to stop at each step to let her internal
organs settle. Her bowels felt weak. She noticed mirror shards
missing from her mosaic. She'd been out of commission for too
long. The house needed her.

"You're still terribly weak." Peter followed right behind.

She reached the top without his help. Pressing against the
wall to support herself, she entered her bedroom. Her bed was
neatly made, with blankets tucked under pillows. But Peter's yoga
mat was spread out on the floor, dirty tissues balled up around it.

The walls were covered with huge photographs, larger than life. Mary naked in a stark light; Mary in her robe, shadowed and soft, reminder of her former abundance and beauty. But a photograph of Cassidy was central. She was naked, in a headstand, her toes spread, feet arched.

Mary lacked the energy to tear the pictures down. She simply rolled into bed. The springs creaked. The sheets smelled of cigarettes and peppermint, of Peter. Assuming he would slip in beside her, Mary shifted to make room. But he didn't. She heard his footsteps descending the stairs. Then she was sitting on the desert sand with three babies beside her. Spiny plants dotted the flat landscape. From the hot, white sky came the sound of chimes. They clanged through her body. The babies didn't stir.

She awoke, achy and squishy in the dark. Her muscles throbbed. She needed her painkillers. Her incision was dripping. Beside her, Peter was snoring, whistling and snorting like a one-man band. As she shook him awake, she could hardly believe she had once found the noise endearing. "You need to sleep somewhere else," she said.

"You're my wife," he said. "Married people sleep together."

"I need a pain pill."

He delivered her tablets and a glass of water. Then he left her alone. Mary fell back into the heat of the desert with her babies beside her, dying in the light.

ANN DID NOT SLEEP anymore, ever. She was in love. Thin and long-limbed, Maria underwent bouts of incessant crying as if angry to be in the world alone, without her siblings. In the dead hours before daylight, Ann held her and sobbed with her sobbing baby. She sat with Maria on the empty hospital bed in the living room and kissed every inch of her skin, pressing her nose into the baby's folds, licking her salty tears.

DESPITE ALL THE DEATH surrounding her, Maria shone with the guiding light of life. *Feed me! Feed me!* her wailing said. But she wouldn't take the bottle. She thrust it away with tiny hands, turning her red face against it. Her whole body shuddered with sobs. Ann was enveloped in a kind of tunnel. Wet and warm, it compressed her in liquid suffocation.

Instinctively, she scooped Maria's legs under her arm. She positioned Maria's nose at her nipple, and tickled her bottom lip. The baby's mouth opened wide and Ann brought it quickly to her breast. A gentle tug and her baby was sucking! She was overwhelmed with gratitude so powerful it bordered on grief.

She had read all about breastfeeding, about the various holds and complications, the danger of thrush and the enormous benefits to mother and child, even though she knew it was impossible for her. She had still wanted to be informed. Now, miraculously, Maria's little hands waved as she sucked. *I wanted this too,* they gestured. Gazing at those unseeing blue eyes to whom she was but a tactile presence, Ann marveled at her baby's animal tenacity. They were suspended in a milky timeless place of sleep and feeding, opalescent at the edges. Outside, a faint yellow hue spread through the darkness, promising dawn. *Thank you,* she whispered.

The next morning, the feeding seemed like a dream. Joel had taken time off from work, and Ann was aware of him puttering around the house while she dozed in the living room with the sun on her face. In the afternoon, when Maria's crying woke her, Ann sat up in the hospital bed. Her breasts had swelled while she slept. They were heavy. A glimpse at her T-shirt showed leaking. The crying came from the kitchen.

Joel stood at the stove, heating the bottle. The baby was in the cradle, miniscule in the huge bed. She kicked and bawled. Every movement of her limbs quivered with intelligence as Ann lifted her out. She held the baby on her lap in a football hold, and brought the baby's mouth to her nipple as if guided by a greater matriarch.

"Whoa, Annie, what are you doing?"

"I'm feeding her." Ann merged helplessly and eagerly with the baby, the ferocious tug at her nipples, the all-consuming physical reality of Maria. Again, her gratitude verged on sorrow.

Joel sat in the chair beside her, clasping the warm bottle. "Is it magic?"

She basked in his wonder. She remembered how Mary would rhapsodize about the holiness of breastfeeding. Ann had resented yet another aspect of womanhood from which she was excluded. Now, she wanted Mary to see her, too. "It's real."

"I feel like we should all be together for this," said Joel.

"Me, too," said Ann. "I was just thinking of Mary."

"I meant the other children." Leaving the bottle on the table, Joel dashed out. She heard him running up the steps. He returned with two urns, which were shaped like oversized cockleshells. They had stored the urns on a shelf in the bedroom closet until they could decide what to do with them. Joel placed them on the kitchen table, encircling them like eggs in a nest with the braided cords from Sage.

But Ann couldn't look at those cockleshells without seeing death. Opal had been thinner than the width of Ann's palm. Ethan's face had turned blue before he died.

Maria began to scream. Her mouth dislodged. No matter how Ann tried to stuff her breast back in, it kept sliding out. "Take them away," she said. "They're upsetting her."

"You're the one upsetting her," said Joel. "You got tense and rigid. She sensed it."

"You're an expert now?" Ann rocked and sang and soothed, but Maria refused consolation.

"Can I feed her?" said Joel. "I was looking forward to it."

"She wants *me*," said Ann.

"She's mine, too," said Joel. "So are the dead ones. They all belong to us."

Loath to release Maria, Ann kissed her eyelids and her cheeks and chin and lips. She pressed her wet face into Maria's belly.

"I was so focused on the birth, I forgot all about dying," said Joel. "Two babies died. We're all going to die. How could we have forgotten about death?"

When she heard him whimper, Ann relented. "Here," she said. "Feed her."

Like an uncertain child, doing everything carefully, holding his tongue between his teeth in concentration, Joel held Maria in his arms and gave her the bottle. Ann rested her elbows on the table. She could see the crenellated fans of the two shell-shaped urns in her peripheral vision as she watched Joel, simultaneously soft and tense, sniffling with tears, and Maria's avid gaze on him, her father. The dead and the living.

ON THE MORNING OF the Autumn Equinox, Mary awoke with a chill, having thrown off her blankets. Cold air blew in through the cracks between the wall and the window frame. Peter stood at the foot of the bed as if he had just materialized. "What are you doing here?" she asked.

"I live here, remember? I'm your husband. I brought you coffee."

"Do you feel guilty or something?" said Mary. "I can make my own coffee."

"You need to create again. Work can get you through this." Peter sat on the edge of the bed, looking proud of himself, as if he'd just delivered a pearl of wisdom she was supposed to be grateful for.

"I'm still recuperating." Mary pulled on her fingers. Yanking her thumb was supposed to dispel worry, according to some eastern healing modality she couldn't recall the details of. Index finger, fear; second finger, anger; ring finger, grief; pinky, tension. Left hand then right, and go around again.

Peter watched her with an intensity that was probably meant to convey the power of his love. Mary couldn't tell true caring from fake, this was her life's lesson. But she knew she hadn't wanted Peter present when they'd taken Ethan off the vent, which made her question whether she wanted him at all.

He dropped back across the bed, clasping his hands behind him, staring up at the ceiling. "I was thinking I'd like to invite the writer for a weekend. She could stay in the old green room. We'll put a bed in there. She wants so much to meet you. She told me she cried when she saw the photographs of Opal and Ethan. I don't doubt her sincerity. She wept on the phone."

Off he went, extolling the virtues of the writer. How could Mary have lost her heart to such a child-man? His enthusiasm jangled painfully at her nerves. "I don't want the writer here," she interrupted, then recoiled in a spasm, as if a giant fist had squeezed her innards out. *Your uterus may continue to contract for a few weeks,* Dr. Stark had said. She remembered everyone touching her at the hospital, their caring faces, Sage's turban, Joel's guitar, Ann's authority. They faded quickly into Dr. Stark's bloodless demeanor. *Opal is dead, Mom. Fluid leaked.*

She rolled over, swallowed a couple of painkillers that she swigged down with coffee, and swung her legs off the bed. Her calves ached, especially the left one. Her incision burned and chafed. Lifting her apron of belly flesh, she examined the inverted 'T' of the cut. It wept clear liquid. She picked up the blow-dryer that she'd been keeping by her bed since she'd been home, turned it on cool and dried off the secretion from the wound. Recommended by the nurses, the cool air gave her shivers.

"Did you take your antibiotics?" Peter sat up. "Is that how it's supposed to look?"

Mary released her flesh so the wound disappeared into her folds. "How should I know what it's supposed to look like?"

"Don't shut me out," he said. "I feel useless."

"This isn't about you." She recalled the golden shimmer of his aura, how her life had seemed to expand just because he'd entered it. He had taken down the huge photographs on the bedroom wall, and carried her statues back upstairs to her altar, which should have pleased her. But she remained unmoved. She picked up her skirt from the floor where she'd left it, holding her belly as she bent, and leaning against the bed as she positioned the skirt low on her hips so the elastic wouldn't interfere with her injury. Her calf cramped and she sank back down. "Shit," she said.

"I'm sad, too." Peter looked crestfallen. "I thought we had a convergence of souls. You are you and I am I and if by chance we find each other…"

For a moment, glancing at the flesh of his thighs, which showed through the rips in his jeans, Mary felt a flaming blaze of desperate love for Peter. It left her drenched in sweat. "You're right," she said. "I have to get back to my jewelry."

"Yes! Your creative drive can heal you. Did I tell you Dr. God has agreed to be interviewed? I'm meeting him next week. I wish we had a decent car."

And he swung like a cradle back to enthusiasm. Hoping the painkillers had kicked in, Mary slid off the bed again. She took a few tentative steps. So far, so good. Peter followed, holding her elbow, talking about publicity and book tours, but she batted him away. She wanted to descend the stairs by herself, and noted again that plaster had loosened and pieces of mirror had fallen out.

When Peter shadowed her into the living room, she lost patience. "Do me a favor? Go to the darkroom or a yoga class, anywhere but here. I love you but I need to be alone."

"I can't leave you like this. You're limping."

"Give me some time with my tools." She stared at her jewelry bench. It stood in front of the bookcase, with her acetylene torch, pliers and hammers, her chair and design books. They accused her of neglect. She'd have to transfer it all back upstairs to her studio. "I'm begging you," she said. "Go."

"Fine. I'll pick up some groceries. I won't be long."

She waited until she heard the rattle of the car engine before she dropped into her pregnant spot on the sofa. Months of excitement and exhaustion had been spent here. The sheer momentum of her pregnancy had kept desolation at bay, and allowed her briefly to celebrate herself.

Mary folded her legs beneath her, resting her cheek on the armrest. Books, crossword puzzles, tarot cards, and her pink vibrator cluttered the end table, evidence that she had frittered her life seeking distraction from her own emptiness, even then, in her happy time. *Get off your duff,* her mother commanded from inside her skull. *Idle hands make the devil's work.* The ache in her legs deepened as she massaged her left calf.

Reluctantly, she dragged herself off the sofa, and settled in the low, castered stool at her jewelry bench, where she opened her wire drawer to an anarchy of dusty spools and broken bits of metal. She slammed it shut. Every single one of her tools required cleaning. *Look, Mama, I'm working.* But Rose had never considered Mary's jewelry as anything other than ridiculous.

She leafed through a Japanese design book. Meaningless patterns wobbled, making her cross-eyed. She sorted through beads and stones, palming first turquoise, then glass, then other stones, one by one. Often, material suggested design. But the rough pearl was cold. Citrine, dead. Jade, overruled. Then she picked up a piece of opal embedded in rock and sadness pulled her back to the hospital bed, with a dead baby inside her blocking the living ones. If she had never gone to the immigration office, would three children be alive, instead of one?

A dry sob formed in her chest. She slid off her seat and crawled to the bearskin rug in the middle of the room, where she folded herself into a child's pose. She remembered Ann holding the dead baby in a bundle. Tears came flooding. She'd lost two babies and one unformed being, and she was empty. Yet, she recognized that her greatest pain came from the loss of her image as a beautiful, bountiful Earth Mother. And she hated herself for that.

When she wiped her eyes with the scratchy wool of her sweater sleeve, she imagined broken blood vessels and cried anew because

Ann had wanted to care for her but Mary couldn't let anyone take care of her. Briefly, she cried because she couldn't cry anymore. Then she shivered in the cold room. Lacking energy to build a fire, she simply took in the infinite variations of gray in the texture and dust of ashes in the fireplace, and waited for more tears.

"Mom? Why are you kneeling in the middle of the room? Are you praying?" Ann startled her from the doorway, looking awkward with the baby in a sling around her front, like a girl pretending to mother her doll. Her little Annapurna.

"You look like a natural," said Mary, wishing to help it happen. She got up slowly, holding her stomach to protect herself from the chafing of the incision. But all suffering had vanished into numbness. "I didn't know I was kneeling. I think I need to sleep."

Passing her daughter and the baby, with a glance at her half-destroyed trickster and its amputated arm, Mary labored up the steps.

"Maybe I should stay with you for a couple of days." Ann climbed close behind. "Joel and I were talking about it."

"Because you feel sorry for me? Well, I won't have it." Mary had to pause at the top to catch her breath. She used to run up these stairs two at a time. Hard to believe she'd been so strong and heedless.

In her bedroom, she was distracted by the leaden sky outside the window. It appeared almost solid above the pale hills. Always, the evolution of the seasons seemed to occur gradually until, suddenly, the new season had unequivocally assumed control. The bedraggled trees shook their fists in the wind, foretelling winter. She saw the Slocombe Builders truck roll over the incline and pull into the driveway. "Joel's here," she said.

Ann didn't answer. Nor did she come to the window. Mary watched Joel step out of the truck and walk around to the back to pull out the huge cradle. Gleaming, polished wood caught the light. "He has the cradle," she said.

He hoisted it over his head like a canoe and carried it to the porch. A moment later, the sounds of thudding and thumping reverberated from downstairs. Joel called, "Hello?"

Mary sank into her bed. All this activity was so very tiring. Rose might have accused her of malingering. "Why don't you answer him?"

"It upsets her when I yell." Ann was unwrapping the whimpering baby from her sling. "Do you want to hold her?"

"As if holding a damn baby will change anything," snapped Mary. Remorse arose immediately. "I'm sorry. Why can't I be nice anymore? Yes, please. Let me hold my granddaughter."

Ann placed the baby on Mary's lap. "Maybe you're depressed. Post-partum."

"How cliché," said Mary. The baby fretted and squirmed, with pursed lips and scrunched eyes. "She might be hungry."

"I fed her before we came. I'm breastfeeding, Mom! It's so incredible. Everything you told me about the experience is true." Ann stood over them, brimming with love.

"That's how indigenous women do it," said Mary. "You put the baby to the breast and milk comes. The miracle of womanhood. The holiest time in my life."

"I thought it was magic," said Ann.

"It is," Mary answered. "In a way."

They were in harmony, the good feelings wrapping them together in soft gauze that Mary wanted never to remove.

But banging and swearing came from the stairwell. Joel maneuvered the cradle through the door and set it down at the foot of Mary's bed. "Thought we'd want this here," he said.

"Are you staying here, too?" said Mary. "You don't like your McMansion anymore?"

"To be honest, we're in something of a fight," said Joel. "I think the baby needs the bottle. She seems like she's always hungry. But Ann doesn't want to hear it."

"I didn't tell her we were arguing," said Ann.

"What in the name of the goddess is there to fight about?" said Mary. "Let him help you. I would have given anything for some help."

The baby released a full-throated bawl, forcing Mary to pay attention to her. She kicked with the strength and power of a Jade, not a Maria. "She *so* doesn't look like a Maria," said Mary.

She heard Ann, as if from a distance. "Did you even bring the bottle?"

"It's in the truck," said Joel.

"Well, could you get it?"

"No one's listening to me," Mary told the baby, who screamed and flapped her arms. Jade was discontented, a lively, creative disgruntlement that would help her grow. Maria, however, would be doomed to tranquility. Her placid nature would quietly suffocate any latent dissatisfaction. Really. These short stubby eyelashes could only belong to a Jade, who would become her own person, charismatic and independently-minded, nothing stereotypical about her.

Mary knew she had to let this name thing go. The baby was not her daughter. Though it might break her heart to watch Jade vanish into a barely remembered dream as Maria came into herself, pudgy and eager to please, she would have to let it go.

She could not let it go.

"No, dammit, this baby is a Jade! You can't make her a Maria!" she shouted. "You can't do that to my girl!"

"Let me take her," said Ann. "She's making you hysterical."

Mary hugged her granddaughter. The baby's cries tore through her skin. Soft bones, malleable skull, pure helpless hunger. "You'll never be an Ann to me, either," she had to yell over the baby's racket. "You will always and forever be my Annapurna."

Annapurna, goddess of nourishment, Mary's little girl. Annapurna, who would never accept Mary's explanations or revelations, forcing Mary to reassess her own life. Annapurna, who embodied the benevolent aspect of the goddess Devi, her father unknown, her person inviolate, a remote mountain range, seeking the sky. She could iron creases in her jeans all she wanted. She could bleach her sneakers white and go to church with Betty and live in a McMansion, but she couldn't wipe out her Annapurnaness.

"I'm Ann. And she's Maria." Ann grasped the baby, trying to take her away.

But Mary held on. "I remember when you were this age, you cried and cried. You couldn't be comforted. It was so hard. I would block my ears and pray for someone else to deal with you because I felt so rejected. I was a lousy mother."

"It's okay, Mom," said Ann. "You don't have to punish me. Or yourself."

Mary lifted the baby. "Here, take her. I'm done."

As Ann bent to put the baby in the cradle, Mary couldn't see her anymore. But the crying continued.

"Don't smother her." Joel came in carrying Maria's bottle. "We don't want another dead one."

"That's a terrible thing to say!" snapped Ann.

"Why can't you two fight at home? I'm too old for this." Mary drew her knees into her chest and slithered down along her pillow. The baby cried and cried. Ann and Joel's voices twanged and clashed. But Mary floated disembodied just above her blankets.

Then she was sitting on the wooden bench at the picnic table in the kitchen at the Peace Ranch commune. The finish was peeling off the wood and she was wary of splinters pricking her bare thighs. Next to her, Sage laid out a runic cross with the tarot cards. *Hold the question in your mind,* she said. Other women watched the reading. Sage flipped the tower card, inciting a collective gasp. *Calamity,* someone said. And Mary was terrified. A baby squalled from a blanket-lined dresser drawer on the kitchen floor. The sound tore through her tendons, her ligaments and bones, and sliced deep beneath her fingernails. Her breasts dampened against her T-shirt.

Go to your baby, Mary, said Sage, gazing at the cards.

But Mary couldn't move, even though she knew the baby suffered. Her infant body was covered in a rash, aggravated by scabs and sores where she'd scratched herself with sharp, minute fingernails. Mary prayed for someone, anyone, to please, please, please deal with the baby so she wouldn't have to.

My cousin's baby had leukemia and her skin was just like that, one of the other women said. A mean-spirited woman with beautiful auburn hair and slender wrists, Mary hated her. But worse, she heard her mother's voice: *You can't even look after yourself, and you have the gall to bring a child into the world?*

She opened her eyes to her own blue ceiling and her dust-covered dreamcatcher dangling from a string. Rolling over, she saw Ann jiggle the crying baby in her arms, milk spurting from the bottle. Ann, too, was sobbing. "She won't stop. She won't take her bottle and she won't take my breast."

"Oh honey." Mary rolled up to sit. But as she lowered her feet to the floor, pain cut through her left calf. "Damn leg!" She kicked to loosen the spasm but kicking seemed to make it worse.

The room spun as she dropped back onto the bed. Joel appeared, then vanished. *Something's wrong with her,* someone said.

Or maybe it was Mary spinning, not the room. Annapurna was quiet now. Tucked in a sling made from several bandanas stitched together, the baby enhanced her status. Everyone smiled when she passed by. She knew she looked good. Her wavy brown hair rippled around her face as she danced and wove her way closer to the stage. She was at a Dead show: Winterland Arena, San Francisco. At first crowds parted. But the nearer she got to the stage, the more frenzied the mob. People flailed and whirled. Someone kicked her in the calf. Pain shot up her leg, through her heart. Onstage they were drumming. A swinging arm struck her baby. Annapurna went berserk. The concert evaporated and Mary didn't know where she was anymore.

I saw angels, I really did, she said.

No doubt. Coyote appeared beside her like a ghost, her first love, the one she left home with, wearing his fatigues painted with white peace signs. *The beautiful lady who digs the seraphim.* He smiled, revealing the slick, dark gap between his two front teeth. *They're with us. They're all around us, all the time.*

"What's the matter?" cried Ann. "Stop doing that!"

For a moment, Mary returned to her bedroom at Sunrise. "Tell me what I'm doing and I'll stop," she said. If only Ann could be happy. But the birds created a ruckus. They sat up in the branches of the giant oak, singing and calling, and all the sharp clear chirps blended into a din of echoes. Mary was sucked into the past again. She couldn't carry everything, not while she held her purse, a big leather bag that she clutched to her side as she stood on the porch. Her mother, wiping her hands on a yellow apron. *You keep hold of your purse, now.* She had to shout above the birds. *Put your money in your shoe, in case of theft.*

The tree was taller than their house. Sunlight flashed through leaves, dappling her mother's face. But even in the play of light, Rose was not pretty. She held her mouth too tightly. The glare of her glasses hid the unforgiving eyes that could detect a stain, a pimple, an errant chin hair. But she couldn't notice everything. Rose had no inkling that Mary had emptied her personal bank account of all the money from her summer jobs, and her purse was full of cold, hard cash that wouldn't fit in any shoe.

Their hug was perfunctory. Mary walked oh-so-casually down the porch steps. She knew Rose was watching so she paced herself, strolling past the shabby vinyl-sided two-story houses. As soon as she turned the corner, out of her mother's eyeshot, Mary's life unfurled like a carpet in a sunlit dreamscape, and she began to run. The rusted blue Pontiac idled by the curb, Coyote's elbow resting on the open window of the driver's side.

Baby, you got a beautiful aura, he said. Snap of the lighter and the joint sizzled. Mary waved goodbye to childhood and suffocating rules, ready to ride headlong into adventure, into life, into the now with the man she loved, her *soulmate.*

Mary, your lips are blue! Busted! She'd been followed. Rose regarded her with sharp, discerning eyes. No, that was Ann, not Rose. She tried to explain the muddle but she coughed instead. She couldn't stop. Her lungs burned. *Are you trying to kill me? What's in this doobie?*

Someone called *Mom!* from another universe.

But Mary was unlatching the door in the back of the Mahayana, emerging from darkness to light to dance among the gas pumps at the rest stop. A refueling. All her lovers gathered: Coyote, Orion, Lars, and the faceless ones between them. America shimmied over, grinding her hips like only America could. Peter stamped his feet, and off Mary spun, lifting her arms. She was flying! Unaffected by gravity or reality, she flew into the light to birth her one and only daughter. And the light expanded and opened and drew her in. *A girl,* they said. *You have a girl.*

THIS WASN'T HAPPENING. ANN could not let it happen. "We need an ambulance right now!" she screamed. "Tell them! She's having convulsions! Now!"

Joel held the baby against his hip. In his other hand, he clenched the phone, giving directions.

On the bed, Mary's body arched up with horrifying stiffness. Blood streamed from her nostrils. Ann remembered a course at the school; all the teachers had to learn CPR. Tilt the head so the tongue won't block airflow. She couldn't hear Mary breathing but her forehead was still warm, and so was her chest. She laid her lips on Mary's and exhaled into Mary's mouth. Pause. Check. Again. Mary tasted salty from the blood. A gurgling sound from her throat gave Ann hope.

Lips on lips. Exhale. Pause. Check. Again. She became a machine, counting seconds. She could not stop. Lights flashed in her eyes, electrical shorts. She was dizzy. *Help me.* She pleaded. *I'm losing her.*

Then she was sucking milk from a warm softness she identified as Mary. She was fulfilled, supremely comfortable. The sound of chimes filled the room. Ann awoke in the passenger seat of a car, crabby and cramped. Thank god it was a dream, a nightmare. *Why are we stopping here?* she asked.

Our house! Mary turned the engine off. Before them stood a ramshackle dump of a farmhouse, sagging porch, broken railings, windows boarded up. *Cheer up, Annapurna. You'll love it here.* Mary left the keys in the ignition, a long colorful lanyard threaded through them. She pushed herself out, getting entangled in her voluminous skirt, falling to the ground and laughing. Her laughter was catching.

Ann couldn't stay crabby, not when the air was so fresh with the scent of resin from the evergreens. The fields were awash in light. Wind chimes sounded from the porch. *We'll paint it purple and make it ours,* said Mary. *We'll call our house Sunrise.*

Hands pried Ann from the dream. She's dead, said a stranger. They were taking Mary away on a stretcher, negotiating the stairs. Someone was screaming, *You can't do this!* Ann realized it was her. Joel held her in a vice grip. *Mary died,* he said.

Ann fought and thrashed and screamed but Joel held tight. He contained her.

Sitting in the Sunrise kitchen where the framed printout of the original multi-celled beings hung on the wall, Ann nursed her baby. She hadn't left Sunrise for days, and neither had Joel, except to fetch the dog. With the baby at her breast, soup simmering on the stove, the murmur from the living room where Joel and Peter were talking, and the whimper of McKenna in his sleep in the doorway, Ann was surrounded by life.

But on the table, next to Mary's tray of candles in assorted stages of hardened melted wax that seemed to foretell death and winter, sat the metal box that held Mary's ashes. Mary had died, officially, of a pulmonary embolism. Her baby stared at Ann with a wide infant gape, blue eyes flecked with green. Her forehead creased with what appeared to be concern, but Ann couldn't sink into a deep mutual stare because she was afraid the baby might not love her now that Mary was dead.

And it felt unfair to love her baby, or even to breathe too deeply, unfair to take pleasure in anything at all. She forced herself to scan her daughter's eyes, which were pools of unfocused strength and innocence, and she knew she would rename her daughter Jade. "You're right, Mom. She's not a Maria." Ann said aloud as she shifted the baby to her shoulder. "She was never a Maria. I see that now."

But Mary, who would have relished this recognition, was absent. Ann could not accept this cold, hard fact, that her mother no longer existed. Nothing echoed. Nothing received.

She could conjure Mary only in pieces, like a montage. Like the fragments in Mary's stairwell mosaic, she remembered Mary pounding her breasts, the stretchmarks like gashes on her abdomen, Mary's eager childlike expression as they joined hands in any ritual, and her strong palms, embedded with black from her metalworking. Jade burped into the towel on Ann's shoulder, drifting into slumber already. Selfishly, Ann didn't want to let her sleep. *Stay with me!* Emptiness threatened to engulf.

She had spent her life fighting Mary's overwhelmingness, knowing Mary only as a mythological force to resist or surrender to. She had never appreciated Mary simply as a woman. Now she'd lost the chance. The link was broken. No one to fight, no one to press up against, no one who knew Ann when Ann was Jade's age. *You're a natural,* Mary had said. But Ann still thought of herself as a daughter, not yet a mother.

I'm the mother. The unique timbre of Mary's voice, so familiar to Ann, it felt like her own, rang through the kitchen. *I don't want to be the crone.*

"You'll never be the crone," said Ann. "You'll always be the mother."

You're the queen now. I gave you my power.

Joel came in. "Are you talking to yourself?" He embraced both her and the baby. He was warm. She gripped his wrists, loving him, needing.

She was also aware of Peter standing behind them. "We're all going to die," said Peter. "What matters is how we live. Mary knew that."

Neither Ann nor Joel responded. But Ann pitied him, as she knew Mary would have, too.

"I think Maria's asleep," Joel whispered.

"Jade," said Ann. "Jade's asleep."

"Can I take her?" said Joel.

Ann relinquished the warm soft sleeping infant to her father.

THE MOON WAS A waning crescent when Ann and Joel scattered Mary's ashes and the ashes of the babies behind Sunrise where Baby Four already lay. Sage drove over from the A-frame, having completed her chemotherapy. Though she was thin, she had regained color in her cheeks and her hair was beginning to grow back, as if life, not death, had won for now. Cassidy brought her children, all dressed up. Cody's hair was slicked back. Sky wore frilly pink. America wore an orange cardigan that had belonged to Mary.

They formed a procession. Ann and Joel marched first. Ann carried the metal box, tipping it to drop Mary's ashes along the path. Joel held the two urns with the babies, the cockles open like mouths to pour out the remains. They were followed by Sage, then America, who wailed and beat her chest like an ancient Greek mourner. Cassidy and her children brought up the rear. At a distance from the group, Peter crouched behind a camera on a tripod.

They had decorated the altar with lilies and poppies. "Let light conquer darkness," said Sage. "Dark sterile mother, bright fertile mother."

"The spirits shall return to the Goddess who gave them," said Ann.

"Mommy, look!" cried Cody, pointing to the sky where a turkey vulture circled. "The vulture teaches us to understand death," said Cassidy.

America cried, "Take her, guard her, guide her. Admit her into peace."

Joel placed a ceramic bowl on the ground below the altar. He shattered it with three blows of a hammer.

Ann gazed at Jade, slung across her chest. She touched her warm skull, her eyelids, the tip of her nose, ensuring that she was still a physical reality. Jade began to cry, squeezing her eyebrows in an expression of hunger. Her crying propelled Ann back to the house. As she heated a bottle on the stove in Mary's kitchen, she took comfort in the smells of food and scented candles. She thought she could smell wishes, filaments of vanilla, orange, and patchouli.

Her milk was not enough to nourish the baby; Joel had been right. It was enough to nourish Ann in the practice, and to bond more closely. She had agreed to supplement with formula. When the bottle was ready, she took the baby to the living room and nestled in the corner of the sofa where Mary used to sit, on the cushion still indented by Mary's weight. The seat was warm, as if Mary had just vacated it. And the jewelry bench in front of the bookcase had been tidied, the hammers arranged in a row, as if Mary intended to work again soon. Jade quieted as her lips tugged the nipple of the bottle.

Peter came in. He twitched. He pushed his hair back. He shifted his weight from one foot to the other. "I loved her," he said. "I honestly truly loved her."

"I know you did," said Ann.

He sat on the sofa beside her, elbows on thighs and chin in palms. His tears ran down his cheeks and over his hands. They dripped along his forearms.

Jade sucked on her bottle with equanimity. Her world stopped at Ann. If Ann stayed calm, the baby would, too. As she stared into Jade's hungry eyes, Ann was absorbed, centered and anchored by her daughter. Ann realized that she herself had provided the same pull on Mary, just by existing. Jade provided a vital force that opposed the black hole of Mary's absence, but Ann understood how difficult the path ahead would be, the unremitting challenge presenting itself over and over: to choose love and life, as Mary had done.

Light poured through the window, reflecting on the amber and amethyst stones on the jewelry bench, warming all the things in the room and everyone still in the world.

ACKNOWLEDGEMENTS

THERE ARE SO MANY people to thank, a world of friends, colleagues and teachers who encouraged, supported and sustained me in the long gestation of this, my second novel. Thanks to Dani Shapiro and everyone in our writing group who read and re-read countless early drafts and provided invaluable feedback: Karen McKinnon, Susie Rutherford, Ellen Schutz, Anda Tal and so many others who helped me shape the text. Thanks to my current writing group, The Exiles, all incredibly incisive, generous, talented writers to whom I'm grateful and beholden: former members whose comments helped me hone many draft: Kate Baldus, Kara Krause, Dana Liu, Jon Mozes, Marysue Ricci, as well as current members who continue to inspire me: Emmeline Chang, Leland Cheuk, Anne Hellman White, Jael Humphrey, Joseph Keith, Jennifer Sears, Rachel Stolzman, and so many others who passed through our group. I'd like to thank my agent BJ Robbins for her generosity and support; and the editors at C&R Press, John Gosslee and Andrew Sullivan, for believing in the work. Thanks to Gina Guidobando for her thoughtful edits and to Babs Griswold for copy-editing and proofreading. For providing magnanimous readings and honest feedback, I'm very grateful to Hillary Jordan. I also want to thank my writer-sisters-in-creativity who have been on this journey with me since 2001, Connie Biewald, Samantha Schoech and Brooks Whitney Philips. And thanks to my family: Bridgit, Ray, Alexis, Julia and Anthony for reading drafts and offering encouragement. I could not have written this or any of my books without the incredible generosity and support of residencies at the Djerassi Foundation, the Millay Colony, Ucross,

Vermont Studio Center and the Virginia Center for the Creative Arts. I also have to thank Steve Adams and all the people I work with for being supportive, creative and flexible with scheduling. I'm grateful to Paragraph and The Writers Room for providing, at various times, a quiet space to write. Thank you to my mother, June, whom I cherish; and I thank always and everlastingly, my beloved husband, Tony.

OTHER C&R PRESS TITLES

NONFICTION

Women in the Literary Landscape by Doris Weatherford et al

FICTION

Made by Mary by Laura Catherine Brown
Ivy vs. Dogg by Brian Leung
While You Were Gone by Sybil Baker
Cloud Diary by Steve Mitchell
Spectrum by Martin Ott
That Man in Our Lives by Xu Xi

SHORT FICTION

Notes From the Mother Tongue by An Tran
The Protester Has Been Released by Janet Sarbanes

ESSAY AND CREATIVE NONFICTION

Immigration Essays by Sybil Baker
Je suis l'autre: Essays and Interrogations by Kristina Marie Darling
Death of Art by Chris Campanioni

POETRY

Dark Horse by Kristina Marie Darling
Lessons in Camouflage by Martin Ott
All My Heroes are Broke by Ariel Francisco
Holdfast by Christian Anton Gerard
Ex Domestica by E.G. Cunningham
Like Lesser Gods by Bruce McEver
Notes from the Negro Side of the Moon by Earl Braggs
Imagine Not Drowning by Kelli Allen
Notes to the Beloved by Michelle Bitting
Free Boat: Collected Lies and Love Poems by John Reed
Les Fauves by Barbara Crooker
Tall as You are Tall Between Them by Annie Christain
The Couple Who Fell to Earth by Michelle Bitting

CHAPBOOKS

Atypical Cells of Undetermined Significance by Brenna Womer
On Innacuracy by Joe Manning
Heredity and Other Inventions by Sharona Muir
Love Undefind by Jonathan Katz
Cunstruck by Kate Northrop
Ugly Love (Notes from the Negro Side Moon) by Earl Braggs
A Hunger Called Music: A Verse History in Black Music
by Meredith Nnoka